ATHERHOOD SURPRISE—

n bachelor doctors to full-time fathers!

onth Mills & Boon® Medical™ Romance
brings you two gorgeous heroes—
and two surprise babies who turn these
op-notch doctors' lives upside-down!

**Enjoy our new two-in-one editions
by your favourite authors:**

**SECRET SHEIKH, SECRET BABY
by Carol Marinelli**

**HIS BABY BOMBSHELL
by Jessica Matthews**

Dear Reader

Welcome to the new look Mills & Boon® Med[
romances!

Now we're offering you two great value editions
two stories in each, double the medical drama
twice as many happy endings. All of your fav[
authors and all the best stories will still be availab[
and with **two double** volumes and **two single bo**
each month, you'll be spoiled for choice!

Look for these great new titles—out now!

HIRED: GP AND WIFE
by Judy Campbell
&
THE PLAYBOY DOCTOR'S PROPOSAL
by Anne Fraser

* * *

PREGNANT MIDWIFE: FATHER NEEDED
by Fiona McArthur

* * *

FOUND: A MOTHER FOR HIS SON
by Dianne Drake

* * *

SECRET SHEIKH, SECRET BABY
by Carol Marinelli
&
HIS BABY BOMBSHELL
by Jessica Matthews

To find out more, visit
www.millsandboon.co.uk/makeover.

Best wishes

Sheila Hodgson
Senior Editor, Medical™ Romance

SECRET SHEIKH, SECRET BABY

BY

CAROL MARINELLI

MILLS & BOON

First published in Great Britain 2009
Harlequin Mills & Boon Limited,
Eton House, 18-24 Paradise Road, Richmond, Surrey TW9 1SR

© Carol Marinelli 2009

ISBN: 978 0 263 86865 4

Set in Times Roman 10½ on 12¾ pt
03-0909-42657

Harlequin Mills & Boon policy is to use papers that are natural, renewable and recyclable products and made from wood grown in sustainable forests. The logging and manufacturing process conform to the legal environmental regulations of the country of origin.

Printed and bound in Spain
by Litografia Rosés, S.A., Barcelona

Mills & Boon® Medical™ Romance brings to you

BILLIONAIRE DOCTORS

Hot, jet-set docs at the top of their game—
professionally…and personally!

These desirable doctors are international playboys—
gorgeous Greeks, sexy sheikhs, irresistible Italians
and Australian tycoons. Their playground might be the
world of the rich and famous, but their professional
reputations are world renowned. These billionaires
dedicate themselves to saving lives by day—
and red-hot seduction by night…

Carol Marinelli recently filled in a form where she was asked for her job title, and was thrilled, after all these years, to be able to put down her answer as writer. Then it asked what Carol did for relaxation. After chewing her pen for a moment Carol put down the truth—writing. The third question asked—What are your hobbies? Well, not wanting to look obsessed or, worse still, boring, she crossed the fingers on her free hand and answered swimming and tennis. But, given that the chlorine in the pool does terrible things to her highlights, and the closest she's got to a tennis racket in the last couple of years is watching the Australian Open, I'm sure you can guess the real answer!

Did you know that Carol Marinelli also writes sensationally sexy, glitteringly glamorous books for Mills & Boon® Modern™ Romance?

Praise for Carol Marinelli:

BOUGHT BY THE BILLIONAIRE PRINCE
'Carol Marinelli's…engaging and sexy couple make for a delightful romantic getaway.'
—*Romantic Times BOOKreviews*

EXPECTING HIS LOVE-CHILD
'EXPECTING HIS LOVE-CHILD is an extremely poignant love story that runs the gamut of emotions.'
—*Romantic Times BOOKreviews*

CHAPTER ONE

THE hotel was stunning.

Dashing through the luxurious foyer, Felicity Anderson would have loved to pause and take in her surroundings—or even, given that she had been caught in the rain on her dash from the London underground, race to the ladies' room and fix her hair and make-up. Her long, wavy blonde hair was tied back, and had early this morning been tamed with hair serum, but the run in the rain from the underground station would have undone all her hard work. There just wasn't time to worry about it. The information session started at ten a.m., and, glancing at her watch, Felicity grimaced because it was already a quarter past. Meticulous and punctual, she had arranged to arrive at nine and linger in a café beforehand, but track works had caused 'unexpected delays' on her train from the north of England, which meant that Felicity was, whether she liked it or not, unforgivably late.

The concierge had pointed her in the right direction for the conference room, and Felicity followed the discreet signs until she found the venue. There a pretty woman who introduced herself as Noor was sitting at the desk outside, and waved away Felicity's apologies.

'We are just glad that you made it.' Noor had thick, long, dark hair that was no doubt rather more neatly tied back than Felicity's. She was wearing an immaculate navy trouser suit, and her manicured hands held out a pen as she asked Felicity to sign the attendance register. 'On now is the introductory presentation about the hospital and the imminent opening of the university.' The dark-haired beauty handed Felicity a heavy bag which contained brochures and forms. 'You can look through them all later—come, I will take you through. Just stand at the back till the presentation ends, and then take a seat. We really are so pleased to see you, Felicity, and delighted that you are considering us. Zaraqua Hospital urgently needs good midwives.'

Felicity was just a little taken back by the warmth of Noor's welcome. But then all her dealings with Zaraqua Hospital had been pleasant. She felt a little bit guilty too—though she *had* explained that she already had a job in the Middle East lined up, bar signing on the dotted line, and was coming to the recruitment information session only out of last-minute curiosity. As a qualified midwife she knew her skills were in heavy demand, and she wanted to be sure she was making the right choice, but really her decision was almost made.

The room was in darkness, just illuminated by the light of the vast screen as Felicity slipped in. Standing quietly, she watched the presentation, her decision wavering as she saw the stunning golden beaches of the Mediterranean sea that gave way to vast, vast desert. The Kingdom of Zaraq was an island with its own royal family, Felicity learnt, and its own deep traditions, though it was progressive too. An all-female university was opening, so the new generation of Zaraq women wouldn't have to leave the island and go overseas to be afforded first-class education. The fact that the university was an all-female environment appeased the more traditional families.

The information about the university was riveting to listen to, but it was the hospital Felicity was especially interested in. Her attention was utterly focussed as she was led through the lavish corridors, glimpsing plush suites, and her eyes widened as the impressive equipment and facilities were listed—this healthcare was available to *all* the people of Zaraq.

So focussed was Felicity that at first she barely registered the person who quietly came in. But as he stood beside her she knew that it was a man without turning her head. A delicious scent reached her nostrils, but more than that there was a presence, an all-male presence, that dragged her attention from the screen. Felicity turned her head and nodded an acknowledgment to the man. But then she couldn't, or didn't, immediately turn her face away.

Even in darkness his beauty was evident. Instead of leaning against the wall, as Felicity was, he stood to an impressive height. His hair was cropped close to his head, and she saw sculpted features, a straight nose, and deep shadows beneath his cheekbones, and eyes that in the darkness momentarily held hers. He gave a brief nod and she jerked her eyes away, turned her supposed attention back to the screen. She felt as if her face were on fire. She held her head rigid and did not allow herself to follow instinct and turn again to look at him.

His presence was devastating—completely overwhelming. It wasn't just his scent, it wasn't just his looks, it was *something* that consumed her as she stood. She had travelled for hours to be here, to learn about the hospital and nursing roles on the island of Zaraq. She had come here so she could make a wise and informed choice. Yet it might as well have been a cartoon on the screen for all the attention she was paying it. He was well over a metre away and yet it felt as if he were right next to her, touching her almost. The darkness was intimate, and she knew—just knew—he had turned his head to her again and was looking at her. She could hardly breathe, hardly swallow, grateful for the wall that was behind her holding her up.

Not once had she felt like this.

Even her ex-boyfriend Paul's most tender administration of affection hadn't elicited even a quarter of this response—their relationship had in fact broken up because of it. Felicity was unable, *physically* unable, to give that piece of herself—and yet, here in the darkness that piece of her she had searched for, the elusive *thing* that every other human on earth seemed to possess, had emerged. Like a shoot after the cold soil of winter, she felt a stir of warmth, the split of a seed, a surfacing that here in the darkness felt surreal.

She was going mad.

Staring at the screen, trying to concentrate, trying to slow her breathing, Felicity thought she was, right there and then, going completely insane. For a full year she'd seen a psychologist along with Paul—had also been to a gynae-cologist who had broken her hymen and given her a strange set of dilators to gradually get her body used to the idea. But nothing—not endless warm bubble baths, nor Paul taking it slowly, not a tranquiliser or a glass of wine, nor a plea to 'just please do it' had worked.

Nothing.

Yet here, standing in the darkness, feeling his eyes on

her, smelling *him*, sensing *him*, had he walked that short distance over and pressed his face onto hers she would have kissed him. She could almost imagine him pushing into her. Her panties were damp just from standing there near him. *How* would it be if he were closer?

And then he was gone.

He just slipped quietly away. A chink of light showed from the door as he made his exit, and finally Felicity could breathe again. She stood for a moment and collected herself before the room was flooded in light, and then she slipped into a seat, her mind, her body still whirring.

'You didn't miss much!' A friendly face smiled, and the man introduced himself as Liam Edwards.

'Just the first fifteen minutes,' Felicity lied—because thanks to the mystery man she'd practically missed all of the introductory presentation.

'Lucky you!' Liam rolled his eyes. 'It was all about the royal family and King Zaraq and his sons. Still, the hospital looks fantastic. I'm a nurse, by the way. I work in emergency,' he added, 'and me and my girlfriend are trying to save for a deposit for a house. This looks like a good way. She's an emergency nurse too. What about you?'

'I'm a midwife.' Felicity's smile was fixed. She wished she'd chosen another seat, not next to this chatty stranger. She was glad when Noor stepped on stage and introduced the first speaker, Judith Lansdon, a woman in her fifties, who was a professor of medicine and in charge of the medical faculty at the university.

Though the professor's talk was no doubt fascinating, Felicity had to force herself to concentrate, still reeling from what had just occurred. Then she asked herself *what* had occurred? She had nothing with which to compare it.

'Now, a few facts about Zaraq before your various specialities are addressed,' the host announced. 'The new all-female university is something we are very proud of on the island. The university has been built beside the hospital in the main city of Zaraqua, which is set near the ocean. Most of Zaraq is inhospitable desert—yet the island has its own economy, its own airport and a thriving tourist industry with stunning seven-star resorts. The compound attached to the university and the hospital where you would be living has every luxury. But be aware that Zaraq holds dear its traditions. Though this is a progressive monarchy, it has its own rules—rules that are outlined in the guidelines you have been given. They are non-negotiable. I strongly suggest that you read them carefully before you consider embarking on this journey. Sheikh King Kaliq Zaraq insists on good healthcare for all his subjects. In fact it is hoped at some time in the future to implement an outreach programme for the Bedouin people, though this is a sensitive area.'

The morning wore on, and gradually the strange encounter faded a touch from her thoughts as Felicity's well-laid plans started to change. Each speaker had her more and more impressed, and with each hour that passed her decision became harder. She had arranged to go to the Middle East for two years to nurse, and her paperwork had been approved, and she was just a couple of days away from signing her contract. But one day her attention had been caught by an article about the new university in Zaraq, and she had looked it up on the internet. She had seen an amazing state-of-the-art maternity hospital. On a last-minute impulse Felicity had rung the information number. On hearing she was a qualified midwife, they had invited her to attend today, and now Felicity, as they all trooped out for a sumptuous buffet lunch, was torn with indecision. Should she just stay with the hospital she had first chosen, or start the process all over again so that she could nurse in Zaraq?

'What do you think?' Liam asked as they stood chatting through lunch. 'The pay's better than at the other hospitals…'

'It looks very impressive. I think it might well be a yes.' Felicity nodded. 'I just hope it doesn't take too long. I'll have to find out more about the application procedure.' She didn't add that her family was desperate for the money this work would bring in. After years of seeing her sister struggle with a severe eating disorder Felicity had taken a vast loan, and Georgie's problems had finally been properly addressed in a top private clinic. Though Felicity considered the money well spent, the fact was, it was money she didn't have. Now it was time to pay it back.

She did not share this information with Liam—not that it stopped him from divulging what was on *his* mind.

'My girlfriend and I will have to get married if we go.' He didn't look too pleased at the idea.

'That's not just in Zaraq.' Felicity frowned. 'If you want to live together in most parts of the Middle East you have to be married. Have you done any research at all?'

'This is it!' Liam shrugged and carried on chatting, but Felicity was lost again. Midway to putting a small, perfectly cut sandwich to her lips, she saw him—across the room, talking to Noor. Worse, he was looking at her, and in the light he was better than beautiful, he was utterly stunning. He had a rakish, haughty face, full, sensual lips—and in four split seconds Felicity achieved more insight into her sister Georgie's eating disorder than she had in all her research and education.

The most natural thing was to carry on, to chat to Liam,

to eat the tiny sliver of bread. But she was so supremely self-conscious, so awkward, so aware of her mouth, her teeth as they bit in, her tongue, her jaw as she chewed, her throat as she swallowed, she gave in, put the loaded plate down, and settled for water instead.

Who the hell *was* he?

It was a question that would remain unanswered. Through the afternoon lectures, despite her eyes scanning the room for him, despite feeling as if she were on high alert waiting for him to reappear, there was no further sign of him. When the session ended at five p.m. it was with a certain reluctance that she accepted she would never see him again. Her mystery man would remain just that—a mystery.

'See you.' Liam grinned, rushing past as she lingered in the foyer. 'But not in Zaraq!'

Felicity laughed. 'Not for you then?'

'Nope. Do you want to grab a coffee?' he offered, but though she would have loved to linger a little while longer, to catch one final glimpse of *him*, her train left in twenty minutes. If she missed that one then she'd miss her connection, and she wouldn't make it back home tonight. Felicity declined, smiling. As she walked through to Reception she could see the grey London streets and the rain threatening. She rummaged in her bag for her small umbrella and heard her phone bleeping.

'Hi, Mum!'

'How was it?'

'Great.' Felicity smiled. 'Too good actually. Now I think I want to go to Zaraq.'

'Well, you're not going anywhere tonight…'

Felicity groaned as her mother continued.

'I looked up the trains and there's been some trouble on

the line. No service till tomorrow. There is a bus, apparently, but it only takes you halfway and you have to change.'

'It will take *hours*.' There was no chance of her getting home before midnight at this rate.

'What are you going to do?'

'Don't worry.' Felicity could hear her mother getting anxious, and as always moved quickly to quash it. 'I'll be fine; I can stay in London overnight.'

'But you haven't booked in anywhere. You don't know anyone!'

'Mum, I'm twenty-six,' Felicity interrupted calmly. 'I'm more than capable of surviving a night in London.'

Her credit card wasn't, though!

Still, as Felicity turned off her phone she was suddenly glad of the train cancellation. The thought of a night to herself was rather tempting—it had been way too long since she'd had one. Her time recently had been taken up with visiting her sister in the eating disorder unit, or stopping by at her mum's for a little pep-talk. Even since Georgie's discharge she hadn't been able to relax, with her mother or sister ringing almost constantly. Then there was taking Georgie to out-patients' appointments, and trying to work overtime as the never-ending medical bills and loan repayments rapidly caught up.

It would be nice to have a night alone.

A night when for once Felicity Anderson could just be that.

Not midwife, not daughter, not sister, not carer, not provider.

Just plain old Felicity would do very nicely.

Karim liked London.

He was an occasional visitor, though recently he had

been coming a lot more often. He had been overseeing the recruitment process for his hospital and university, as well as visiting his mother and checking on several investments and businesses he had stakes in. He wasn't busy enough though for his liking—not in the way he was in Zaraq, or had been. Karim blew out a long breath.

It was hard to get excited about million-dollar deals when they were but a drop in the ocean of his family's vast wealth. Hard too to inject enthusiasm into the recruitment process. The hospital and the university had been his inception, both ideas had fired him up at the time—but Karim didn't want to be watching films or looking at brochures of well-equipped hospitals. He wanted to be working in one. He wanted to stretch his brilliant mind with a complicated diagnosis, or to immerse himself fully in a long operation. But thanks to his status those opportunities were getting fewer and further between.

Still, he loved the relative anonymity London gave him. Here, though he worked seemingly hard, there was no real responsibility. Here he was carefree—a playboy prince who regularly indulged. It was so very different from his rigid, high-profile life back home. Here he could walk the streets unrecognised—which his security team hated him doing more than anything. Karim refused to bend. Dressed in a dark suit with a full-length overcoat he actually enjoyed the rain, enjoyed the changing seasons he witnessed when he came here. Late autumn was a season he liked, perhaps the most. This weekend he would drive to the country, get out of the city…

As his phone bleeped he gave it a cursory glance and then rolled his eyes. It was Leila again—he would have his aide, Khan, speak with her and forbid her from pestering him.

Yes, he would drive to the country—and, he decided, he would not go alone…

Karim thought only briefly of the rather difficult conversation he had had with Leila earlier this week, telling his long-term mistress that her services were no longer required. She hadn't taken it at all well—but then, what woman ever did?

Karim enjoyed and had bedded many women, though he believed absolutely in monogamy. After all, he always ensured the fling, or relationship, or whatever it was called, was confirmed as over before he readily moved on to the next! But not for much longer. He was being pushed further and further towards marriage by his father—something Karim was doing his best to avoid. Leila had delusions of grandeur—had thought that their three-month fling might be leading somewhere—and was refusing to listen now Karim had told her that marriage to her was not and never had been his intention. Over the past two weeks she had become demanding. When Karim didn't take her calls she would pester his aides—and, most importantly to Karim, the sex hadn't been that good!

Well, it had been good, Karim corrected—it had just taken too long! He was a marvellous lover—he had no issues there—and he lavished his lovers with attention. He did all the right things, and they certainly wept for more. It was really a time issue. With an appetite as insatiable as Karim's sometimes there simply wasn't *time*, and Leila had been insisting recently on the full theatre, when for Karim sometimes all he needed was her mouth.

Enough, he had decided. It was over and he had dealt with it—to his father's dismay. His father had told Karim in no uncertain terms that it was time now to find a bride—

which was why he'd flown to London. For one last play, one last feast of indulgence, before duty caught up and he married a suitable bride.

When he had slipped into the meeting room and been greeted by that stunning blonde he had felt the attraction—*how* he had felt it. And at lunchtime he had been sorely tempted to walk over. Still, when Noor had explained she was there to consider working in the maternity section of the hospital, Karim had decided it might be rather messy should he see her at work. He had decided that an afternoon stroll might be safer, so he'd rung Mandy, whose eyes weren't quite as blue and whose hair wasn't naturally blonde, and arranged to see her tonight. Even if she wasn't *her*, Karim was blessed with a good imagination—if he could stop Mandy talking for half an hour he would have a good night!

He'd headed back to the hotel only once the information session was over—happy with himself until he saw the real thing, walking out of the hotel and looking straight towards him.

Karim smiled and walked towards her. Why should he settle for a poor imitation?

It had been raining, Felicity realised, and it was about to seriously pour again. The sky was heavy and dark, the streets wet and uninviting. And then she saw him, walking towards her, dressed in a long black coat. With his dark hair he should have blended in with the rest, but he stood out, luminous almost in the grey and gloomy day.

And he saw her looking.

The underground was across the street and to the left. There was a moment for Felicity—a mysterious, inexplicable moment—when she knew she could walk down the steps and turn left, could turn her back and that would be it; or she could stand still and see what happened.

It was bizarre, watching as the rain started to fall, as everyone else hastened their speed or paused and put up umbrellas. His stride never changed. He just walked towards her with purpose in his eyes—determination, almost—and with a stab of regret she knew that it was pointless. Even if he engineered a conversation, asked her to join him for coffee or dinner, even if he was as stunning to talk to as he was to look at, all she would do in the long run was disappoint.

Mission pointless, Felicity realised, shaking herself out of her momentary trance, and she went down the steps and turned left.

There was Liam, walking out of a coffee shop over the road with a large muffin in his hand. Everybody was going back to their lives, and so too must she. As she pushed the traffic light button her head was whirring, trying to define what it was she had turned her back on—because not a word between them had been said.

The lights were changing, cars, taxis, cyclists and buses all slowing down and the green light was about to flash to tell the pedestrians to walk. She almost *wanted* his hand to come on her shoulder, for this mysterious man to haul her back to his world.

There was no hand on her shoulder. It was self-preservation that caused her to step back. In fact Felicity pulled an elderly lady back too, as she saw that one car wasn't slowing down—if anything it was speeding up. In the small amount of time it took for it happen, Felicity saw everything. The female driver, her head back, jerking at the wheel, the slide of the car over the crossing, and the horrific sound of a revved engine. It was like a missile turning and randomly choosing its course. It could have ended up anywhere—on the crowded pavement, in a packed café window. With no time to move, to register, even to run, an eerie silence descended. And then came a ripping sound of metal that went on for ever, a thud of impact as the small car slammed into a bus, its wheels still scratching and spinning, its engine still revving.

Then people moved.

The chance of an explosion was imminent.

As the crowd scattered, a few people ran forward.

Felicity could see the hotel doorman and Liam, running towards the centre of the bus, pulling on the closed doors. *He* was running too—but to the crashed car, as was she.

'She was fitting,' Felicity called out to him. He was leaning in the car as she sped over, her smart high heels hard work in the rain. She realised she hadn't been heard above the scream of the engine as she reached him, and shouted again. 'She was fitting!'

He had reached in and turned off the engine, but still it was dangerous and he told her so. 'Get back—this could go up at any time.'

It was the first time she had heard his voice. Deep and accented, it was telling her very clearly to leave the scene. Liam was telling her the same, having helped off the passengers after he had dashed to the centre of the bus. Seeing just how dangerous it was, he told Felicity to get the hell out.

'They're all off the bus. Driver's got minor injuries. The fire engine will be here in a moment—it's unstable…'

It was—smoke was billowing from the car engine. Felicity could hear sirens in the background. Help was never far away on busy London streets—except the streets were packed, and the short distance between help and the accident was blocked with cars.

'Go!' *He* didn't turn to say it—he was supporting the woman's head; she was breathing but unconscious—but he made his orders clear. 'Get back *now*!'

So she did—albeit reluctantly. Felicity knew it was up to the experts, that if he chose to risk his life then that was his choice. And then she heard it, the shrieks of a newborn baby. Not fearful, stunned shrieks, but like those of a wounded animal, and she could no more walk away now than fly.

Liam was calling her back, telling her not to be foolish, but Felicity ignored him. *He*, the beautiful stranger, didn't question her decision as she approached. He was still holding the woman's head but he was also assessing the car for an opening, trying to locate the piercing screams of the baby. He didn't order her to leave again—knew perhaps he would be wasting his time—and time was of the essence.

Felicity wrenched at the crumpled car door and tried to get her head in the small gap she created.

'The baby's bleeding.' Though it was wrapped in a blue blanket, the little white baby suit was dark with blood on the arm. Felicity's head couldn't fit fully in, but she could see a shard of metal sticking out of the babe's arm, and even though the blood loss looked relatively small, for such a tiny infant it was substantial.

'There's a piece of metal…'

'Felicity.' She was surprised that he knew her name, but he said rapidly, 'I'm Karim. Can you get your arm in? Can you reach?'

She was already trying—only she couldn't see and stretch inside at the same time.

'I can't get in!'

'No.' His voice was calm and assured. 'Turn around and put your arm in that way. You will be able to reach; you will be able to hear me.'

'But I can't see.'

'I will guide you.' His voice was accented, rich and strong, and so assured, it reassured *her*. It made Felicity think that she could do it.

She had no choice *but* to do it.

One last glance at the baby to get her bearings showed her the patch of blood was spreading. She could see the shard of metal in its arm and knew she had to apply pressure.

She turned her head, the rain lashing her face as her arm slid into the dry confines of the car.

'Lower your hand,' Karim ordered. 'That is the base of the crib.'

Crib? The baby seat, Felicity translated to herself. He was holding the patient's head and ducking his own in and out of the vehicle, so that he could be her eyes on the inside and speak to her on the outside. Inch by inch her fingers crept forward.

'Now to your right. Feel his foot? That is his right foot. Move up.'

The injured arm was the baby's left one, and Felicity slowly moved her hand upwards with Karim's guidance. The baby had stopped screaming now, and was just making little noises—which was even more worrying than the crying. Without Karim's instruction her fingers located the sternum, the neck, and tried to move to the left.

'I can't reach,' Felicity said. 'I can't.'

'Two inches,' Karim said, and she was grateful then for her high heels—and for Karim urging her on. 'Careful,'

Karim warned, but because she had seen, she knew where the metal was. She slipped her fingers into the babe's axilla and pushed upwards.

'Is it stopping?'

'I don't know,' Karim admitted. 'Just keep pushing.'

So she did.

For what felt like for ever.

The emergency services had arrived and the passenger door was peeled back a touch further. She could get her head inside now. She couldn't move to cover the baby with a blanket as the firefighter punched in the rear window— Karim did that. A paramedic had put a collar on the mother, and she had been extracted, but instead of stepping back, Karim climbed in further, covered the baby with an ambulance blanket, and covered Felicity's head too.

'She needs a hard hat,' a fire officer called.

'There's no room for a hard hat,' Karim responded. 'Turn your head,' Karim said to Felicity, which she did. Screwing her eyes closed, she tried not to move as the emergency crew created rear access to the baby.

And Karim stayed with her in the strange little tent.

He talked her through it, as her hand was numb and she wasn't sure if the baby was alive or dead.

'The firefighters have doused the engines,' he assured her. 'It shouldn't be much longer now.'

'My legs are freezing,' Felicity admitted.

'It will be over soon.' He held her eyes, black on blue, and it helped. She could hear the chatter of the firefighters and the paramedics behind her, but it was Karim's voice she was listening to. 'They are giving oxygen to him now.' It was as if he was her translator, and she could only listen to him, only trust what he was telling her, because he had been her eyes. 'They want to put IV access into his scalp before they move him. Can you hold on a little while more?'

Her whole arm and shoulder weren't only numb now, they hurt. Her body was trying not to shake, though she was frozen. She thought of all her mums in the last throes of labour, when it was all too much, when it was impossible, and yet still, with encouragement, somehow they pushed on.

'You *can* hold on,' Karim said, and she listened to him instead of to her body, that wanted to stop. She told herself it wasn't for much longer and pushed on.

'Got him.' A hand was over hers, pushing where she had, and a nameless voice told her she could let go now.

'Move her slowly backwards,' Karim ordered whoever was supporting her—because now she *could* let go Felicity was unsteady. She had to be pulled back rather than just remove herself from the car. Then she stood massaging her arm, tears pricking at her eyes as Karim climbed out too.

'Well done,' he said, and then changed his mind. 'I told you to get back. You should think before you rush in.'

'Did *you*?' Felicity commented.

'You should be more careful—there could have been more victims.'

What made the rules different for him? Felicity thought, and then winced as blood rushed back to her numb arm. She stared down at her soaked, filthy clothes. Her hair and face were drenched, and suddenly she didn't need scolding. She was close to crying, and he must have seen that because he changed tack.

'Go into the hotel,' Karim instructed. 'I will come and speak with you there.'

'I'm fine…' Felicity attempted, but gave in because

clearly she wasn't—not that Karim was listening. His attention was back on the accident scene.

Felicity looked on. The world was coming back into focus now, as her circulation returned. The street was awash with fire trucks and paramedics. The little babe was being lifted out in his intact child seat, loads of hands gently guiding the little life to safety. It was like watching a baby being born—a long, silent pause, then relief from the crowd, from everyone, as he was safely delivered from the confines of the car. A blanket had been put around her shivering shoulders and Felicity just stood and took it all in. But not Karim. Even though there were doctors and paramedics, all waiting to assist, he didn't relinquish control. He snapped out orders as Felicity continued to stand and watch.

Just who *was* this man?

Only when the ambulance doors closed—when the siren blasted and the police directed it away—only then, when there was nothing more either could do, did he come over to Felicity and without a word guide her inside the hotel.

Just as she had known he would.

CHAPTER TWO

'WELL, I don't think we need to check your references!'

They were sitting in the sumptuous hotel lounge; Felicity had relinquished her blanket and was shivering as Karim rapidly ordered drinks. Piping hot chocolate appeared in a moment. Soaking wet and shivering, and completely out of place in such surroundings, she must have looked a sight—but because Karim didn't turn a hair, neither did she. For now.

He gave her a kind smile and it dawned on Felicity where she was—not her surroundings, more the company. She was sitting with the man who had captured her attention for the entire day—the man she had chosen at the last moment to avoid. Now here she was, sitting drinking hot chocolate, the sole focus of his attention.

And she had every right to be nervous!

Now that everyone had stopped looking at her, she was able to look at him—and he really was the most heart-stoppingly beautiful man she had ever seen. His coat had been removed by a waiter, and his gorgeous ˙harcoal suit— apart from damp cuffs—was completely unscathed. His short black hair was glossy and wet, and his tie and the top of his shirt were loosened. He might have stepped out of a board meeting. The superbly cut suit accentuated his long limbs, and his olive complexion was set off with a crisp white shirt and gunmetal tie. His eyes were black, and they were kind, but they were not friendly. There was an elusive quality to him that Felicity couldn't quite put her finger on. An air of superiority that had Felicity fast realising that she hadn't a hope of relaxing and enjoying his company!

'Allow me to introduce myself—I am Karim. I oversee recruitment for the university and the hospital.'

Which was a rather vague introduction. Felicity frowned.

'You're a doctor?' she checked. He had known what he was doing out there, had retained control even when the emergency services had arrived. He was more than a recruitment consultant—of that she was sure.

'A surgeon.' Karim nodded. 'Though I rarely practise now. Recruitment is my focus.' He changed the subject. 'And you are Felicity Anderson, a fully qualified midwife who has all her paperwork up to date and is ready to leave.'

'How do you know?'

'Because I checked who you were with Noor.'

'Oh!' She blamed it on the hot chocolate, but she felt pink returning to her pale cheeks.

'I asked her to point out any midwives or emergency nurses. We are very short of both.'

'I see.' Felicity nodded. So that was why he had been looking. She only had her imagination to blame for thinking otherwise. Curiously deflated, she sat there, exhausted now, as the adrenaline that had seen her through the accident fully wore off.

'You did very well out there.' Karim looked her over approvingly, but sadly, Felicity realised, he was assessing only her nursing skills. 'Without you the baby would have exsanguinated.'

'I just hope I did enough soon enough.'

'I will ring and find out later,' Karim said, looking forward to the prospect—perhaps they could do that from his room! 'So, do you live in London?'

'Unfortunately, no!'

'Unfortunately?' Karim checked.

'I live in the north, and my train just got cancelled.' She was drained at the prospect of finding somewhere to stay, but Karim clearly thought he had the answer.

'Stay here tonight, then.'

'I don't think so!' She gave a small laugh; certainly she'd love to stay here—would love to peel off her damp, muddied clothes and climb into a fluffy white bathrobe rather than trudge the streets searching for accommodation that was rather more basic. But it was impossible, that was all! At that moment her phone rang. Not wanting to be rude, Felicity ignored it, and Karim gave a slight frown.

'It's my mum!' she said, by way of explanation.

'Shouldn't you speak with her?'

'I did a little while ago,' Felicity said, and then relented a touch. 'She suffers with anxiety. It's easier if I ring her when I've found out where I'm staying.'

'You just have,' Karim said. 'You will stay as our guest.'

'*Our* guest?'

'Zaraqua's guest!' He spoke as if the city was a person. 'We invited you to attend today's information session; now you have missed your train and you have also saved a baby's life. Of course it is our responsibility to ensure you get safely home. If that means you stay in London tonight, then so be it…'

'I couldn't possibly.' Felicity shook her head.

'This is how it will be.' Karim stood up. 'Excuse me for one moment.'

Felicity watched his broad back as he strode through the lounge. He really did have the most amazing presence. Every head turned as he walked past. She sat quietly, determinedly ignoring her phone, which was ringing again. She wished her mother would wait a little. Felicity *would* ring her, she resolved again, when she knew what was happening herself.

'Here.' Felicity jumped slightly and put down the scone she was eating as Karim returned and handed her a neat navy folder. 'It has all been arranged.'

It had too! She opened the folder, saw her room number and a swipe card, and could scarcely believe it. She was also just a little nervous as to what she was being offered. 'Are you sure?' Felicity frowned, completely unused to being spoilt, to things being sorted for her—normally that was *her* role. Still, the incident had shaken her up enough that she didn't have it in her to protest too much! 'Are you sure about this?'

'Absolutely.' Karim nodded. 'You cannot go home in wet clothes. Use the laundry service, and you have full use of the facilities—perhaps visit the spa… After today, you deserve to relax, And,' he added, 'may I say again well done. They are both very lucky that you were there.'

She deserved this, Karim thought. This woman who had just saved a life should not be stranded in London. She deserved to be spoiled, pampered. He insisted to himself he would have done the same for any attendee, but as he had arranged her accommodation he had shamelessly upgraded her—several notches, in fact. A rather confusing thought had occurred to him. Karim remembered the moment before the accident—the moment this woman had turned her back on him.

'Well, thank you,' Felicity said, retrieving her bag from the floor. 'It will be nice to get out of these clothes…' She stopped abruptly, a little embarrassed at her choice of words. 'Thank you again.'

She was going, Karim realised with a frown. Her words *had* been unintentional. There was no hint of flirting, no lingering to see if he might ask her to join him later…

'Would you like another drink?' Karim asked, but she shook her head.

'No, thanks.'

'Perhaps later?' When again she shook her head, Karim couldn't be bothered to pursue it. He was here in London for fun, and this was starting to feel like hard work.

As Felicity stood to go the waiter came over.

'Will you and your guest be dining with us tonight, Your…?'

He was frowned into silence. Karim had given strict instruction that his title was not to be used within the hotel—his security team were miserable enough with his jogging and walking the London streets, without alerting the public that there was a sheikh royal prince in their midst.

'Sir!' The waiter changed his words with a cough.

Karim was about to decline. He thought of Mandy, ever ready and waiting, and then looked to where Felicity stood. Her face was blushing scarlet, her eyes so startled he half expected her to turn and run. Maybe he should just let her. But he remembered again the attraction that had flared in the presentation room, that unacknowledged arousal between them that had rendered him so hard he had to get out. He decided the effort might be worth it—he wanted to go there again.

'Would you like to join me?'

He saw the dart of her eyes, and—always smooth, always polite—said the right thing. 'Forgive me—that was crass. Of course you do not have to join me. There is no obligation.'

'I know…' Felicity managed a small laugh as he voiced her urgent thoughts and then checked herself. Her accommodation was sorted, and now the most impossibly attractive man was asking her for dinner… So what if it couldn't lead to anything? So what if there was no point in pursuing a romance with this man? She hadn't had a night out or off in months.

Staring into his black eyes, at that moment the answer was easy. 'I'd love to join you, except…' She gestured to her crumpled and soaked linen suit.

'The hotel will sort that…' He waved his hand as if it *were* that easy. 'And I can give you an update on the mother and baby over dinner.'

'Thank you.' Felicity nodded.

'We will meet at eight,' Karim said. 'Here?'

'That would be lovely.'

It *would* be lovely, Felicity thought as Karim stalked out of the hotel lounge. But, glancing at her watch, she realised she had only just over an hour to prepare! So, after ringing her mother to tell her a rather loose version of her plans, Felicity snapped into urgent mode and dashed to a chemist. She bought some stockings, a toothbrush and paste, and some hair serum, and then went up to her room.

Only it wasn't a room—it was a suite. A vast sprawling

suite, with flowers and chocolates and even a bucket of champagne cooling in a silver bucket.

And then someone knocked at the door.

Her heart stilled. She was nervous that it was Karim, that she had misinterpreted the exceptionally friendly gesture after all.

But it was a woman with an instant wardrobe on a trolley, that she wheeled into Felicity's room. Felicity just stood there as she was informed to help herself, and told that her own clothes would be laundered and back to her by morning.

She couldn't get her head around it. She was used—too used—to being two steps ahead of everything, to being the one who anticipated problems, the one who sorted things out. Yet since she had stepped into the hotel—since her first greeting from Noor—she had been looked after, her needs anticipated, and she had been rewarded for a job well done too.

It felt nice.

Unfamiliar, but very, *very* nice.

Peeling off her damp clothes, Felicity took in her suite.

It had everything—and she hadn't needed to worry about the toothpaste and brush. The little basket of goodies in the bathroom contained everything a girl might need, Felicity thought as she found a teeny pump bottle of hair serum. And even things a girl didn't need too…

Like condoms!

Oh, Karim had assured her there were no obligations, but that wasn't why she dropped them like a hot coal. Whatever Karim might be expecting from her, it was never going to happen.

Felicity sat, deflated, on the edge of the huge oval bath and stared at herself in the mirror.

Her blonde hair was tumbled, there was still a flush of excitement in her cheeks, and her blue eyes were glittering at the prospect of dinner with Karim. But, as Paul had found out, dinner was all it would ever be. What if tonight went well? Felicity worried. What if he asked to see her again? And what if they went out for a few weeks…? She screwed her eyes closed at the prospect. At what point did you tell someone? She knew it was impossible for them to have a relationship, knew it was pointless to pursue it, but she *did* want dinner with him…

And dinner was all it could ever be for her—even with a man as dashing as Karim.

CHAPTER THREE

HE WAS waiting for her.

Karim stood as she walked into the hotel lounge, and his decision as to his choice of date for the night was instantly confirmed as the right one.

She was wearing a pale grey woollen dress, a modest dress—yet it clung nicely to her trim waist, and Karim noticed the scooped neckline. It accentuated her full bust…

He had idly wondered what she would achieve in an hour. Used to summoning mistresses, he had women on tap and permanently ready. This one was not used to his ways, and yet she had done exceptionally well! No one would possibly guess that just a short while ago she had been saving a life in the driving rain.

Her hair, that had been tied back in all of the short time he had known her, was loose now. Soft and newly washed, it fell over her shoulders. Her long, slim legs were encased in stockings, her feet in dark grey stilettos.

Yes, he was glad of his choice of company for the night. But as he placed his hand on her elbow and guided her through the restaurant, and she shot forward at the slight contact, he knew it was going to be a long one! Unashamedly he had checked her CV. He knew that she was twenty-six and single, yet she was acting like a gauche teenager on her first date.

Oh, well, Karim decided glancing at his watch. If they weren't in bed by eleven he could be at Mandy's by twelve!

He'd give her three hours!

The menu was impossible. Oh, there was plenty that at first glance she liked, but sitting opposite Karim made the simplest decision impossible. He was wearing a different suit, had used his hour to shower and change too. Felicity could see that—and smell it. She was somewhat relieved and a little irritated too when his phone rang. He answered it, and after a brief apology spoke to whoever was on the line in rapid Arabic.

'I am sorry about that.' He put his phone down, and then picked it up again and turned it off. 'That was an old friend and colleague of mine. He is working at the hospital the casualties were taken to—he always speaks in our own language.'

'How are they?' Felicity asked, glad now that he had taken the call, but worried as to what she might hear.

'The mother has regained consciousness. She had another seizure on arrival, but she is doing well.'

'And the baby?'

'Is in Theatre now,' Karim said. 'It will take a while, but the surgeons are very hopeful.'

'Did he regain consciousness?'

'Yes!' Karim nodded. 'They resuscitated with fluids. There is one problem…' He paused for just a moment and Felicity held her breath. 'He's a *she*!'

'Oh!' Felicity blinked, remembering the blue blanket. 'Well, there's a reminder never to assume!' She smiled, and he did too. He had lovely white even teeth, with just a tiny irregularity. But even that made him more exquisite; this was no capped, manufactured smile, and he really was, as she had first realised, devastating.

With only brief consultation he took care of the wine and the ordering, and was such pleasant company that by the time she had struggled through the entrée and moved onto the main Felicity was almost able to relax.

But not fully—because always, *always* her mind was on the end of night, or the next night, or the next.

This *was* a date.

A real one.

And real ones—good ones—led to more dates…

'You may find things different in Zaraqua,' Karim warned her, after he had pressed her about her work and she had told him how she was a strong advocate for natural childbirth with minimum intervention. 'We have top-class facilities and equipment, and we do tend to use them.'

'I have thought about that,' Felicity said, 'and I'm not looking to change the world. I work in a low-risk birthing centre at the moment—hopefully I'll come away from Zaraq more informed, which can only be good.'

'You have an open mind.' Karim smiled. 'You would not make a good surgeon.'

'I'm a good midwife, though,' Felicity said, and smiled back.

'Did you tell your mother you were staying here?'

'No!' Felicity said. 'I just told her I had found somewhere.' She saw his slight frown. 'She'd only worry more if I told her about the crash.'

'It must be hard, having a parent who worries so.'

'It is,' Felicity admitted, and thanked the waiter as her main course was taken away. 'And I'm still not sure if I'm doing the right thing, going overseas. My sister hasn't been well for a couple of years,' she explained. 'She's doing fine now, but there have been a lot of expenses. This way I can really tackle them. Only…' She hesitated. The practical solution she had come up with for her family had been a sensible one, but there was an emotional side to it too—one she had never shared and certainly not with a stranger.

'Only…?' Karim checked.

'I'm not sure I'm doing the right thing—I'm not sure how they'll manage. Georgie, my sister, has an eating disorder. She's doing brilliantly now, though.' She swallowed uncomfortably, nervous of voicing her innermost fears. 'I'm just worried that my leaving will set her back. But I don't really have a choice.'

'Georgie has,' Karim said as a white chocolate mousse drizzled in hot raspberry sauce was placed in front of her. 'She can choose to stay well or not—you cannot do that for her.'

He was right—of course he was right—only it wasn't so straightforward.

'You don't understand…'

'I can assure you I do!' Karim responded. 'I know all there is to know about duty and family. And I know how it feels to be the strong one.'

Karim had declined dessert, and was working his way through a cheese platter. Now her dessert bowl was empty, it merited just a little look from her. He pushed the platter forward and, to her own surprise, instead of refusing and saying she was fine, Felicity took a cracker and helped herself.

'What about your father?' Karim asked, watching as the cracker paused midway to her mouth.

'He died a few years ago.'

'I'm sorry. That must have been hard for you all.'

She stared across the table at him, stared into black, assessing eyes that gave absolutely nothing away—eyes that judged but were somehow not judging. Instead of taking the easy option and accepting his condolences, after a brief hesitation she responded.

'Don't be sorry. He caused this mess. What about *your* family?'

He gave a brief shrug. 'There is not much to tell.'

'Oh?'

He stabbed a piece of cheese with his knife and smeared it on some bread, then took a sliver of quince jelly and topped it with that. He handed it to her and then did the same for himself.

Karim never usually shared—he was generous with gifts, he just never shared what was his.

But tonight he did.

'I have two brothers. My mother lives here in London—my father is in Zaraq.'

'Are they divorced?' For a second she was sure his face tightened, and she thought she must have said the wrong thing. It was an entirely natural assumption—just the wrong one.

'There is no divorce in Zaraq. My mother, even though she lives in England, gave my father four sons. She deserves his support and respect.'

This was a rather different way of looking at things than Felicity was used to hearing in the maternity wards! But he'd confused her now.

'Four?' She crinkled her nose. 'I thought you said that you had two brothers?'

'I do.'

She knew then she had definitely said the wrong thing, and immediately apologised. 'I'm sorry…'

'You weren't to know.' He didn't elaborate straight away, and neither did Felicity push, but after the longest pause it was Karim who broke the silence. 'I am the third son. Ahmed was the second. Zaraq is seventy percent desert. Ahmed was into desert racing. He was practising. His vehicle broke down and help did not get there in time.'

'I'm sorry.' She said it again and he held her gaze, even opened his mouth for a second to speak, then changed his mind.

Don't be. He'd been about to repeat her very words. *He caused this mess.*

There was no bill to summon—just separate rooms to go to.

It was the part of the night she always dreaded.

They walked slowly to the lifts, where a few people were waiting, and Felicity's heart was hammering in her chest as he stood and faced her.

'Thank you,' she attempted, 'for a wonderful night.'

Karim was about to say that it didn't have to end there, but he hesitated. She was jangling with nerves, so he decided to soothe her with his mouth; he would play with her hair, his skilled lips moving in… He would let this lift go, Karim decided as the doors pinged open. His lips would meet hers and then he'd take her to his room in the next one!

His mouth was moving in. She was his sweet dessert to linger over—he had waited twelve hours, and he was more than ready to be rewarded for his good behaviour now.

For Felicity, there was just a sliver of indecision. She felt the weight of his lips, the bliss of his mouth on hers, then relaxed and gave in. They were alone at the lifts now, his hands loosely on her hips as his mouth worked on. Fear was replaced by pleasure, and a tiny curl was unfurling in her stomach. An empty lift opened, and she pulled back her head and stared into his eyes—because if he asked to see her again, even though she lived miles from London, even though it would be difficult, maybe she would say yes…

His mouth was on hers again, pulling her closer in, and it felt sublime to kiss him back without thinking. It was tender, but with intent, his tongue sliding between her lips, the thick scent of arousal suddenly closing in as if suffocating her. She jerked away again, because even if it wasn't tonight with Karim it would be soon. The inevitable day would come where she'd have to tell him she was frigid. She simply couldn't face it.

She saw the whip of confusion in his eyes as she fled to the lift and he called her name.

'Just leave me,' she sobbed, tears blurring her vision as she tried to make out the floor numbers. She ended up pressing more than half the buttons, so that the lift stopped and started almost at every floor. She wasn't scared that he'd chase her, just mortified by her own fear, choking down sobs as she swiped her card and stumbled into her room.

It was hopeless!

Soon her stunning grey dress lay in a puddle on the floor. Sheathed in lacy underwear, she lay under the sheets, curled into a shameful ball. She was ashamed of her own behaviour, knew she'd made a fool of herself and embarrassed him—he'd been kissing her goodnight, that was all.

It scared her how much she'd enjoyed it.

But she'd been stupid to try, Felicity was fast realising. Stupid to try and pretend that she was normal.

And very foolish to pretend with a man like Karim.

CHAPTER FOUR

STEPPING out onto the freezing grey street and heading for the underground, Felicity just wanted to get home.

Her clothes, as promised, had been laundered and delivered, and looked better than when she had put them on this time yesterday morning. She had set her alarm for six, determined to get out early and not to have to suffer the embarrassment of seeing him at breakfast.

She'd overreacted appallingly—she knew that.

A simple goodnight would have sufficed.

But it wasn't his kiss that had terrified her, it was the thought of where it might lead—where, with a man like Karim, it *would* lead. She couldn't stand the shame of a disappointing end. Better to just walk away now. Karim oozed sexuality—and she could hardly beat him down with a stick, hardly keep chatting her way through dinner only to dodge his caress at the end of the night.

'Morning!' She hadn't noticed him jogging towards her, and she jumped when she did. He was dressed in grey sweats—a world away from the suited man she had dined with last night, but still impossibly gorgeous. Slightly breathless, he gave her a guarded smile. 'Off to get your train?'

'The line's running, apparently—I just rang and checked.'

Karim couldn't be bothered with small talk. He was annoyed, and glad that he'd caught her so that he could tell her so.

'You really didn't have to run off crying last night—saying no works very well for me.'

'I just…' She screwed her eyes closed in confusion and embarrassment—because she *had* kissed him back, for a moment had actually forgotten. He deserved some sort of an explanation—except it was impossible to come up with one. 'I just felt things were moving along too fast.'

'It was a kiss,' Karim said. 'And good kisses tend to move things along.'

He was still annoyed—but not just with her.

She was a *nice* girl. And nice girls wanted romance, kisses, flowers, phone calls—none of which Karim minded. But he wanted sex too. He stared down at her miserable face and it moved him—because if he'd had time on his side she might very well have been worth the effort.

Only he didn't have time.

'I've got to get going,' Felicity said, and he had to get going as well—back to his last taste of freedom before he took on the full weight of the crown.

So why was he calling her back? 'What if I want to take you for dinner tonight?'

'You'd have an extremely long drive!' Felicity attempted a smile, but it wavered when he shrugged.

'I don't mind travelling,' Karim said.

'Let's just leave it.' Tears stung her eyes as she stared at this beautiful man, who deserved so much better than her truckload of issues. 'Look, it isn't you, it's me!'

The pedestrian crossing was bleeping, the little green man waving her over—she could see the underground and just wanted to dive into it, wanted to fade into oblivion in the crowd. She shook him off and ran—but she was wearing heels and he was wearing running shoes. The crowd swallowed her, and she hoped she had disappeared into a mass of dark suits as she took the escalator.

Karim was enraged—confused and enraged! Who *was* this woman who used his lines? Who *was* this woman who denied his kisses, his invitations? Did she know who he was? He plunged into the underground. Okay, she didn't know just *who* he was, but that was part of the game—he won on charm alone.

Except with Felicity he wasn't winning.

'What's that supposed to mean?' He was beside her, with people tutting as he stood where they wanted to walk. He pressed in beside her, taking the escalator with her.

'Just leave it!' Felicity hissed.

'I don't want to.'

'And you always get what you want, do you?' Felicity's voice was curt—derisive, even—as she looked at him and saw him for the rich, spoilt playboy that he was. 'Well, not this time.'

They were off the escalator now, and he took her wrist. 'What are you running from?'

'You!' she said loudly. 'You just assume that I'll sleep with you because you bought me dinner—'

'I just offered to drive for hours to take you to dinner again…' Okay, he'd had no intention of driving—his pilot would have taken care of that side of things—but he had offered her way more than he intended and yet still she refused him. 'What's so scary about that?'

'Nothing,' Felicity snapped. 'Can't you accept that I'm just not attracted to you?'

It was a lie, an utter lie, and he dashed it with his mouth, kissing away her fibs. She could hear the tube train screeching into the station, feel the rush of wind around her legs, the thick flow of people walking past. But they all faded as he pressed hard into her. His tongue parted her lips and she felt flames lick around her stomach, felt a stroking deep inside that she'd never felt before, that none of Paul's fruitless attempts had ever yielded. And still Karim kissed her, his mouth capturing hers so thoroughly she couldn't breathe, didn't want to breathe, could only think about kissing him back.

'I beg to differ.' He pulled his head back.

She broke down then, in a way she never had before.

Karim stood for the longest time, then pulled out an immaculate handkerchief and flinched just a touch as she blew her nose on his royal coat of arms. He should walk away—because it wasn't his problem, and clearly there *was* a problem. He was here for his final fling, his last taste of life before he took on full royal responsibility.

But he felt responsible *now*.

Tears rarely moved Karim. Hers did.

Walk away, a voice told him. He could not.

After a brief hesitation he took her in his arms, curiously relieved that she didn't stiffen or shrug him off. Unfamiliar tenderness—compassion, even—was filling him as he led her away from the underground and further complicated his life.

CHAPTER FIVE

'SHE didn't suffer...' Karim said to Felicity, but for the benefit of the curious onlookers as they took the lift to his suite. 'We have to take solace in that.'

Her face was in his chest. Her tears were at the gulping stage now, and from the depths emerged the glimmer of a smile. It warmed her that he would do that for her—would soothe the sting of shame as her private misery was momentarily on public display.

She could only vaguely remember getting back to the hotel, with him holding her, leading her through the streets. She had baulked at his offer of a secluded table in the restaurant, and she might live to regret the folly of her ways, but at some very deep level she trusted him. After last night she knew that for Karim no meant no, and the fact he was a doctor helped too. But it wasn't just that. Yesterday something had been triggered inside her, and Karim was the source—the source of a feeling that had always eluded her. And though she'd tried to walk away, now she willingly walked back.

Even in her highly emotive state there was a slight flash of wonder as they stepped into his suite—if hers was gorgeous, this was truly a palace—yet all she felt was safe.

There was actually nothing sexy in it. She sat on his sofa and centred herself for a few moments as Karim rang down and ordered breakfast, then poured her a large brandy. She shook her head.

'It's seven a.m.!'

'We don't choose when these things happen!' Karim said, and so she took a sip, and then another. She shivered as violently as she had yesterday, after the accident, despite the warmth of the room, but it was she who broke the gentle silence.

'I shouldn't have accepted your invitation for dinner.'

'Are you involved with someone?' Karim asked, because that would make sense. Their attraction had been so fierce it would have been hard to deny it—easier, perhaps, to lie a little, to give in to the forces that had propelled them from the moment he had walked into the conference room.

'We broke up.' Felicity took another sip of her drink, then put it down—because nothing could calm her till she admitted the truth. 'I'm not very good at relationships.'

'Neither am...' Karim started, but then halted. Because even gentle humour was out of place at this time.

'There's no point starting something. It's not fair to you and it's not fair to me...' She wasn't making much sense. 'Paul and I were together for a year and we weren't able to... I mean, *I* wasn't able to...'

She actually couldn't say it, but Karim got to the painful point. 'You were unable to have sex?'

'Yes.'

'You know I am a doctor?' He watched as his words were absorbed and she nodded. She understood that at this moment he *was* a doctor—which was maybe why she felt safe, maybe why she had let him lead her to his suite. He was a doctor—*another* one who would tell her it could be sorted. 'And I am telling you—you are not frigid.'

She shook her head. She had heard it so many times before.

'Felicity.' His voice was firm and so assured—so absolutely assured that she wanted to believe him. 'You are *not* frigid.'

Yet no matter how she might want to believe him, how assured he sounded, she knew better.

'I've seen doctors, psychologists. I had a boyfriend for a year and we tried everything. All I ever feel is scared.'

'Did they work out why?' He didn't flinch as she spat out a mirthless laugh. 'Your sister is ill?'

'She's anorexic,' Felicity said. 'Well, she's recovering.'

'And your mother suffers with extreme anxiety?'

'I know all that.' Felicity clawed at her scalp—because she was sick of it—sick of going over and over it in the hope of a different outcome. Always the result was the same. 'My father was a controlling drunk. There was no abuse as such…' She hated all the questions, the assumptions—because they were all wrong.

'Abuse does not have to be sexual or physical to be abuse.'

'No…' Felicity breathed, glad that at least he understood that—that her father's controlling ways had been enough to damage her in a way that wasn't as obvious as her mother's or Georgie's. She had been left with an intense private fear of giving trust, of losing control, that couldn't be logically explained.

He didn't make her try.

'You have never once felt aroused?'

'No. Never.'

'Not once in your life?'

'No…' Her eyes darted to his, and then back down. This was the reason she was here—because yesterday she *had*! Yesterday Karim had flicked a switch. She didn't know how, but she wanted to know why.

He stood torn with rare indecision. He was moved by this beautiful selfless woman who delivered babies, who had so bravely saved a life yesterday, who put her family first and was, for whatever reason, holding a part of herself back, too nervous to trust. The clock was ticking on his last days of freedom. He could be out there enjoying himself, but he actually wanted to be here. He wanted to spend his last days with this shy, deep stranger, to bring passion and joy into her life—and of course there would be a reward for him too!

'I'm not being a doctor now,' he said. 'Because as a doctor I cannot speak like this. But as a man I can fix it.'

'Paul said the same,' Felicity sneered—because his was a typical response, such an arrogant thing to say, and it told her he didn't really understand.

'I'm not Paul, though.'

She pressed her fingers into her eyelids, because he had made a vital point.

'And I am telling you that you are *not* frigid. I assure you, this can be fixed.'

'How do you know?' She was angry at his assumption. 'How do you *know* that I'm not just going to feel worse if the world's sexiest—?' She stopped then, watched his beautiful mouth curve into a smile, and she cringed back on the sofa but sort of smiled too.

'Compliment accepted,' Karim said—and then he stopped smiling, serious now, and knowledgeable too. 'I can fix it. Because to be frigid, or whatever you choose to call it, means you are unable or unwilling. You think you are unable, but you *are* willing. In the lecture theatre, when we stood in the dark near each other, were you aroused then?'

'I don't know—I don't know…' She was trying to stand up, like an animal trying to escape, mortified, confused. He held her wrists.

'Suppose we took it slowly…' Karim watched her through narrowed eyes. 'Suppose you said yes to dinner tonight.'

Tears were spilling out of her eyes as he deliberately said the wrong things, and he knew he was right then— knew he was right to say what he said next.

'So why don't we get *it* out of the way—and then…' He forced her chin up to see his smile. 'You can actually enjoy dinner.'

'I don't know…' she breathed. 'I don' t even know how I felt yesterday.'

'You *were* aroused,' he said. 'I could feel it, I could smell it, and I could taste it.'

'How?'

'Because I was aroused too.'

So she hadn't been imagining it.

And as he watched his words settle in her mind, Karim knew he was right to do what he did next.

'*This,*' Karim said, guiding her hand to his thigh, 'was how you were feeling.'

She could feel him beneath her hands, long and thick and hard, and so huge it really brought her no comfort. She went to pull her hand away—because if she hadn't been able to accommodate Paul, then how the hell could she accommodate Karim—but he was speaking on, talking in low, sensual tones that held her hand there. 'As I stood in that room I could feel it, and I could feel *you*. I wanted to go over to you…' She could feel him stretch beneath her fingers, feel a stirring in him just as she had felt herself. She felt him harden as he spoke, yet still her hand stayed. 'I could of course do nothing about it. I stood there like this and saved it for later.'

'For later?'

He glanced to the left, to the bedroom and the massive rumpled unmade bed. 'Last night after dinner I could have called many women. Yet I wanted *you.*'

She could feel his manhood steeling upwards, feel the strength of his erection beneath her fingers. A sick excitement built in her as she pictured him on that very bed. She was not even looking at him now, just holding him and staring at the bed.

'I *had* you last night, Felicity.'

Oh, she could feel a terror building deep within—only it didn't exactly feel like fear, more a nervous flurry that was usually evident in her chest, but was much lower now, as his voice rumbled on, as he grew in her hand.

'I stroked myself and thought of you, and I know you did the same.'

'No.' She jerked her hand away. 'I didn't. I *can't,*' she begged.

'But do you *want* to?'

Did she?

It was a dangerous situation, and yet somehow she had never felt safer. He was beautiful, and for the first time she was starting to feel it was not impossible.

'Yes…' It was the most honest she had ever been— because right here, right now, she *did* want to. With him, with this man who knew how to hold her, how to kiss her, how to talk with her. This man who had known to take her by the hand and walk her back to the hotel. It was reckless and dangerous, and there wasn't a hope of justifying it, but if she couldn't do it with him today then she could never do it with anyone.

Here, with this beautiful man, was her chance to start her life over, to cast aside the demons that plagued her. She had never been so attracted to anyone. Oh, yes, physically—but *everything* about him enthralled her. His rich voice, his piercing eyes. And as for his smile… A smile that was turned on her now…

'What if I can't?' Felicity asked—not angrily this time, but because it was what was worrying her the most.

Still Karim smiled. 'You worry too much.'

Someone knocked at the door and Karim stood. Felicity's eyes glanced down to his groin, to all that she had felt, but there was no real evidence of it now—just a long shadow against his lean thigh. As Karim called the butler in, it was like a bubble bursting, and real life invaded. Terror caught up with her as she realised what she had agreed to.

'I am going now for a shower.' He gestured to the table that was being laden with food fit for a king. 'You will eat.'

As the butler exited discreetly, Felicity stood, unsure what to do.

'Eat!' Karim called from the shower, as if he could read her mind.

Eat?

She didn't want to eat, she just wanted to get it over with—which was undoubtedly the wrong way to think, but it was how she felt. She was tempted to turn tail and run, listening to the running water. Oh, Karim didn't know the extent of her *problem*, couldn't understand just how real her fear was. That despite honest, desperate efforts by Paul she was so closed up he couldn't enter.

Karim took his time showering. He wondered, as he dried off and pulled on a bathrobe, if she would still be there when he came out.

Last night he had wanted her, yet he had sensed her nerves, and as his guest it would have been wrong…

He had wanted her, though.

She had him curious.

Karim shaved himself, and thought about her, then grinned in the mirror as he recalled her words and nearly cut himself as he stared at 'the world's sexiest man'!

She was cute, Karim decided, paying closer attention to his heavy overnight growth but his mind was still on Felicity.

Karim read women well—he'd had plenty of practice. Yet Felicity was a challenge—which suited Karim fine.

He loved two things in life—women and challenge. Felicity was both.

He knew she was terrified, knew she was probably expecting him to lie her on the bed and devour her for hours, yet he also knew that would be pointless. She wouldn't relax when in the back of her mind she would be waiting. Despite her protests, despite her insistence that she didn't like it, he *knew* he had aroused her back there in the lecture room. And Karim mused on *that* as he walked out of the bathroom, to see her nervously sitting there, as if she were waiting for a dental extraction. He realised that only when it was impossible to do anything did she relax.

'I have to make some phone calls,' Karim said. 'Important calls. I am sorry, I cannot avoid them.'

'Of course!' Felicity smiled, but inwardly her heart sank.

As he leafed through his diary—no doubt wondering

where he could pencil in their 'sex hour'—he chatted away in Arabic on the phone, and then switched to English. 'Tell him to call me back in five minutes!' His voice was dark and full of foreboding. 'If he calls back one minute later the deal is off!'

He turned to her. 'Why don't you have a bath and relax while I make these calls?' Karim offered.

Though he probably thought he was saying the right thing, Felicity was tempted to pick up her bag and run. If only it were so easy, she thought wryly. How many bubble baths had Paul run for her? There was no chance of her relaxing, knowing what was coming…why couldn't anyone understand?

'Look—' she gave a brittle smile '—I really think I ought to just go…'

'One moment.' His phone was bleeping again, and he took the call. But with his free hand he pulled her towards him, rolled his eyes at the intrusion, and chatted as he idly stroked her face. Then, still in between talking, he kissed her cheek—lots of tiny little kisses as he spoke on. When the call had ended, he kissed her more thoroughly.

'Have a nice bath, and then I will be free…'

'Okay…' He was so nice to kiss. Clean-shaven now, he smelt of soap and cologne. His hair had been damp against her cheek as he'd kissed her neck, then returned to her face.

'Stay there,' he growled as his blasted phone rang again. He put it on speaker phone, rested it on the dressing table behind them, and proceeded to kiss her again as a nasal voice droned on in the background. 'They will be calling me back in a few moments.' Karim smiled at her as he barked his instructions to the phone. 'Bath!' he ordered—only she didn't want to go.

She could feel his arousal pressing into her, could feel his tongue mingling with hers, and it was like being back in the tube station. There was a delicious pull low in her groin as he pressed himself into her.

'Were you really?' Felicity pulled away. 'Last night—were you really thinking of me?'

'Oh, yes…' Karim said, lifting her onto the dressing table. He parted her knees slightly, pulling her skirt up around her hips, and Felicity felt her stomach tighten. 'When you lie in the bath, think of me as last night I thought of you. Like this…'

Fascinated, terrified, she stared down as he parted his robe, her throat constricting at the sight of him. Fear and hopelessness gripped her because she could *never* accommodate him. And yet he was so exquisitely beautiful. His hand stroked his magnificent member, his fingers loosely gripping the dark skin that she wanted to touch too.

'I thought of you in that dark conference room. I imagined forgetting everyone was there and walking over…' He was slowly nudging her knees apart with his hips, stroking against the silk of her knickers. She badly wanted to touch him. 'I thought of lifting your skirt…' He could see her arousal on her panties, and he touched it with his tip. He took her hand and guided it to him. She bit on her lip as she felt his velvet-soft skin and the power beneath it.

'Later,' Karim said, 'when I am not so busy, when I have taken this call and you are nice and warm from your bath…'

He was fiddling with her panties, pulling them down in one lithe movement, taking them over her ankles. Then he returned to stand before her, stroking her intimately with the tip of his erection. 'When there is no chance of us being disturbed…' He undid her blouse, shrugged it down to her shoulders, then unhooked her bra so her breasts were loose. Lowering his head, he suckled slowly on one nipple, dragging it out as still he pressed at the top of her legs. Her body twitched with each feather-light stroke. Then his mouth returned to hers, kissing her deeply, his tongue probing her, darting in and out as she unfurled inside.

Karim was always prepared, always aware of the value of his seed. Condoms were dotted everywhere in his life, and easily he opened a drawer as still he kissed her. 'Here.' He handed her a condom.

'We can't *now*…'

'Of course not. We will take our time—we have all morning—but it is good to practise.' He unwrapped the tiny parcel. 'Later, after your bath, you will slide it on like this…' Her hands were shaking so much she almost dropped the slippery thing. 'When you know how to do it, it will be much easier. I will show you…' He placed it on his tip and then took her trembling hands. 'Now, roll it down…'

She was terrified she'd scratch him, but she did as told, watching it unfurl over his gorgeous length. 'See,' Karim said. 'It is easy.'

Karim was glad it was on as he parted her and ran his erection over her sweet place; he knew that precious warning drop had already escaped. He *had* imagined her last night—but she was so much sweeter in the flesh. So pretty and pink and wet, and she was a virgin. Well, suffice to say he was ready! He stared down at her tentative hands and hoped he was doing right by her—because her beauty deserved it. He could hear involuntary moans escape her lips as his thumb worked her clitoris and his fingers crept to her entrance. He felt her tighten, felt her tense refusal, and knew rather than hoped then that he was right to do it this way.

She felt his fingers *there* and she panicked. But as they moved away she relaxed a touch.

His blasted phone was ringing again, and she knew he had to get it—except she didn't want him to, was kissing him hard as he pulled back.

'I have to get that!'

'I know.'

But he was still kissing her as the phone clicked off, kissing her harder and harder as the message bank bleeped.

'He'll call back…' Karim groaned his apology. 'Bath, Felicity.' He was right at her entrance, smiling a rueful smile. 'You deserve my full attention, and when you come out…'

He was right there, right *there*, just nudging a little, with tiny, tiny thrusts that went nowhere and yet shot her to orbit, giving her a glimpse of what maybe could be done. Then the blasted phone rang—their five minutes were clearly up.

'I will just take it… You go and…'

'Okay…'

'I really must take it.'

'I know.'

He was staring down at his sheathed erection, just there at her entrance. Felicity did the same.

'Soon I will have the whole day.'

'I know.'

The phone was silent again. He was a tiny way inside her, just the tip of him nudging her, and she was still staring down. His phone would start trilling again soon, and she knew when it did that he'd have to answer. But she didn't want him to.

'Look!' Karim gently ordered her, and she did, staring down at where he was, watching as he pulled out a little way and then pressed in a little more. He shrugged off his bathrobe, his whole delicious naked body in front of her, and she could feel her thighs shaking, feel a pit of want as he slid in just a little more. It was starting to hurt, and she knew she would spasm, but she was saved by the phone. There was utter regret in his eyes as she looked up.

'Now, if you will forgive me, I really have to…' And he did. Holding her eyes, he thrust deliciously in, watched the shock of fear as he stabbed inside her, watched the surprise, the bemusement and then the wonder. If it had been anyone but her he would have come at that second, it was almost killing him *not* to come, and yet he wanted her to relish this moment. There was no triumph, just tenderness as he saw the rapt expression on her face as she looked down.

Oh, it had hurt—did hurt—yet it was a delicious hurt. For Felicity it was like a bizarre out-of-body experience. She was watching it, feeling it, yet unable to comprehend that it was happening to *her*. He absolutely filled her, guiding her hands to feel him, to feel him slide in and out, till she could look no more—because she was weak, leaning on his shoulder and sucking it—biting it, maybe— as her legs wrapped around his back. And then she felt it.

The *it* she'd never felt was emerging, the tremble in her thighs spreading, a flash of heat darting up her spine as he bucked fiercely within. And it wasn't gentle, it was *fabulous* as he pulled her off the dressing table, and finally she came. Karim pressed her right into him, holding her, supporting her, as her body gave what she thought it never could—the delicious stabs of her first orgasm. She wanted to scream, but she held back. And then he was groaning and thrusting. And, yes, she could scream now—but instead she sobbed, a deep, sweet sob as he climaxed inside her.

Karim was dizzy.

He came often. But not like this—never once like this. He felt depleted—his thighs ached, the small of his back ached. It was as if he had dragged on hidden reserves to deliver all of his best. He couldn't even take her to his bed for a moment, just stood as he lowered her down.

'Thank you…' she gasped, as weak and as dizzy as him. She stood till the world caught up, and then let him take her to his bed. She sat on the edge as he undressed her, garment by garment, kissing each newly exposed part of her body and then lying down on the bed beside her. He held her in the crook of his arm and felt her warm skin. 'I loved it…' Her voice was more normal now. 'I never, *ever*, even in my wildest dreams…'

Her hand slipped down. He was about to tell her no, that it was too soon, too tender—but nature never ceased to amaze him. Her pleasure was so transparent, her wonder so catching, and he watched as he rose to greet her. And for Felicity—for her—he knew that he could do it all over again.

CHAPTER SIX

FOR three years, at some level, Karim had known this day would come.

Late afternoon his phone had buzzed quietly—not his regular phone, which he had long since turned off, but the one phone that he never could.

He had taken the call in the lounge, listened to the news and sat with his head in his hands in silence for a full five minutes afterwards. Then he had walked back into the bedroom, his gaze falling to where she slept, and all he'd wanted to do was climb in beside her, rest next to her soft skin and disappear. He wanted to wake with her in his arms and smile in relief as he realised it was just a dream. But to sleep now would have been to waste what he knew was his last taste of freedom.

The last few minutes in his life of being Karim—because, despite being the third-born son, he was being groomed to be King.

This day that should never had come—had never, when Karim had been a child, been anticipated. The third of four boys, relatively safe from the prospect of succession, he had run free. His mother had loved him with more abandon, the press had been less interested in the dark, wilful young Prince than in his elder brothers.

His elder brothers, Hassan and Ahmed, had been groomed, of course—Hassan the successor, Ahmed just in case. But for Karim, and later Ibrahim, there had been more freedom. It was a freedom that their mother had fought and begged for, and had been won only for her younger sons. Three of the boys had inherited some of their mother's features. Hassan, the eldest, had her piercing blue eyes but none of her joy or lightness, Ahmed, the second boy, had a lighter complexion and hair and had inherited her high-strung personality too.

And young Ibrahim was a true mix of both—royal and abrupt, like his father, yet dashing and wild, like his mother.

Karim, though, was truly his father's son.

He was, his father had said in a pensive moment, the one who would make the best King.

Decisive, arrogant, Karim held an innate strength, a deep streak of privacy that belied his public persona. Even when his mother's indiscretion had been exposed and she had fled, shamed, to England, Karim, the closest to her, had been the only brother who had refused to cry.

It was how it had to be.

There could be no pardon, no erring from the rules— she was the wife of the King.

To Karim it was simple.

And, as third in line, it *was* simple: he could indulge his passion. While after their mandatory stint in the army his older brothers had studied politics and history, the young Karim had indulged his desire for medicine, heading to the UK, spending time with his mother, causing a stir on the social scene. A dashing Prince, he had had the young fillies of London eating out of his manicured hands.

At what point had it changed?

Staring out into the darkening London skies, Karim rested his forehead against the cool window and watched the cars, taxis and shoppers below enjoying the anonymity London afforded. He remembered the first time he had felt it, that shiver of realisation, a feeling he would later recognise as dread, sliding like black fingers around his heart. He felt it occasionally at first, then more regularly, until now each morning he awoke with a tight band around his heart.

Hassan had married. Karim remembered well the pride and the jubilation in Zaraq. Remembered too laughing at his father's concerns when it had been two years and no heir.

'There is plenty of time…'

Then it had been three years, then four, and then finally the news the country had waited for.

A baby due in April.

In February he had come—too soon for the little scrap of life named after the King. Karim had held his tiny nephew, Kaliq, on that last day. As a doctor he had known at first glance that no machines or technology could help. When neither Hassan nor his wife, Jamal, had been able to face it any longer he had held Kaliq in the palm of his hand, stared at the little life that was too weak, too frail, and yet so wanted, then held him to his cheek as his life had slipped away.

Those first voices of dread had started to speak up, but he had quashed them, dismissed them out of hand. Because if Hassan could not produce, then long in the future, if the King should die, there would be Ahmed.

Ahmed. Despite the grooming, despite the bravado, Karim had always known that his brother was fragile emotionally—just how fragile Karim had refused to consider.

Burdened by the prospect that one day he might be King, Ahmed had one day taken his four-wheel drive into the hostile desert. Suicide was a sin, so it had been called 'heat exhaustion'.

By November the country had been plunged into mourning again.

Nothing was ever voiced.

Nothing had ever actually been voiced.

As third in line, Karim had always indulged in his passion for surgery, but as the line of succession had shortened, so too had his theatre and patient list. Slowly he'd been moved away from the hospital and from direct contact with patients. Instead he built a new hospital and a new university, trying to ignore the voices. Because if he acknowledged they were real…

Today they were real.

Today they spoke.

You are strong, Karim said to himself. You will be a good leader for the people.

He knew he was strong. And he wouldn't acknowledge, even to himself, the deep and buried truth.

Instead he pushed it aside and chose to get on with what he had been summoned to do.

The room was still and dark when Felicity awoke, stretching luxuriously. For that moment all she felt was peace—not a smudge of regret for what had taken place.

Karim was standing by the window, staring out on to the street below. Just as she was about to smile and greet him, she stilled. She saw the grave expression on his face, the weary set of his shoulders, and a chill of foreboding swept through her.

'Karim?'

He came over, forced a half-smile on his grim face, and sat on the bed beside her.

'You looked so peaceful that I didn't want to disturb you.'

'Is something wrong?' There was a different energy to him. They had made love on and off throughout the day, and Felicity had shared with him not just her body but her mind. She had told him how she adored her family, how it was tearing her apart to leave them even for this short while, how she adored her work, her friends. Bit by bit she had revealed herself to him, but now, as she stared up at his strained face, despite his tender words she realised Karim had revealed so very little.

'My father is ill.'

'I'm sorry.'

'He has been ill for some time, but I have just found out that he has been admitted to hospital. I have to leave tonight for Zaraq.' His face was stamped with pain.

Felicity knew he was telling the truth, and she moved to comfort him as he had her, but even as she held him, he was unreachable. There was tension in his shoulders, and when he pulled back his voice sounded formal rather than tender.

'I don't know when I will be back.'

'Will you call me?' Oh, of course one should never sound needy, but she *was* needy—needy of him.

'I did not expect to have to return so soon. Felicity…' He wasn't finding this easy—wasn't finding any of it easy. He stared at her. She looked confused and gorgeous, and he wanted to take her with him, but he couldn't. She didn't even know who he was—and more than that he couldn't inflict it all on her. She wanted romance, flowers, phone calls, Karim reminded himself. She wanted her family and her friends and the freedom in her body that he had just given her. He couldn't, wouldn't do it to her. 'It will be busy when I get home. Things are very different for me there.'

'So that's it, then?' Hurt, angry eyes met his, yet there was a dignity to her as she dressed, a proud dignity as she pulled on her clothes. And there was something else about her too—since this morning she had grown up. Before him now stood a proud, strong woman, and Karim knew that this day had played a large part in that.

Felicity knew it too. Oh, she was hurt, and bitterly disappointed, yet somehow she also felt strong. Of course he must go to his father. Of course they could never be…

But something beautiful had been taken away too soon, and it was with that sentiment that, instead of storming out, she walked over to him. And Karim held her. He held her in his arms as if he never wanted to let go.

'I will have a car take you home.'

'Karim, I live miles away…'

'You are not getting a train.' His phone was ringing again, and this time he answered it, talking for a second or two before clicking off. 'My plane is being prepared.'

'*Your* plane?'

He checked himself, determined not to confuse her further. 'I am sorry. Sometimes my English is confusing. I have to be there soon. I have booked my ticket. I have to leave in half an hour.'

He didn't want to go. She knew that. She could feel it in the hard kisses that he showered on her, in the desperate lovemaking that ensued, could even feel it as he took her down to Reception and saw her to a waiting car.

The journey home was long, but Felicity wanted it to

be. She needed to get her head around all that happened in the last twenty-four hours.

She didn't even know his surname—yet this man had changed her.

To anyone else it would sound cheap and sordid—a day of no-strings sex, with someone she would never see again—yet Felicity felt no need to justify to herself what had taken place.

Especially as, after she had taken the lift to her apartment and rummaged for her keys, when she paused in the middle of the corridor and saw a most exquisite bouquet at her door.

They must have cost a fortune, soft pink blooms of orchids, and with tears in her eyes Felicity read the note.

Never forget.
Karim x

How could she ever forget? Felicity thought, letting herself into the flat, staring at the blinking red light on the message machine and listening as Noor offered her a position in Zaraq.

The money was more than she'd been expecting; the only blight was that she had to leave within a week. Felicity knew it couldn't have been Karim's doing as, from the time of recording, the message had been left immediately after the information session.

Her mother's message urged her to ring the second she was home. Instead she crossed her modest flat and stared out of the window into the cold night sky. She imagined Karim up there, flying back to his sick father, and wondered if they might meet again. Because even if his life was complicated, for Felicity it was actually rather simple. She read the card one more time.

Never forget.

Oh, she'd never forget—because every second of their encounter was etched indelibly on her mind. And anyway, Felicity realised, letting the tears spill now, she'd never forget because already she loved him.

CHAPTER SEVEN

THERE was no time to dwell!

Not a single thing she could do about it!

In the week she'd had left she'd had to fill in paperwork, decline her prior job offer, and attend endless friends and family farewells—as well as reassure her mother and sister that she wasn't disappearing for ever.

And even though she knew she'd be back it was so hard leaving.

Standing in the airport, Felicity hugged her fragile sister close.

'Look after the flat,' Felicity said, trying to pretend she wasn't worried about how Georgie would cope living alone.

'Of course I'll look after it! I'll be fine—stop worrying.'

'I'm not worried,' Felicity lied. She wished for the same lucky star that had sent her Karim to shine on her sister, wished Georgie's problems were as easy to solve and she prayed that Georgie would be okay, that this essential separation wasn't going to set her back. 'You stay strong,' Felicity said.

'I will.'

'You'll ring as soon as you get there?' her mother fretted.

'I will,' Felicity assured her. 'But, Mum, I won't be

ringing often—and you can't ring me on my mobile. We can't afford it.'

'I know,' she breathed. 'We'll be okay, darling.' Felicity's heart twisted with pride as her mother did her level best to be strong and brave. 'And so will you.'

Felicity hugged her mother and then she walked away, through the security checks and barriers with all the other tense passengers. And as she entered to the boarding lounge, despite her doubts and worries, there was excitement too.

This was *her* time. This was *her* adventure.

For Felicity it wasn't about making money and saving for a deposit on a home, it was about clearing debts, about cleaning up the past and moving onto the future. And also, though she tried to curb it, there was a sliver of hope too as she boarded her flight—because, despite his firm words, there was surely a chance she might see Karim again.

It was a long journey but a comfortable one, even in economy class. Zaraq Air looked after its passengers.

Just, Felicity thought, as Karim had looked after *her* that magical night and day.

Putting on her headphones, Felicity flicked on her little screen, smiling at the tourist information film about Zaraq. She gazed at the images of sandy beaches, deserts and mosques, excitement building. Soon she would really be there…

It was talking about the royal family now. She listened as the narrator explained about the ancient kingdom, with a royal blood line so pure that its founders had passed on their proud name—each King a true Zaraq. It was riveting. Felicity watched the screen as soldiers marched smartly outside the palace, with the King of Zaraq waving to his subjects from the balcony, his family beside him.

And then Felicity's heart stopped.

Because there, smiling from the seat-back in front of her, dressed in full military uniform and looking stunning, was—as the commentator informed her through her headphones—Sheikh Prince Karim of the Kingdom of Zaraq.

It was as if her bowels had turned to ice.

Karim was a *prince*.

No wonder he had warned her they could never be together. It wasn't just miles that separated them, but a heritage that went back thousands of years.

'Your seat belt?' Felicity blinked as the stewardess reminded her, snapped on her belt, and sat in stunned silence as the plane began its descent.

Her first glimpse of Zaraq was through disbelieving eyes. She watched the blue Mediterranean ocean give way to yellow sands. The plane circled in a wide flight path, as if to mock her, letting her glimpse all the power behind the man and the vast abyss that separated them.

Golden sands as far as the eye could see one minute, and then, as the plane dipped to the left, she glimpsed Zaraqua, its ancient buildings huddled together. The cabin lights dimmed, and it seemed wrong somehow to be encased in metal, seeing medieval mosques, colourful markets, from such a modern invention. And then for a second she glimpsed it—the most spectacular building of them all, rising as if from the dust with the ocean as backdrop. What must surely be the palace.

That was Karim's home.

As the tyres hit the tarmac, as the brakes screamed and Felicity was pinned to her seat, it was nothing to the impact she was feeling as she landed in Karim's world.

As she entered the Kingdom of Zaraq.

CHAPTER EIGHT

'LEILA?' Her back was to him, and Karim watched his ex-mistress jump as he walked into his bedchamber. 'What are you doing?'

'Waiting for you.' She turned and smiled.

'You were not invited.'

'So?' She pouted. 'That never worried you before. I heard about the King, and I wanted to be here for you, to give you some comfort during these worrying times.' She ran a hand over his chest and Karim grabbed it.

'Leave.'

'Karim…' Her other hand moved to his crotch but Karim blocked it. 'Leave, Leila. I should not have to say it twice.'

'One last time,' she pleaded. 'Make love to me one last time—we were so good together, Karim.'

And they *had* been good together—at least Karim had thought so at the time. Yet since Felicity there had been no one, no desire, no need for another woman. And it confused him, because there *was* desire and need but it was aimed solely at her.

At Felicity.

'Leave.' Three times Leila made him say it, and Karim's voice was black. Her tears didn't move him; her sobs only enraged him further. Karim summoned his guards to remove this woman from his life.

He would find another, of that there was no doubt, but the next one had—according to his father—to be his bride.

The thought made him shudder. His brilliant mind was bored easily, and the thought of waking to the same woman every morning chilled him to the marrow. He could take a mistress—he would probably *have* to—Karim conceded. And his mind, as it always seemed to these days, flicked to Felicity.

He was tempted to ring her, to check with Noor if she had accepted the job at the hospital. But, no, it was too dangerous a time right now. Maybe when these next months were over, maybe when there was a suitable bride-to-be in the palace, when things were more stable, he would allow himself that indulgence.

Maybe, Karim thought, lying back on the bed as Leila's sobs faded in the distance, he could *keep* Felicity in London.

Pleased with himself, liking his idea, for the first time in a hellish day Karim smiled.

Felicity soon found out the meaning of hitting the ground running. She was met at the airport, as promised, by a fellow English nurse. Relief flooded her as she saw her name on a card being held up by a dark-haired smiling woman who introduced herself as Helen.

'Thank you so much for this…' Shy, awkward, and still stunned at discovering who Karim really was, Felicity had great difficulty listening to all Helen was saying.

'Don't worry; you'll be greeting people yourself in a few months. It's a great system. After orientation you'll be buddied up with me for your first few shifts.'

'How long have you been here?'

'Nearly a year,' Helen said. 'I'm going home for a visit in a few weeks, and then I'm coming back for another year. I only intended to stay for one, but I love the place.'

There was so much to take in.

Her accommodation was fabulous. She had a small apartment on the same floor as Helen's, and there was a gym and two pools—one for women, one for men. It was *bliss*, Helen told Felicity as she showed her around the complex, to dip into the pool after a hard day on the ward.

'You work hard while you're at work, but there's loads of leisure time too,' Helen explained. 'It really is wonderful once you get used to it.'

And for those first few days it really *was* just that—wonderful. Helen introduced Felicity to loads of ex-pats—friends waiting to be made—and gradually, as Helen took her to some other haunts, as she discovered the colourful, loud bazaars and blinked at the contrast to the designer boutiques in town, Felicity came to believe this was the best decision she had ever made. So busy was she by day she didn't have time to stop and think about Karim. She almost forgot she was here in his country, that he was nearby. It was only late at night that her mind wandered.

A shiver of excitement and fear filled her as she lay in bed. Here, in Karim's world, the palace was her view from the bedroom window. She ached for him, and some nights actually got up, pulled by strange longing, to stare out of her window and imagined him sleeping.

Or not.

Resting her head on the cold window didn't cool her as she thought of him lying on a bed not so far away. Maybe lying there thinking about her…

* * *

Her orientation days had been informative, but Felicity knew the only way she would really fit in was when she actually started working. She was grateful when Helen knocked on her door early for her first real shift, and walked with her through the hospital grounds and into the hospital. It was immaculate, like the most luxurious private hospital, except this was accessible to all.

'Except the royal wing,' Helen explained. 'If you think this is fabulous, you want to go and have a peek up there. It has its own nursing staff. It's used for royalty and diplomats and the like. The King's a patient there right now.' She nudged Felicity's attention to the tented city beyond the hospital walls. 'They're keeping vigil for him—he's very ill, apparently.'

'What about his sons?' She couldn't stop herself from asking, but Helen didn't turn a hair, just kept on walking. 'Do you ever see them?'

'Prince Hassan has been visiting daily, while the King is a patient, and there's always a bit of a stir when he arrives…'

'Isn't one of them a doctor?' Oh, so casually she said it—but Helen gave Felicity a small nudge as they walked. 'Hands off Karim! He's mine.' She grinned. 'Who told you about him?'

'I can't remember.' Felicity blushed as pink as her uniform. 'One of the girls said that one of the princes was a surgeon.'

'He used to be,' Helen said, 'and he still does the occasional list. But he doesn't do much now, so he's rarely around. He's too busy being a royal, unfortunately.'

'Unfortunately?' Felicity checked, her throat tight.

'I miss my fix.' Helen nudged her again, not noticing

that Felicity wasn't smiling. 'I miss swooning in the corridor when he stalks past—not that he'd acknowledge me, of course.'

'Because he's royal?'

'No!' Helen laughed. 'Because he's a surgeon—they're treated like royalty the world over. Karim fitted in here perfectly. Now, did you bring all your documentation, like I told you?'

It was to Felicity's intense relief that Helen changed the subject then. It took her till the middle of the morning to work out that for the first time in her life she'd been *jealous*!

Her first shift was spent mostly getting security tags and photocopying paperwork. For safety Helen locked it all up in the ward safe, and gave Felicity the duplicates. There had been a couple of instances of credit card theft on the compound, but security were on to it, Helen assured her.

Her pale pink uniform was practical and comfortable, and Felicity soon found out that pregnant women were the same the world over. Some were thrilled, others excited, some stunned and a few upset. By the end of her first week she had dealt with them all, and was that day working a shift in antenatal.

'Mainly this clinic deals with ex-pats from the UK or America,' Helen explained. 'Dr Habib speaks perfect English and has an excellent reputation, so we tend to do the clinic this way. It gives women from the same background a chance to meet mums in the same situation.'

Certainly, from the lively chatter in the waiting room, the theory was working well.

'For the first visit we check obs and weight, and do a routine urine and pregnancy test,' Helen went on as they worked through their busy morning.

Felicity ticked little boxes, checked dates, and tried to ignore the little voice inside that kept reminding her that her period was due.

Late, even…

Felicity glanced at the calendar, trying to tell herself she was only a teeny bit late, and assuring herself that she was being completely paranoid. Still, by the time lunch came around it was nice to take a break away from the ward.

'I'm on the labour ward tomorrow,' Felicity said as she and Helen paid for their meals in the large canteen. Though *canteen* wasn't the word Felicity would use for it, because it was nothing like the one in her old hospital. The room was spacious and airy, the food was prepared by chefs instead of being delivered via vending machines, and was quite simply delicious. Already Felicity was getting to know a few people, and she smiled to a couple of familiar faces as she and Helen walked over to a table. 'And then I'm in Theatre the next day.'

'And after that you're on your own—I bet you can't wait.'

'I've loved being supernumerary, and I love that I haven't been thrown in at the deep end, but I really am looking forward to working on my own.'

'And delivering your first Zaraquian!' Helen grinned and drained her cup. 'Okay, back to it.'

A hefty nudge in the ribs as they walked out had Felicity looking up, and her face paled as she saw the subject of Helen's attention. Dressed in a suit, chatting and laughing with a colleague, he was focussed on his conversation and heading towards the surgeons' lounge. Corridors could feel like very long things at times—because Karim saw her. His eyes frowned, his voice halted mid-conversation—and then normal services were resumed. He swept towards her as if she wasn't there, completely disregarded her.

As, of course, any surgeon would a nurse they supposedly hadn't met.

'Didn't I tell you he was gorgeous?' Helen said when they had passed, but Felicity didn't answer. She had caught a waft of his cologne as he breezed past, and her cheeks burned.

Karim had very clearly set down the rules. Yes, corridors were very long things. Because, had he chosen to, had he cared even a little about her, there would have been plenty of time for a brief smile.

'I'm just going to the loo.' They were back at Maternity, and Felicity needed a moment to collect herself.

'Again?' Helen grinned.

Yes, again, Felicity thought. Because even though she didn't actually need to go, she did need to check.

Again.

And *again* there was nothing.

She was being ridiculous, she told herself for maybe the hundredth time.

They'd used protection. Karim had been so careful. Her period was one day late, for goodness' sake—hardly anything to worry about, given the move, given the flight. Yet she took out the little specimen jar from her pocket, because she just wanted her mind to be at rest. It was no wonder she felt slightly sick. The different food, jet lag… She was being ridiculous and soon she'd have proof. Wrapping the jar in toilet tissue, Felicity placed it back in her pocket.

She didn't want to take a test home with her—there were Security everywhere and what if they checked her pockets?—but neither did she have the confidence or knowledge to go to a local pharmacist. Would they ask questions? Could an unmarried woman even purchase a test? She truly didn't know.

But though her head was in many places, her mind was still on her patients.

'Blood pressure's fine…' Felicity smiled at the chatty woman beside her. Jessica Hammel was forty-two, had four sons in high school, and was about to welcome baby number five.

'It doesn't feel as if my blood pressure's fine!' Jessica rolled her eyes. 'I can't believe I'm going to be looking after a tiny baby again.'

She blinked at the enormity of it all.

'I had a tummy tuck two years ago. Fat waste of time that was!'

Felicity smiled and waited for Jessica to speak further if she wished.

'I'm okay with it. A bit stunned, I suppose. Everybody thinks I want a girl.'

'Have you found out?' Felicity asked, checking her patient's scan report.

'Nope!' Jessica said firmly. 'Because, as I've told everyone, all I want is for it to be healthy. Though…' she caught Felicity's eye '…after four boys a girl would be rather nice. I think I've earned a bit of pink!' Her voice was a little anxious now. 'Dr Habib said that if nothing happened by this visit, then I was to be admitted and induced.'

She looked over to Felicity, who was eyeing the CTG reading and almost willing it to change. But this baby looked very comfortable where it was for now. If Felicity had her say, it would stay put for a little while longer. Still, she didn't have a say, and, as she had told Karim, she wasn't here to change the world. She took her patient off the monitor and chatted away to her, trying, as she always seemed to be these days, not to let her mind wander to Karim.

Felicity took a pipette and did a routine pregnancy test on her next patient—one of the lecturers from the university who had been undergoing IVF. She happily ticked the little box on the chart as the pink cross came up and signed her initials, before throwing the card in the bin. She turned to go, then changed her mind and opened up the cupboard that held the pregnancy tests, worried about taking one. Where she'd used to work nurses did it all the time—it was for that reason the tests were generally locked up. But she was here in Zaraq and she simply had to know!

She pulled out the little jar, seeing her hands were shaking, and performed the simple test. She jumped guiltily when Helen breezed in, pulling out trays and looking for some batteries for the Doppler machine. Felicity joined her in the search, as she was still trying to get acquainted with where everything was kept.

'You're doing really well. The clinic is running smoothly.' Helen smiled. 'Tonight there are a few of us going out for dinner—you should come along…'

'I might ring home tonight,' Felicity said. 'But thanks for the invite.'

'There'll be plenty more.' Helen shrugged. 'We're a friendly lot, all in the same boat…or the same desert. Who's that for?' she asked casually as she found the batteries and walked out, glancing over her shoulder at the test card.

For Felicity there was the most appalling moment—because a negative test would cause confusion, given they were in the antenatal ward. But Helen didn't notice the silence, just glanced at the patient file and answered her own question.

'She's a nice lady, isn't she? Dr Habib will probably send her straight for an ultrasound, just to put her mind at rest.'

'Sorry?' Felicity croaked.

'IVF patients,' Helen answered patiently, as she had all Felicity's questions through the week. 'They can't believe they're pregnant till they see it for themselves on screen.'

Despite the cool air-conditioning Felicity felt as if she were standing in the heat outside, as if the sun was beating on the back of her head. She was drenched with nausea and fear, and tried to walk casually across to the bench to comprehend why Helen was talking as if the card indicated positive.

'Let me know if you change your mind about tonight,' Helen said, walking out of the room, utterly oblivious to the chaos she'd left behind. The heavy door softly closed behind her.

Picking up the card, Felicity stared at the pink cross, telling herself she must have mixed the specimens up. But that argument failed in a trice—she was meticulous at that type of thing. Jessica's specimen had been thrown away before she'd even retrieved her own.

The card was wrong. Felicity's heart lurched in hope. Maybe it was a faulty batch. And then her heart sank again—because that would mean every test she had performed this morning had been on a non-pregnant woman—which, given they were in an antenatal ward…

Her mind just staggered from hope to hope, like a lost child running frantically in the supermarket for his mother, tugging every familiar coat and then recoiling when it wasn't her.

She *couldn't* be pregnant!

She couldn't be trapped in this country with no ticket home and not enough money for one either.

She couldn't be having Karim's baby.

A baby!

There was no comfort in that thought, no sweet feeling of peace or surge of maternal protection—her only feeling was unadulterated fear.

Two weeks ago she'd never even met him.

Two weeks ago she'd been a virgin.

Now she was in a strange country, where they didn't tolerate pregnancy out of wedlock, and if that wasn't bad enough she was pregnant by one of the family who made the rules.

She stared down at the card and the unpalatable truth hit her.

Yes, she was pregnant.

Pregnant by Sheikh Prince Karim of Zaraq.

CHAPTER NINE

It was the longest, loneliest night of her life.

She rang her mother, trying to sound upbeat and happy, trying not to think about telling her.

Or Georgie.

She'd have to ask a friend to loan her some money for a ticket home. Or work for a few weeks and then break her contract and fly back.

To what?

She was already in debt up to her eyeballs. Lying on her bed, Felicity was shell-shocked, completely overwhelmed by it all. She stared over at the palace and thought how it mocked her tiny flat.

Single motherhood versus his kingdom.

He was responsible for this too, Felicity breathed.

She wouldn't make a fuss—would disappear with her baby from his life if that was what he wanted—but he had every right to know, and he was in every position to help. Slowly, slowly she calmed down…

For about eighteen seconds.

* * *

Someone else, Felicity realised as she was given handover on her early shift the next morning, hadn't had a very good night either.

Jessica Hammel had been given gel to ripen her cervix the previous evening and had spent an uncomfortable night. She had just started to complain about her contractions and had vomited, but there were no regular strong contractions to speak of, and Dr Habib was on his way to see her.

'Just keep an eye,' Martha the charge nurse said.

It was obviously nice for Jessica to see Felicity's familiar face when she walked in to greet her and her husband, Garth.

'How are you doing?' Felicity asked, but Jessica didn't answer. She closed her eyes and clutched her stomach as a wave of pain hit.

'They're coming more regularly now,' Garth said to Felicity, rubbing his wife's back, as he had done on four occasions before.

Instinctively Felicity's hand moved to the patient's stomach, to feel the strength of the contraction.

'She doesn't look well,' Garth said, and privately Felicity agreed with him. Helen was standing by the bed, assessing her new midwife, and Garth was concerned for his wife and trying to tell himself he was imagining things. 'Mind you, it's been a while…'

Felicity nodded, worried that there was no tightening. She looked over to the CTG to confirm her findings. Jessica wasn't having a contraction, although clearly she was in pain.

'Helen?' She gave that wide-eyed smile that was familiar to nurses the world over, which meant help was required, and then smiled back to her patient, who was opening her eyes now that the pain had passed, two hands on her stomach now, both Felicity and Helen, assessing the odd situation.

'I'm paging Dr Habib now…' Helen said—not that Jessica noticed. She was vomiting again, and her blood pressure was low as Felicity checked it. Far from being supernumerary now, she laid Jessica down and applied oxygen. She tried to comfort Garth too as she inserted an IV, and Helen urgently typed in the message to be sent directly to the doctor's pager.

'What's going on?' Garth was taking deep breaths, trying to stay calm, and all Felicity could do at this stage was answer him honestly. 'I'm not sure, but Dr Habib is on his way.'

'Is it the baby?'

Felicity's eyes flicked to the foetal monitor, to the strong, regular heartbeat, and swallowing a fraction she shook her head. 'The baby seems fine. Dr Habib will be here soon.'

In moments in fact, and Dr Habib was instantly concerned. He examined his patient and it was clear his excellent reputation was well earned. He didn't dither. Instead he told Helen to summon the on-call surgeon, and Felicity's heart tightened several times as she heard the word *Karim*.

He must have rolled out of the on-call bed instead of his undoubtedly more luxurious one at the palace, because he was there in a matter of moments, dressed in navy theatre scrubs. Instantly he commanded the room. And yet in an unexpected but very kind touch he nodded to Garth and very briefly shook his hand, explaining who he was, before he palpated Jessica's abdomen.

'I'm Karim Zaraq—the surgical consultant on call.'

Whether Garth knew of his title was irrelevant to him and irrelevant to Karim at this hour. Felicity watched as a very calm surgeon assessed a very ill patient and came to a rapid decision.

'Your wife has to go straight to Theatre. Till I get her there I cannot be sure, and there is no time to confirm my diagnosis with ultrasound, but I believe your wife has an intestinal obstruction. I need to operate—along with Dr Habib.

'Ring Theatre and alert them.' Karim nodded to Helen, who was already on it as Felicity prepared a trolley for the urgent run to Theatre. 'I need you to sign a consent form,' Karim said to Jessica's stunned husband, scribbling on paperwork as he spoke. Calm but concerned, he explained that though he had a provisional diagnosis until he operated he could not know exactly what was wrong—and that it was better in this case to act rather than wait and investigate. He held the man's eyes as he offered the pen, and added that he would do everything he could to save Garth's wife and his baby. Garth didn't hesitate.

Felicity and Helen both dashed with the patient to Theatre. Jessica bypassed Reception and was moved straight through to the operating room. Felicity and Helen pulled on shoe-covers and caps, and helped the porters and theatre staff to move the patient to the operating table as the rest of the theatre staff methodically and rapidly set up. The anaesthetist was lovely—Felicity caught a waft of an American accent as she chatted to her semi-conscious patient—and then it was all under control. Jessica was Theatre's patient now. An anaesthetic was about to be administered; her stomach was being prepped. Felicity and Helen were politely thanked, which meant they must leave, because—as the theatre charge nurse said—'We'll take it from here.'

Felicity wasn't looking for him, but her eyes found him.

She saw him scrubbing up at the sink, washing each nail in detail. He glanced up and for a second held her eyes. With her eyes she wished him all the best for the operation, told him that she missed him, that she needed to talk to him, and his eyes told her the same.

And then he was back to his nails, back to doing what surgeons did—saving lives.

Jessica got the little girl she was hoping for. She was a gorgeous baby too, bonny and pink and covered in vernix. The baby was soon returned to the labour ward, where Garth met his daughter and spoke to Dr Habib, and then came the arduous task of waiting for news on his wife.

She *had* had an intestinal obstruction, Dr Habib explained, and considerable adhesions which had been caused by the tummy tuck. It would be a complicated procedure but, Dr Habib added, 'Her surgeon asked me to pass on that he is quietly confident that your wife will be fine.'

Felicity watched as Garth blew out his breath and she did the same. She was so grateful, as she popped in regularly on father and daughter, that Karim hadn't kept this man waiting. He had been aware of the agony of waiting and had offered some much needed hope.

It took a couple of hours for hope to be formally delivered.

Karim, tired but elated, smiled as he walked into the nursery, where Felicity was checking the baby's temperature as Garth watched anxiously on.

'Your wife is fine.' He got straight to the point. 'It was a difficult operation because there were a lot of adhesions. I had to remove some bowel, but I achieved a healthy anatomises—' He frowned and checked himself. 'A good union. There is no colostomy.' He carried on with the good news as Garth stood, tears streaming down his face, and then Karim moved onto the not so good—which, after all Jessica had been through, sounded like a walk in the park. 'She will stay in Recovery for a couple more hours and then she will be looked after on my surgical ward by my team. Of course she is postnatal, and has had a Caesarean section, but I would prefer that my team watch her. They know my ways, know the things I like to be called for…'

Helen was here now, telling Felicity to go on her break, and Karim didn't hang around—as Felicity moved off, so did he. Her respiration rate increased as she walked towards the staffroom, her heart pounding as she felt his eyes on her, heard footsteps behind her. She paused as he called her name.

'Felicity…'

She went to turn round, and it was at that point it all caught up with her: yesterday's shocking news, her sleepless night, the warmth of the theatre and Karim's black eyes waiting to meet hers. She was drenched in cold sweat, could feel it running between her breasts, breaking out on her forehead. Leaning against the wall, she was glad to see Helen over his shoulder, hear the question in her voice as she took in Felicity's grey face. But Karim was already on it, seizing her arm before she fell, breaking her fall as the floor slammed up to meet her.

He somehow guided her to a side room with only the minimum of fuss. Not that Felicity cared by then. She was completely out of it. She came to at the horrible plastic smell of an oxygen mask, and saw Helen's kind, worried face as she let down a blood pressure cuff.

'Low!' She smiled at her colleague. 'My fault for not sending you for your break earlier.'

'I'm fine.' Felicity tried to sit up, but Helen pushed her down.

'It happens to all of us—the food, jet lag. Rest there…' She stopped talking then. Chatty, effusive Helen was suddenly silent. Karim had come back from wherever he had been.

'I have spoken with the nurse co-ordinator—you are to be moved to a side ward. Staff health—'

'I'm fine.' Embarrassed now, Felicity sat up, but Helen pushed her down, her eyes warning Felicity to be quiet. 'It was a simple faint. I really don't need—'

'I have said what will happen,' Karim broke in. 'You are to be admitted.'

'I don't want to be admitted,' Felicity argued. Helen's eyes widened in horror, but she didn't care if she *was* arguing with a surgeon—or a prince, come to that. All Felicity cared about was *not* being admitted. Because there were many reasons for her to faint, but she knew the real one. 'I just want to…'

'Excuse us, please.'

She saw the dart of confusion in Helen's eyes at his request to be alone with Felicity, but Helen took her own advice and didn't argue. She slipped out of the area and they were alone. Felicity wanted him to scoop her into his arms, wanted him to hold her, to say that he had missed her, to say anything at all. All he did was stand there.

He gave nothing away—could not smile, could not hold her. Couldn't because if he did he would surely snap. He had operated throughout the night on what was meant to be his last 'on call'. The operation had been long and intense, yet he had loved it. He had stood under the lights and performed in *his* theatre as only a surgeon could. *His* choice of music playing, *his* team—the team that *he* had individually chosen. They had worked together for the very last time and then he had walked out to Recovery to speak with his patient—a halal butcher from the main street of Zaraqua, a man who had held his hand and thanked him not as a royal prince but as a doctor.

Unusually for a consultant, he had stayed at the hospital, had lain on the bed where he had slept as an intern, deciding he would hold onto his pager till nine—because he just couldn't stand to let it go.

At seven fifty-five he had been summoned.

He had run through the hospital with adrenaline chasing his heels, had walked into crisis and felt calm, had seen Felicity there, reassuring husband and patient. If there was one day in surgery he could capture this would be it…

This *was* it.

And now he had to walk away. He stared at her pale face on the pillow, knew he could drag her in deeper—or let her walk away.

He chose to give her no option.

'Tell me now why you do not want to be admitted.'

'I don't want any tests.' Her eyes were blinking rapidly.

'Because?' His mouth that had been wet was suddenly dry. He wished that she would answer, wished that she would prove his mind wrong.

'Because I'm pregnant.'

He heard the prison doors slide closed, heard the turn of the key not imprisoning him but *her*, his child. And he couldn't stand it. His mind flashed to Kaliq—to the frail babe he had held in his hand, the tiny babe who should have lived to be King. How proud Karim had been of his nephew as he had slipped from this life to the next.

No, he would *not* tolerate prison for his child, so he refused to even consider that it was his. She had to leave, had to go away—and *he* had to ensure that she did.

'Don't.' His voice was like ice. 'Don't even try it on me, Felicity. Don't even think of playing games with me.'

'It isn't a game…' Her voice was bewildered, reaching out to him, and he couldn't stand to see the pain on her features. 'Karim—I found out yesterday. I know we were careful…'

'Careful!' Karim breathed, angry now, in fact enraged—because she *had* to be lying, because this couldn't be true. 'I am more than *careful*! Do you know how precious my seed is? I don't go to the local chemist for protection. Do you think I would take risks with a whore like you?'

She couldn't believe the brutality of his words. The sexy, tender lover who had won her heart so easily was unrecognisable now. Each word spat a warning, each growled sentence told her not to even attempt to argue. 'Did you find out who I was, Felicity, at that introduction day? Use your little sob story, your ways, your wiles and pretend to be a virgin?' It was so much easier to loathe her than to love her, so much easier to send her away than to claim her now.

'I am…' she sobbed. 'I *was*.'

'Please!' Karim sneered. 'There was no evidence…' He shooed her away with his hand, dismissed her sobs, her story, as easily as he would swat a fly. 'There is no place for your sort here in Zaraq. I could have you arrested.'

This was a different man—a completely different man from the one who had held her. 'Karim, please. If you will just listen—'

'No. *You* listen.' He was standing directly over her, his menacing face silencing her. 'I will not let you smear my name with these lies. Because I know the consequences a woman in your position faces, you will be admitted tonight under my care. I will arrange for your contract to be broken. Your things will be packed and you will fly home tomorrow. A car will collect you. I will arrange your ticket.' He stared down at her and forced himself to say it. 'You will be generously remunerated for your services that day.'

'Karim!' she begged.

He was unmoved by her pleas. Whether or not she was telling the truth, in time she would realise he was actually doing her a favour. 'Enough—you do not argue with me. Tomorrow, Felicity, you leave Zaraq. If you choose to stay, then you deal with this dilemma alone.'

CHAPTER TEN

THIS wasn't the first woman who had lied to Karim.

And by the time he hit the changing rooms he had convinced himself she was a liar.

Because all women lied, Karim told himself as he showered and dressed.

His mother, who had kissed him goodbye as he left for school and said that she would see him that afternoon, had lied.

His father's lovers, who'd feigned interest in the young Prince only to discard him when his father summoned them.

And later his own lovers.

They swore he was their first, or that they understood it was just sex—they too lied, because always they wanted more from him.

And now Felicity.

Sweet, virginal Felicity, the most precious of his memories, tainted now. She had no doubt been pregnant already and looking for a father. Who better than a royal prince?

Did she think he was a fool?

It was so much easier to be angry, so much easier to not believe.

All this whirred in his head as he marched through the hospital with his entourage. Khan, Karim's senior royal aide, had told him that the King had asked to see him.

He visited his father daily, but this time he had been summoned.

His father had asked that the nurses and the aides all leave, and seeing his gaunt, strained face, Karim fleetingly wished for the problems of a moment ago—how much easier *they* were to deal with than this was surely going to be.

'I have spoken with my surgeon.' The King's once strong voice was now thin and reedy, and Karim stood, his back straight, his face an impassive mask, as the news was delivered. 'At this stage surgery is not an option.'

'Surgery is your *only* option.' Karim's voice *was* strong, his bedside manner steadfast and absolute—as it would be for any patient facing the appalling truth. A strong doctor, a strong man was needed to give bad news. The only indication that it was his father he was talking to was a flicker of muscle in his taut cheek. 'To live you need surgery. The tumour is getting bigger.'

'My heart is too weak. If they operate now I will die on the table.'

'I will arrange another opinion—' He stopped then. There had been so many opinions, and Karim trusted only his own. '*I* will operate.'

'Karim!' There was some strength still in the King, and he used it now. 'You are to stop this nonsense. You are a surgeon, but you are not a god. You cannot make miracles. I will not let you operate; I will not give you the guilt that will come when surgery fails. I am to rest, to be built up, given medication, and if my heart is strong enough *then* there will be surgery.'

'You might die waiting.'

'Karim, *this* you cannot control.'

'That is not your teaching—'

'It is the truth.' The King's response was direct. Two proud, strong men were facing the future and did not like what they saw. 'Karim, I am not scared of death. I am scared for my people, for my sons, for the turmoil I am leaving behind.'

'There is no turmoil,' Karim lied.

'Please—there is no time for lies or sugar-coating the truth. Hassan and Jamal—well, since Kaliq…' His voice faltered then, and both men remembered the tiny scrap of a baby who had lived only two days, the weak offspring Hassan had produced, too fragile to carry the hope of the nation. 'There is still no sign of a baby—which means after Hassan there is no heir, no hope for the people. I know you do not want to be King, but that is why I have pulled you back from your work. You, my son, will have to step in. I have spoken with Hassan, and reluctantly he agrees that for the people of Zaraq there must a strong ruler, one who can produce heirs. Not him.'

'Then don't die yet.' Karim said, because to him it was simple. 'Just refuse to.'

'I will try not to,' the King said, 'but I will rest easier if I know that my affairs are in order, that the people have a future. You must marry, Karim. Your playboy ways end now—this very day. You will take a bride, you will produce children. Hassan will step aside. Even though he begs not to, he knows he must step aside…'

'What if Hassan *did* produce an heir?'

'We know that is not going to happen—again Jamal weeps this month. The people need to know that if their King dies the Zaraq line will go on.'

Karim was never swayed by emotion. He stared out of the tinted windows at the vigil that was being held, at the people who had no idea what the future might be without their strong King. An idea was forming in his mind, a germ of an idea that was growing even as he stood. It wasn't a new one either. A conversation like this had taken place years ago, but the strategy had been discounted. Karim resurrected it now.

'What if I told you there will be an heir?'

'I have said already—Jamal cannot—'

'There is a woman,' Karim broke in. He could not stand to picture her face as he said it, so he stared at his father—his King, his ruler. 'She says she is having my child.'

There was just a beat before his father answered. 'Then marry her, Karim, and Hassan will step aside.' To the King it was simple.

'What if it is not mine?' Karim challenged, hoping it would terminate the conversation, that somehow he could set her free. But the King on his deathbed would settle for a lie if it meant that his people had hope.

Oh, it had been done before. The pure bloodline the people of Zaraq were so proud of was littered with hidden secrets. There had been affairs everywhere. Even his own brother Ahmed, so much fairer, so much paler than the rest…though doubts had never been uttered.

Karim could never raise a child that wasn't his own. But Hassan could—if it meant he would be King.

'You will do right by the people. I know that, Karim.'

Karim didn't answer straight away.

What if it *was* his?

Hassan would step aside, and Karim would be a better King, perhaps, with Felicity by his side. No woman had taken him to the heights she had, and he could have that again and again. There would be no need to stray. He could groom her to be a suitable wife, could teach her, make love to her... And as for their child... He leant against the window, because letting his mind go there brought him no peace at all. He couldn't even allow himself to think of that—couldn't allow feelings to enter into this at all.

He paced for a moment and then stilled, rested his gaze on the south-facing window, away from the people and the ocean to what mattered most...

The desert. It would not change in his lifetime.

Oh, the sands lifted and swept and moved in a blink—yet the constants remained.

He stared at the canyons that would remain for his lifetime.

He was a constant.

It was better that it *wasn't* his.

There would be a test soon, to confirm that fact. Felicity would see reason. What poor single mother wouldn't want a kingdom for her child?

Maybe his father would live, Karim thought for a wild moment. But without the peace Karim must administer to him now it was surely impossible.

'You have to do the right thing for our people.' The King broke into his thoughts. 'I cannot rest till I know that the future of Zaraq is safe.'

Karim watched a small sandstorm settle—a regular event in the desert, blinding, paralysing, but temporary.

He stared at the canyons unchanged, at his grief that didn't matter in the scheme of things, and then he headed for a different window. Karim watched a wave pull back into the ocean, saw the swirl of a turning tide, and in that second his fate was sealed.

'Then rest,' Karim said simply. 'I will take care of everything. Rest and get strong, Father, knowing that whatever happens our people, our ways, are safe.'

CHAPTER ELEVEN

SHE'D told him.

Whatever his response, Felicity felt a certain relief that she had done the right thing—had given him the opportunity to be a part of his child's life and he'd declined it.

Maybe it was better this way, she thought, choking back tears as Helen came to see her early the next morning.

'Your things were packed last night…' There were tears in Helen's eyes as she spoke, but she was trying to smile. 'I grabbed a change of clothes for you. I figured you wouldn't want to sit on the flight in your nurse's uniform.' And then she was serious. 'You should have told me,' she said. 'I could have helped.'

'You know?' Felicity blinked.

'Well, most people don't faint and then leave rapidly in the first few weeks unless they have good reason. It is lucky that Karim dealt with you—he's spent enough time in London not to judge.'

Helen gave her a final cuddle, and it dawned on Felicity that it would never enter Helen's head there had been anything between herself and Karim.

'Here—I got these from the safe on the ward.' She

handed over Felicity's paperwork. 'You wouldn't have got far without them.'

Another nurse wheeled her to the lavish hospital entrance, and to the limousine waiting to take her to the airport.

Her things had, as Helen said, all been packed for her. The driver told her they were in the rear of the limousine as she stepped out of the wheelchair the hospital had insisted on and climbed into the cool air-conditioned vehicle. She craned her neck for a last glimpse of the hospital, realising that in a few hours she would be gone from Zaraq.

But at least she would be on her way home.

Just another single mother-to-be, another father who didn't want to know. She hadn't been here for very long— no one would miss her.

Especially not Karim.

Zaraqua really was stunning, and Felicity watched it speed by for the last time through tear-filled eyes. Vast freeways sliced through the edge of the desert. How she would have loved her year here, Felicity thought, wondering about the sights she would now never see. She stared at the deep blue sky, the harsh landscape. This was her child's home. She tried to imprint it on her mind, so that one day she could tell her child about its origins—because its father clearly wouldn't.

She hadn't remembered the journey from the airport taking this long, and it was twenty minutes later that concern started to register.

The road signs were in Arabic, but there were pictures of planes to indicate the way. The driver seemed to have ignored them, turning off the main road and heading towards the glittering ocean.

Perhaps this was a quicker way? Felicity told herself. But, no, there was another sign for the airport indicating left. The driver was going straight ahead.

'The airport,' Felicity said, unsure if he could hear her through the glass partition. 'How far is it to the airport?'

On he drove. Felicity caught him looking at her in the rearview mirror, and suddenly she was nervous. She banged on the glass, demanding his attention, but still he drove on, and somehow, even before the white building loomed into view, even before they swept into a vast drive with the blue ocean glittering in the distance, Felicity knew where he was taking her.

Zaraq Palace.

She had seen it in the brochures, on the tourist film, from her bedroom window, but nothing could have prepared her for the imposing grandeur of it as they neared.

What did Karim want?

Her hand moved to her stomach. The tiny life inside her was the answer.

How foolish to think she could tell him and just leave.

How foolish to think it might be that easy.

As a midwife, Felicity chose to expect things to go smoothly, but she prided herself on being prepared for when things might not go well. It was important to smile and stay unruffled even when you were concerned.

She could see the driver's eyes on her in his rearview mirror, and knew he was waiting for her to react—she refused to.

She had nowhere to go—all her things had been packed and loaded and were in the car, and her documents were in her bag. Her passport was in there too, and apart from the life inside her it was the most precious thing she possessed right now. No one knew she had it. Everyone assumed that she only had the copies, not the originals, and instinct told her it must stay that way.

It was the one thing she clung to quietly as the gates slid open. The limousine glided past armed guards at checkpoints, and Felicity sat, her forehead beading with sweat, trying to wonder what Karim would have to say. Maybe he wanted to say goodbye, she told herself as the door opened and the driver came round to let her out.

A woman who introduced herself as Jamal greeted her, smiling warmly, but Felicity was unable to return it.

'Come.' Jamal led a shaking Felicity into the palace. The cool marble, the height of the ceilings—everything was daunting. 'We will have some refreshments…'

Tea was poured, mint tea that was refreshing, and Felicity didn't waste her breath asking about the purpose of the detour, knowing it would be in vain.

A man in a suit came then, and spoke for a minute in Arabic to Jamal who briefly translated.

'Karim will see you now—Khan will take you.'

She was guided through corridors with pictures of ancient ancestors hanging on the walls.

He rose from a low sofa as she entered a room, and he was wearing traditional black robes and a black and white chequered *kiffaya*. Tall, imposing and grim, he looked nothing like the man who had once held her—nothing like the man she had seen laughing and chatting—and Felicity knew she was meeting Sheikh Prince Karim Zaraq of Zaraq and it unnerved her.

His black eyes loathed her, as they had yesterday, and his brief smile was a fake one, of that Felicity was sure.

'Have a seat.'

He dismissed the man in a suit, then halted him. 'Would you like tea? I can ask Khan…'

'I've had tea,' Felicity said quickly. She just wanted to know was going on.

As Khan left, Karim turned and faced her.

'You say this is my baby?'

'It *is*,' Felicity said, glad of the chance to talk, to end things on more even terms. 'Look, I understand it's difficult and I don't expect—'

'Then we will marry,' Karim interrupted, and her eyes widened. 'Today, in an hour, we will be married.'

'We don't have to marry!' Felicity was flustered. It was the twenty-first century, for heaven's sake, they had been together for one night. He didn't have to do this. 'I just need help to get home. Maybe we can work out—'

'If this is my son, then you are pregnant with a royal prince. Of course we must marry.'

'No…' Felicity shook her head, ruing her own stupidity. She had frowned at Liam for not doing his research, for not knowing Zaraq's rules, and now she had in turn gone and done the same. She should have told Karim from England, Felicity realised, her panic growing. The palace was huge, but it seemed to shrink then, as she recognised the prison she had just walked into.

'If this is my child then there is no question that we marry—and the sooner the better. We will just have to hope that the baby comes a little late.' He flashed a very black smile. 'My guess, however, is that this baby is going to come early. Still, we will know where we stand in a few weeks.'

'A few weeks?'

'You will have an amnio, of course, and a DNA match will be performed.'

'No.' She stood up. 'Absolutely not.' She said it again. *'No.'*

But Karim just shrugged. 'Come—the papers have been drawn up. You will be prepared for marriage now. Hassan and his wife, Jamal, will be witnesses.'

'Karim, no!'

'Felicity!' He snapped the word—an impatient snap that silenced her. Then the room fell silent and he spoke again. 'You do not argue with me. I do not discuss things with you. But, given you are new to our ways, I will explain things to make you feel better. I will look after your family.' Karim stared coolly at her. 'There are merits to our ways, and looking after the extended family is one of them. Our marriage will bring peace to my father in his final days. In return, whatever the test results, I will secure your mother and sister's finances— yours too.'

'There won't be a test.' She wasn't going to take a test simply to satisfy his curiosity. 'This is your child, Karim.'

'Then,' he said patiently, 'there is no question that you can leave.'

It was like talking to a stranger. The beautiful, rational, sensitive man who had held her, to whom she had entrusted her body, must surely be there beneath the surface. But all Felicity could see was a strange clone of him.

'You come to this country, you live by our rules. We will marry today. When questions are asked, we will say this is a honeymoon baby. And if it is not mine…' Karim did not continue. Now was not the best time, perhaps, to tell her of his intentions for her bastard infant!

'Won't your people expect a big wedding? How are you going to explain?'

'My country is holding its breath for the King. It would

be crass to hold a party now. For now we will be discreet, and in a few weeks we can arrange DNA testing.'

'No.' Her eyes shone with tears. On this she would not bend. 'No—it could be dangerous to the baby.'

'It is a routine procedure. We will then both know where we stand.'

'No.' She knew the more she resisted, the more Karim thought she was lying about him being the father—but there was no way Felicity would allow him to risk her child, *their* child, just so that he might believe her.

'Felicity…' He was bored with explaining now. 'You say that you are having my child—you demand that I believe you—and then you resist my proposal of marriage.' Karim truly didn't understand. He accepted he had been less than enamoured with the news she had delivered, but now that he had proposed, now that he was offering a *commoner* marriage, he could not fathom her resistance.

He was right. Slowly it dawned on her—she was having his child, was pregnant by a prince. There wasn't much she could dispute.

All her clothes and her belongings had been brought to a vast bedroom. Her life was contained in one suitcase and the handbag a maid had placed in a large wardrobe. A scented bath had been run, and in minutes she had been relieved of her clothing. The handmaidens now chatted excitedly as they prepared the bride for their Prince. They oiled her body, and her scalp too, and then tied her hair so it hung in a long coil over one shoulder. They rouged her lips and cheeks, and kholled her eyes, then dressed her in her wedding costume—a white beaded hand-embroidered gown that looked heavy but, when slipped over her head,

Felicity found was actually light. Her head was wrapped in a veil, and her feet were placed in beaded slippers.

She was ready to meet her groom.

She stood and sat as instructed.

She knew that in this she had no say—but her mind was working overtime.

Karim was her baby's father.

Despite his harsh words yesterday, despite his cool demeanour today, somewhere within was the man she had fallen in love with. Somehow she knew she must reach him, and this was her only way.

It felt surreal as she walked into a large study. Jamal was smiling, greeting her, and a man who must be Hassan nodded. Karim merely gave a nod of approval as she entered.

It did nothing to soothe her nerves.

'Karim…' Her eyes met his as she made a request she was quite sure he would refuse. 'Can I ring my family first?'

'Of course.' Again she had read him wrong. He even helped her dial, and she stood dressed in her finery, in a study looking out over the desert, her groom by her side, and heard her mother's anxious, excited voice at her daughter's unexpected call. Felicity closed her eyes and knew she couldn't tell her. Knew that until she had sorted things out with Karim she couldn't burden her family with all this.

In minutes she was married. The celebrations would take place later. She put her thumb print on a document and apparently she was his. And now, unless she wanted to jump out mid-flight, she had no choice but to sit as a helicopter whirred them deep into the desert towards the red setting sun and Karim's vast tented kingdom.

Her first true glimpse of the desert was at dusk. Stepping

out of the helicopter, she felt the sting of sand around her cheeks, the whistle of wind in her ears and the heat of the day that had been absorbed by the land. Then she felt his hand on her elbow as he guided her across the sand to a huge tent. As they reached it, they stepped into a small entrance and Karim instructed her to remove her slippers.

'Here,' he said. 'Put these on.' Her feet were slipped into another pair of jewelled slippers, which seemed rather pointless, but as he parted the drapes and she padded through she understood why. There was no sand inside—the desert floor was smothered in thick patterned rugs, the walls of the tent too. Lanterns cast light and shadows as Karim parted swathes of silk and led her deeper within his desert abode.

Somewhat shaken and stunned, she stood quietly as he introduced her to his staff: a woman called Bedra and her husband, Aarif. They seemed delighted by their arrival, and guided them further into the bowels of the tent, where a lavish feast awaited them.

They were seated on cushions, apart and opposite each other, and a heavy purple runner was laid between them as Bedra served food and drinks on a low tray.

Felicity was poured some tea, and Karim instructed her to drink the syrupy brew that tasted of mint and sugar. Each mouthful, Karim explained to her, was part of a necessary ritual.

The food was endless, all eaten with the hands: Bedouin bread with olives and camels' milk cheese, pitta wrapped around richly spiced lamb. It was delicious, but she was too nervous to eat. Still she tried, because Karim was eating, and she was sure it would be rude to refuse. Yet the more she tried to eat the more Bedra served and the more Karim ate—until she was sure it would never end.

'Karim.' She gave a nervous swallow, not wanting to offend. 'All of this is delicious, but...' She couldn't speak of the baby in front of Bedra, but she truly couldn't eat another thing or she might offend him in a way that was unthinkable.

Karim, the haughty Prince who had rebutted her in the hospital, who had married her because he could, was now smiling. 'You are full?'

'Yes!' she hissed in a loud whisper. 'I can't eat another thing. I don't want to be rude...' She shook her head as he pushed his plate away and summoned Bedra to clear the tray. 'You carry on, though.'

'I'm not hungry either. But you see...' He was almost laughing, and that beautiful smile she had once been privy to dazzled her now again. 'I must not rush you. Custom says I should eat till my bride or my guest is full. Only when you are finished...'

She was almost smiling too—well, not almost, she *did* smile. 'You could have told me that before the camel milk cheese!'

And she glimpsed him again—glimpsed the Karim she had so quickly and heavily fallen in love with, the man who was the father of her child. And somehow, somewhere deep inside, Felicity knew this could work.

As Bedra approached, she took Felicity's reluctant hands. 'She is going now to paint you,' Karim explained. 'Henna for beauty and luck and health.'

Bedra painted Felicity's hands, and her feet as well as an intricate coil of flowers that crept up her calves and forearms. Yet all she wanted was to be alone with Karim.

'They are our witnesses,' Karim explained. 'Soon we will be alone.' Karim took her hand, slid on her finger a silver knotted ring that was studded with turquoise and agate and decorated with symbols. Karim's voice was serious. 'This symbolises not just two lives, but two families that are now intertwined.'

'Meaning?' Felicity asked. Perhaps not the most romantic response, but she wanted to know—wanted to know about his ways so that she might understand him better.

'It means that your celebrations I applaud and your problems I help with.' He stared into her eyes. 'Your family is mine. There is no burden that is not shared. This is what it means to be loved.'

She must be drunk on mint tea, because calm invaded her. This was her love that greeted her. This was the father of her child. And, yes, he was different here, yes, tradition invaded, but as she was taken aside—as Bedra smeared her body in fragrant oils and slipped a flimsy white muslin gown over her head and then directed her to his sleeping chamber—she was barely nervous. Because finally they could be alone.

He watched her walk over, her hennaed feet and hands stunning on her pale skin, her blue eyes dazzling, and the thin nightgown revealing her feminine shape.

Every night she would be his.

The rules had been waived now that she carried a child, and it meant that every night he could have her.

He must be gentle, Karim reminded himself as she padded towards him. His needs did not matter when the kingdom was at stake. He must remember that she was with child.

And then she was at his bedside. Shy and nervous, but decorated for him and forever his.

He pulled her down beside him. As he kissed her he

could smell the oil in her hair, could feel the body that had aroused him so, and for once duty was a pleasure.

For Felicity, any nerves had vanished when he held her—just as they had the first time they'd made love. He slid off her nightgown and kissed each waiting breast in turn. His lips moved up to her neck and then on, deliciously, to her waiting mouth. And finally he was kissing her—heavy, deep kisses that urged instant response. Her body leapt at the memory of him. Here in bed they could communicate. Here they could discover each other again and work out their differences.

As his fingers went to a place that was already moist, Felicity knew that this was the one thing they had in common. Her legs were parted by his knees and she let them relax. She was having his baby. He was her husband.

His hand reached over her head, and at first Felicity didn't know what he was doing. As he opened a small drawer in the heavy wooden bedhead and produced a sheath she was confused.

'It's a bit late for that,' she pointed out breathlessly.

'It is not just for—' He didn't get to finish. She slapped her hand hard across his cheek.

'How dare you?' She spat, then recoiled on the bed at his expression. Felicity wondered, in fact, how dared *she*. But she would not be so insulted.

'How do I know?' he demanded of her. 'Have you any idea the number of women who try this? Two weeks!' He shook his head at the improbability of it. 'I was using protection.'

'Then why marry me?' Felicity demanded—but Karim couldn't answer.

She was covering herself with her nightgown, her face wounded and angry, tears in her eyes. He wanted to believe her, yet he could not allow himself—because if it *was* his child she carried then unbeknownst to her everything had already changed, would change again.

He had to believe the baby was going to be Hassan's. Had to detach from the baby she grew inside. Because one day so must she.

He climbed out of bed, and when she saw he was holding a dagger, running his finger along the blade, there was a terror in her soul that she had never before experienced. Here in the desert, here amongst his people, who would respond to her scream? She watched. The blade was so sharp as he ran it along his finger that blood trickled, and then he looked over, saw her fear, and his face was as cold as granite as it registered.

'You imagination runs too wild. You are not a prisoner. I would never force you,' he sneered. And just as quickly as that he lay down the dagger, walked over to the bed and smeared the silk sheet with a trickle of his blood. 'I cover for your lies.'

'Why won't you accept that this baby is yours?'

'When I get the test results, then I will believe it.'

'There will be no test.'

'You do not argue with me.'

'Oh, but I do, Karim,' Felicity said. 'You *chose* to marry me today. You *chose* me to be your wife, and now you have me. I will respect your ways and your traditions in public, but here in private I will always speak—this is me. There will be no threat to my baby's safety just to satisfy you, and there will be no condoms just because you cannot trust that you have been the only one. So,' Felicity concluded in a voice that was shaky but somehow assured, 'it looks like there will be no consummation.'

'You do not leave here till our marriage is consummated.'

'Then we'll die in the desert,' Felicity replied.

Karim just shrugged. 'I have told you how it will be,' Karim said, and then he climbed into bed and turned his back to her. 'When you're ready, you will come to me.'

CHAPTER TWELVE

MAYBE they *would* die in the desert.

As the days moved slowly on, it became clear that neither of them had any intention of changing their mind.

Absolutely *she* would not give in—would not sleep with a man who offended her.

And absolutely neither would Karim.

He took her out sometimes. This land that looked so barren and bare was, Karim explained, full of gifts if only you knew where to look.

He was right.

In the seemingly bare desert he showed her landmarks, canyons that moved maybe ten inches in a lifetime, and the simple, endless rule of a sun that rose and set and always offered direction.

There were oases too—a full day's walk from each other. He took her once in his four-wheel drive, and they picnicked by one.

'They prove the land is fertile,' Karim said, stretching out on his back and staring up to the sky. 'You just have to know how to treat it.'

There was a response there on her tongue, but to her

credit she chose not to offer it. She was biding her time till the Karim she loved returned again.

Bedra was her only real outlet. They chatted as Bedra dressed Felicity, or did her hair. But Bedra was always covered in a black *abaya*. How Felicity wished she would take it off, so she could see her face when she spoke to her. One day she asked Bedra about it.

'I do not wear it at home. There I can be myself,' Bedra explained. 'But here, at work…'

This upset Felicity—not a lot, but it niggled. For all their chatting, for Bedra it was work, and Felicity didn't want it to be like that. Bedra's husband, Aarif, tended to Karim, and sometimes when she was resting in the afternoon, while Karim wandered in the desert, she heard Bedra and Aarif laughing. She wanted it to be the same for her and Karim—because Aarif treated Bedra as if she were golden.

She asked Karim when he returned that day from the desert.

In a black robe and unshaven, he didn't look very approachable, but still Felicity asked—although she didn't much like the answer.

'Of course he is nice to her,' Karim said. 'Why would he not be? She is a good woman, a nice lady.' He frowned down at her. 'Why would he *not* be nice to her?'

'Well, you're not exactly nice and communicative with *me*.'

'Till our marriage is consummated you're not my wife.' Karim shrugged. 'Anytime you're ready, Felicity, you can find out how *nice* to my wife I can actually be.'

As the days ticked on occasionally they spoke, and sometimes even laughed, but both remained immutable on that point. And the more they spoke, the more he taught her of his people's ways and he learned of hers, the more impossible it seemed to be.

'Poor Hassan.' She was lying on the cushions eating figs, which Felicity had found out she liked—not just liked, *loved*. Pregnancy cravings, along with morning sickness, were starting, and figs—sweet, juicy figs—were the only food she could keep down. There was a lot to stomach now, and her head reeled as Karim told her about his family and what was expected of them.

'Why poor Hassan?'

'To *have* to be King.'

'He is honoured that he will serve his people. There can be no higher honour,' Karim said sharply.

'Then poor Jamal.' She refused to be quiet, even though she knew she was angering him. 'I don't blame them for not wanting children.' She shuddered a touch. 'It would be horrendous.'

'How dare you?' Karim barked. 'How dare you say our ways are horrendous? Their baby would be born to be King.'

'Which to me—' Felicity smiled '—would be *horrendous*. I'm just glad—infinitely grateful, in fact…' she paused as she took another bite of her fig '…that when you concealed your identity—'

'I did *not*.'

'When you *forgot* to mention you were a royal prince, I'm just glad that your name didn't happen to be Hassan.' She shook her head at the horror of it all. 'I could think of nothing worse. At least you get your freedom, get to follow your career…' Felicity frowned at that very thought. 'Why don't you practise any more?'

'It is not for me.'

'But you did?' Felicity pushed.

'For a while.' Karim shrugged. 'Then I realised I could do better for my people by overseeing the commissioning of the new hospital and university.'

'Do you miss it?'

He didn't answer.

'I mean, you're a surgeon...'

'Enough.' Karim terminated the conversation.

'I was just—'

'Then don't.' Karim clipped. 'When your husband says enough, when a royal prince says enough, you do not argue.'

'Oh, but I do. As I have repeatedly said—I will respect your ways in public, but in my home, which this blessed tent is for now, *my* husband will give me trust and respect and conversation.' She gave him a brittle smile. 'We're getting nowhere, I'd say.'

She slept in his bed, for the sake of the staff, but she would never give herself to him. The barrier he insisted on wearing was a barrier to her heart. Sometimes there was a fleeting glimpse of the man she had fallen in love with. Sometimes she would awaken in his arms, feel him wrapped around her, and wonder how she had got there, wonder for a moment what had taken place—yet sure that nothing had.

Safe.

Lying there one night, feeling him breathe, feeling his skin next to hers, she wondered how it could be. How, despite his vile accusations, despite his refusal to trust, despite everything, in the middle of the desert, deep in the dark with Karim, for the first time in her life she felt treasured and safe.

Karim wondered too.

Eternally vigilant, he felt her awake beside him and he

wondered as to her thoughts, as to what Felicity lay in the dark thinking about. He wondered whether she was missing her family, and he knew she must surely be confused and scared.

He pulled her in just a little closer. Warm, relaxed bodies were so much easier to move.

Could her baby be his?

His hand went to her stomach, to stroke the little scrap of life that was there inside, but he stopped himself. He could not let himself give in to emotion, because if it was his child then its fate was the same as his—and if it wasn't...

Karim's eyes opened and he stared into the darkness. The back of her head was inches from his face. How he wanted to bury his head in her hair, to kiss that neck. He could feel her warm bottom against his stomach. The hand that was wrapped under her held her shoulder loosely, and he was hard now. His fingers wanted to stroke at her breasts...

What if the baby *was* his?

Karim didn't do sentiment.

He never had and had thought he never would.

Speaking with his father, he had allowed his calculating mind to come up with a rapid solution.

For the sake of their people he would carry the weight of the lie, as would Hassan, and the King would take it to his grave. Once Felicity's test was taken and the baby proven not Karim's, Jamal's belly would appear to grow and the people would cheer.

Felicity offered a solution.

And now he'd had to go and do something stupid—like care. Care about the effect it might have on her. Every day she made him laugh inside, chatting away to herself even as he refused to answer. Every morning was better for waking up with her. Of course there were differences. He had assumed he would iron them out of her, but now he didn't want to.

How did he tell her that the career she loved must now end? How could he tell her that she was not just a princess but might one day be Queen—that her every last freedom would be gone?

She stirred a little beside him, and there, lying in the darkness, he didn't care about the people of Zaraq for the first time in his life. He didn't care about the people, he cared about *her*. Neither did he care if this child was a boy or a girl, he just wanted it to be *his*—wanted Felicity to be his too.

He felt her breathing grow shallow and quicken. His hand moved on her waist, bypassing her stomach and moving down, down, to her sweet, warm place, feeling her thighs part a fraction.

Tonight he would love her, Karim decided, and tomorrow he would tell her. And if she couldn't do it, didn't want to do it, then; maybe they would work something out.

He was right there, at her entrance, his tip already moist, could feel her oiled and ready beneath his fingers. So easy would it be to slip in, to sink in, to share and to trust…

Not a word had been spoken, not a kiss had been shared, yet she had never felt closer to him. She knew he was awake beside her, had known when it started that this was no idle, sleeping erection. And she knew too that he was thinking of her, even loving her a little bit. She had felt his fingers ponder over her belly and then move down, felt him softly stroke her, felt his mind wander and then return to her.

Parting her legs, she could feel him now, feel the swell of him, the tip of his erection nudging at her clitoris and then moving a tiny way back. She rocked against him, willing him, wanting him, desperate for him.

'Make love to me, Karim…'

'Your Highness! Forgive the intrusion…' Aarif was sobbing.

Karim swore violently in Arabic.

He was cursing and furious. How *dared* a servant intrude? If his father were sick his aide would ring. Nothing, *nothing* should disturb him in his chamber.

'Please forgive me, Your Highness,' Aarif pleaded. 'But Bedra is dying, bleeding….'

CHAPTER THIRTEEN

In a trice he dressed and sped through the tent. Felicity took a few seconds longer, but almost as soon she raced into the servants' quarters.

Bedra lay collapsed, her huge brown eyes terrified. Karim deftly examined her belly, and it was only then that Felicity realised Bedra was pregnant. The *abaya* had concealed it. Karim was speaking in Arabic, then quickly translating for Felicity.

'She is about six months pregnant.' There was blood everywhere as Karim delivered his stark diagnosis. *'Abruptio placentae.'*

In a hospital Felicity would have known what to do. There Bedra and her baby would both have a chance. But here in the desert, with help miles away, it was clear from the extent of bleeding they would rapidly lose them both.

Felicity rolled the woman on to her side, to help with oxygen delivery to the baby, and Karim barked rapid orders to a tearful Aarif, who quickly ran off.

'Should we drive her?'

'There is not enough time to get her to the hospital.' In one deft movement Karim scooped up the woman, carried her through long white corridors of tent. Felicity followed, confused as to where they were going. The desert was dark and cool as they stepped outside, and she was even more confused—because Karim had said it was too late to transport Bedra anywhere and yet one of the large four-wheel drives was speeding towards them. It stopped. Aarif jumped down and opened up the rear, and Karim ran towards the vehicle with Bedra in his arms. As Karim lay Bedra down in the rear of the vehicle Aarif was already pulling at leads, while Felicity stood, her nightdress billowing in the wind, unsure as to what exactly was going on.

Karim snapped her out of it. 'Felicity—come on.' He was strapping on a tourniquet as Aarif opened large labelled boxes, pulled out drapes. Here, right here in the desert, a mini operating theatre was being created. 'We must operate *now*.'

He was a surgeon, yes—but to operate, to perform a Caesarean section here…

'I am a surgeon,' Karim said, his eyes locked with hers. 'I know what I am doing.'

Aarif, on a strange kind of auto-pilot, where he was detached from his wife and baby in the hope of saving them, was slapping at Bedra's arm, trying to find a vein. It was then that Felicity stepped in. How and why didn't matter for now. They were in the middle of the desert in a four-wheel drive that looked like a mini-ambulance—and Karim about to perform a Caesarean section!

Karim was drenching Bedra's belly in iodine; Aarif was pulling up drugs. 'I cannot give them,' Aarif said, handing her the vials, and Felicity looked at them. A strong analgesic, and a relaxant that would cause temporary amnesia. It wasn't a general anaesthetic, but in such a strong dose it would compromise her airway.

'Give them,' Karim said, setting up his instruments. 'Aarif will watch her airway. Felicity, get ready to receive the baby.'

His authoritative tone was welcome now. On Karim's instruction she shot the drugs into Bedra, but she was acting on her own instincts now, opening up a large resuscitation box and selecting the smallest equipment. Aarif took the ambu bag and bagged his wife, delivering vital oxygen as if he had done it a hundred times before.

The surgery was urgent and basic. It had to be. It was a classic Caesarean, a vertical incision, performed for haste. In seconds Felicity was being handed a scrap of life, and Karim delivered the placenta that had been ripping away from the uterine wall. It was the only way to stop Bedra from haemorrhaging to death.

Felicity worked on. The baby was flaccid, but responding to her resuscitation. She tried not to think, just to *do*.

Still her heart went out to Aarif. He looked over a few times, his eyes blank. This quiet man was guarding his emotions because it wasn't safe to have them yet.

Karim was calling to Aarif to give him more drugs, then packing the abdomen to prepare Bedra for transfer. Just as Felicity was about to ask Karim how she should summon help she heard the sound of a chopper landing.

Here in the desert Karim had saved not one life but two, against impossible odds, and now help had arrived.

He was shouting rapid orders to a doctor Felicity recognised from the hospital. It was Dr Habib running from the chopper to the four-wheel drive, but thankfully he didn't glance at Felicity, just headed straight for the mother. A paediatrician came to take over the infant's care. Aarif must have seen the fear in her eyes, and Felicity wondered whether he understood or misinterpreted it as shame at being uncovered. But he threw her a drape and hastily Felicity put it over her head.

Just not in time.

She saw the absolute shock on Helen's face. There was a stunned, questioning second, where both women swallowed the response on their lips. Then Felicity gave Helen a quick, urgent shake of her head, to indicate that this must not be acknowledged, and they did what they had to—got on with the job of preparing the little babe for urgent transfer. He had pinked up and was crying, but his cry was weak. To Felicity he looked around twenty-six weeks' gestation, and the paediatrician agreed.

Karim only relaxed when Bedra was under full anaesthetic and blood was dripping into her veins. Resting back on his heels, he stared over at the incubator, stared at the little life he had saved, and remembered his nephew, Kaliq, whom his brother had refused to hold. He remembered too Jamal's wailing, his father's tears—the whole country had been in mourning for the tiny little baby that had died in his hands.

And then he stared over at Felicity, chatting with the paediatrician, her eyes watchful on the child, and he knew that it would kill her to give her child away.

He straightened his back, refusing to let sentiment in. Because… Well, she might have to.

Only when they had loaded the mother and infant into the rescue chopper, the blades whirring as it prepared for takeoff, did Felicity manage to utter a few vital words to Helen—her only link with the real world, the one woman who could understand her predicament.

'I'll make contact.'

CHAPTER FOURTEEN

IT SHOULD have brought them closer, what they had shared, what they had achieved. Karim had been about to make love to her before the interruption, of that Felicity was absolutely sure, but as for the first time in his life Karim prepared his own bath his silence spoke volumes. He stonewalled her questions, pretending to be asleep by the time she'd bathed and returned to his bed.

'Karim?' She spoke to tense broad shoulders. 'You did so well out there…'

Yes, pretending to be asleep. Because in response to her question he proceeded to snore. And for all his ruthless ways, there were some redeeming features—and one of them was that Karim didn't actually snore.

It was worse than being told to be silent.

She persisted in her own way. She refused a husband who was less than he could be, refused to live with his silence. So at various times, as the days dragged on and they were truly alone in the desert, she chatted happily though mostly to herself.

'I've cut myself,' she said—and she had, lounging on cushions, reading a magazine. She had a tiny paper cut that really didn't need anything doing to it, but she mentioned it just the same. 'I wonder if there are any plasters…' He was reading a thick black book, and he didn't look up as she stood, just lay stretched out on cushions. 'I know!' Felicity said brightly. 'They'll be in the fully equipped mobile theatre which just happens to be close by. I might go out and look…'

There was a ghost of a smile on the edge of his mouth as she walked past him.

'No, don't bother getting up, Karim. I'll get them.'

He caught her ankle, smiled up at her, and it was brighter than the sun outside. Scorching, warming, and it dazzled.

'You talk too much.' Still he held her ankle.

'You talk too little.'

'Sit.' He let go of her ankle and patted the cushions beside him, but she just kept on walking. 'Felicity,' Karim said with a rather strained sigh, 'why don't you have a seat and we can talk for a while?'

It was a little like being back in the restaurant—formal and awkward at first. But they avoided hot topics, like sex and babies, and given there wasn't much else between them spoke about the one other thread they had in common—their work.

'I just always wanted to be one,' Felicity answered when he asked. 'I think I was *born* wanting to be a midwife. I love pregnant women, and I just adore newborns.'

But that was about babies… At every turn they couldn't avoid their issues, couldn't talk about her hopes to work in a natural birthing centre when she returned to England, because somehow it was too much to acknowledge that that hope was now gone. And she couldn't talk about her family, about her father and the legacy his alcoholism had left, because that would mean she trusted Karim.

And she didn't.

Finally, after a few stalled attempts, they spoke about Karim—which didn't help either, because the more that was revealed the more she liked him.

And the more confused she became.

'So you practise medicine out here?'

'With Bedra's help.'

It was Stockholm syndrome, Felicity told herself—where you fell in love with your captor. Only she'd loved him long before that, and every moment he intrigued her more.

'It is like a mobile hospital,' Karim explained. 'I cannot practise any more at the hospital. It is not appropriate.'

'But you trained as a surgeon.' Felicity blinked. 'You *worked* as a surgeon.'

'I cannot be accessible to the people.' He frowned at her, and she chose to stay silent—chose instead of arguing just to listen. After a long pause, Karim delivered perhaps his first honest admission. 'I do miss it at times.'

Felicity blinked at the revelation, at his first display of emotion, feelings—proof that this remote man was actually real.

'You do not choose to be a surgeon. I believe it chooses you. And yet my country, my role, for reasons you do not understand make it impossible to do both. But here in the desert…' He was silent for a moment, as if drawing on the vastness. Even the wind wailing outside hushed for a moment as he centred himself and drank from the endless cup of wisdom this hard land brought. 'I can fulfil both. I can be a royal and I can heal—Bedra is a doctor,' he explained. 'She trained overseas and has returned to Zaraq to help her people. That is why I chose her to be here. The palace staff think she and Aarif are really servants. The Bedouin people are proud and remote, they would not line up at a royal tent for help, so Bedra takes help to them. That is the vehicle you saw, and with GPS she can summon assistance from the hospital. Sometimes, for things Bedra cannot do—she is not a surgeon—I go out with her…'

'You run clinics?'

'My family do not know. You are not to say anything,' he warned. 'I am working on a project to send doctors into the desert as part of the hospital rotation. However, for now I am servicing that need quietly.'

He made it sound as if he were running a brothel instead of practising medicine. How could saving lives be a *secret*?

'Change has to be slow,' Karim said at her furrowed brow. 'But there is change. There is the university, the new hospital. Women will not have to go overseas to study. I can work as a surgeon, and of course save lives, or as a royal prince I can slowly implement programmes that will change lives.'

As King he could just *do* it. Karim swallowed on that uneasy thought.

As King he could make more progress than his father or Hassan ever would. He loved his country, the traditions, its ways. But at times, at certain points, it frustrated him—angered him, even. Progress was so slow, yet as King himself more good could be done.

But it couldn't be about what he wanted, and it had nothing to do with Felicity, so he stood up and ended the conversation there.

Felicity didn't understand. He made her head spin. At every turn it was a different Karim—the man in England, the Prince in his palace, and this doctor in the desert. But she wanted *him*—all of him. She wanted the blurred image to focus, for the many facets of this man to join into one.

She wanted *him*.

'I have to leave tomorrow.' He offered no explanation other than that, but this time Felicity refused to stay quiet. He always did this, Felicity was beginning to realise. Gave a little of himself and then regretted it, withdrew further and confused her more.

'Where are you going?'

'That is not your concern.'

'Karim, please…'

'My father has surgery in a couple of days.'

'And you didn't think to tell me? Karim, I am your *wife*.'

'A wife who refuses sex is a poor wife.'

'A husband who doesn't trust is a poor husband!' Felicity retorted, but he was prowling the tent now.

'When the helicopter comes to collect me, they will bring staff to take care of you.'

'No!' She hurled herself off the cushions towards him, scared of being left in the desert with strangers. 'No, Karim. I won't stay.'

'You will do as you are told.'

'No!' she begged. 'Surely your wife should be with you? Surely your family will expect that?'

His family expected *nothing* from her. He stared at her with black soulless eyes, held her wrists as she attempted to claw at him. Could she not understand that his family did not *care*, that all that was wanted from her was her baby—be it as Hassan's or his.

His.

For a second he relented, let go of her wrists and let her beat at his chest.

They did not care about her and *he* must not, Karim told himself, holding her arms again. But she kicked with her feet, beating her way into his closed heart.

'Let me come with you, Karim. Surely I should be—?'

Only his mouth could silence her, and it felt so good to feel her. He held her angry body in his arms and kissed her quiet. Every time she pulled back he kissed her harder. Now he could taste her, his tongue curling around her rigid one, pressing her right into him so that she could feel what she was missing, feel the heat that had been building for so long now. It was a heat he had refused to douse himself, relishing the challenge like a fast in the desert— because when she came to him, and she *would* come, how much sweeter victory would taste.

Her mouth was softer now, her body more pliant in his arms. But then she resisted again—and Karim dropped her.

'I have told you already—the desert is our home till the marriage is consummated. It is entirely up to you.'

CHAPTER FIFTEEN

SHE *had* to get back to Zaraqua. Would not be left in the desert alone.

Felicity lay in bed, pondering her baby's future. She wanted to give it the best chance to have a father, a loving father, and to grow up in a happy, loving home, yet it was up to Karim to take that chance—to trust in her.

How she hated him. Yet somehow she couldn't completely…

She closed her eyes as she recalled his lovemaking, the tenderness he could at times display, the insight that had freed her from her fear of sex only to plunge her into another prison.

He had to trust that this was his baby. On that she refused to waver. Karim had to make love to her without protection or tomorrow she would be left alone.

As Karim prayed for his father and his country, Felicity drew her bath.

She had no seduction routine, no experience, but, drying herself off, she stared at the rows of glass bottles Bedra had prepared her with on her wedding night. She had poured rose water into the bath and Felicity did the same, then stepped into the fragrant water.

After, as she dried herself, she remembered Bedra's excited chatter as she had massaged Felicity's pulse-points with oil from tiny glass bottles. *Attar*, Bedra had explained—mixed fragrances. This oil was a heady mix of sweet amber, *oudh* and musk that would please the Prince.

'*Oudh?*' Felicity had asked.

'Wood,' Bedra had said. 'And I will place this dish of almond oil by the bed…'

'For perfume?' Felicity had asked, sniffing the bland dish, but Bedra had just laughed.

It seemed strange to Felicity to be massaging her pulse-points with oil of wood, but the fragrance was heady, and she remembered again him holding her that night, before it had all gone so wrong. She did what Bedra had done, and placed a slim silver dish of almond oil by the bed, waiting for him, as nervous as any bride on her wedding night.

He was 'too tired' to talk when he came to bed. He shrugged onto his side, with his back to her, and promptly feigned sleep. Yet she could feel his tension, could feel the black energy in the bed. When finally he did sleep he rolled over and held her, just as he did most nights. His hand in sleep on her belly made her weep.

She was protecting him from himself, Felicity knew. The man he really was would never jeopardise the safety of his baby. She turned over and stared at him.

She touched him.

She felt his body, reluctant, angry, even in sleep.

'I won't have the test, Karim.' She spoke to darkness, and didn't know whether or not he was listening, but she told him, warned him, begged to his soul to listen to her plea. 'I will not take the risk, however small, just to appease—'

'Felicity.' Annoyed with himself for having rolled

towards her, he turned away from her again. 'Can we get through these next days?'

He willed sleep to come again. For Karim it was going to be a long night, made bearable only by having her beside him. He had considered taking a wife, but only for the sake of duty. There would be no real benefit to him. There had been so many lovers, so many women, and he had felt so many pleasures. Yet after the grim conversation he had had on the phone to his brothers insomnia had beckoned. He had never expected to feel peace this night—his father's operation looming, so many decisions to be made. Yet climbing in beside her, angry with her, with himself, with his brothers, with his father, suddenly all there was was the dark tent and silence, and the musky scent of her that gently spirited him to a better place. Hearing her breathe beside him had brought a rare peace that was unexpected.

Perhaps the future was a touch more bearable with her in his bed at night. And then she had awoken him.

And now he couldn't sleep.

He didn't want the test either—didn't want to find out the truth. This wretched time was only bearable because of her. Her scent was too heavy, too much woman lay untouched in the bed beside him. He considered asking her to go and bathe, to remove that fragrance so he might rest, except he didn't want to.

'I cannot sleep,' he admitted, half an hour of silence later.

'Would this help?'

'What?' He heard the nervousness in her voice.

'This.' Her hands were at his shoulders and softly she stroked them. She could feel the knot of tension in the muscles beneath the silken skin, felt him arch his neck as she smoothed a hard knot. 'Does it help?'

And because it seemed it did she gently guided him to turn to his stomach. She wanted this closeness as much as him—wanted this chance for Karim to see sense before morning came.

She knew what Bedra had meant now, was glad for the silver dish of almond oil that was by the bed. Felicity dipped her fingers in it, rubbed it the length of his back, moving her thumbs along his vertebra, her oiled fingers pushing into his loins then up towards his shoulders. She felt the tension seep slowly from him, and when it had, when he was relaxed beneath her, she peeled off her night-gown and turned him over. She dipped her fingers back in the oil as those black eyes caressed her body. She rubbed the sweet potion into him, slid it into the thick black hair, and cupped him tenderly in her hand.

'You know too much.' He grabbed her wrist. 'For one so innocent, you know way too much.'

'I know nothing,' Felicity corrected. 'Except what my body tells me—what your body shows me it wants.'

She meant it. Always sex had been feared, yet with Karim it was instinctive, her body, her hands, guided by more than her mind, by more than just thought.

The oil in her palm made him slide through her fingers, no grip in her hold as she touched him. Her two hands slid in perpetual motion, feeling him grow. Even as he slipped out of her grip the other hand was waiting to slide up to his peak, an endless tunnel that closed around his member. She was enchanted, feeling him grow strong in her hand, feeling his mind weaken. This proud, contained, distant man was coming close now to the man she had first met, the man she had first loved.

His eyes were soft as he took in her body. 'Your body

is changing.' It was his first real acknowledgment of her pregnancy, and it made her melt.

'Feel it, then,' Felicity whispered, because touch brought closeness.

He oiled his palms with what she'd left on his body and slid his hands over hips that were rounder and softer now, then up to her breasts. Still her own hands worked on. He rubbed her breasts until she felt her thighs grow warm. His fingers stroked her tender nipples, slowly, slowly letting his hands take in the changes. He moved down to the soft curve of her stomach, his thumbs meeting in the middle, where their baby lay beneath. He stroked her pale flesh, and for Karim, for a dizzying second, there was a flash of a life that wasn't about duty or honour or country. It was about trust, doing things right by her. He could not stand the thought of a needle in her pale flesh, piercing into her uterus, disturbing their baby's slumber.

Their baby.

'There will be no test.' He said it, and then he said it again. 'There will be no test.'

She felt all woman, felt a shift between them. They could, here in his bed, be equals. It was something to build on.

'Felicity…' Her hands were like magic. A silver pearl of moisture was at his tip, and she rubbed it in till he thought he might weep. But Kings did not weep—nor Princes, nor men. With her, in that moment, maybe he could. 'I do not want to be King.'

She smiled down at him, held him with her eyes as still she stroked him.

'I would give *anything* not to be King.'

'You don't have to be….'

She didn't understand, and he was too far gone to

explain, reeling from his own admission. From somewhere deep within she had reached in and pulled out the truth. Relief washed through him, allowing him to discard facts and believe she was right, that all he had to be was with her.

He did not want her hands around him now. He wanted *her*.

Her hips were slippery from the oil, but he lifted her, watched the glorious triangle of her thighs part over his erection. He massaged her clitoris, holding her there for a moment, because as soon as he entered her Karim knew he would come. He had never felt a woman around him without barrier, and as he lowered her onto him, felt the delicious grip of warm muscle, he thought he might die from the pleasure of a sensation he didn't want to end. He was stroking her inside and he could feel every twitch, every clench of intimate muscle, her delicious grip as he raised her hips and lowered her again and again. He refused to give in to his intense need, sliding her up and down his length and staring at her—at this woman who blurred everything, who made light of rules that were ingrained. How, *how* he wanted to trust.

She didn't need his hands to guide her now. Felicity was locked into a delicious rhythm. He was stroking her *there* now, but still looking at her, and she could feel the first waves of orgasm. She wanted him to come with her, her eyes pleading with him to join, to trust…

'I want to feel you come.'

Still he held back.

She was coming, so hard it made her scream. This was what he did to her. Took everything from her and yet held himself back. She was sobbing his name, begging him to believe that he was the only one, that this was *his* child to love.

He raised his hips and shot into her. He could do this every day, every night, for ever, if only he could believe.

He held her afterwards, his hands exploring her body as he wrestled with the demons of his mind.

His father had never forgiven his mother—had lived a lonely life since.

For what?

Karim had not slept well for two nights, he was aware of that. This crazy word *love* kept bobbing into his head, but he told himself it was lust as his hand crept between her sleeping thighs. Lust would have him hard again, lust would have him waking her from her necessary rest when now all he wanted to do was hold her.

CHAPTER SIXTEEN

IT WAS better with her here.

He had kept his word and brought her back from the desert—for how long he did not yet know. But as Karim visited his father it was easier knowing she was in the plush waiting area outside. Hassan was there too, and Jamal. Ibrahim was flying in and was due to arrive soon.

He didn't know in what way it was better, but as he stepped out of his father's suite his eyes went to hers first, blue jewels that shone from beneath the *abaya* she had chosen to wear, it was.

'How is he?'

'Weaker,' Karim said. 'They should have done this weeks ago, when I first said.'

'His heart would not have taken a long anaesthetic then.'

'Hassan and Jamal are going back to the palace once they have seen him,' Karim explained. 'I am going to meet with the surgeon and discuss his plans for the procedure.'

'I'd rather wait for you.'

'I may be some time.'

'Then I'll wait.'

After a moment's pause he nodded.

'Could I visit Bedra?'

He shook his head. 'It is too soon for the people to know. You might be recognised…' He stared into her eyes and relented. 'For a little while. Tell her I pray for her and her son too.'

The maternity ward was busy. Visitors were in each room, and nobody gave her a second glance as she strolled through the familiar ward—dressed in an *abaya* this time.

Aarif recognised her, though, bowing, overwhelmed that she would visit. Felicity quickly told him not to make a fuss, and then she saw Bedra, pale and tired on her pillow, but alive.

Her soft brown eyes filled with tears as they met Felicity's. 'Thank you!' she wept. 'For what you did. You saved our son.'

'How is he?' Felicity asked.

'Small, but very brave. The doctors say that he has a strong will, that he is a fighter. We have named him Karim.'

Felicity left her to rest then, glad to have visited. But it wasn't only because Bedra was tired that she chose not to linger.

'Helen!' She watched her colleague frown and turn round. 'Helen—it's me. Felicity.' She saw her friend's eyes finally widen in recognition.

'Thank goodness,' Helen said. 'I've been walking past the royal wing every break I get. What on *earth* is going on?'

'I don't know.'

They sat in a small annexe off the maternity ward, and nobody gave them a second glance. The *abaya* provided anonymity, and Felicity was grateful for it.

'This is my last shift.' Helen shook her head helplessly. 'I leave for the UK tomorrow. I can tell your family…'

'I don't want to worry them.' Felicity's voice was shaken. She was relieved, almost, that the story was out, but guilty for her imposition on a friend and guilty as to how bad Karim's actions sounded when she repeated them. 'Things seem better now. He has said that I don't need to take the test.'

'If you're sure it's his, why don't you?'

'I am not risking my baby for a man who refuses to believe me. I don't know what is going on. He said today that I should return to the desert once the King's surgery is over—that it is better for the people if they don't know of me yet. I feel as if I am being hidden.'

'Can you talk to him about it?' Helen asked. 'Can you tell him how you feel?'

A bitter, mirthless laugh shot out of her lips, and Helen gave her a sympathetic smile. 'I'm sorry. Of course you can't. I forget sometimes just how different it is here.'

'He's nothing like the man he was at home,' Felicity said. 'But sometimes…' Her voice trailed off as she recalled the tenderness of last night, but she was too muddled to think. 'I need to get away. I need to think. Maybe once the operation is over…'

'Has he taken your passport?'

'No.' Felicity shook her head. 'I don't think he was expecting to bring me back here to the palace, but I've checked and it's still there amongst my things. I have no money, though.' She laughed again. 'I have every luxury you could want, but no money. I can rustle up some back in England…'

'I cannot help you,' Helen said. 'If it ever came out, I could never return and work here again.'

'I understand.' Defeated, Felicity moved to stand. 'But thank you—thank you for listening.'

'Felicity, sit down,' Helen said. 'Tomorrow is the King's operation. Everyone will be distracted. It is your only chance.'

'You said you couldn't help,' Felicity said. 'And I truly understand. I don't want to involve you.'

'You had no choice but to involve me, but it has to be kept quiet.' Helen eyes held hers. 'This conversation never happened. You need a suitcase; you need to look as if you are flying home for a family emergency.'

'To who?'

'To the people at the airport—when you buy your ticket.' It was Helen who stood now. 'I am coming in to say goodbye to everyone tomorrow. I'll leave a case here in the annexe at midday, with money in it. But please, Felicity, don't acknowledge me at the airport. They will watch CCTV if you get away.'

'I can't leave tomorrow.' Felicity shook her head at the impossibility. 'I'm not leaving Karim on the day his father has surgery.'

'I think you ought to…' Helen ran a nervous hand through her hair. 'Felicity, I think you need to. Then you can sort things out. You have to think of the baby.'

'I *am* thinking of the baby. It deserves a father.'

'Is Jamal pregnant?' Helen's worried eyes met hers. 'I know it is wrong to ask, but surely you can trust me that it will go no further—*is* Jamal expecting a child?'

'No.' Felicity shook her head. Jamal had a trim figure, and only this morning she had wept quietly and told Felicity about her shame at not being able to give Hassan a son. She had said that she was glad and grateful that Felicity understood.

'There are rumours that she is,' Helen said.

'Then the rumours are wrong.'

'These are rumours that come from the palace.'

'But why would they…?' Her voice trailed off. A

thought so vile it didn't bear thinking started to trickle in, and she blocked it.

'If Karim believes it is not his child…' Helen gave a tight shrug. 'They need an heir, Felicity. These are turbulent times, and the people need to know there will be an heir.'

'No.' She refused to believe it of Karim—remembered his hands on her belly last night, tender hands that had cradled the life within. 'He said I didn't need to take the test last night. He said that…' She recalled his words, and then she recalled something else.

I would give anything not to be King.

Was that what Karim had meant? In the throes of near orgasm had he admitted his dark truth? That he would give away his own flesh and blood rather than be King?

Was *this* the man she had thought she loved?

'You'll lend me the money?' Felicity could hardly believe the strength in her voice or the plans that were being laid. 'You hardly know me.'

'I believe you, though,' Helen said. 'And your situation is impossible otherwise.' She gave her friend a pale smile. 'Try to talk to him tonight—try one last time to find out his plans. But don't get too upset. If he gets any indication you are planning to flee, then he'll be watching you like a hawk. And if you can't talk, if you can't work things out…' Helen gave her a quick hug. 'I'll see you in the UK.'

CHAPTER SEVENTEEN

THERE wasn't any time to talk.

When she returned to the royal wing Jamal and Hassan had left, and even though she felt as if she had been gone ages her absence did not seem to have been noticed.

Karim came out from speaking with the surgeon, and then they were driven back to the palace, where Ibrahim had just arrived.

He was far friendlier than the rest—more western in his ways—but the brothers all headed off to discuss their father and their country as the women sat and chatted, mainly in Arabic. On the rare occasion they did translate, it only upset Felicity more—because they all spoke beautiful English.

Really she might as well not be there. So she removed herself.

She lay in Karim's bed in the palace and pondered her future—wondered if she had so spectacularly misread him. Her hand moved down to her belly—it was definitely starting to swell now, and she truly loved it.

She loved her baby with a passion she had never anticipated.

Oh, all mothers loved their babies—even reluctant ones often wept with relief when they held their infant after birth. But now Felicity understood how a woman could lift a car if their child was trapped. She lay in awe at the surge of maternal instinct to save, to protect her child, that flooded her body.

When Karim came to bed he refused to talk. He had argued with his brothers, Karim said. There had been enough talk for today.

He removed her nightdress.

And she let him.

She let him make fast, urgent love to her. Still he moved her, still as he slid over her and deep inside her she could not believe Helen's words were true. That the man who was groaning her name, holding her so closely, begging her to come with him, could ever do that to their child.

Her orgasm was intense. She clung to him in the most intimate way possible—because she needed to believe *he* was real. And afterwards she lay beside him, tried to keep the fear from her voice, tried to make tender post-coital conversation, asking a question surely any mother-to-be would.

'What do you hope, Karim?' Felicity asked against his chest as he held her. 'What do you hope for our child?'

'Everything,' Karim answered. 'For our child, I hope for everything.'

His words brought no comfort—no comfort at all.

CHAPTER EIGHTEEN

KARIM needed to think.

His prayers were for his father this morning, that he might live. And not for selfish reasons either.

He wanted his father to have time—to amend the past, to meet again with the woman who had loved him even when she had strayed. Deeper into prayer he went, round and round in circles in his mind. He asked that he might forgive, that he might trust even if the answer wasn't the one he craved.

And for a surgeon that was hard. For a reluctant king it was harder.

He sat on the terrace and looked over to the desert, handing over the control that he had always lived by.

She was pale, sipping on her tea, her eyes downcast and shy. How he wanted to confide in her—and yet he didn't want to cause her pain.

He did not want this, the greatest honour that could be bestowed upon him, and what Karim was now contemplating made him feel sick at the chaos it would create. Last night he had broached his plan to Hassan and a shouting match had ensued.

He stared out to the desert and felt its call. His last visit there had been dishonest. He must return and take counsel from the land, let it guide him to the right decision. Not just for himself, not just for his country. His eyes went to Felicity, to one woman versus a whole nation's hopes, and he was angry. He was angry because without her there would be no decision to make.

Without her, duty would be done so much more easily.

'Karim…' Her hand was shaking as she placed the tiny jewelled cup down. 'What you said last night…'

'Felicity,' he interrupted, 'today my father undergoes surgery…'

'What happens then?' she pleaded—because she had to be sure. Her last chance to leave was today, and she wanted his assurance, wanted the man who made love to her at night to return by day. She was too scared to trust him. 'Are we to have our wedding celebration? Am I to be announced to the people?'

'There is no time for discussion now,' Karim snapped. No one argued with him. No one except her. At every turn she challenged not just his words but his mind. 'Can we just get through today? And then…' He closed his eyes, made himself say it, forced the words out. 'I will tell you tonight.'

'Tell me what?'

He opened his eyes and she was still there. Time was running out, and whether his father lived or died he had to tell her the truth. 'I will tell you everything.'

But she needed everything *now*—and there wasn't time. That much she understood.

A maid came in and announced that his brothers were ready to go to the hospital. Karim dismissed her before addressing his wife again. 'We will talk tonight. But I must leave now. Today I must show the country our family is strong. You will wait here.'

'I'm coming with you,' Felicity said. 'I want to be with you.'

He paused; he had always thought that he would have to face this day alone. This life, this pain was so much easier with her beside him.

'Very well.'

The maids slipped her *abaya* over her head, and as they were driven to the hospital Felicity's mind was in turmoil. Last night's assurances were so much sketchier by day. Still she had no idea of the fate that awaited her. He had promised they would talk tonight—but what was it he wanted to tell her?

She had a voice, Felicity assured herself—with Karim, she had a voice.

Helen had surely got things wrong.

'Karim?'

He didn't even turn his head, just stared out of the window, completely immersed in his own thoughts. And of course she was ignored as they walked through the hospital and sat in the lavish lounge as the King was prepared for surgery. Hassan didn't look up as they entered and Jamal it seemed deliberately wasn't looking at her. The tension in the room was unbearable as the hour approached. Felicity was sure it wasn't just to do with the King. None of the brothers spoke or acknowledged each other. Even Ibrahim sat with his head in his hands.

It was an appalling, oppressive place to be, and Felicity was tempted to stand, to go for a walk—anything that would break the stifling silence. But then she felt something so strange, so unfamiliar and unexpected, it made her breath catch in her throat.

Karim's hand was in hers.

This strong man was holding on to her. And all Felicity knew was that today she couldn't go—couldn't add to his pain, to his grief. She knew that somehow she had to trust that beneath it all the Karim she loved was still there, and he would do the right thing. Her fingers gripped his. This display of affection was so out of place in this country, with this man, and it moved her.

'The King would like to speak with his sons.'

Hassan stood, looked over to Karim and spoke in Arabic. There was challenge in Hassan's voice as he spoke, but Karim didn't rise, just sat in stony silence.

Hassan went in first, and his face was like chalk when he came out.

And then it was Karim's turn. There was no emotion to be seen. When he returned his face was a mask, his back so straight. Felicity took his hand again. He needed her.

And then in went Ibrahim. He was there for a long time, and his eyes shot daggers at Karim when he came out. Karim didn't look up, just stared fixedly ahead, only jolting when Khan spoke again to his wife.

'The King wishes to speak with you, Sheikha Felicity.'

She felt his hand grip hers. Her eyes flew to his.

'I will come with you,' said Karim.

'He wishes to speak with the Sheikha alone.'

'I will come with her.' Karim stood up, but Khan shook his head. The King had given his orders. 'He insists on speaking to the Sheikha alone.'

Khan had told her how she must greet the King, saying that she must tell him she would pray for him and that he would be cured.

'Thank you.'

He was so much older than the images she had seen of

him. Feeble and pale, he lay on the bed. The attentive
nurses and his aide disappeared. His speech slurred slightly
as he greeted her, and his eyes struggled to focus. No
doubt, Felicity realised, from his pre-op medication.

'You are a good woman,' the King said. 'I can see that.
Karim has told me that.'

'Thank you, Your Majesty.'

'You carry a great gift; you must take care of the baby.'

He *knew*! Her eyes whipped to his, to eyes as black as
his son's, and she was touched that Karim had confided in
his father. It was right he should die knowing of his grand-
child's existence.

'I hope for a son.'

Felicity smiled. He did not mean to offend. She understood that much of their ways, at least.

'Our people need a son, an heir…' He was closing his eyes,
then forcing them open, and Felicity felt the first prickles of
confusion. 'They need to know that there will always be the
King to guide them after I am gone. Hassan was raised to be
King.' He smiled at her pale face. 'Karim would never say
his first duty is not to his people—he would never say it. But
I know he does not want to be King. This way, because of your
gift, our people will get an heir and Karim can have the life
he wants. I know Hassan will be a fine father to your infant.'

'Hassan?' She wanted to be sick. It was *true*! It was true
and it had all been decided.

'When I close my eyes as they put me under I will pray
for our future King…' He gave in to the drugs then, and
Felicity just stood there. She wanted to shake the old man
awake, demand to know what the hell he meant. Except she
knew already. Full realisation was hitting her with devastating force.

This was not her baby to them. This was a solution.

This was what Karim was going to tell her tonight.

She stood frozen as the truth dawned bitterly. Karim had *told* her that he didn't want to be King. He hadn't been relenting, as she had thought. The results of the DNA test didn't matter—the baby she was carrying was a mere solution to them.

This was not a living, breathing child, but an heir to the throne—at whatever cost.

So *this* was what Karim had been planning: to hide her away until she gave birth. This was what he was going to tell her tonight.

This was the man she had thought she loved.

It was imperative that she leave—essential that she act completely normal as she walked out and joined Karim in the lounge.

'What did he say?' His question was low, but urgent. She saw the dart of worry in his eyes and knew he was worried what his father had said. Never had she been more grateful for the *abaya*. She only had to lie with her eyes. But still that was hard.

'To take care of you.'

'He said that?' Karim sounded surprised. 'What else?'

'Nothing…' She lowered her gaze. 'He fell asleep… the drugs…' She couldn't maintain normality, but for her child she *had* to—for the sake of her child she *had* to leave.

A few moments later the King was being wheeled to Theatre, and the clock-watching began. If a doctor appeared too soon then they'd know the operation had been hopeless.

There was a sliver of hope as an hour passed—but not for Felicity.

She stared at the clock, watched it inch past eleven-thirty. This was her chance.

'Karim…' She blew out a breath. 'I don't feel well. I feel a bit sick.'

He frowned at her strained, breathless voice. Felicity wasn't putting it on—her breathing was coming short and fast through fear, and she was so nauseous she felt she might really vomit. His concern was genuine, but Felicity realised it was for the baby rather than her. Karim told her he would summon a nurse, or a car would take her to the palace.

She shook her head. 'It's morning sickness. I might just have a walk in the gardens, like I did yesterday. It helped,' Felicity said. 'I want to be here to hear the news.'

'It could be hours…' Karim started, but Felicity halted him.

'If I need to go back to the palace I will get a driver to take me. You just worry for your father.' And he *was* distracted, Felicity thought as she walked away. Because usually she would be sent with an escort. Or perhaps after last night, he thought he had won her over…

He almost had.

Just as Helen had promised it would be, there was the case. Felicity opened it, grateful it was filled with clothes. It looked exactly as if someone had packed it in a hurry, and there too was a wad of cash.

Taking off her *abaya*, Felicity hung it on the back of the door. Picking up the case, she walked out.

She was just another relative, just a blonde woman who turned a couple of heads, but there was nothing unusual in that, even though there were cameras set up outside the hospital, giving the people updates as the country prayed for its King.

She climbed into a taxi and asked to be taken to the airport. The driver started the engine. He was listening to the news, which, from the teeny bit she could make out, was about King Zaraq.

It *was* the right time to flee; the airline staff were all watching the news too, barely listening as Felicity explained that her sister was ill and that she *had* to get the next flight home.

She held her breath, wondering if her name would set off alarm bells, if Security would suddenly grab her. But then there was a ticket in her hand, and she was going through.

Cold sweat drenched her as her passport was checked. At every stage she expected a hand to be placed on her shoulder.

There was Helen—their eyes met for a second, but Felicity quickly looked away. She sat tapping her foot, and faced the interminable wait for the flight to board.

If he rang, her heart would surely stop—because if she didn't answer it would cause alarm. And if she did he might hear the background noise of the airport. Armed guards were everywhere. She felt as if everyone was looking—as if everyone must know.

She tried to walk nonchalantly to the restrooms, then locked herself in a cubicle and waited the hour out. She stared at her phone. If he was going to call then it was better it was now. He called.

'Felicity?' It was almost a relief to hear his voice. Then there was a terrible struggle to remember her place, to be the suitable bride, not to ask but to be told. Only that wasn't her, and Karim would notice the change.

'How is he?' she asked—because that was what the old Felicity would have said. The old Felicity, who had cared.

'It is three hours now since they started.' She could hear

the strain in his deep voice, but it didn't move her. Her hand over her stomach, she remembered what really mattered. 'How are *you*?' he asked.

'Tired,' Felicity said, staring at the wall in front of her and closing her eyes at the horror of it all. 'Just tired.'

There was a pause, an interminable pause, and then he spoke. 'Felicity, my—'

Whatever he was about to say was drowned by the flushing of the toilet in the next cubicle, which made Felicity's heart race. She tried to smother the phone. Instead of questions she got an apology—clearly he thought she was still feeling sick.

'I will go. You need your space. Try to rest. If you need anything…'

And as she said goodbye, as she clicked off the phone, it was for all the world as if she had been speaking to a man who trusted in her.

But she was running away.

Even as the plane taxied down the runway, still she expected it to halt—for police or soldiers to flood the aircraft. Then they were in the sky; the seat belt sign was pinging off. Only then did it dawn on her.

She wasn't safe.

She could never be safe.

She had taken away their King.

CHAPTER NINETEEN

'ARE you okay?'

They were standing in the line for the plane's toilets when Helen first spoke to her.

'I feel sick,' Felicity admitted. 'I'm not sure if it's nerves or morning sickness.'

'You'll be home soon,' Helen said.

So would Karim. Maybe she was being paranoid, Felicity told herself as she locked herself in a cubicle. Maybe he would just accept that she had gone. After all, his mother had left…

And then her thought processes stopped. The red on her panties she had wished for in those early days was there now. And fear of Karim's wrath was nothing compared to the fear mingled with grief that hit her as she felt a low, cramping pain in her abdomen.

She was losing her baby. The very thing she had fled to protect was slipping away, and there was nothing she could do.

Nothing.

Helen frowned as her friend came out of the bathroom.

'What's wrong?'

'Nothing.' She didn't want to involve Helen.

'Felicity, there's something wrong; you're as pale as anything.'

'I'm bleeding.'

The staff were lovely. They moved her up to business class, where she could lie down, pulled curtains around her. But really there was nothing anybody could do. She stared out of the window as she slid through the sky, the cramp in her abdomen telling her nurse's brain this was real.

And she couldn't weep—because if she started she would never stop. She had to try and hold it together as the plane landed, then had to wait for everyone to offload so they could bring a stretcher on.

The case Helen had packed for her still had to be collected, Customs regulations still had be adhered to, but it was all dealt with efficiently and speedily.

She was in England. She was home.

An ambulance was waiting, and the paramedics told her to rest on the stretcher as they put in a drip because her blood pressure was low. Still she didn't cry.

It wasn't an emergency, the bleeding had stopped now, so there were no lights or sirens. Only with the airport out of sight did she dare to turn on her phone. Texts and voice-mail messages bleeped, filling her inbox. In a matter of seconds it rang, and only then did Felicity fall apart.

'I lost it.' She hated him so much in that moment, she screamed her torment into the phone. 'I lost it on the plane. You can hate me and you can find me, but I don't care. I hate you, Karim. I hate you for never trusting me.'

CHAPTER TWENTY

Felicity.

As he'd sat in the hospital awaiting news of his father still his mind had been on her.

She gave him strength.

A different sort of strength from the type he was used to. Holding her hand today had helped him.

The surgery had been long and delicate. For twelve hours the country had paused, and so too had Karim.

Refusing food, he'd drunk only water. Hassan hadn't been talking to him, Ibrahim had been immersed in his own thoughts, the aides and servants had stayed silent.

Oh, there had been many hours to think.

He'd rung her once, but she was resting, so he'd left her alone to do that. She would need all her strength for tonight, when he must tell her. Whatever the outcome, she had to know the plans that had been laid. How reckless he had been with their baby and the decision he had made.

Their baby.

It had been at the forefront of his mind even as he'd spoken with his father's surgeon. He hadn't spoken with his brothers or his aides. He'd walked out of the hospital with apparent dignity. Yet he had felt filthy inside. He'd wanted to fall into bed and into her arms instead of telling her the truth. But he wanted it out all the same.

But she was gone.

There was no fresh scent in the bedroom, no movement in the bed. Even as he demanded answers from Security, from his drivers, from the airport, even as all the accommodation at the university and the hospital complexes were checked, he knew that she was gone.

Every minute he rang her—and it nearly killed him when she finally answered.

His baby was gone. Before he had even acknowledged it. Before he'd had a chance to love it. Felicity too. They had both gone, never to return.

The news was confirmed by the airline. Yes, a Miss Felicity Anderson had suffered a miscarriage on the plane.

Except she was a sheikha, Princess Felicity Zaraq. Had he alerted them, had he kept her in the desert, maybe they would both still be here?

'It is probably better.' Hassan now spoke to him. 'She was weak. She would have revealed—'

It took Ibrahim's hand to block Karim's punch.

'I must go to her.'

'Why?' Hassan frowned. 'Our people need you here. You don't even know where she is. She would be a fool to go straight home. Get security to trace her, and then you can decide her punishment.'

'She's just lost a baby.'

'It probably wasn't even yours.'

This time Ibrahim's block was too slow.

His mother was kinder, her voice at the end of the phone gentle and worried, and Karim knew she was speaking the truth.

'Is that what you really wanted for her? To keep her trapped in the desert or locked in your palace with the airport on alert? That is not how you love a woman. It is how you keep her, perhaps, but that is not love. Let her go, Karim. For two years I lived in fear of your father finding me. If you really love her, ring her or write to her and tell her that you are letting her go. Zaraq's ways are too different for some. I loved your father, I tried to fit in, but I couldn't. I am ashamed of what I did, but I was bored, unhappy. Your father was always in demand, myself always silent. Is this the life you want for the woman you love?'

'It would be different for Felicity. I would change.'

'Your father promised me the same.'

His mother's voice brought him the closest to tears he had ever been in his life.

'I am sorry you lost the baby.'

He had doubted Felicity and now he was paying the price. But there had been *so* many women, and never an accident. Karim dredged his memory bank, and as he sorted the blitz of emotions and feelings into slightly neater order he suddenly *knew*.

Opening his bedside drawer, he pulled out a condom, opened it and headed for the sink, filled it with water and watched its slow leak.

Leila. He remembered her jumping when he'd caught her in his bedroom, understood now her reluctance for anything oral. She had been damaging the condoms, procuring his seed, doing her best to ensure that the marriage he had been resisting would take place with her.

He just wished he'd worked it out earlier.

Wished he had had it in him to believe in Felicity sooner.

It would be easy to lie down now, to give in to tears, to

follow all the advice. But that had never been Karim. Picking up the phone, he listened to his heart and summoned the royal jet.

CHAPTER TWENTY-ONE

THEY kept her in for two days.

As she lay there, Felicity decided to lie to her mother, to ring her as she had from the desert and pretend that she was fine. But mid-conversation she couldn't do it. She broke down. And even if her mother was anxious when she arrived at the hospital, even if Georgie was in tears, crying on a nurse, somehow it was worth the pain she had caused.

It was such a relief to be in her mother's arms.

Later, she took a call from Georgie at the flat, and answered calmly when she was informed there was a man called Karim at the door and Georgie asked should she call the police or let him in.

'Let him in,' Felicity said calmly. 'Tell Karim that when I am ready I will talk to him—you go to Mum's.'

Her eyes screwed closed as she hung up the phone. Even with freedom beckoning, still her mind searched for closure.

She went from the hospital to her mother, and let herself be looked after. She refused to call Karim, and he, as requested, did not call her. The waiting game they had played in the desert was being repeated again.

'Here.' Georgie brought her a tray laden with toast and scrambled eggs and a vast mug of tea. 'You're to finish it,' she instructed, and it was nice that finally it was Georgie telling Felicity this and not the other way around. As Felicity ate her lunch she glimpsed a future that was better—where the Anderson women were stronger—and knew that day was about to come.

But she had to deal with something first.

Stepping into her flat on day five, she was ready to face him.

He looked terrible.

Sitting on her sofa, wearing jeans and a T-shirt, he looked like a man who hadn't slept in a week. Or shaved, come to that.

'I'll never go back,' she said. She dropped her handbag on the floor next to Helen's case and told him, 'Nothing you can say will make me go back—you'd have to kill me first.'

'You really think I would do that?'

'I'd rather you didn't,' Felicity said. 'But, frankly, I'm so tired right now I actually don't care.'

'About the baby…'

'I *hate* what you were planning.' She watched him flinch. 'If you want to do your precious DNA test, if you need to check, then you still can—at the hospital.' She was talking as if she didn't care, except tears were rolling out her eyes and she spat out her words. 'It was *your* child—and you would have given it to Hassan rather than be King yourself.'

'No!' He was on his feet. 'When I thought it might be another man's, *then* we spoke of it…'

'Do you think that helps?' Felicity demanded. 'You would have done that to me—you would have ripped my baby from my arms and given it to your brother just so Zaraq had its heir.'

'I wouldn't have.'

'Your father told me your plans.'

'I wouldn't have,' Karim said again, his voice strangely calm. 'I thought I would. I thought I could. But, no. That night we were together, I knew that I could not.'

'Please,' Felicity scoffed. 'You told me you didn't want to be King—and without an heir, without *our* baby, Hassan couldn't be either.'

'No!' He demanded her attention, his black eyes fierce—not with anger, but with something she couldn't interpret. 'I did *not* want to be King. Have you any idea how hard that is to say? If I didn't hand over the baby Hassan would have stepped aside and I would have been King. It was my duty, it was my role and yet it was the last thing I wanted. And if it is the last thing that *I* want, how could I wish it for my son?'

And for the first time he cried.

'I did not want that future for him,' Karim explained. 'I did not want it because I knew what was coming—the burden that it would place not just on him but on you.'

She recalled her own words and realised how hard it would have been to hear them. Every cell in her body paused as he told her the truth.

'I told my brothers the night before my father's operation that the baby would stay with me. Hassan and Jamal were furious. They want to rule, they were bred and raised for it, yet I was denying them the chance. They kept telling me that it wasn't even mine...' He was silent for a moment. 'And I told them that even if it wasn't mine, I would rather love it than lose you.'

She turned to his proud face, looked at the tears that had dried on his cheeks, and prayed she would never have to see them again—would never see this proud man reduced by her doing.

'I told them too that I would not be King.'

'Then who?' Her mind darted, remembering the daggers Ibrahim had thrown at his brother. 'Ibrahim?'

'We did not know.' Karim shook his head. 'We chose to keep the decision from my father before surgery, but when he came round we told him what had happened.'

'He's alive?'

'He has many years left in him,' Karim said firmly. 'And Hassan has many years more.'

'Hassan?'

'He loves Jamal—that stuffed shirt of a guy actually does have feelings, and he loves Jamal. Even if she can't give him a son. Infertility happens to everyone—and if the people of Zaraq can't accept that yet, then there are many years left to educate them, to work out a solution.' His eyes met hers. 'To learn that there are other ways of doing things.'

And she wanted to believe, wanted to tell him so, but she was too tired to think straight, too tired to trust in her own heart.

The Sheikh, Prince Karim of Zaraq, would just have to learn patience.

'I'm tired, Karim.'

She slept in her own bed for a day and a night, and a day and a night more. She padded out occasionally, to the loo or the kitchen, and always he was there.

A sexy sheikh, topless in jeans, struggling to squeeze a teabag.

Once she had to smother a smile as she walked past and saw Karim on his knees, trying to work out how to change the loo roll.

He didn't really know what to say when she wept, so instead he just held her or, when she didn't want him, pushed a tissue under her bedroom door. And then, when she emerged from her room for longer intervals, he sometimes patted the sofa and sat silent as they watched a movie.

And she healed a heart that was broken, because that was what women did.

There was a lot of healing still, but Felicity knew she was starting to get there one morning when she laughed at a silly joke he had made. And later that day when she glanced out of the window to smile at a daffodil.

She healed, and he let her do so at her own pace—until the third night, when she sat on the sofa beside him and he said those three words that she wasn't sure she was ready to hear.

'I love you.'

She stared at the TV screen, at her favourite soap, and wondered if they got it in Zaraq. Then she remembered who he was—a sheikh, a prince, a man who could do anything. Of course she'd get her programme. He had just given her his heart.

'I will stay here as long as you want me to. I will stay here for ever if you will have me. I have duties and commitments, but they are nothing compared to my duty and commitment to you.' And then he said it again, but this time he added her name. 'I love you, Felicity.'

'Say it again.' Still she stared at the screen, the indecision that had plagued her these last days fading as over and over he said it.

'I love you… Felicity, I love you… I love you, Felicity.'

Every way possible he said it, and whatever road her mind darted down, he blocked it with his words.

And then she turned and faced him.

'So you should, given I'm your wife.' She accepted his

nod, and then she said it, tears streaming down her cheeks as she let herself trust him. 'And given that I'm having your child.'

'You lost it.'

'No.'

'You told me…'

'I thought I had…' Felicity gulped. 'When I rang you, I truly thought I had.'

His eyes were stunned. 'You let me grieve. You let me think I'd lost my child!'

'Because you almost did,' Felicity said angrily, because it was essential that he see how close he had come to losing them both. As little as fifteen minutes ago, still she had had doubts, wondered if he was just saying and doing the right thing in order that the Prince could collect his wife. 'I had a placental abruption, like Bedra, only not as severe. I was told to rest and heal, told that there could be no stress if I wanted to hold on to my baby.'

He closed his eyes. He understood why she had done it to him after all he had put her through, could see why she had felt unable to tell him.

'When I was having the scan, and I realised the baby was alive, I promised her I would never go back, promised her that I would keep her safe. I promised her I would never let you know…'

'Her?'

It had never really crossed his mind that they might have a girl!

His hand moved to her belly, uninvited but very welcome.

'Meet your daughter.' She handed him the ultrasound photo from her purse, and watched as his face softened and a tender smile spread across that haughty face.

A smile reserved for the daughter who would unashamedly melt his heart and twist him around her little finger.

'I am perhaps the only royal prince who would rather have a daughter.'

And the sofa was too small, so despite the early hour he took her to bed, just so he could hold her properly. And he remembered the first time he had realised he might love her—the night when he had held her without lust—and he closed his eyes in sweet relief as he did it again.

He held her close and relished that he could.

And because she should rest, because she was dozing, it was Karim who reached out and answered the phone, speaking for the first time to his mother-in-law. She wasn't anxious, as he'd expected, in fact she was very assured. She told him in no uncertain terms how she expected him to treat her daughter. Karim held the phone from his ear as Felicity lay half awake, smiling.

'Give me that.' She took the phone from Karim and spoke to her mother as he lay back on her rather small bed and stared up at her. His throat tightened when he heard her words. He was humbled at how far her love went.

'I really am, Mum—once the baby's a bit stronger...' She smiled at her man and he smiled back. 'I'm going to live in the Kingdom of Zaraq.'

EPILOGUE

'I CAN'T do this!' Jamal screamed.

And she might have been raised to be Queen one day, but Felicity and Dr Habib shared a hint of a smile as this very prim lady uttered a few choice words.

'I should be in the Royal Suite!' Jamal demanded.

'It's being painted,' Felicity soothed for the fiftieth time. 'For your baby's arrival!'

'Well, it's coming *now*,' Jamal said, her face darkening as she bore down.

Five weeks premature, the future King had caught Zaraq on the hop!

The suite wasn't being painted—that was a midwife's lie—there had been a shift in the building and it had been closed off. But Jamal didn't need a long explanation. Jamal just needed to concentrate on the important task at hand.

Felicity had wanted to be there. In the past year or so she and Jamal had put aside their differences and become friends, and Felicity had been building up to asking if she could attend the birth. But babies came when they were ready—and this one had decided to make its entrance sooner rather than later.

Karim was in the middle of operating, Hassan was in

the middle of a speech on the other side of Zaraq, and the King was over in London—as he seemed to be rather a lot these days. So not only was Felicity birthing coach, she was also shouting orders to Khan through the labour ward doors between contractions, telling him that Hassan must hurry if he wanted to see his child born.

'He is here!' Khan said excitedly.

'In a few more minutes he will be allowed in…' Dr Habib said, because traditionally males didn't enter till the very last moment.

But Jamal had other ideas.

'Hassan!' She screamed for her Prince, and who was Felicity to deny her? She invited Hassan in to share in the miracle of birth. And as cameras were set up at the entrance to the hospital, and people buzzed with rapid excitement, a strange peace filled the room as a baby was born.

Yes, he was destined to be a king. But as his mother scooped him into arms that had ached for ever, as Hassan wept and finally got to hold his son, he wasn't a king, he was something greater—a baby, a miracle. With tears in her eyes as the family entered, Felicity was grateful for the arm that wrapped around hers as she and Karim both remembered the day they'd first held their own gift.

'Georgie's got her outside,' Karim said, stroking his nephew's cheek and blinking for a moment, remembering little Kaliq and praying he was safe and loved too.

Georgie had come to help with her niece. Felicity didn't want a nanny, or a maid, she wanted her sister. And there was Azizah now, cooing and blowing bubbles in her auntie's arms. Felicity scooped her up, surprised at how heavy she felt after holding Jamal's baby.

They had chosen Azizah's name carefully. It meant

precious and cherished, which she was every day. Both her parents knew what a true gift she was. It had been a difficulty pregnancy. Karim had refused to listen to her pleas to attempt a normal delivery, and after her Caesarean Dr Habib had told Felicity that her husband had been right.

They had both listened, and they both learned from the other.

Karim could be a prince and a surgeon too, so long as at home his only duty was to love her.

'Did I get here in time?' Ibrahim arrived, neither present nor correct to meet the new King. He reeked of perfume, and Felicity smothered a smile as she spotted the smudge of a fresh bruise on his royal neck.

'Go and tidy up!' Karim growled to his younger brother, and Ibrahim walked off to do just that. Then Karim saw her pensive face and knew what was coming. 'Are you okay?'

'Fine. Can we talk?'

'Sure,' Karim said, although he wasn't.

'Could you watch Azizah? Karim and I want to go for a walk,' Felicity said to her sister, and then saw Georgie's pink face, and the rather wide eyes that lingered where Ibrahim had been. She had only been in the country for two days, and so far Felicity had managed to avoid them meeting, privately worried at the scandal those two might create. 'Don't even *think* about it.'

'I'm not,' Georgie said. 'Here—give me Azizah.'

They walked in silence to the gardens, Karim in his navy theatre scrubs, Felicity in her pink maternity ones— just a nurse and a doctor walking and talking, a husband and wife enjoying each other's company, but also a prince and his princess too.

'You want to go back to midwifery.' It was Karim who broached the subject, and for that she was grateful.

'I enjoyed today so much. I knew I would. I've been looking forward to it.'

'You miss it?'

'Yes.' Felicity nodded. 'I didn't think I would. I mean, Azizah is three months old now, and I love spending time with her—I can't believe I want to go back to work. But maybe just one shift a week…' She turned troubled eyes to him. 'Is it impossible?'

A year ago the answer would have been yes, of course it was impossible. But times had changed since then.

He had listened to her, had let her lead him to his own conclusions and had told his father he could be both prince and surgeon. The news had been more acceptable, perhaps, because Jamal had announced she was pregnant…

He loved it.

He walked into the hospital in the morning and stretched his brain, and then came home to his family at night, which made his royal duties a doddle.

'Of course it is possible,' Karim said, hoping he'd catch his father in a good mood when he rang him in London tonight—though recently the King's mood had been excellent! 'Anything is possible,' he said firmly.

But his words didn't soothe her. Protocol Karim would take care of, but it was as wife and mother that she turned to him. 'Can I be all four?' she asked, and Felicity truly didn't know the answer. 'Sheikha, wife, mother, midwife?'

He took her by the hand and added to that list—tossed in a few balls more, knowing she would always juggle them. 'Sister, daughter, lover and friend…'

There was peace in his soul as he gazed down at her.

'Felicity, you can be anything you want to be.'

And she could...with Karim beside her.

HIS BABY
BOMBSHELL

BY
JESSICA MATTHEWS

MILLS & BOON

First published in Great Britain 2009
Harlequin Mills & Boon Limited,
Eton House, 18-24 Paradise Road, Richmond, Surrey TW9 1SR

© Jessica Matthews 2009

ISBN: 978 0 263 86865 4

Set in Times Roman 10½ on 12¾ pt
03-0909-54284

Harlequin Mills & Boon policy is to use papers that are natural, renewable and recyclable products and made from wood grown in sustainable forests. The logging and manufacturing process conform to the legal environmental regulations of the country of origin.

Printed and bound in Spain
by Litografia Rosés, S.A., Barcelona

Jessica Matthews's interest in medicine began at a young age, and she nourished it with medical stories and hospital-based television programmes. After a stint as a teenage candy-striper, she pursued a career as a clinical laboratory scientist. When not writing or on duty, she fills her day with countless family and school-related activities. Jessica lives in the central United States, with her husband, daughter and son.

Praise for Jessica Matthews:

FOR A CHILD'S SAKE
'Jessica Matthews tugs at our hearts with
FOR A CHILD'S SAKE… Ms Matthews creates an
absorbing premise and a strong emotional intensity.'
—*Romantic Times BOOKreviews*

'Jessica Matthews entertains readers
with compassionate characters, lively scenes
and sparkling dialogue.'
—*Romantic Times BOOKreviews*

To my husband Terry,
my personal 'go to' guy for my golfing questions.
To my daughter Jessica, for all those golf tournaments
I was privileged to watch you play,
and to my son Matt, for the music you bring to my life.

CHAPTER ONE

SABRINA HOLLISTER knew she'd eventually see Dr Adrian McReynolds again, but she'd never dreamed that moment would come unexpectedly at a golf course or that she'd knock him senseless in the process.

After a year of leaving her equipment in the back of her single-car garage to collect dust, her friend and fellow nurse Kate Ostmeyer had convinced her to brush off the cobwebs and participate in the First Annual Pinehaven Health Center Benefit Golf Tournament.

Although her first- and second-hole scores weren't anything to brag about, she'd parred the next few before shooting an unbelievable eagle on seven. Not bad for a woman who hadn't swung a club since early last season.

Between the excitement of continuing her game from where she'd left off and the thrill of being outdoors, instead of stuck inside on this beautiful summer day, life couldn't have been better.

Until the eighth hole.

Sabrina took her first tee-off practice swing seconds before Kate completely shattered her concentration.

"Mercy Memorial is loaning us one of their ER docs," Kate announced, clearly proud of her news scoop.

Sabrina froze and she felt her palms break out into a sweat inside her gloves. *Steady*, she cautioned herself. *Don't jump to conclusions.*

Determined to only sound mildly interested instead of frantic, she asked, "Really? They've never loaned us one before."

"There's a first time for everything," the OB nurse remarked cheerfully. "And why shouldn't Mercy send us a doctor? They're part of our consortium and the corporate folks decided that every hospital in the group would take their turn helping cover our ED until we hired a permanent physician. It's Mercy's turn."

Mercy's turn or not, Sabrina scolded herself for leaping to conclusions. The man she'd known at her former place of employment surely wouldn't be the one who would come to her new stomping ground. However, her reassurance didn't stop her from mentally crossing her fingers as she struggled to inject the right note of idle curiosity into her voice. "When is this happening? Not for a few weeks, I hope."

"Oh, he's already here. Started today. In fact, he's playing in this tournament. Apparently our chief of staff wants to make a good impression so he insisted on including him as a member of his foursome."

Sabrina didn't care what Dr Mosby wanted. She did, however, care about working with whomever Mercy had sent. As a member of the nursing float pool, Sabrina was temporarily assigned to the emergency department until one of the regularly assigned nurses returned from maternity leave. Which meant she'd be sharing space with the new guy for the next three weeks.

Don't let it be Adrian.

Sabrina gritted her teeth and asked the obvious. "Do you know who he is?"

"I forget his name," Kate admitted sheepishly. "But, hey, you worked there before you joined us, so I'm sure if you mention a few, I'll recognize his."

"I've been gone for ages," Sabrina pointed out. "Turnover was high. The ED folks I knew probably aren't there any more."

She wasn't telling a lie. Mercy always had new ER docs coming and going, although it boasted a core group who'd remained the same over the years. If hospital administration had been asked to supply a physician, most likely the ED director would assign one of the newbies. Those with seniority wouldn't be sent to another facility without good reason or unless they'd volunteered. She couldn't imagine Adrian offering to leave his house and his job when his gesture meant he'd be an hour and a half away from his family.

Family. She was both envious that he had a family to call his own and bitter that he'd refused to share it with her. But both of those emotions were counter-productive, so she stuffed them back into the mental box where she stored "subjects not to think about".

Kate tapped a forefinger on her chin in obvious thought. "All I remember is that it started with an 'M'."

Sabrina ran through the few names she recalled, eliminating one in particular. "Monighan, Miller, Magee…"

"Close, but not quite. Mac something, I think."

Her chest tightened as only one person fit Kate's criteria. "McReynolds?"

Kate snapped her fingers. "That's right. Dr McReynolds."

Sabrina's entire world suddenly changed from living

color to shades of gray. Blood rushed through her ears, drowning out all sound, and her heart seemed to thump through her chest.

Adrian was coming. No, he was already here.

Heaven help her!

She'd wanted to put off meeting him in this lifetime until she was mentally and emotionally prepared to face him again—preferably in about fifteen or twenty years. Clearly, she'd have minutes or at most twenty-four hours, which wasn't nearly long enough for her to develop any sort of game plan.

She'd dated Adrian for about six months and by the end of that time their relationship had subtly shifted to the point where they'd discussed theoretical topics such as how many children they'd like to have, the sort of house they'd want to live in, which area of Denver had the best elementary schools. They'd been on the verge of a commitment, she believed, when everything changed in an instant.

While riding his motorcycle, Adrian's twenty-four-year-old brother Clay had been sideswiped by a minivan on Interstate 70. He'd come into the ER more broken than whole, with his prognosis of being a paraplegic if his broken vertebrae had damaged his spinal column. Only time would tell.

Determined to help the man she loved to bear the burden of caring for Clay, she'd been crushed when Adrian had broken off their relationship because "he had to focus completely on his brother". Although she'd tried to convince him that she wasn't asking him to put her ahead of his brother's needs, each passing day and failed attempt to see him had caused her hopes and dreams to slowly die: Finally, she'd surrendered to the inevitable and gave up trying to talk to him. Determined to avoid reminders of the man she'd grown to love and the places where they'd spent happy hours, she'd resigned her position at Mercy Memorial and headed for the growing northeastern suburb of Pinehaven, where she'd moved on with her life, just as Adrian had wanted.

Now he had the audacity to appear and upset her hard-won composure. Yet she couldn't deny the hope that suddenly blossomed in her chest. Could he have volunteered because she was here and he wanted to see her? After all, as an ED physician with seniority, he normally wouldn't have been chosen for an assignment like this.

But as the possibility raised her spirits, she warned herself to be cautious. Better for her to keep her imagination under control and not jump to conclusions. Extremely high hopes had a tendency to fall hard and land more painfully.

When she really thought about his arrival logically, it didn't make sense for Adrian to tie himself to a job for three months just to see her again when he could have found her quite easily by other means. She may not have specifically given him her new address, but she hadn't moved to Pinehaven in secret—any number of her ex-coworkers knew her destination. If he'd wanted to talk to her, he would have telephoned, emailed, or appeared on her front porch before now, especially if one considered how Pinehaven Health Center wasn't far from Mercy—a mere ninety minutes' drive if traffic was heavy, less if it wasn't. No, if Adrian had truly and temporarily relocated here, he'd only come under duress.

The realization hardened her heart.

"Do you know him?" Kate asked, curiosity coloring her face.

Did she know Adrian McReynolds? What a question!

She knew details. He liked his coffee black, his food spicy, his work and living spaces clean and neat. He wore boxer shorts to bed, had silky smooth hair on his chest, developed five o'clock shadow twice a day, had the faintest scar near his left temple's hairline and a birthmark on his right hip, and was a fantastic lover. He was charming, had a wonderful sense of humor, was devoted to his younger siblings, and locked away his deepest feelings behind a wall of stoicism that only a few could breach.

On the job, he was a perfectionist and demanded the best for his patients. He was completely immovable once he'd made a decision. At one time, she'd admired the trait because it showed tenacity, persistence and strength of character. Now she only saw it as a flaw of closed-mindedness.

Did she know Adrian McReynolds? Apparently not as well as she should have or as well as she'd once thought.

She hesitated before answering. Until she considered the ramifications of what his presence would do to her life, she refused to admit anything but the barest of details. She didn't want people to know they'd once been quite close or that he'd ended the relationship because he didn't want to make room in his life for her, so she stretched the truth almost to the breaking point.

"I've run into him a few times," she said instead.

"Then I'm sure he'll appreciate seeing a familiar face now that he's here for the next few months. And speaking of faces, the stranger over there with Dr Mosby's team must be our fellow."

Sabrina lowered her club to study the group approaching the thirteenth green about fifty yards to her right.

Instinctively, her gaze homed on the tall individual she hadn't seen in thirteen months, one week and two days.

Even from this distance, she recognized his confident bearing, his long-legged walk, and his lucky black-and-purple Colorado Rockies baseball cap.

It was Adrian. The man she'd never expected to see until she'd plotted out every second of their next encounter, until she could think of him as a casual acquaintance rather than a lover, until she could face him with the cool indifference he deserved.

As aloof as she wanted to be, as often as she'd told herself she'd relegated him into her past and moved on with her life, seeing him with hardly any advance warning brought all of those painful emotions to the surface.

Her chest hurt as she realized his presence affected more than her own heart. His untimely arrival complicated everything she'd built for herself during the past year. She'd prided herself on her ability to work with anyone and everyone, but working with Adrian on a daily basis for several weeks was a punishment she didn't deserve.

If disrupting her professional life wasn't enough, he'd turn her personal life into a shambles, too. Pinehaven might be a suburb of Denver, but the people in this community were a close-knit group. Secrets were impossible to keep. All he had to do was ask the right question, and well-meaning people would share her meticulously vague story.

The same story to which only he could piece together all the bitter details.

Thank goodness his name had never crossed her lips. No one would associate him with the fellow who'd dumped her, not even Kate, her best friend and the OB nurse who'd coached her through her labor.

Tears of frustration blurred her vision and she rapidly blinked them away, hating the inevitability of Adrian turning her world into chaos after she'd finally, and with extreme effort, whipped it in order.

Instantly, her lungs seemed to deflate and she ran through the full gamut of emotions before finally settling on panic.

"Are we going to play or stand here all day?" Molly Blake, a third member of their Rusty Clubs foursome, whined as she swiped her forehead. "You guys might prefer to swelter under the sun, but I'd rather hang out in the air-conditioned clubhouse."

Sabrina's flight-or-fight response kicked into high gear. The only thought running through her mind was to escape before Adrian saw her. Contrary to what Kate might believe about familiar faces, Sabrina needed to postpone their imminent reunion so she could mentally prepare herself.

Numb, Sabrina stepped up to her ball and swung blindly. As soon as her driver made contact, she knew without even looking that she'd sliced the ball.

Time slowed as she watched it head in Adrian's direction like a computer-guided missile searching for its target. Oh, surely fate wouldn't be that cruel!

"Fore," she yelled just before the projectile struck her nemesis on the side of his head.

He dropped like a rock and lay motionless on the manicured grass.

Horrified, Sabrina's club slipped from her hand as her heart pounded. Dear God, she'd killed him!

She'd killed the father of her son.

"What the—?" Adrian squinted up at the blue sky, seeing stars when none had been a few moments ago. His head throbbed in time to his heartbeat and something warm trickled down his ear and neck.

"Just lie still for a few minutes, son." A worried face hovered over his, blocking the sun from his eyes. "Give yourself a chance to recover."

The world spun at all sorts of crazy angles, so he gratefully complied. "What happened?"

"Golf ball." Mosby pressed a semi-clean golf towel to a spot above Adrian's left ear. "How's the head?"

He took stock. "Sore."

"Any dizziness, nausea?"

"Some," he admitted, hoping the power of positive thinking would slow down the spinning and churning of his internal amusement park ride from Tilt-A-Whirl to a sedate carousel.

Mosby peered into his eyes. "Pupils are equal and reactive, so you can rest easy on that account."

"I'm OK. Just give me…a minute."

"Take all the time you need," Mosby advised, placing a hand on his shoulder. "An ambulance is on its way."

"Not necessary," he croaked, hating to appear weak, especially on his first official day in town. "I'm supposed to *work* in ER, not check in as a patient."

"It's very necessary," Mosby assured him. "We take care of our own, and as of eight o'clock this morning, you're one of us."

Adrian folded one arm over his eyes, too befuddled to argue and quite content to lie on the grass until his wits returned. He heard voices and tried to focus on them through the pounding in his head, but none seemed to make any sense until he heard one so familiar it haunted him in his dreams.

"How is he? Is he OK? He's breathing, isn't he?"

Sabrina.

He'd known he'd see her again—the hospital wasn't large enough to avoid it—but he wondered if her breathless concern would fade as soon as she realized that *he* was the one lying on the ground with a goose egg on the side of his head.

He lowered his arm and opened his eyes to see her face above his. Through his slightly blurry vision, he recognized her retroussé nose, high cheekbones, kissable mouth and eyes as black as midnight. "Yeah, I'm breathing and talking," he answered for himself. "In a few minutes I'll be walking, too."

"That was one helluva slice," Mosby commented. "I wonder who hit it?"

Even with his head feeling as if his brains had been run through a blender, Adrian was alert enough to watch color wash over Sabrina's face. "I did," she admitted.

Of all the people in this tournament, Sabrina had knocked him senseless? He wanted to laugh at the irony but his skull hurt too much. The best he could do was smile, and that turned out to be more grimace than grin.

As he covered his eyes with his arm once again to wait for the paramedics, one thought ran through his mind as clearly as a church bell on a calm summer day.

Paybacks were hell.

After seeing Adrian awake and alert, Sabrina felt marginally better, until she saw his ashen face and the blood trickling past his ear and down his corded neck to stain his shirt collar. In spite of everything that had gone wrong between them, in spite of past hurts, she'd never dreamed of physically harming him. Not that he didn't deserve it, of course…

"I'm so sorry," she murmured. "It was an accident. Honest."

"Of course it was," Mosby declared. "No one deliberately slices the ball."

"That's right," she concurred, hoping Adrian wouldn't accuse her of evil intent, at least not in front of this crowd of witnesses. "If it's any consolation, I've never hit anyone before."

"Or you haven't been told," Adrian remarked dryly. "That would have been quite a drive if it had gone straight."

"Probably," she agreed.

An ambulance siren wailed in the distance and he visibly winced, then sighed. "For me, I suppose."

"Afraid so," Mosby said.

"What if I don't want it?"

Sabrina ignored his petulant tone. He'd hated receiving attention and today's incident would forever mark him in the hospital staff's collective minds. As a man who preferred to remain out of the limelight, he'd never forgive her for the notoriety.

Then again, he had worse things to hold against her than being the subject of well-meant gossip. Never telling him about their son topped this incident by a country mile. Oh, he'd no doubt be furious, but she'd endured too much during and after her pregnancy with no one but herself to rely upon to be afraid of his reaction. She'd had her reasons and as far as she was concerned they had been the right ones, but her bravado didn't stop her from checking his hand for a wedding ring.

No ring. Not even a pale tan line marked his third finger. How curious, especially after what she'd seen…

"Sorry, young man, but when you go back to Mercy,

you'll go none the worse for wear," Mosby replied. "If everything checks out, you can report for work in the morning."

Either Adrian recognized the finality in Dr Mosby's voice or he'd realized that an ambulance ride wasn't such a bad idea because he didn't argue.

"Sabrina?" Mosby turned his attention to her. "Follow Adrian to the hospital and make sure he's given VIP treatment. Nothing's too good for our newest physician."

Oh, sweet baby Jane. "Me?" she protested, before she realized that refusing would only foster unwanted speculation.

Mosby studied her. "Why not you?"

Why not her, indeed? She could give him a specific reason—Adrian had told her that he didn't want her in his life—but mentioning their volatile past wasn't appropriate under the circumstances. Fortunately, the perfect excuse popped into her head.

"I'm not sure he'd appreciate me doing the honors when I'm the one responsible for his condition." She glanced helplessly at Adrian, hoping, *expecting* him to refuse her company.

"Nonsense," Mosby declared. "Dr McReynolds is a professional as well as a golfer. Accidents happen. He won't hold this against you."

She wasn't as certain, but she bit back a reply because anything she could have said would have raised questions she didn't want to answer.

"I suspect you won't play worth a hoot after this anyway, so your team will probably thank me." The chief of staff added with a twinkle in his eye, "It may also be safer for the masses if you aren't swinging a club."

Great. She'd never live this incident down, either. For a

woman who'd won regional tournaments in both high school and college, she'd rather be known for a brilliant achievement instead of a hapless slice that had knocked out a fellow golfer and sent him to hospital.

Mosby laid a hand on Adrian's shoulder. "Never fear. We won't abandon you. Will we, Sabrina?" he asked with a pointed glance in her direction.

She glanced at Adrian, wondering why he consented to Mosby's plans. While he truly wasn't in a position to refuse any more than she could, she wondered if he was simply too confused to realize what was happening. Accident or not, she felt guilty for causing his injury.

"I'll get my things," she said reluctantly, hoping she wouldn't be forced to contact his sisters with bad news. Conditions such as skull fractures, subdural hematomas and nerve damage were serious possibilities. Although it was a shame he hadn't shown initial signs of amnesia. It would solve a lot of my problems, she thought wryly.

"Good. I'll check in with you as soon as we've finished our round. We'll have test results by then."

"Paramedics are here," someone said, and the small crowd parted.

Sabrina stood off to one side, watching the emergency personnel apply a cervical collar and prepare Adrian for transport. The grim set to his mouth and his one-word replies suggested his head hurt worse than he cared to admit. Surprisingly enough, his vulnerability tugged at her heartstrings.

You'd feel the same for any injured person, she told herself, refusing to believe she held any tender feelings for him at all. After the way he'd treated her, thrown her love away like yesterday's garbage, how pitiful would she be if she did? In another lifetime, she would have been more than happy to escort him to the hospital and act as his hospital liaison, but too much had happened since those blissful days. Far better for her peace of mind if she treated him warily or, at best, as a familiar stranger until she discovered why he'd taken this temporary position at Pinehaven Health Center.

An uneasy thought came to her. Did he know about Jeremy?

No, she decided. She hadn't mentioned her pregnancy to anyone before she'd left Denver. Since then she hadn't run into any of her old friends and her new ones had never heard Adrian McReynolds' name until today. For the moment, her secret was safe, although she'd have to deal with it sooner than she'd anticipated.

She caught a ride back to the parking lot in a tournament official's golf cart, loaded her clubs, then followed the ambulance to the hospital.

By the time the paramedics had unloaded Adrian and installed him in a trauma room, he sported an IV in his hand, a pulse oximeter on his finger, and a long-suffering expression on his handsome face.

The old Sabrina would have teased out a smile because she hated to see him ill at ease, but the new Sabrina refused to let herself feel anything but objective concern. As far as she and the rest of the world were concerned, he was just another patient, even if he could legally use the initials "MD" behind his name.

"Would you like me to call anyone for you?" she asked politely after the ER doctor had examined him and they were waiting for the lab and radiology staff to arrive. "Your wife? Girlfriend? Or a family member?"

"No." His blue-gray gaze met hers. "Don't call a single soul."

"I'm sure someone would want to know what's happened."

"There isn't anything to tell to anyone," he said shortly. "This is a minor injury and not worth the trouble it would cause."

So much for finding out if he'd ever replaced her… "Suit yourself, but if you should change your mind, let me know."

"I won't."

"As stubborn as ever, I see," she remarked, already breaking her first rule to treat him as a stranger she'd met a few minutes earlier.

"I just want to play the hospital's game so I can go back to my apartment where I can recuperate on my own."

Knowing Mosby as she did, Adrian wouldn't be heading back to his apartment as quickly as he thought, but someone else could break the news. On the other hand, Adrian hated not being in control, so if she planted the idea, maybe he'd resign himself to his fate before he got official word from The Man himself. Why she wanted to prepare him for the eventuality, she didn't know, other than dealing with his surliness ranked at the bottom of her list of things she wanted to do.

There was a silver lining, though. She hadn't wanted to be Adrian's guardian angel in the first place, so if he gave her the slightest bit of trouble, she'd shovel it right back, in spades.

In fact, now that she thought about the situation, he wouldn't have to complain too much for her to do so.

"Dr Mosby may decide to keep you overnight," she mentioned offhandedly, testing his reaction.

He frowned. "Why? You don't admit every person in the hospital for a bump on the head."

"No, but you aren't just any person." She ticked off the reasons on the fingers of her left hand. "One, you're a doctor, which means you get special consideration. Two, Mosby is determined to treat you like spun gold, not only because he wants to impress you but because he wants you to speak fondly of us when you go back home."

"Ah. For recruitment purposes, I presume."

"Probably," she agreed. "This position has been vacant for some time so I'm sure he intends to take advantage of whatever opportunities he can to show us in a good light. The question for the moment though is, who would monitor you through the night if Dr Mosby discharges you? Unless, of course, you aren't staying alone." She raised an eyebrow.

"Fishing, Sabrina?"

"Not at all," she said, airily indifferent, although deep down she wanted to know if he had allowed a significant other into his life. Not that she cared one way or another, of course. She was only being curious.

"Your living arrangements don't concern me. However, they could factor into Mosby's decision, so I thought you might appreciate the advance warning. If not, pretend I didn't say a word."

He fell silent as if mulling over his situation. "I don't suppose the crickets count as companions?"

"Not unless they can take your vital signs and call 911 if necessary."

"I was afraid you'd say that." He sighed. "Then, yes, I'm all by myself."

"I'm surprised." She hadn't realized she'd spoken aloud until he answered.

"Why would you think that?"

She evaded the question. "I assumed you would have brought Clay with you." After Clay's discharge from hospital, Adrian had moved him into his own home to oversee and assist in his rehabilitation.

"He's living by himself these days."

Relief at the news made her forget to treat Adrian with cool disdain. "Oh, Adrian, I'm so glad. Then he's all right? I've wondered and worried about him…" Realizing she'd said too much, she cut herself off. When Adrian had severed their ties, he'd also severed her relationship to his family members and she missed them almost as much as she'd missed Adrian. Oh, she could have kept in touch with Clay, but it would have been an awkward situation for both of them, so she hadn't.

"He hasn't completely recovered," he admitted. "It took awhile before he could start therapy and then his progress came slowly, but he's graduated from a walker to a cane, which was quite a cause for celebration."

"I can imagine." And she could. She pictured Adrian, Clay, Marcy and Susan barbecuing in Adrian's back yard. Adrian liked to wear his "Kiss the Cook" apron and chef's hat and monitor the status of his burgers with the same intensity as an anesthesiologist monitoring a surgical patient. Clay had often stolen the green olives out from under Marcy's watchful eye while Susan had scolded him for spoiling his dinner. Adrian's portable CD player had usually provided the ambience while Sabrina had acted as the official and unbiased taste tester of Marcy's culinary concoctions.

She wondered who did the honors now, then jerked herself off that fruitless and painful path. The McReynolds family wasn't part of her life and never would be. For her own peace of mind, she had to remember that.

"In any case…" She steered the conversation back to the original topic. "If you're living alone, I'd plan to spend the night in a luxurious private suite on our spacious second floor."

"If it's a matter of having a babysitter, you could do the honors," he said in a clearly hopeful tone.

Coming from anyone else, she would have laughed and countered with a saucy answer, but the offer came from Adrian, which made his suggestion no laughing matter. If he didn't look so pathetic, she'd tell him exactly what she thought of his idea, using words capable of blistering the walls' semi-gloss enamel paint.

But he *did* look rather forlorn and pitiful and she let her opportunity slide. There would be plenty of others when she could fully vent her anger and not feel lower than pond scum for verbally attacking a concussed man. A confrontation was inevitable.

"Sorry, but I don't do private nursing. And even if I did, I have laundry waiting at home."

"You wouldn't have to stay," he coaxed. "Just long enough so Mosby thinks I'm not alone."

She eyed him carefully and forced herself not to succumb to his pleading, puppy-dog-in-the-window expression. "I won't put myself in the position where you can tell the chief of staff I ran out on you halfway through the night."

"I wouldn't."

He must think her to be a complete fool if she'd trust him the minute she'd laid eyes on him, and she was not a fool. "Sorry, but that's the sort of favor I'd only do for a friend."

"We were friends once."

"We were," she conceded, "but not any more. Considering our past, aren't you afraid I'll slip arsenic into your coffee or smother you in your sleep?"

"I'll take the chance, Bree," he said dryly, "because we both know I won't get any rest here. And…" He paused. "I'd hoped we could…talk."

So Adrian wanted to talk, did he? She'd suffered through too many hurts to think that a simple heart-to-heart at this late date would clear the air and heal old wounds. He'd betrayed her trust and she couldn't imagine any way he would possibly earn it again.

"You aren't in any condition to carry on a conversation," she said calmly, grateful for her ready-made excuse because the thought of discussing anything more serious than a weather forecast released a flock of butterflies in her stomach. The day for an in-depth conversation would come, but only when she was ready.

"Maybe not at this moment, but—"

"I'm not interested in rehashing ancient history," she warned. "Not now. Not ever."

"A year isn't ancient history."

"It is to me." That year was a lifetime ago—Jeremy's lifetime. Events before then weren't worth the time or energy to dwell upon.

"Sabrina—" he began.

The curtain swooshed and a young man carrying a phlebotomy tray walked in. "Oh, my," she said in a too-bright tone that hinted at her eagerness for the interruption, "Lab's here. It's Dracula time."

Seizing the opportunity to gain much-needed breathing space, she walked out of the trauma room while the technician drew Adrian's blood samples. Unfortunately, physical distance didn't settle her thoughts, as she'd hoped.

Wishing she hadn't sliced the ball like a novice and landed in her present position, Sabrina idled away the hours while he was poked, prodded, and CT-scanned. From time to time, like any good nurse, she exchanged his magazines from the waiting room's well-thumbed collection, brought ice chips when he complained about being thirsty, and covered him with a warm blanket when she found him huddled under the sheet, half-asleep. Although she'd like to leave him to his own devices, Dr Mosby would ask Adrian about the care and personal attention he'd received, so she simply gritted her teeth and treated her nemesis as if he truly were a VIP.

Although, she decided with wicked glee, in his case the "I" stood for "irritating" rather than "important."

Through it all, and somewhat to her surprise because Adrian didn't accept defeat easily, he dropped the subject and stared impatiently at the clock. His gloomy mood didn't improve until Dr Beth Iverson returned with his results.

"Do you want me to stay or leave you two alone?" Sabrina asked before the doctor could share anything that Adrian might consider a violation of his privacy.

"You may as well hear the verdict for yourself," he grudgingly offered. "Go ahead, Doctor. Tell me what I already know—I'm fine. No cracks, no nerve damage, nothing!"

"At the risk of making your head swell more than it has," Beth said cheerfully, "you're right. Lab work looks great and no skull fractures or hematomas appeared on the scan. Your cut bled a lot and you can get by without stitches, although I'd like to put in a few to prevent the edges from separating too easily."

Adrian looked quite smug as he met Sabrina's gaze. "What did I tell you? I have a hard head."

In more ways than one, Sabrina silently agreed.

Beth continued. "You'll probably have a headache and some nausea for awhile—concussions will do that, you know, and as yours is mild, those symptoms shouldn't last long. Continue with the ice packs and acetaminophen for the pain."

"Will do. Now, if someone will give me my clothes, I'm going to my home away from home."

Beth shook her head, her eyes apologetic. "Sorry. John wants to keep you overnight. As a precaution."

"You don't need someone as healthy as I am taking up bed space," he coaxed in the charming manner that allowed him to get his own way more often than not.

Beth smiled. "I have my orders. There's a bed upstairs with your name on it."

His smile turned into a frown. "This is so unnecessary," he groused.

"Take it up with the boss," the doctor advised. "I'm just the hired help. After I stitch up your head, Sabrina will see you're settled in your room. If you need anything, call me. I'm on duty until seven."

She quickly closed the gash with neat sutures. After pronouncing her work finished, she breezed out of the room and left Sabrina to deal with an unhappy Adrian.

"Wheelchair or gurney for the next leg of your trip?" she asked, relieved to know her golf ball hadn't done lasting damage. She wouldn't admit it either, but she was privately glad he'd be under close observation for awhile. Problems weren't always detected immediately and could develop over time. It would be far better for him, and for her peace of mind, to spend his first night in Pinehaven under a nurse's watchful eye.

"I'll walk."

She shook her head. "Not on my watch, buster. Physician or not, you're a patient, which means I'm in charge for the moment. Nor will I let it be said that I don't abide by the rules. So what'll it be? A wheelchair or a gurney?"

He glared. "Wheelchair."

"Then sit tight and I'll be right back."

Transferring him to the medical floor went smoothly and silently, which came as a relief. She wasn't in the mood for small talk and clearly he wasn't either. However, once she'd braked his wheelchair and pointed to the hospital gown on the edge of the bed, he shook his head and crossed his arms.

"I may have to stay here unnecessarily, but I'll do it in my own clothes," he stated regally.

"And how do you propose they get here?"

He raised an eyebrow. "Need you ask?"

She held up her hands to object, but he didn't give her the opportunity.

"You landed me in these spacious accommodations with your wicked slice," he reminded her. "In my books, that's a debt you have to pay."

"If every other patient can wear the stylish apparel we so thoughtfully provide, so can you. And if you're worried about your hiney showing, stay in bed."

"*Hiney?* My, my," he said dryly, "your professional vocabulary is amazing."

"That's what continuing education is for."

"Whatever you call my hiney, buns, or posterior, there's the matter of you being responsible for my VIP care. As a VIP, I want my own shorts and T-shirt, not a flimsy, see-through, doesn't-close-in-the-back hospital gown."

No question about it—the "I" definitely meant irritating.

"But you don't sleep in anything except your boxers," she blurted out.

"At home, I don't. Does this…" he waved his arms in an all-encompassing motion "…even remotely look like home?"

Sensing the futility in arguing—apparently he'd decided that if cajolery wouldn't get what he wanted, arrogance and his rank would—she heaved a sigh. "OK, fine. I presume you also want a change of clothes for tomorrow and your toothbrush?"

"Yeah. Don't forget my electric razor either." He dug in his trouser pocket and tossed a keyring at her before he sank gingerly into the bed. "Thanks. I'd be grateful if you'd bring them within the hour."

She caught it in mid-air, irritated by his demand. She couldn't possibly meet his hour deadline even if she'd wanted to because she was due to pick up Jeremy from the hospital's day care. Chafing under his order, she chose not to warn him she'd be late. Better to ask forgiveness after the fact than to beg permission beforehand.

"I'd also like a pizza," he informed her.

"Our cafeteria has good food. The patients all agree."

He eyed her loftily. "If I can't sleep in a real bed, then I want to eat real food. Sausage, Canadian bacon and mushrooms."

She ground her teeth. "Pizza it is. Anything else for our most illustrious personage?"

With that detail apparently settled to his satisfaction and apparently not put off by her disrespect, he closed his eyes. "No, but if I think of something, I'll call you. You do still have a cellphone?"

"Yes, I do. Who doesn't these days?"

"I'd like the number, please."

She didn't want to give it to him, but she really didn't have a choice. A notepad wasn't in sight and she didn't have a pen, so she recited the seven digits from memory.

He listened intently before satisfaction showed on his face. "Same as before."

His comment caught her off-guard. "I'm surprised you remember."

"I remember a lot of things."

"I'm happy for you," she said tartly, but a new set of questions suddenly popped into her head. If he'd wanted her out of his life so badly, why had he remembered her number? Knowing that he'd never acted on the information at his fingertips only made the intervening months of silence more painful to think about.

The sudden pressure in her chest demanded she escape before he saw this new hurt he'd caused without even trying. Immediately, she pivoted on one foot and headed for the door.

"Sabrina?" he called.

Reluctantly, she paused. "Yeah?" Sounding hoarse, she hoped he'd attribute it to grumpiness.

"For what it's worth, it's good to see you again."

She'd spent the last year shoring up her defenses against his anger and rejection, but had built nothing to protect herself against unexpected kindness. Not trusting herself to speak over the sudden lump in her throat, she simply fled.

CHAPTER TWO

"YOUR father isn't playing fair," Sabrina railed aloud as she drove to Adrian's home-away-from-home while Jeremy fussed in his car seat. "After being such a jerk, he has no right to suddenly act like a decent human being."

Jeremy chewed on his little fist and grunted as he kicked his legs and squirmed.

"I don't know what he's up to, but I'm not falling for it," she mumbled as she parked in front of the apartment complex next to Adrian's recognizable black Toyota Avalon. Apparently John Mosby had served as Adrian's taxi service and given him a ride to the golf course. "I don't care if he had a change of heart. It's too late. Too late, I tell you.

"And frankly," she continued her rant, "I'm glad my ball hit him on the head. He deserves some pain and suffering for everything he's put me through!"

Buoyed by her thoughts, she lifted Jeremy out of his car seat, hoisted him on one hip, and headed up the sidewalk. "Come on, little man. Let's get this nasty old errand done so we can go home and play."

Carefully, she inserted the key and stepped inside.

The place reminded her of a hotel room, but Adrian had

only arrived that weekend. He hadn't had time to stamp his presence on the hospital's apartment. Certain she'd find personal articles in the bathroom, she headed there first.

His toiletries lay on the counter, but she hardly noticed because the familiar scent of his favorite brand of soap hung in the air.

"What do you want for your birthday?" she asked as she cuddled against him on her sofa. *"It's coming up, you know."*

"I have everything I need right here." Adrian nuzzled her neck.

She giggled as he focused on a particularly ticklish spot. "I'm serious. There has to be something you'd like or need."

"Soap. Bath soap, in particular."

Sabrina pulled away to study his face. "You're kidding, aren't you?"

He shook his head. "Nope. My sisters usually shop for me and they're always buying the girly, flowery-smelling stuff."

"Ask them to choose a different scent."

"And hurt their feelings when they're trying so hard to be helpful?" He sounded horrified. "No can do. But if someone should happen to give me a case or two and I rave about how good it smells, they'll get the hint."

"You're quite a mastermind, aren't you?" she teased.

"I raised a younger brother and two sisters," he said matter-of-factly. "It was the only way I could stay one step ahead of them."

And so Sabrina had bought a dozen bars of sandal-wood-scented soap which, surprisingly enough, he still used. After he'd dismissed her from his life, she would have expected him to toss out all reminders of her, including the soap, but perhaps he'd forgotten she'd gotten him hooked on it in the first place.

Idly, she grabbed his razor and his toothbrush and headed toward the bedroom. As Jeremy reached for the things in her hand and grunted his give-me noise, she allowed him to clutch the fluorescent blue toothbrush in his fierce, baby grip.

Adrian's suitcase lay open on the queen-sized bed, still containing the clothing he hadn't taken time to unpack. As she rummaged through the contents one-handed in search of underwear, socks, and the athletic apparel he'd requested, it was as if his fragrance had followed her, evoking more bitter-sweet memories—memories of soaping his back in the tub because he'd won their round of golf, celebrating her pay raise with champagne and strawberries, watching TV in his bed while feeding each other popcorn.

"You can't go back," she scolded herself. "You've moved forward, remember?"

Pushing those memories aside along with the pile of clothes she planned to deliver, she grabbed a pair of dress slacks and a short-sleeved pale green shirt from the closet, as well as his highly polished dress shoes.

He'd always polished them while he watched the evening news, she recalled, just as his father had taught him and just as he'd taught his brother Clay.

The question was, who would teach *his* son?

She glanced down at the bouncing twenty-pound joy of her life. "Sorry, kid, but spit-shining shoes wasn't part of my education. It'll be sneakers for us."

He waved the toothbrush and chortled, scraping her face with the brush end before accidentally running it through his hair like a comb.

"Be careful with that, young man," she said, smoothing down the light brown wisps on his scalp as he stuck the smooth end into his mouth.

She placed him on the floor with his temporary toy and her set of keys while she went in search of a bag to hold Adrian's clothes. Coming up empty, she returned to the bedroom, dumped the rest of his clothes on the bed and refilled the suitcase with the things she'd selected. But when she took Adrian's toothbrush away from Jeremy, he screamed. She closed her ears to his vocal protests until she noticed several distinct tooth marks on the handle.

Great. As observant as Adrian was, he'd see the ridges and wonder how they'd gotten there. Unable to dream up a plausible explanation—it was too bad he didn't own a dog she could blame for the marks—she simply had to purchase a new one, even if it meant fighting the crowds at a store with a baby who didn't handle shopping trips very well.

By the time she had loaded Adrian's suitcase and her son into the car, Jeremy was yelling for his dinner. Adrian's specified hour was nearly over, but he'd have to wait a bit longer, she decided grimly. Jeremy's needs were more important than Adrian's comforts.

Two hours later, after dinner and an unscheduled bath to wash the strained peas out of Jeremy's hair and after she'd ordered Adrian's pizza and ran into a drug store to select a bright purple toothbrush from the hundreds on display, she pulled into the hospital parking lot. With any luck, Adrian had either slept the entire time or had gotten so engrossed in television that he hadn't noticed she was late. If he had, though, too bad. Impressing him with her efficiency and dancing to his tune weren't on her list of things to do.

Balancing a well-fed and now-happy Jeremy on her hip, she went inside.

* * *

Sabrina was late. By nearly two hours. Adrian had dozed off and on during the three hours she'd been gone, but with all the staff fluttering around him, checking his vitals, quizzing him on what day it was, did he know his birth date, how his headache and nausea was, he hadn't been able to rest for more than fifteen minutes at a time.

He grumbled aloud at how he could look forward to this well-meant but unwanted solicitous care for the remainder of the night as he pressed an ice pack to his head. The situation was enough to make a congenial man grumpy, and for the past several months he hadn't been known for his congeniality.

Oh, he may as well be honest. His good humor had disappeared about the time he'd driven Sabrina away a year ago. Most people had attributed his curtness to his concern over Clay, but as time had marched on and Clay's condition had improved, Adrian's mood had not. In fact, it had worsened.

His siblings had compared their amateur psychology notes and had decided he needed a woman in his life to smooth his rough edges. However, after one date, he'd realized he'd spent the entire evening quietly comparing her to Sabrina. He'd suspected the poor girl had known it, too. Because no other female had interested him, his dating days had ended as abruptly as they'd begun.

Their next theory was that subconsciously he was expressing his latent anger and frustration over his broken relationship with Sabrina. That he was still mourning his loss and taking out his emotional distress on his hapless colleagues and staff members. Their answer? To get him back together with Sabrina.

Naturally, he disagreed. He was simply working too hard and doing too much. As for the ER staff, the skills of the people being hired simply weren't up to the hospital's formerly high standards.

As for his relationship with Sabrina, he believed he'd taken the high moral ground by ending it when he had. Clay needed his attention and he didn't feel it was fair to expect Sabrina to put her life on hold or be relegated to the fringes of whatever life he was free to give her. For all he knew, Clay would never leave his wheelchair and would require years of intensive therapy and personal attention from experts as well as his family.

Fortunately, his fears never panned out. While he was glad Clay's health problems hadn't turned into the worst-case scenario, as his doctors had warned, Adrian couldn't undo the past. He simply had to console himself with the knowledge that he'd made the best decision based on the information he had at the time and live with the consequences.

For him, those consequences turned him from being 'that nice Dr McReynolds' to a physician who caught nurses drawing straws in the employee lounge to see who would work with him. Even Clay's slow but steady recovery didn't improved his mood. Only one thing would—apologizing to Sabrina—but pride wouldn't allow him to take that step. What was done was done. End of story.

But it wasn't the end because his boss intervened.

"We've cut you enough slack, Adrian," Carter had told him bluntly on Friday afternoon. "I've talked to you about your attitude and you've attended several human resource seminars on interpersonal relationships, but nothing seems to be working. I don't know why you can't pull yourself together, but I'm giving you your last chance."

"Which is?"

"Our sister hospital in Pinehaven needs a temporary

ER physician and we've been asked to provide one. I'm sending you."

"Pinehaven?" The name of the town caught him by surprise and Adrian shook his head. "I can't go there."

Carter crossed his arms. His jaw was squared as he narrowed his eyes to study him. "Why not?"

"Because..." He drew a bracing breath. "Because my ex-girlfriend works there. Our parting didn't...go well." What an understatement! He'd been rude and obnoxious to make his point and he wouldn't be surprised if she threw a bedpan at him.

At first Carter didn't reply. Then he straightened in his chair and fixed his gaze on Adrian's. "Then this will be a good time for you to work out your differences, won't it?"

He initially balked at the Pinehaven assignment, but then he realized it was exactly what he needed. First, he'd swallow his pride and apologize for his former rudeness and salvage enough of their relationship so they could work in the same facility without coming to blows. Maybe, if all went well and the fates were kind, they would at least become the friends they had once been instead of remaining the bitter enemies they were now.

Secondly, as soon as he saw proof that her life was every bit as wonderful as she deserved it to be, he could finally rest knowing that he'd made the right decision. His worries and wondering would be over and he could return to Mercy Memorial emotionally whole, no longer venting his frustration on the people around him.

So far, his plan was stuck at square one. For supposedly being his liaison, she avoided him as much as possible and when she couldn't, she talked to him as eagerly as she'd participate in a rattlesnake round-up! As much as he hated having this bump on his head, his injury had paved the way for Sabrina to be his captive audience this evening. Courtesy of a talkative nurse, he'd learned Sabrina was scheduled to cover the ED this next month, which made negotiating a truce even more critical for both their sakes. Sabrina's, because she hated being a subject on the hospital grapevine and his, because if he went back to Mercy Memorial in disgrace, he'd be hunting for a new job.

Impatient and bored, he glanced at the clock once again as he tossed the ice pack onto the bedside table. Just when he began to worry about her being delayed by something horrible like a car accident, she rushed in.

"Sorry I'm late," she said, hoisting his suitcase onto a chair. "The last few hours have been absolutely crazy."

He eyed her carefully, relieved to see her. Her shoulder-length dark brown hair was tousled, as if someone had run his hands through those soft tresses and she hadn't taken time to find a comb. She still wore the same yellow Bermuda shorts and polo shirt he'd seen earlier. And her face looked strained, as if she'd been running at full speed all day. Or, at least, since he'd seen her last.

For an instant, he felt guilty for asking her to fetch his personal things, but if he wanted to establish their personal ceasefire, he had to take advantage of whatever opportunities came his way.

Heaven help him, but after regaining his wits and seeing the wariness in her eyes, as if she expected him to act as boorishly as he had before, he *wanted* to redeem himself.

"I wish I could say the same," he remarked. "The only crazy thing I can claim is being stuck in this hospital bed for no good reason."

"How's the head?"

He didn't want to discuss his aches and pains. "Getting better as we speak," he prevaricated. "Did you have any trouble finding my stuff?"

"No, but I had a slight problem with your toothbrush and had to buy another. It's the same brand as the one you had, just a different color."

He raised an eyebrow, unable to imagine anyone having a problem with a toothbrush. It wasn't a normally break-able item. "What happened?"

She avoided his gaze. "Long, boring story. Not worth mentioning."

"Dropped it in the toilet bowl, then had second thoughts?"

"If I had, trust me when I say I wouldn't have bothered to replace it," she said tartly.

He grinned. Every now and then he caught a glimpse of her simmering temper, which meant she was probably keeping her full fury in check because of the bump she'd given him. There weren't any thrills in kicking a man when he was already down, so he was more than content to play the injured soul until she'd vented a portion of her pent-up anger.

"So what happened?"

"What's with the third degree?" she asked, clearly ex-asperated. "It wasn't a priceless Ming vase, Adrian. It was a cheap toothbrush that you would have replaced in a few months anyway. You should be grateful I went out of my way to buy you a new one. I didn't have to, you know."

"I'm grateful. Really. It's just that I never knew you to be accident-prone."

Her face colored. "Yeah, well, life happens. Today just hasn't been my day. In more ways than one," she finished darkly.

He glanced around. "So where's my food?"

"I didn't order it in time to pick up before I came. They should deliver it before long."

"Good. I'm starved."

A baby giggled in the background, sounding as if it was right outside his room. "I didn't realize you admitted babies to this wing," he mentioned.

"Oh, we don't," she said lightly. "Peds is to the left of the elevators. You know how sound carries."

The baby cackled again. "This place has terrible acoustics if people can hear the kids throughout the entire floor," he said.

"He did seem close by," she admitted. "One of the nurses is probably walking around, trying to entertain a fussy one."

Her story didn't quite ring true. A nurse might be strolling a colicky baby around the hallways, but she wouldn't expose an already sick infant to the germs on an adult ward. She would have remained on the pediatrics wing. Neither did it explain Sabrina's hurried glances toward the doorway, but at this moment, he had more important issues to tackle.

The infant's laugh suddenly became more of a shrill, happy scream. Adrian winced as the pitch caused his head to throb. "If that child is fussy, I'd hate to hear him when he's happy. In fact, he doesn't sound like a sick kid at all. Do they allow visitors to bring babies on to the floor?"

"Sometimes. Under extenuating circumstances." She rushed to close the door. "There. The noise shouldn't bother you now."

"I didn't say it bothered me," he protested.

"Whether it does or not, you need peace and quiet," she

insisted. "And you really need to reconsider your decision to work tomorrow."

"I won't."

She muttered something about mule-headed doctors, then sighed. "I didn't think you would, even though we both know it's for your own good."

"I'm fine now and I'll be even better in the morning." He changed the subject, tired of having his health the sole topic of conversation. "I hear you're scheduled to work Emergency for the next month."

"Unfortunately, I am." She sounded resigned.

"Unfortunately?" He studied her closely. "Don't you like covering that department or are you afraid to work with me?"

"Afraid?" She sputtered, and bristled like a porcupine, which suggested he'd nailed the reason for her concern accurately. "I may not *want* to work with you, but I'm not afraid to. I'm a good nurse. A *careful*, meticulous, nurse. Just ask anyone. If you're not convinced, feel free to ask the director of nursing to reassign me while you're here," she finished caustically. "It wouldn't be the first time you pushed me out of your life."

He started to shake his head, then stopped as his skull protested. "Ask to reassign you? Not a chance."

"Oh, I get it. You're just planning to question my nursing skills and nitpick everything I do to death so that *I'll* ask for a transfer."

"I won't."

She eyed him dubiously and he continued, "Working together will be good for us."

Her jaw dropped. "You clearly need another CT scan. Your brain is obviously bruised."

Adrian laughed at her response. "I'm serious."

"So am I."

The apparently happy baby now yelled its rage so loudly Adrian heard him through the closed door.

"I have to go," she said instantly.

She couldn't leave yet! He hated the idea of spending the rest of the evening with only the television, his thoughts, and the eager-beaver nurses for company. More importantly, they hadn't had time to talk about his idea of starting over with a clean slate.

"What's the rush?" he asked. "It's still early. You can share my pizza."

"It's later than you think," she mumbled before she lifted her chin in defiance, "and I'm not hungry. Besides, I have things to do and…and someone's waiting for me."

The news caught him by surprise, although it shouldn't have. Bree, as he'd called her, always had a lot of girlfriends coming and going and he said so.

She bit her lip. "It's not a friend. He's my…guy."

He'd been celibate since their break-up and the idea of Sabrina having a relationship burned like a hot poker in his gut. After giving her the freedom to date someone else, his response was completely illogical. "Someone special?"

"Someone I love very much."

His spirits deflated like a punctured inner tube. It was depressing to think she'd moved on with her life so easily when he'd struggled. For now, he simply summoned a smile to hide his resentment and disappointment. "Be sure to introduce us."

"Yeah. Probably. Some day. I have to go."

"See you tomorrow."

"Right. Tomorrow."

Adrian watched her scurry from the room like a mouse

escaping a cat before it could pounce. Sabrina had never been secretive before and if she'd been a typical woman scorned, she would have rubbed his face in the fact that she had a new man in her life. Yet she hadn't. She hadn't bragged or said anything about him—hadn't even mentioned his name—which seemed odd. In his experience, the women he knew never stopped talking about their latest love interest, whereas Sabrina had practically run away before she could.

Now that he thought about it, shouldn't she also have acted *grateful* toward him? After all, if they'd stayed together, she wouldn't have had the opportunity to meet this new man of her dreams.

Curiouser and curiouser.

Whether she had a boyfriend or not, he'd come to Pinehaven to do his job and salvage his career. For the sake of everything he held dear—his profession and his family—he had to make his peace with Sabrina, then leave the past where it belonged.

You should have told him about Jeremy, Sabrina's alter ego scolded in the dark of the night, long after she'd finally tucked her son into bed. *You had the perfect opportunity.*

No, I didn't, she argued back. The perfect opportunity had been when she'd first learned she was pregnant, but at the time he'd still refused to talk to her.

In the days immediately after Clay's accident, she'd done everything she could to help Adrian and his family during their crisis. She'd sat by Clay's bedside so he wouldn't be alone, even though he'd been too groggy from pain meds to know she was there. She'd fixed meals for Adrian because he'd focused completely upon Clay to the exclusion of everything else. She'd run errands and washed a few loads of Adrian's laundry so he could spend more time with Clay. She'd understood his need as Clay's elder brother and head of the McReynolds family to be at the hospital every chance he could.

She'd also tried to be the emotional rock they'd needed, encouraging them to think positive and not give up hope when the experts had admitted there was a chance that Clay might be a paraplegic.

Little did she know that this news became a turning point for her. Two days later, Adrian told her to stay away; he was ending their relationship because Clay required all his attention and energy. He didn't have room in his life for her, he claimed.

She argued her case that she could help, that she knew and understood how Clay was his priority, but he remained adamant. She begged and pleaded and told him how much he meant to her, but none of her entreaties made an impression.

He refused to reconsider. It was for the best, he told her.

From then on he didn't answer her phone calls, return her messages or speak to her in the hall. It was as if she had become a complete stranger.

Deciding she was only setting herself up for more pain, she changed her schedule so their paths couldn't accidentally cross, only visited Clay on a rare occasion when she knew Adrian wouldn't be there, and erased Adrian's number from her cellphone directory. Meanwhile, she prayed he'd come to his senses and kept her distance in every way possible.

Until the little test strip turned blue.

She waited outside the hospital after his shift had ended,

hoping to catch him on his way to his car, but before she could rise off the park bench, a tall, beautiful redhead burst through the ER entrance doors and rushed after him. He turned, they talked, then he grabbed her close, swung her around with such exuberance that Sabrina could hear their laughter across the lawn.

His apparent no-time-for-romance philosophy only seemed to apply to her. Her spirits crushed, she slipped away before he could see her.

Pride stopped her from trying to contact him again. If he didn't have time for her, he certainly wouldn't have time for a baby. During her weak moments she debated about sending him a letter, but she was afraid his over-developed sense of family would force him to propose out of a misguided sense of obligation. She wasn't about to marry a man under those circumstances. After her mother had died, her uncle and his wife had taken her in because they'd felt they had to, and she'd been reminded of their sacrifice too often. Asking her child to suffer through the same was out of the question.

Another possibility was that he'd offer financial support, but strings always came with money. She'd have to share her baby with him and she wasn't inclined to do that either.

He'd wanted to go separate ways, so she'd honor his wish. Having made her decision, she planned her future to become a single mom.

She arranged for a transfer to another hospital in the same consortium in order to maintain as many employee benefits as possible, announced her departure, hid her condition, which wasn't easy because she'd been so ill, then moved to Pinehaven to start over.

Now Adrian had arrived and no doubt would muck up her new life.

As she stared at the dark ceiling above her bed, she wished he'd never left Denver. The reasons for his arrival didn't matter, but what concerned her now was how he'd respond when he learned about his son.

Although Sabrina didn't expect Adrian to stay home the next day and give himself another twenty-four hours to recover, she hoped that good sense—or John Mosby—would rule the day. Unfortunately, Adrian reported for his shift bright and early at six a.m., looking quite strong for a man who'd spent the night in the hospital under observation.

"What are you doing here?" she asked as he caught her reviewing the contents and arrangement of the trauma-room cupboards.

"My shift starts at six, remember?"

"I know that," she said stiffly, "but Dr Mosby couldn't have discharged you already. He doesn't make rounds this early."

"John called after you left last night. He said, and I quote, 'If you don't have any problems, you can leave first thing in the morning'. So I did."

"I doubt if he meant for you to check out before dawn."

"As far as I'm concerned, five-thirty can be considered 'first thing'. Just so you know, my vital signs passed muster all night, so after finding my way around the doctors' lounge to shower and change clothes, here I am."

And, indeed, here he was, wearing a long white lab coat over the pair of tan trousers and pale green dress shirt she'd delivered to him last evening. Surprisingly enough, he appeared well rested, which was hardly fair when *he* should have been the one to suffer a sleepless night instead of her.

He frowned as he studied her with similar intensity.

"No offense, but you look more frayed around the edges than I do. A stiff wind would blow you away."

To think she'd spent extra time this morning with her make-up to hide those dark circles under her eyes! She'd obviously wasted those minutes, along with her beauty products. As for the stiff wind, she'd lost all of her pregnancy weight and then some, because, for her, coping with a job and a newborn all by herself had been a terrific diet plan. Hating that he'd noticed, she changed the subject.

"I thought you're supposed to attend orientation this morning," Sabrina said, irritated because she had to share her first morning in the ED with him. As a floating nurse, it usually took her a day or two to fall back into the rhythm of her new assignment and she didn't want Adrian finding fault before she'd re-established an efficient routine.

"I am, but the session doesn't start until eight. I thought I'd orient to my own department before I learned about the rest of the hospital. So what's up?" He glanced at the board where all the current patients were listed, along with their preliminary diagnoses.

"As you can see, we're empty at the moment. This might be a good time for Hilary, our nursing supervisor, to give you the grand tour."

He grinned. "I already asked. She sent me to you."

"Oh, really?" Sabrina wasn't convinced.

"Yes, really. If you like, you can confirm it with her. She's in her office, mumbling about the schedule and sounding quite ferocious about staff hours and budget cuts."

"What about Dr Beth?"

"She's breakfasting in the cafeteria, or so I've been told."

In the time it took Sabrina to talk her way out of this little task or find someone else for the dubious honor, she could be finished, so she gritted her teeth and vowed to give him the fastest orientation in the ED's history.

"As you can see, this is the trauma room, complete with everything you could possibly need." Her gaze landed on the crash cart within easy reach.

"Our second trauma room is next door." She led him into the corridor. "And it can accommodate three patients, too. We also have six cubicles for walk-in patients and two that are set up for pediatrics.

"We have electronic record keeping, so all your reports can be found by accessing the hospital information system. I'm sure someone from IT will assign your password and explain how to navigate the software."

By the time she'd answered his questions, referred those she couldn't to Hilary and showed him around the entire department, it was time for his orientation session.

As soon as the double doors closed behind him, Sabrina sank bonelessly into a chair behind the nurses' station and rubbed the tense muscles in her neck. She'd known that working with Adrian underfoot would be tough, but these past two hours had been more difficult than she'd imagined. Not because he'd been rude or sullen or looked through her as if she didn't exist, but because he'd done the complete opposite! She didn't want him to be congenial, polite, or study her thoughtfully from under his incredibly long eyelashes.

She grabbed the receiver out of its cradle and prepared to dial her director of nursing when she suddenly hesitated. Asking for a transfer was like admitting to fear, and she wasn't afraid. She was anxious, wary, and cautious, perhaps, but she had faith in her abilities even though she had to work with a man who upset her composure just by standing in the same room. She would simply grit her teeth and suffer his presence for the next 3 weeks. After all, it wasn't for ever.

"You chose a good day to start in the ED," Hilary remarked as Sabrina joined her at the nurses' station.

Sabrina glanced at her supervisor, grateful that the woman was a congenial sort whose interest in her patients and staff was sincere. "How so?"

"It's a slow morning, our new defibrillator is on its way down from our bio-med department, and we have a new, handsome doctor in our midst."

"Oh, yeah. Right." Immediately, Sabrina felt Hilary's gaze rest upon her.

"You don't think the new guy is handsome?"

"Beauty, or handsomeness, is only skin deep," Sabrina returned.

Hilary chuckled. "You're too young to be so cynical, girl."

Sabrina grinned. "I am, aren't I?" Then, because she didn't want to discuss Adrian McReynolds, she asked, "Is there anything new I should know about?"

"Nothing I can think of at the moment, but feel free to read through our department manual."

"I will," Sabrina told her. She would do whatever was in her power so Adrian wouldn't find fault with her performance.

As it usually happened, their slow morning turned into a busy day and Sabrina could only spare those manuals a longing glance. A patient with a kidney stone was followed by a man who needed stitches after trying to sharpen his lawnmower blade by himself. After that came a chest-pain case, a teenager with strep throat, and an elderly man who'd fallen out of his bed at the nursing home and broken his hip.

Just as Sabrina was about to slip into the lounge and eat her late lunch, or early dinner, depending on how one described a mid-afternoon meal, a well-dressed woman in her sixties rushed through the emergency room doors, dragging two young children with her.

"Please, you have to help us," the woman begged as soon as she saw Sabrina.

Sabrina pushed aside her plans to put up her feet and enjoy her carton of yogurt. "What's wrong?"

"These two grandsons of mine…" the woman shook the arms of the two boys who stared at their surroundings with wide eyes "…got into my purse and ate my digoxin pills."

Sabrina immediately ushered them toward the pediatric trauma room, then flagged down the passing ward clerk. "Send Dr Beth, stat," she murmured before following them into the room where she hoisted each of the boys, approximately three and four years old, onto a bed. "How many did they swallow?"

"I just came from the pharmacy to refill my monthly prescription. There are only five left. Between the two of them, twenty-five are missing."

"And you're certain the boys ate them."

The woman nodded, her eyes frantic with worry. "They were playing doctor. I don't know what possessed them to take the bottle from my purse. What's so awful is that I've always asked the pharmacy to use snap-on lips instead of the childproof caps for my pills. You see, I live alone and my arthritis makes those lids difficult to open." She sniffled. "This is all my fault. I should have moved my purse or put my pills in the cupboard where they couldn't reach."

"Kids can get into trouble in the blink of an eye," Sabrina said.

The woman nodded, then squared her shoulders as if drawing on her emotional reserves. "As soon as I saw how many they'd eaten, I brought them straight here. If anything happens to Corey and Casey, I'll never forgive myself." Her voice cracked and her lips trembled. "I'm Edith Gilroy, by the way, and I'm watching my grandsons because my son and daughter-in-law are attending a funeral in Oklahoma City."

"We'll do everything we can," Sabrina told the trio as she began taking vital signs, noting the absence of any abnormalities.

"They look so healthy. Maybe those pills won't hurt them?" Edith asked hopefully.

"They will, I'm afraid. An overdose of digoxin will produce cardiac toxicity which manifests itself in a number of ways, depending on the amount ingested. If we can get those pills out of their system before the drug is absorbed, they'll be fine."

Sabrina watched the two closely for the less serious symptoms of nausea, vomiting and a headache, hoping they could prevent the more severe ventricular tachycardia or fibrillation. So far, these two looked more scared than ill, although the time for symptoms to develop could be anywhere from thirty minutes to hours. Regardless, those pills had to be removed. By the time these two went home, they would never play doctor with their grandmother's medicine again.

"Should I have just gone to the drug store and given them syrup of ipecac?" Edith asked.

"No," Sabrina told her. "Vomiting can make any abnormal heart rhythms worse, which is why in cases of digoxin poisonings we often do a procedure called a lavage where we rinse out their stomach contents with fluids. Then we give activated charcoal to adsorb any of the drug that may have gotten into the bowel."

"Oh."

When Adrian walked in as she finished her treatment overview, her surprised heart skipped a beat.

"What do we have?" he asked in the calm, quiet voice she remembered so well and had tried so hard to forget.

Wondering if he'd skipped out on his orientation class, she shoved her question aside to answer his. "Corey and Casey ingested a number of their grandmother's digoxin pills about thirty minutes ago." She glanced at Edith for confirmation and received it. "So far, they aren't showing any cardiac symptoms."

"And you're sure they swallowed them."

"I only have five left in my bottle," Edith interjected.

He turned to the two youngsters. "What were you boys doing?" he asked, while Sabrina worked in the background to retrieve the necessary supplies from the cupboards and shamelessly eavesdropped on his conversation with his little patients.

"Playin' doctor," the eldest said, his gaze intent on the stethoscope hanging from Adrian's pocket. "Are you a real one?"

Adrian smiled. "I am. And what did you do when you were playing doctor?"

"Corey here…" he glanced at his brother "…was pretendin' to have his arm broke and his throat hurt. I was goin' to give him a shot." He pulled a toy syringe from his pocket. "But he started to cry. So I told him I'd give him pills like Mommy sometimes takes." Casey's lower lip turned into a pout. "I wanted to give him liquid in the alligator spoon like Mama uses, but Grandma doesn't have a spoon like that and her juice was all gone."

Edith gasped in the corner and Sabrina saw Adrian fight a smile at the boy's petulant tone.

"I'll bet the pills you found tasted nasty," he commiserated.

Corey shook his head. "Nope."

Sabrina exchanged a glance with Adrian. Digoxin tablets were tiny but, if chewed, were bitter. She couldn't imagine the boys gobbling them up and from the expression on Adrian's face he couldn't either.

"Then how did they taste?" he coaxed.

"Like apple sauce," Corey answered.

Once again, Edith moaned in the background, shook her head and covered her eyes.

"Apple sauce?" Adrian asked, clearly surprised.

Casey stared at him as if the man who towered over them should know that. "Mama puts pills in apple sauce, so that's what I did with the cups Grandma gave us for our snack."

"How many did you put in the cups?" Adrian pressed.

Corey held up two fingers. "Eleventeen."

The twinkle in Adrian's eye belied his serious expression. "That many," he said.

"I would have put more in, but Corey dropped the bottle and the pills rolled out. We tried to pick them up, but they were so tiny we just pushed them down the hole in the floor where the air comes out."

"The floor vent?"

"Yeah." Casey studied his shoe. "We didn't want Grandma to know we lost her pills 'cos she'd get mad at us."

"I see. How many went down the floor vent?" he asked. "A few or a lot?"

"Only a few."

"Did you eat any of the apple sauce, Casey?" Adrian asked.

"Not when I was the doctor. Doctors only give out medicine." He stared at Adrian as if he should know that.

"Did Corey pretend to be the doctor, too?" he asked.

Casey nodded. "My pills tasted like apple sauce, too."

Adrian turned to Sabrina. "It's hard to guess how many they ate and how many disappeared into the ductwork," he said wryly, "but we can't assume anything. Call in reinforcements so we can get started. I also want a baseline basic chemistry panel and digoxin levels on both boys."

A gastric lavage was the next step and with two patients they needed twice the number of hands. While Adrian explained the procedure of inserting a gastric tube into each boy's stomach in order to rinse out the contents, Sabrina recruited Dr Beth and Hilary to help.

Corey and Casey's blood samples were drawn and stomach contents flushed out until four of the missing twenty-five pills were accounted for—three from Corey and one from Casey—and the returned fluid ran clear.

Without a way to prove they'd removed all the medication, Sabrina administered activated charcoal, which the boys deemed "nasty" and refused to drink until Adrian warned them he'd insert the tubes again. Amid much gagging and misery, they complied. A laxative came next, which they downed most unhappily. While the two looked quite pathetic in their miniature hospital gowns as they waited dejectedly for the medication to send them to the toilet, Adrian called for the lab results and watched their heart monitors closely.

She'd expected him to pop in and out of the room, but he never left. He talked with the boys about television shows and the books their parents read. She was surprised to hear him recount the adventures of *The Berenstein Bears* and *Clifford, the Big Red Dog* as easily as he discussed cardiac arrhythmias. And when Casey began to retch, Adrian was there with a basin.

"Hey, now, buddy," he said as he patted the boy's shoulder. "I know this isn't fun, but it will be OK. I promise."

From Sabrina's position, she saw Casey's gaze meet Adrian's and an encouraging smile settled the deal. The youngster relaxed and all was well. From then on, whenever the children started to panic, he held hands, patted heads and shoulders, rubbed backs and told the occasional knock-knock joke to coax a smile.

The children kept him in their sights, as if he were their savior.

For a moment she pictured Adrian bouncing Jeremy on his knee, tickling his toes, and cradling him in his strong, capable arms. Until now, she'd justified her decision to keep her son's presence a secret, but years from now, when Jeremy asked about his father, would time prove her reasons to have been selfish? She'd ponder that question when she had a private moment.

Finally, she administered the digitalis-specific antidote. "Do you want to send them upstairs to Peds so they can monitor their drug and potassium levels?"

"I really think we flushed out their systems enough to avoid any problems, so if we have the bed space, let's keep them here for the next few hours," he said. And they did.

It didn't take long for the boys to get bored with only their grandma for company. When the latest lab results yielded numbers in the normal range, Adrian agreed to send them home.

"No more pills when you play doctor, OK?" he told the two sternly.

Both bobbed their heads.

"We don't want those tubes down our throats again," Casey assured him.

"Good decision. It wasn't fun, was it?"

"No. When I'm a real doctor, I can give pills, though, can't I?"

Adrian ruffled his hair. "You bet, but not until then."

Edith clasped his hand. "Oh, thank you for everything."

He smiled. "Just doing my job, but after meeting those two, I think yours is harder than mine."

She laughed. "Casey's definitely too smart for his own good, but trust me. I'll keep them on a short leash now."

After restoring the treatment room to rights, Sabrina's shift ended. As she headed for the exit, Adrian fell into step beside her. "Going home?"

"Yes," she said, feeling a little guilty for not admitting she was stopping by the hospital day care first.

"Do you have plans for dinner?"

She almost chuckled. Leftover tuna casserole and heating Jeremy's baby food didn't come close to the concept of "plans". Yet she knew where his question was leading. "I'm not interested in going out or having company."

"What about tomorrow night? I'll take you to dinner."

She shook her head. "Sorry."

"Thursday."

"I don't think so."

He frowned, clearly frustrated by her lack of cooperation. "You can't ignore me for ever, Bree."

"Oh, yes, I can," she retorted, meeting his gaze with a steely-eyed one of her own. "I learned how from a master. Goodnight, Adrian."

Unfortunately, as she reflected on the successes of the

day, his kindness and concern for the two inquisitive and rambunctious boys gave her second thoughts about Adrian's request. No matter how hard she tried, she couldn't shake the picture of Adrian stroking Corey's hair or wiping the tears on Casey's face out of her mind. Was she doing the right thing by not telling him about Jeremy? Could she live with her decision?

On the other hand, and perhaps more importantly, could she share her son with a man she didn't trust? Considering how important family was to him, would he fight for custody, or would he decide he didn't have time for a son and leave the two of them alone?

She hoped for the latter because the possibility of losing her little boy was too frightening, too untenable to imagine, which was why she'd hadn't planned to inform him about Jeremy until he was at least eighteen. Unfortunately, with Adrian underfoot, she couldn't hide Jeremy's existence for more than a day or two. A conspiracy of silence involving all the hospital staff would never last for Adrian's tenure. Her only option was to break the news under her own terms.

As she reached the automatic doors, she realized that spewing caustic and bitter remarks just might make him defensive enough to fight her for custody on principle alone. Being congenial might go a long way to convince him to cooperate with her. She simply couldn't afford to antagonize him.

Resigned to being more amicable, she pivoted in his direction and tried to talk herself out of her impulsive decision.

He hadn't moved from the spot. She still could have stopped herself, but the bleak expression in his eyes melted the final strands of her resistance. She only hoped she could live with the consequences of what she was about to do.

"Friday," she said, aware that after he visited her house her life would change again. "You can come over on Friday."

His smile slowly grew wide, then he nodded. "Friday it is."

CHAPTER THREE

ADRIAN returned to the nurses' station with a definite spring in his step and a jaunty whistle on his lips. He'd survived his first day on the job with Sabrina and the day had gone far better than he'd hoped for or expected. Other than her obvious disdain when they'd been alone, they'd functioned as a cohesive medical team. Sheepishly, he admitted that he should have known she was a professional through and through, that she wouldn't be so petty as to allow their personal conflicts to interfere with the job.

In any case, come Friday evening, he'd find out if she was happy and had adjusted to her life. As much as he'd hated to let her go, knowing that his sacrifice hadn't been in vain would go a long way toward helping him find closure.

Hilary glanced up from her computer monitor. "You're in an especially jovial mood all of a sudden."

He smiled broadly. If the staff at Mercy Memorial had seen him, they would have wondered if he'd finally snapped. He hadn't earned the moniker of The Doctor To Avoid At All Costs by being a friendly sort over the past year. Now, being one step closer to mending his fences made him feel like the old Adrian McReynolds when everything in his life had been running as smoothly as well-maintained diagnostic equipment.

"I am," he admitted before he lowered his voice to a for-her-ears-only volume. "I have a date. With Sabrina."

Hilary stared at him as if he'd just sprouted an extra eye in the middle of his forehead. "You don't say."

"Yeah. Friday night."

"Wow. I'm impressed."

He was puzzled. "Why?"

"Because she doesn't date."

"She doesn't?" he said, wondering how the guy Sabrina had met last night after leaving him in his lonely hospital bed had fallen beneath her colleagues' radar.

Hilary shook her head. "Not that I've ever heard and, believe me, if she did, the news would travel faster than instant messaging."

"Are you sure?"

"Absolutely." She studied him closely. "You must have done something right if she accepted your invitation."

Actually, he'd done everything wrong, but the details weren't for Hilary's ears.

"I, for one, am glad she's finally willing to do something just for herself," Hilary continued. "She's a sweet girl and considering everything she's been through, there isn't a person in this hospital who doesn't want to see her happy."

Everything she's been through? What was Hilary talking about? Had she been ill? Could that explain her frail appearance, the tired circles under her eyes? It had been easier to think she'd simply moved away without incident. To hear otherwise would only drive a few more nails into his guilty conscience, but curiosity drove him to ask and caution warned him to brace himself for bad news.

"What has she gone through?"

"She's had a tough time since she got here, so if you cause her grief, you'll have a lot of folks who won't take kindly to you," Hilary continued, apparently choosing not to share specifics, which frustrated him to no end.

"I don't intend to cause problems."

"Good, because she doesn't need any right now."

Somehow, he felt as if he was missing an important piece of the puzzle, but he let that topic slide. "Are you certain she isn't seeing anyone? I could have sworn she'd mentioned something last night about meeting a guy." Someone she loved dearly, he recalled rather morosely, although he didn't know why the idea pained him when he'd wanted her to find a deserving fellow.

Hilary laughed. "She says that a lot to keep men away."

Hope sprang in his chest. "So there isn't a fellow in her life?"

She eyed him carefully. "By 'fellow', I assume you mean 'romantic interest'. If she did, she wouldn't have agreed to go out with you."

He grinned sheepishly. "I guess not." As it wouldn't hurt to ensure she didn't change her mind before their date on Friday, sending flowers might be a point in his favor. "By the way, she forgot to mention her address. Do you know where she lives?"

Apparently Hilary thought he was trustworthy, because she rattled off the location. "I can't remember the exact number, but she's in the housing development at the corner of Madison and Poplar. She has several potted plants on the front porch and a ladybug windsock hanging from the eaves. You can't miss it."

"Thanks."

Although he was eager to find a florist, duty tethered him to his post for another hour. Finally, after he'd completed his notes, he handed off the last patient—thirty-four-year-old Alan Cavendish who'd come in complaining of intense headaches, dizziness and nausea—to his evening shift replacement. Cavendish was already on his way to Radiology for an MRI and his blood tests were in progress. Dr Lehrer assured him he could handle the case from here, so Adrian gratefully left the hospital.

Driving down Central Avenue, he passed a grocery store sign that advertised a bakery, a hot food buffet, and a floral department. A quick decision sent him veering out of traffic into the parking lot. A few minutes later, he stood in front of the refrigerated case, studied the arrangements and debated between fresh flowers or potted daisies or carnations, a single bud or a bouquet. In the end, he asked the clerk for a dozen roses in assorted colors.

Impatient to see the look on Sabrina's face, he chose to deliver them now rather than wait until later in the evening. With luck, he might coax her into joining him for dinner tonight after all.

After punching the intersection Hilary had mentioned into his car's GPS system, he followed the directions. Five minutes later, the disembodied female voice announced he'd reached his destination.

However, as he gazed at the shabby duplex surrounded by several other equally shabby duplexes, he was certain he'd come to the wrong place. The peeling paint, sagging shutters, and yard that boasted more weeds and bare dirt than grass all testified that this was a low-income housing complex. He could only imagine what the inside looked like. Surely Sabrina hadn't moved *here*, had she? Nurses were paid well these days and he knew of her obsession with creating a nest egg for that proverbial rainy day.

If she lived here, her rainy day had clearly come and gone.

But rainy day or not, the ladybug wind sock that Hilary had described hung in full view above a potted plant. This was definitely Sabrina's place.

Determined not to judge by outward appearances, he strolled up the walk and knocked on the door. After a long minute without a response, he raised his hand to pound again when suddenly the door swung wide.

"Sorry to take so long," she said breathlessly, but her smile soon died as she remained framed in the entrance.

He'd expected to see her alone, not with a gurgling baby on her hip. Immediately his dinner plans evaporated. "Hi," he said inanely.

"Adrian," she said, her eyes wide. "What are you doing here?"

He held out the roses. "After everything you did for me yesterday, I thought flowers were in order."

"Ah, thanks."

"Your hands are full," he said smoothly. "Why don't I bring them inside and help you put them in water?"

"Now isn't a good time," she began.

"Don't worry. I left my white gloves at home," he quipped, knowing how she hated visitors when her house wasn't spotless.

"Truly. I'm not prepared for visitors. Thanks for the flowers, though."

He should have left then and there, but he discovered that he couldn't. Seeing her in a pair of cut-offs and T-shirt with her hair loose and feet bare was a real reminder of the Sabrina he'd once known so well.

The baby on her hip began babbling, as if trying to talk, and Adrian stalled his exit for another minute. "Cute kid. From his blue romper, I assume he's a boy. What's his name?"

"Jeremy."

He tickled a spot under Jeremy's chin and elicited a hearty laugh. "So you're babysitting tonight."

She paused. "No. Jeremy is…"

Adrian glanced at her expectantly. "Jeremy is…what?"

"He's mine."

Words temporarily failed him as his head spun. "Yours? You have a baby?"

"Yes."

The news struck with the same impact as yesterday's golf ball and left him reeling. "How?"

She shrugged. "The usual way."

At first, he felt guilty because he'd obviously pushed her away and she'd found comfort in someone else's arms— someone who'd taken advantage of her, then left. But as he guessed Jeremy's age and mentally counted backwards, a sense of foreboding swept over him.

He stared at the child, this time seeing what he hadn't noticed before. Jeremy had the classic McReynolds chin, the same eyes and nose. In fact, he came close to looking very similar to himself in his own baby photos.

"How old is he?" he asked hoarsely.

"He's not quite seven months. He was born in January."

Still unwilling to believe his own suspicions, he met her gaze. "Is he mine?"

She squared her shoulders and lied. "No."

"Don't play games, Sabrina," he warned her. "He looks like the pictures of Clay and I when we were his age. I'm his father and don't deny it."

"Oh, all right. I'd like to say he isn't yours, but I can't," she snapped. "It's quite obvious just by looking at him that you were the sperm donor."

Hearing her confirm his status should have been a reassuring moment. Instead, Adrian's head felt as if he'd suffered another concussion.

He was a father. To a boy. A *son*. Another generation of McReynolds had arrived.

Immediately, he flashed back to the afternoon before his very first date with Marilyn Carstairs, a blonde who had been fifteen and built like she was twenty-five....

"I imagine you've learned all the physical mechanics of the birds and the bees by now," his father said.

"Yes, sir."

"There's a responsibility that comes with that sort of activity. Did your biology classes teach you that?"

Adrian met his father's sober gaze. "No, sir, but you have."

He nodded thoughtfully. "Keep in mind that accidents happen, no matter how careful a fellow tries to be. The best way to avoid it is to keep the horse in the barn, if you catch my meaning."

"I do."

"The consequences will last a lifetime," his father continued. *"If there are any, a real man won't shirk his duty..."*

He swallowed hard, shaken by his memory.

Sabrina peered at him, clearly concerned. "Are you OK?"

"I'm fine. Just surprised."

But other emotions soon followed. Anger that she hadn't told him she was pregnant. Guilt that she'd gone through her pregnancy alone. Fierce pride and joy that he had a son. Another bout of anger when he realized how easily he might never have known this earth-shattering piece of news. More anger as he reflected on how he'd heard his own child giggling and laughing last night and she'd refused to tell him. Refused to *introduce* them.

He purposely held onto his temper as he watched the baby that had instantly captured his heart with his chubby little face and drooling smile. Forcing his attention back to Sabrina, he saw her fearfully wide eyes. At the moment she had every right to be worried because this was a slight he couldn't forgive or ignore.

"Why didn't you tell me?" he demanded.

Ever since she'd collected Jeremy from the day care, Sabrina had agonized over her decision to tell Adrian about the baby they'd created. Her heart had told her it would be better if he heard the news from her because he'd find out anyway, but she hadn't forgotten those days when she'd had nothing but righteous anger to sustain her—when she'd been so ill with morning sickness and had worked her shift instead of curling into a fetal position and staying in bed; when she'd had to quit work a few months later and survive on her small nest egg and the generosity of others. Knowing Jeremy would be *hers* and hers alone until *she* said otherwise had given her a lifeline to hold onto when the world had seemed bleak and threatening.

Now her best-laid plans had vanished and she needed to devise a way to regain control of the situation.

"Why didn't you tell me?" he repeated.

"How? After our *enlightening* conversation, I rarely saw you and when I did, you weren't ever alone."

His jaw held a stubborn set. "You should have made the effort. Sent a letter. Done *something*."

"Done something?" she asked, incredulous. "You didn't

answer my phone calls or respond to my emails. What would have been my clue that you would have welcomed a letter?"

He didn't answer, so she continued, clutching the flowers until she felt the thorns poke her palm through the protective plastic. "And why should I have bothered? You didn't have time for a relationship, you said, because you'd be too busy with Clay. Using your logic, if you didn't have time for me, then you certainly wouldn't have found time for a baby."

"A baby changes things," he insisted.

"Oh. So you're telling me now that after you'd decided you had too many demands on your time for me—an adult who helped you any way I could—you would suddenly have been able to share your free hours with a helpless baby?"

"You still…" He stopped in mid-sentence. "Can we take this inside or would you rather air our dirty laundry in public?"

As she sheepishly noted they hadn't moved off her front porch, she glanced toward the other half of her duplex and saw the curtains rustle. With a sinking heart Sabrina realized her neighbor was not only aware of their argument but had probably also heard the reasons for it. As a young mother who'd never had a single man darken her door since she'd moved in, the conversation that the elderly Mrs Owens overheard would end up as great gossip. Wordlessly, Sabrina stepped back and allowed him enough room to sidle inside her small home.

"Have a seat," she offered with chilly politeness as she motioned to the lumpy recliner that he probably remembered from their times together. It was one of the few pieces of furniture she still owned from her life BJ—Before Jeremy. She would have sold both it and the bed where she'd spent so many blissful hours with Adrian in her effort to wipe every trace of him out of her life, but she couldn't afford replacements.

Jeremy gurgled and blew bubbles, seemingly unaware of the undercurrents in the room, so she set him in his playpen with a few of his toys and hoped he'd continue to be more enthralled with his plastic rings than with the man who'd arrived.

She straightened to find Adrian slowly perusing her small living room, certain he noticed it only contained the recliner he was currently enjoying, a wooden rocker she'd bought at a garage sale, an umbrella stroller and a larger carriage, Jeremy's infant car seat, and a toy chest.

Even without her sofa, television, and other household effects, she'd taken pride in the cozy space she'd created, but Adrian's presence seemed to draw the walls closer and turn her haven into the size of a matchbox.

"Nice place," he commented.

"It suits us," she defended, well aware it didn't compare as favorably to her apartment in Denver, but this had been the only available apartment to fit her tight budget. "As you can see, I've decorated in Early Baby." Actually, she'd sold her own furniture to obtain the money to purchase the things Jeremy had needed, but Adrian didn't need to know that. She didn't want his pity.

"It's hard to believe one little person needs so much," he said simply.

"It is," she agreed, "but as one of my elderly patients once told me, 'Good or bad, this too shall pass.' I'm not as old as she was, but she made a believer out of me."

"For the record," he began, "when I broke off our relationship, I was trying to spare you."

"Spare me?" She stared at him, incredulous. "From what? From sharing my life with you when I thought we'd enjoyed being together? From helping not just you but Clay, who was more than your brother to me? He was a *friend*."

He fell silent and when he spoke he'd softened his tone. "I saw everything you did for us and I appreciated it more than you know, but once I knew Clay would need extensive rehab, I had to give all of my time to him. You would have been tied to a man who simply couldn't be there for you."

"Did I complain?"

He fell silent.

"I understood what would be involved, Adrian. I didn't ask you to choose between romancing me and supporting Clay, did I?"

He hesitated. "No."

"You didn't have the right to make that decision on your own."

"It wasn't like we had made any promises to each other," he defended. "I was trying to do the honorable thing."

She raised her chin ever so slightly. "You failed. We may not have gotten to the point of being engaged, but if I hadn't lo—" She bit off the word *love* because she wasn't about to give him the satisfaction of knowing that she'd been head over heels for him. "If I hadn't felt something for you and thought what we had would continue to grow, I never would have slept with you in the first place. You, of all people, knew I didn't have indiscriminate or casual sex."

His skin turned ruddy, as if he'd conveniently forgotten that her first sexual encounter had been with him. A twenty-nine-year-old woman waiting that long for intimacy should have proved her character and established her principles.

"So, you see, Adrian, your brilliant idea to 'spare me' so I could create a wonderful life with a different guy who wasn't potentially saddled with a disabled relative was flawed from the beginning. If you ask me, you knew we had something good and suddenly got cold feet. Clay's accident just gave you the excuse you'd been looking for."

"No!" He shook his head. "No."

He sounded so horrified and so vehement that she might have been convinced had she not remembered the painful scene she'd witnessed. Unfortunately, nothing either of them said would be able to sway the other's opinion at this point. Replaying everything was only stirring up emotions that were better left at the bottom of the pot.

"Look," she said tiredly, "we can both rationalize and accuse and second-guess all we want, but it won't accomplish anything."

He frowned as he reached for the stroller parked beside him and rolled it back and forth. For a few seconds the only noises in the room consisted of Jeremy's gurgles and squeaky wheels. "I still wish I'd known you were pregnant," he said quietly.

His voice carried a wounded quality, as if he recognized exactly how much he'd lost by his magnanimous gesture and now regretted his choice.

"Just for the sake of argument, let's say you had known." She eyed him carefully for his response. "What would you have done, Adrian? Would you have had second thoughts or blamed me for getting pregnant? Or would you have felt guilty enough to marry me because it would have been the right thing to do? And if we had, would you have felt trapped?"

"No." He shook his head. "Never trapped."

His words were bitter-sweet, and suddenly she wanted to get everything out in the open, once and for all. "You say that now, Adrian, but I saw you with a redhead and she seemed quite important to you."

He appeared startled and a thought wrinkle marred his forehead. "A redhead? I don't know a redhead…"

"As a matter of fact, I *did* try to contact you. I waited outside the ER one night at the end of your shift. You had just come through the doors and were on your way to the parking lot when this woman ran after you. The two of you talked, then you hugged and kissed her before you swung her round and laughed as if you didn't have a care in the world."

To her surprise, mentioning what she'd seen was almost as painful as observing it for the first time. "You didn't have time for a romance with me," she continued, "but you obviously found the time to be with another woman."

He was clearly at a loss. "I didn't. There hasn't been anyone. You must have mistaken someone else for me."

She raised an eyebrow. "Then you have an identical twin who also owns the same green scrub suit with the bleached out spot on one pocket."

Still puzzled, he shook his head. "I don't remember…"

Somehow, his memory loss irritated more than it consoled or explained. "Did you go out with so many women that you've forgotten this particular lady?"

"No!"

He sounded so appalled she almost believed him, but the same pride that had stopped her from telling him about their baby rose again. "In any case, you'd obviously moved on with your life, so I made the choice to do the same."

"You didn't have to leave town."

"I wasn't a glutton for punishment, Adrian. I couldn't

stay, but my transfer wasn't a secret." She met his gaze. "Considering how many months have passed, you can't claim you rushed to mend fences. Why did you come now?"

He leaned back. "My boss twisted my arm because I haven't been the easiest to work with. He thought I'd benefit from a change of scenery."

"Chewed out one too many nurses, did you?"

"Nurses, colleagues, it didn't matter. I was on the fast track to losing my position. As crazy as it sounds now, I was eaten up inside by not knowing how you were doing and I took out my frustration on my staff. I had to see you again, to reassure myself I'd done the right thing, but enough time had passed that I didn't know how to make the first move." He managed a smile. "As it happened, my boss took matters into his own hands.

"What's important now," he continued, "is that I *am* here, regardless of the how or the why."

She begged to differ. "If you say so."

"While I'll have to live the rest of my life with the reasons why you didn't tell me you were pregnant before you moved away from Denver, you could have told me about our son last night. The baby I'd heard outside my room *was* Jeremy, wasn't it?"

She heard the chiding note in his voice and it irritated her to think that he had the audacity to question her decisions when his own had been so faulty.

"Yes," she agreed defiantly, "but your head had just been sliced open by a golf ball, you had an entire drum corps pounding in your head and were under observation for a concussion. As I told you last night, you weren't in any condition to hold your end of a serious conversation and you certainly weren't able to handle additional shock and stress. In fact, I'm not sure you should be hearing this tonight, either."

"Believe me, *not* hearing this tonight would have been much worse." He paused. "Were you *ever* going to tell me about him?"

"I'd planned for the two of you to meet on Friday." At his dubious expression, she shrugged. "Believe me or not, I don't care. Introducing you to Jeremy was the only reason I agreed to see you. As for him being 'our' son, he isn't. He's *mine*."

"A judge might feel differently. Fathers have rights these days, too."

She squared her shoulders, raised her chin and bluffed. "Threaten all you want, Adrian, but intimidation won't work. I don't scare as easily as I did then."

This time, *he* bounded to his feet and rubbed his neck in obvious frustration. "Look, I don't want to fight about this. I'll admit I may have made a mistake—" At this she scoffed, but he continued, "But I don't want Jeremy to grow up with his parents at odds with each other."

Part of her wanted to rant over his naive belief that she could pick up where they'd left off on the strength of his I-may-have-made-a-mistake statement. The other part told her that carrying a grudge wasn't healthy for Jeremy, or for her. Frankly, she didn't have the energy required to fuel this level of animosity indefinitely.

"In my head, I know I should forgive you," she began tiredly, "and someday, Adrian, I probably will, but today my heart won't let me."

He accepted her reply with equanimity. "I'm asking for too much too soon, but I'll do whatever it takes to make it up to you."

She didn't think that would ever be likely, but his voice carried a note of promise, as if he was making a solemn vow to both of them. Before she could guess at or ask what he had planned, he spoke again.

"The big question at the moment is, what do we do next?"

His use of the plural pronoun irritated her. How like him to barge in and take over as if he were riding a white horse to the rescue!

"*We* don't do anything," she said firmly, determined to hold onto her position. "*I* will raise my son and you're welcome to visit him as long as you're in town. After you return to *your* family—" she couldn't resist throwing his long-ago reference back at him "—I'll drop you a postcard every now and then."

His eyes narrowed. "I want more than a postcard. Jeremy is part of my family, too. I'm as responsible for him as you are."

"No, you aren't," she argued. "You relinquished your claim a year ago."

"I. Did. Not!" he roared.

Jeremy immediately burst into a howl and Sabrina rushed to cuddle him against her chest. "Sorry, little man. He wasn't yelling at you, just at Mommy." She kissed the top of his head and wiped away the tears clinging to his eyelashes before she snarled at Adrian, "Would you please control yourself?"

To his credit, he appeared completely repentant. "Sorry. I didn't mean to shout."

Sabrina sat in the rocker, holding a wary Jeremy on her lap. "What if Clay suffers a relapse and he has to live with you so you can personally care for him again? I won't be put in the position of explaining to our son why his father doesn't want us except when it's convenient."

"It wouldn't be like that."

She turned a steely-eyed gaze on him. "Sorry, but I'm not convinced and I'm not willing to take the risk. For Jeremy's sake."

Jeremy began to fuss and the noise drew her attention as well as Adrian's as they watched the little boy, who'd suddenly become distracted by his bib and was currently stuffing the fabric into his mouth.

"Children need both their parents," he said simply. "I want Jeremy to know who I am."

"Certainly. Feel free to send a picture every now and again."

He shot her a look of disgust. "I'm supposed to be satisfied with Jeremy knowing me from a *photo*?"

"OK, fine. You can visit after you've gone back to Denver," she offered generously. "And I'd be happy to drop by whenever we head in that direction." Of course, she *never* drove near Adrian's house or Mercy Memorial and didn't intend to do so either. In fact, she hadn't traveled outside Pinehaven since she'd moved here.

"Not good enough, Bree," he said, unaware that his pet name for her irritated more than it soothed. "I can't be a face in a snapshot to him. I want to be his dad, in every sense of the word. Not just the sperm donor."

Obviously, her previous description had struck a sore spot in his ego. Studying him with suspicion, she said, "Your life isn't in Pinehaven, Adrian. How do you propose to be his dad when you're hours away?"

"I don't have specifics," he said, clearly exasperated. "If you recall, I haven't had a lot of time to digest the fact that I have a son. But I can tell you this. Being an absentee father isn't in my plans and I'll do whatever it takes so it doesn't happen," he said grimly, as if preparing himself for battle. "I'll drive back every weekend if necessary."

She shouldn't have been surprised by his offer. His strong sense of family had cemented her attraction to him long ago, but she'd hoped Adrian's animosity toward her would be enough to convince him to maintain his distance.

"You can't have one of us without the other," she said firmly. "I'm not going to turn Jeremy over to you whenever you roll into town. Nor will I send him back and forth between our homes like a package, so don't waste your time suggesting it."

"You may not have a choice."

She met his gaze. "If you want to fight this, I will." She didn't know how or where she'd find the money if he pursued legal action, but she would.

To her surprise and relief, he backed down. "Let's not overreact. I've only known of Jeremy's existence for…" he glanced at his watch "…two hours. Logistics and legalities can come later."

Meaning that at some point in the relatively near future he wouldn't be satisfied with hovering on the fringes of Jeremy's life. As she wasn't willing to share, a no-win situation loomed.

"While I'm in town, though," he continued, oblivious to her thoughts, "I intend to catch up on everything I missed."

She could either cooperate or not, but his demand made it plain that one way or another he wouldn't be thwarted. Unfortunately, sharing her son with Adrian was easier said than done.

"Catching up on Jeremy's short life is impossible tonight," she said, flatly. "It's getting late, I haven't eaten all day, and it's time for Jeremy's bath."

He didn't move. "I know I'm wearing out my welcome, but I'd like to stay and help with his nighttime routine. I promise not to get in the way or disrupt your schedule."

"You already have."

"Probably," he agreed, "but…please?"

Months ago, she would have been happy to hear Adrian beg, but seeing him humble himself as he already had several times tonight only made her uncomfortable. She had enough faults without adding cruelty to the list. Besides, what would it hurt? If cooperating now meant he wouldn't fight for custody later, then she would.

"You'll get wet," she warned. "'Splash' is Jeremy's middle name." Adrian's subsequent grin reminded her of happier times when her future had seemed safe and secure in his hands. She pushed aside those bitter-sweet memories.

"I won't melt," he promised, rising to stand beside her.

As difficult as it was for her emotionally, she placed Jeremy in Adrian's arms, careful to avoid physical contact because she didn't want to remember how good it had felt when he touched her. Stepping back, she watched him hold their son like the priceless treasure he was.

The awe in Adrian's eyes and in his expression as he gazed at his bundle brought a lump to her throat. She saw his steady hand tremble as he caressed Jeremy's cheek and touched his tiny fingers. Jeremy stared at him in silent wonderment, as if he instinctively sensed the connection between them.

She held her composure until Adrian's eyes developed an unmistakable sheen.

"Bring him into the kitchen when you're ready," she said hoarsely before she fled. She was generously giving them a moment alone to meet each other, she told herself as she plucked Jeremy's bath towel and washcloth off the rod in her bathroom. It had nothing to do with the emotional moment of a father holding his son for the first time.

As she passed through the living room on her way to the kitchen, the sound of Adrian's baritone almost undid her as he sang a child's verse about the things Papa would buy him. What hurt worse was how Jeremy gazed at his father with undivided attention and a toothy smile, as if he loved hearing this new and more interesting voice than his mother's.

Sharing her flesh and blood with a man she couldn't trust had become even more difficult that it had a few minutes ago. She wanted to snatch Jeremy away because Adrian didn't deserve such instant and unconditional adoration, but she couldn't. She'd suffer through, for Jeremy's sake.

She should be thrilled Adrian would be a part of Jeremy's life because her son wouldn't grow up without knowing his father. She should be ecstatic at the prospect of sharing the responsibilities of raising a child. She should feel vindicated that Adrian wanted to make amends and had admitted his mistakes, but she didn't feel any of those things. She only felt empty inside.

He was beautiful, Adrian decided as he cradled Jeremy against him, handling his little body for the first time. He was disappointed for missing out on Jeremy's first months, but he couldn't blame anyone except himself. If he hadn't been so eager to put his life on hold to ease his guilt over Clay's accident, things would have turned out differently. He never should have loaned him the money to buy the motorcycle in the first place, but Clay had set his heart on one in spite of Adrian's warnings about the inherent dangers. So he'd given in and his worst fears had come to pass.

Determined to appease his conscience, he'd focused on Clay at Sabrina's expense. Now he had to save Sabrina from making his mistake. Contrary to what she might believe, pushing him away as he'd pushed her wasn't in anyone's best interests.

Part of him wanted to appeal to the court system and force her to give him a piece of Jeremy's life. Unfortunately, doing so would alienate her and place Jeremy in a position where he'd feel disloyal if he loved both his parents. His best option was to stay calm and cooperate with her so she didn't feel threatened. Once the pain of their past faded, they could readdress the visitation issue.

As Jeremy stopped chewing on his fist to gaze at him with complete trust, Adrian's chest swelled with love and commitment. "Your mom and I are going to work this out. One way or another. I promise."

Jeremy grunted and Adrian kissed his forehead, reveling in his baby scent. "Come on. Your mom's waiting."

He carried him into the kitchen and ten minutes later, as Sabrina had predicted, most of Adrian's clothes were soaked.

She smiled as she wrapped Jeremy in a bath towel. "I told you so."

"I'll wear swim trunks next time."

"That won't be necessary," she said quickly, as if she remembered what had happened the last time they'd both worn bathing suits. "Just wear old clothes."

He grinned inside, pleased she was giving him another opportunity to take part in Jeremy's evening routine.

"I'll slip on his pajamas if you'll warm his bottle." She pointed to the stove as she stood poised in the doorway. "It's in the refrigerator, ready to go."

He eyed the pot of water on a front burner. "Will do, but

don't you think it's too hot for jammies?" The room's temperature was definitely warmer than what he considered comfortable, and he had the added bonus of having damp clothing to cool his overheated skin.

"He wears a diaper and a T-shirt," she called over her shoulder, "not footed flannel sleepers."

He opened the fridge and found the bottle, then paused as he noted the sparse contents. A few apples, a bag of carrots, a carton of eggs and a near-empty quart jug of milk didn't come close to filling the space. Just thinking of food made his stomach growl a reminder that he hadn't eaten, either.

Quickly, he closed the refrigerator to conserve its cold air, plunked the bottle inside the pan and set the water to boil, then called in a pizza delivery order courtesy of a number he found in the phone book. With their upcoming meal under control, curiosity drove him to check out her cupboards. Their sorry state matched the refrigerator's.

Before he could snoop around a bit more, the bottle was ready and Sabrina appeared in the doorway with Jeremy gnawing frantically on his hands and smacking his lips. "How are you coming?" she asked as she bounced him on her hip.

He shook a few drops of formula on his wrist. "I guess this is warm enough. Want to check for yourself?"

She did, then pronounced it acceptable. "Would you like to feed him?"

He heard a trace of reluctance in her voice, as if she hoped he'd refuse, but he couldn't. "I'd love to."

Once again, she handed Jeremy into the crook of his arm, but this time his fingers brushed against the soft swell of her breast and she gasped. Afraid to move for fear he'd drop the baby, he froze.

Immediately, blood rushed to his groin and his body responded as if they hadn't spent the last year apart. Saints in heaven, he'd missed the feel of her skin against his, the way her fingertips had glided across his abdomen, the sensation of taking her in his mouth and driving her wild.

She moved just enough to break contact. "Do you have him?"

The breathless quality in her voice suggested that the accidentally intimate touch had rekindled those memories for her, too.

"Yes," he said, hoping she wouldn't notice how his trousers had suddenly tented.

"Take the rocking chair. And be sure you burp him every few ounces because he feeds too fast. If you don't, we'll be giving him another bath," she advised wryly, "and you'll be wearing 'eau de formula'."

Adrian obeyed. Silently and under Sabrina's watchful eye, he fed and dutifully burped as instructed. Apparently satisfied by his efforts, she eventually disappeared into the kitchen. He was flattered that she trusted him, but the bleakness in her eyes suggested another reason. Perhaps she couldn't sit by and watch the man who'd rejected her so completely fall instantly and irrevocably in love with their son.

He may have wedged his size eleven foot in the proverbial door to get this far, but he had a lot of penance to complete before he could step inside.

Jeremy had emptied the bottle and was asleep by the time she returned.

"What now?" Adrian whispered.

"Lay him in his crib," she answered. "It's in my bedroom."

He followed, loath to let the little boy out of his arms, although he couldn't and shouldn't hold him all night.

Just as he was about to lower Jeremy onto the mattress under Sabrina's watchful eye, the doorbell awakened Jeremy. He wrinkled his face and screwed his mouth into a wail.

"Who's that, I wonder?" Sabrina spoke in a near whisper.

He kept his voice low, too. "Probably the pizza I ordered."

She stopped in her tracks. "You ordered pizza?"

Adrian heard the surprise and displeasure in her voice over Jeremy's unhappiness. He shrugged as he soothed the baby against his shoulder and tried to console him with a pacifier. "What can I say? I was hungry and I assumed you were, too."

She lowered her gaze to a point somewhere near his breastbone. "I…um, I can't pay him."

"I didn't expect you to feed me," he told her. "My billfold's in my hip pocket. Take what you need." He turned to give her easy access.

She gingerly removed the wallet, as if she was afraid to touch him, then disappeared. As he crooned softly to Jeremy and the youngster settled down once more, Adrian studied the room. Zoo animals dotted the bedding and a mobile featuring similar creatures hung from the headboard. The rest of the room was filled with more baby paraphernalia, a small dresser and her bed.

Jeremy seemed to own all the equipment necessary for a baby, but Sabrina definitely lived a spartan existence. Before he had a chance to work the inconsistency out in his mind, she reappeared.

Without his wallet, he noticed wryly. Clearly, she didn't want to return it to the place where she'd found it, although he'd rather hoped she would. He missed her touch, even as impersonal as it would have been.

"Is he asleep?" she asked.

"I can't tell for sure, but he hasn't moved, so I think he is."

Ever so gently, he placed Jeremy on his back and covered him with a light cotton sheet. For a long moment, he stared down at the miracle of his son.

Unable to stop himself, he snaked his arm around Sabrina's waist and pulled her close, allowing himself a few seconds to revel in the moment. "Thank you," he whispered.

"For what?"

"For having him," he said simply. "Under the circumstances, it would have been easier to choose another option. I'm so glad you didn't."

Her smile wobbled as she gazed at the tiny figure in the crib. "There wasn't another option," she said simply. "He was all I had."

CHAPTER FOUR

ADRIAN had always prided himself on achieving his goals, but his success at pushing Sabrina out of his life so she could have a clean start had been an expensive accomplishment. The experiences he'd lost as a result were priceless. All these months, he'd imagined her happy, prosperous, and relieved that she'd escaped a half-hearted relationship. Instead, he'd found her struggling on her own to maintain a home and a job as well as being a single mother to *his* son.

Oh, yes. His so-called victory was hollow indeed.

He tightened his grip on her waist to hug her. How could he ever undo the damage? It was obvious from their earlier conversation that he could talk until he'd used his last breath, but words wouldn't heal her mistrust. Action was the only thing he had left to prove he'd changed.

However, as he gazed down at her, his intention to devise a strategy faded. If the anguish on her familiar, pixie-like face had haunted him before, he'd never be able to sleep again after seeing her somber expression or her pain-filled eyes. Her mouth trembled, drawing his attention to those sweet, warm, moist lips that had always driven him wild.

He wanted to kiss her, to "make it better", as his mother

had always done whenever he'd sported a new scrape or a painful bruise. Before he could debate the pros and cons of taking the liberty, he simply took it. He lowered his head and gently brushed his lips against hers.

Nothing happened. Just when he was ready to concede defeat, her lips parted. As he hauled her closer, he sensed her rising on tiptoe to meet him.

Aware of her response and gratified by it, he continued his light pressure, knowing she was near tears and hoping his non-verbal apology could stem the oncoming tide.

Slowly but surely, her response changed, as if she'd understood and accepted what he was trying to say without words. Her hands slowly came up to rest on his chest and she molded her mouth to his.

An instant later, she jerked herself free, horror written on her face. "We can't. No." She shook her head and took a step back. "This doesn't solve anything."

Not everything, he mentally agreed, but in his opinion they were certainly heading down the right path. "I know it doesn't," he admitted, "but—"

She rushed out and he followed her to the center of the living room where she stood with her arms folded around her as if she'd drawn inside herself.

"Why did you come?" she asked in a trembling voice. "Why couldn't you have stayed away?"

"Because—"

As if she'd gathered every bit of strength from within, she squared her shoulders and her eyes flashed fire. "You need to go. Out of my house. Out of my hospital. Out of our lives!"

"I know this is tough—"

"You have no idea," she said bitterly.

"But it isn't easy for me, either. I'd go if I could, but I can't, Sabrina," he said flatly. "Not after knowing we made a beautiful boy. Don't ask that of me because I can't give you what you want. I just can't."

I can't give you what you want.

Adrian's comment echoed through Sabrina's head as he waited for her reply. Given his sense of responsibility and his devotion to family, she truly hadn't expected him to walk away so easily. Neither would he be satisfied with her doling out Jeremy's time with an eyedropper. Unfortunately, although she'd suspected he'd respond exactly as he had, she'd *hoped* he'd do the opposite.

She chewed nervously on her lip, resigned to the prospect of his steady presence and taking an active role with their baby while he fulfilled his contract in Pinehaven. However, it was anyone's guess what he might do or want after he returned to his position in Denver. For a while he'd probably phone every evening or organize weekend excursions. He might even set up one of those webcams in order to see Jeremy in real time as he talked to him, but the novelty of being a long-distance parent would wear off as soon as he got tired of dealing with the logistical problems. Or so she hoped.

Until then, though, he'd be underfoot. What she truly hated about having him in her home on a regular, if not daily basis, was that she wasn't as immune to him as she'd believed. At the moment she didn't know if she was upset with him for kissing her or upset at herself for responding.

She tucked a loose strand of hair behind her ear with a shaky hand. "I had to ask."

He nodded, as if he understood how desperately she

wanted her life back—the life she'd had before he'd rolled into town. "As long as you know I'm in this for the long haul, we're both on the same page."

"And how long will that be?" At his protest, she held up her hands. "It's a fair question. I thought we were in a relationship for the long haul, too, and we both know how quickly that changed."

"Nothing, short of my death, will keep me away."

It was a vow, she sensed, spoken firmly and with sincerity. One thing she knew about Adrian—when he committed to something, nothing would sway him from his decision. Whether that character trait was a positive one or was a flaw, his set jaw and determined demeanor telegraphed how completely immovable he was on this subject.

If she had to surrender this battle, she would surrender under her own terms.

"All right, but we need a few ground rules," she told him, noticing how the tension seemed to leave his shoulders and relief appear in his eyes, as if he'd expected more of a fight. "We've both seen or known families torn apart by strife and I don't want Jeremy to live in the same state of uncertainty when we're together."

"Neither do I."

"And no more of what just happened in my bedroom. We both reacted to the emotional moment. That's all it was," she insisted. "I'm not interested in picking up where we left off before Clay's accident. The relationship we once had is over."

He opened his mouth as if to protest, but she glared at him. "OK," he said. "We'll take that as it comes. Anything else?"

"No."

"Good. Then let's eat."

Eat? He wanted to *eat*? The knots in her stomach made it impossible to digest food. "I'm really not hungry—"

"I ordered your favorite. Pepperoni and mushroom."

He'd remembered her weakness. She might have been able to resist the temptation, but she hadn't indulged in the extravagance in a very long time because her budget didn't cover such luxuries, and the scent alone was causing her mouth to water.

"Come on," he coaxed. "We're starting over, remember? Most dates involve a meal where the two people can talk and get to know each other."

"We aren't dating."

"Whatever. Regardless, we're going to spend a lot of time together unless you're willing to let me take Jeremy back to my place."

She snorted. "As if."

"I thought not, which means it will be very awkward if we only talk to Jeremy. Eventually, he'll wonder why his parents never say more than two words to each other."

Years would pass before their son would notice that sort of detail, but as someone had once said, "A journey begins with a single step." So she might as well begin hers now. For Jeremy's sake.

"OK, I'll share your pizza, but then we'll have to call it a night. My shift starts early in the morning."

"Fair enough."

They sat down at her kitchen table where she'd covered most of the scratches, knicks and gouges under the cheery yellow sunflower place mats she'd sewn, and he began firing questions with a boyish eagerness that brought a smile to her face.

"Tell me about your pregnancy. How was your labor and

delivery? Has Jeremy changed a lot since he was born? Do you have photos?"

"We agreed to catch up tomorrow," she reminded him.

"I know, but I can't wait. Surely you can share a few things," he coaxed.

She hesitated. Waiting another day wouldn't change anything and Jeremy *was* her favorite topic of conversation, so she bowed to the inevitable. After all, cooperating with Adrian would only serve her best interests, she reminded herself for the umpteenth time.

Choosing to answer his last question first, she said, "Of course I have pictures. I have them in the other room." Carrying her pizza slice with her, she located an album on a shelf in the living room and carried it to the table. "Here. Take a look."

Immediately, he stopped eating to open the padded book. Reverently, he turned the pages, stopping at several to comment. Surprisingly enough, he paused at the images taken at her baby shower. "You didn't gain much weight," he remarked.

She hadn't. For starters, she'd been so ill up to her fifth month that her obstetrician had threatened to admit her to hospital. And after that she'd developed high blood pressure, which heralded pre-eclampsia. Although she'd cut back her hours to part-time work, eventually her condition had progressed to the point the doctor had prescribed bed rest. Fortunately, Jeremy had decided to arrive two weeks early, otherwise Dr VanderWaal would have performed a Cesarean section.

"I got fat and waddled like every other expectant mom," she said lightly, hoping he wouldn't notice she hadn't shone with the expected glow of impending motherhood.

She'd been allowed out of bed for her two-hour party and then, like clockwork, Kate had driven her home. While she'd rested, her friends from the hospital had carried in all the presents and stowed everything away.

He frowned as he studied the snapshots. "You look pale. Were you anemic? Did your doctor prescribe vitamins? Better yet, did you take them?"

"You can't diagnose me from a photo taken in bad lighting," she protested, although she hadn't looked her best that day. "I did have a few problems, but they all worked out. As for labor, it went fairly quickly. One of the OB nurses, Kate—she golfed with me yesterday—acted as my coach.

"Anyway." Her voice softened as she reflected on those hours after his birth. "Jeremy was this tiny baby with a few strands of the darkest hair." She flipped another page and pointed. "See?"

Adrian groaned good-naturedly. "Someone curled it. Who would do such a traumatic thing to a boy?"

"Kate. She thought it made him look cute—more like a baby and less like a little old man. Everyone remarked on how he seemed to know what people said to him, probably because he always looked directly at the person talking."

"Intelligence shows." He grinned. "He gets that from his dad."

"He definitely inherited your disposition," she said wryly. "He's easygoing until he wants something, and then you'd better give it to him right away, or else. As small as he is, he doesn't mind throwing his weight around."

His skin turned ruddy. "We'll have to work on that together." His watch beeped the hour and he frowned as he checked the time. "I guess that's my cue to go," he said, clearly reluctant to cut short their evening.

"Take the album with you," she said magnanimously. "If you'd like copies of the photos, I saved them to a CD so you can make prints. I put the camera you gave me for my birthday that year to good use."

"I'm glad."

"Oh, and speaking of gifts…" She hurried into her bedroom, rummaged through her sock drawer, and returned with the tiny box containing an expensive diamond pendant in a double-heart design that he'd given her for Christmas. "I almost forgot. This is yours."

He stared at the jeweler's box as if it were a canister of anthrax, then met her gaze. "You should keep it."

"What for?"

He shrugged. "Save it for Jeremy."

"No, thanks." She reached out, grabbed his hand and placed the case in his palm. "Please take it. I have no use for a necklace like this. If I should ever meet anyone else, I'd feel too awkward to ever wear it."

"Keep it," he repeated.

She held up her hands and backed up a step, out of arm's reach. "I should have returned it before I left Denver, and I would have but… Anyway, just take it. Give it to your…to someone else who'll appreciate it."

In her dreams, she'd always imagined herself handing the gold pendant to him as carelessly as if it were a piece of costume jewelry. In real life, however, transferring ownership hadn't been as satisfying as she'd imagined. Perhaps she should keep it—for Jeremy—but the necklace was simply too painful a reminder to accidentally run across. The interlocking hearts had seemed so appropriate but apparently she'd read far more into the meaning behind the design than Adrian had. To her, the shape had been a sign of their feelings for each other, while to him it had meant nothing. Removing the pendant from her drawer only marked The Official End to a relationship that had precipitously ended a year ago.

Instead of feeling liberated and relieved, she felt…lost and depressed, which was ridiculous. Disposing of this gift was supposed to be part of the healing process. Wasn't it?

His fingers closed over the small square box and he slipped it into his pocket. "Do you need anything? Anything at all? Anything like…" He glanced around the room as if searching for ideas, "I don't know, formula or baby stuff, or even a sofa?"

"Jeremy and I are fine. We don't need a thing," she said firmly.

"I feel as if I owe you something."

How typical to think money would solve their problems when it would only ease his conscience. "You don't."

He looked thoughtful, but didn't argue. Thank goodness, because she wasn't ready for a full-scale argument. He only said, "If you don't mind, I'll check on Jeremy one more time and then I'll get out of your hair."

"OK."

He didn't stay long in Jeremy's room and left after delivering a curt "See you tomorrow". After she'd closed the door behind him, Sabrina tidied her tiny home and removed all traces of their impromptu dinner. However, as the pizza scent lingered in the air after she'd stuffed the box in the trash can outside, so did the memories of his strong, steady embrace and the kiss that had curled her toes and reawakened her hormones.

She couldn't forget the instant when he'd splayed his hand across her back to anchor her tightly against him or how her own body had betrayed her as she'd risen on tiptoe to meet him halfway. Luckily, her good sense had kicked in and stopped her from allowing the situation to escalate. They'd only been reacting to the emotional moment, she told herself for the tenth time. As sizzling as the kiss had been, it didn't mean anything.

How embarrassing to think that even with their history she still responded to his touch and his non-verbal signals so easily. How pathetic was that? Pathetic enough to wish for a carton of either fudge ripple or chocolate chunk ice cream to magically appear in her pitifully empty freezer.

Over the next couple of days, in spite of berating herself for being so weak, in spite of Adrian subsequently acting like the perfect gentleman, or perhaps *because* he acted like the perfect gentleman, those living color memories resurfaced at the oddest times. Like now, when she should be concentrating on Mrs Gardner in room four.

The woman had come in with sudden indigestion when she hadn't eaten for hours, a squeezing sensation in her chest that continued into her throat and both jaws. Although the symptoms weren't typical for a heart attack, Adrian seemed in favor of the diagnosis after reviewing her EKG. Now Sabrina was checking the computer for the lab's cardiac enzyme results and waiting for a cardiologist to arrive.

"Yo, there, Sabrina." Hilary bustled up to the other side of the counter. "If you're relatively caught up, I want you to handle the walk-in we're getting. A woman was found wandering the streets, confused and possibly assaulted. The cops are bringing her in."

"No ambulance?"

"The paramedics are tied up at a warehouse fire, so the police decided not to wait for them."

The automatic ambulance bay doors opened and two uniformed officers escorted a petite woman inside. "They're here," Hilary announced. "I'll find Dr McReynolds and send him in ASAP."

Sabrina strode toward the trio, noting the woman's bloodied face, torn clothing, and the way she clutched the blanket around her as if it were armor. "I'm Sabrina," she said gently as she touched the woman's shoulder to guide her into a nearby exam room. "I'm going to be taking care of you. Meanwhile, would you like me to call your family, or a friend?"

The woman simply stared at her with panic in her eyes. "I don't—I can't…"

"We don't know who she is," the middle-aged Officer Malone, according to his nametag, volunteered. "The victim says she can't remember her name. You don't by any chance recognize her, do you?"

Sabrina studied the thirty-ish brunette's battered features. When the swelling subsided and the bruises faded, she'd be quite attractive. "Sorry."

"We're hoping you folks find a distinguishing mark or two to help ID her if anyone files a missing persons report."

"I'll see what I can do." She closed the door behind them and coaxed her to release the blanket.

The woman's clothes, although torn and bloody, were of a much higher quality than most. Her neck sported a number of red marks, suggesting someone had ripped off her necklace. Her hands were devoid of all jewelry, although her left hand's ring finger showed a distinctive band of white.

Helping her into a hospital gown was like helping a two-year-old. The woman had definitely been traumatized.

"Why can't I remember? I want to," the woman said on a near sob. "I remember being in a car and then walking, so I should be able to think of my own name, but when I try, my head hurts."

"You have a nasty bump," Sabrina told her kindly. "Sometimes those injuries can cause temporary amnesia."

"How long is 'temporary'?"

"It depends," Sabrina prevaricated. "A neurologist can give a better answer than I can. Meanwhile, you simply have to give yourself time to heal, both physically and emotionally. You never know when a conversation, a sound or a smell might trigger your memories."

"I suppose." She didn't sound convinced.

"First things first," Sabrina declared. "Have you eaten?"

The woman shrugged. "I don't know. I think so. Whether I did or not, I'm not hungry."

"A snack always helps," Sabrina told her. "After the doctor is finished, I'll scrounge something from the cafeteria. Maybe soup or a sandwich, along with tea or coffee. Or does a soda sound better?"

"Cherry cola would be nice. It's my favorite." Her face lit up as soon as she spoke, then her smile became a frown. "How can I remember what I like to drink when I can't remember who I am?"

"The mind does unusual things during times of intense stress," Sabrina said. "The good thing is that you *are* remembering little details. Chances are good the rest of your memory will return soon. As I said, the specialist will be able to answer all of your questions." She took her clothes and placed them in a proper bag to be used as legal evidence.

Adrian walked in at that moment, along with a striking blonde in her forties who wore a police badge. "I'm Dr

McReynolds," he said in a low, soothing voice, "and this is Detective Harper. If you're ready, I'm going to examine you and then you can shower and change clothes. Sabrina will find something for you to wear."

He raised an eyebrow at Sabrina and she nodded. They stored a few scrub suits for occasions like this.

The brunette's mouth quivered. "Thank you."

He gently examined her as Sabrina stood by and noted her injuries. In addition to the obvious scrapes and contusions, she had distinct marks on her arms, indicating that at least one person had grabbed her. Two of her ribs were separated—fortunately, neither had punctured a lung—and an angry-looking cigarette burn marred her left thigh.

As Adrian performed a pelvic exam, his sober glance at Sabrina said it all. The woman had been sexually assaulted.

In his quiet baritone, he explained everything he was doing while Sabrina carefully labeled the samples he'd collected. Detective Harper's sharp-eyed gaze followed the proceedings as she murmured encouraging words to the victim.

In a remarkably short amount of time they'd finished treating her injuries, obtained blood and urine samples to check for medical conditions, and administered the appropriate prophylatics to guard against HIV and hepatitis. The only real surprise was that Jane Doe's pregnancy test result had come back positive.

"The real kicker is that she probably wouldn't have known even if she hadn't lost her memory," he remarked after they'd sent her to X-Ray for chest films. "Her beta-HCG level is very low, which suggests she's only days into her pregnancy."

"Will she miscarry?"

He shrugged. "We wait and see."

"What will happen in the meantime? We can't discharge her when she can't fend for herself."

"We won't," he promised. "I'll admit her for observation because a concussion could have caused her memory loss. With luck, the police will locate someone who knows her before being homeless becomes an issue."

"I saw the white line on her finger. Whoever hurt her probably stole her wedding ring."

"That's my theory, too. According to the police, she was wandering around in a residential area, probably trying to get home."

Sabrina nodded. "I should have asked Officer Malone what they'll do to find her family."

"If no one files a missing persons report, they'll look for abandoned cars."

"What if the bad guy stole that, too? Or if she walked?"

"Then they may issue a press release asking the public for information."

"And if no one comes forward and we can't find a reason to keep her?"

"I imagine she'll go to the local women's crisis shelter. We won't turn her out to fend for herself."

"I should hope not! I feel so sorry for her husband. Wondering where his wife is." The idea of being separated from one's family sent a cold shiver down Sabrina's spine.

"No one lives in a vacuum, Bree," he said kindly. "Think positively. Someone's sure to notice our Jane Doe didn't come home when she was supposed to and he'll report it."

"I hope you're right," she said fervently, disturbingly aware that if this situation had happened to her, it would take a while for anyone to notice and sound an alarm. More importantly, what would happen to Jeremy? She hadn't recorded a name in the "next-of-kin" box on her employment form. Neither would Jeremy's birth certificate give any clues because she'd left the space for the father's name blank, too.

"This case really bothers you, doesn't it?" he asked, uncannily accurate.

Sabrina shrugged. "I can normally be objective, but this time…I feel so sorry for her and her family. She's a lost soul and I can't imagine what her husband must be going through."

"You always cared about your patients more than most," he said. "Are you sure that's all it is?"

She refused to admit that this scenario had awakened fears that she hadn't considered—fears that should be addressed relatively soon to ensure Jeremy wouldn't be left in legal limbo. While she didn't look for tragedy at every turn, it was an equal opportunity event—no one, no matter how careful he or she was, was safe from misfortune.

Explaining that, however, would only make her appear paranoid. As thoughtful and considerate as Adrian had been these past few days, she wouldn't show any weakness that he could exploit. She'd experienced firsthand how quickly he could turn on her, so trusting him was too risky.

She drew a bracing breath. "It is. You know me," she said lightly. "I always get too wrapped up in my patients' problems, but you're right. We have to be positive and I need to stop imagining the worst-case scenario."

"I can help you with that," he said. "Let's take Jeremy to the park tonight. He wants to have a picnic."

She grinned at his matter-of-fact revelation. "Oh, he does, does he? I suppose you have a special skill and insight that allows you to understand baby-speak?"

"I do," Adrian said self-importantly. "I asked him if he

wanted a trip to the park and he jabbered at me for a full five minutes. The translation definitely involved a trip to the park."

His good humor was infectious. "Really."

"Yeah. He also said that his mommy wouldn't want to go, but I should persuade her because she needs the fresh air. So, how about it? We both clock out at six. I can pick you up at half past and we'll be on our way."

Relaxing in the shady confines of the park after being cooped inside all day sounded heavenly, but spending evening after evening with Adrian wasn't wise. He'd wiggle his way into her life and then leave a gaping hole when he left.

Yet what choice did she have? She understood his need to spend time with his son. After being away from Jeremy all day, she treasured their evening hours before he fell asleep and the day's routine of work and day care repeated itself.

She had one problem. More than one, actually, but the two were intertwined. "Without going to the grocery store first, I don't have anything for a picnic."

"All right. We'll spend this evening at the grocery story and save our picnic for Friday."

"It doesn't take an entire evening to go shopping," she pointed out.

"Maybe not for groceries, but there are other things I want to shop for," he said firmly.

"Then you don't need us along. I've learned that shopping with Jeremy is an exercise in patience."

"Yes, but that was when you went alone. You aren't alone any more."

But for how long? she silently wondered.

CHAPTER FIVE

ADRIAN bounded up the sidewalk to Sabrina's door some thirty minutes after he'd left the ER at six, grinning like a loon with excitement. Granted, a shopping expedition wasn't normally something he enjoyed, but he planned to accomplish two objectives in one swoop.

Naturally, he also hoped for the perfect opportunity to kiss her again. Oh, he remembered what she'd said—no more kissing—but after their first experience, it was the only thing he could think about. Tasting her, feeling her body against his, only whetted his appetite for more of the same.

It was amazing how quickly he'd fallen into his old habit of wanting her so badly he ached. He'd only been deluding himself when he'd thought they could work together in the same facility on a platonic basis. They'd always been fuel to each other's fires and limiting their contact to the hours of their shifts wouldn't have changed that.

If not for Jeremy, though, he'd be in a position of only looking and never touching because he wouldn't have been able to convince Sabrina to see him once her shift ended. While he had to proceed slowly and tread softly, now he had unlimited possibilities to remind her of how good they'd been together.

In the back of his mind a little voice taunted him. *An honorable man would respect her wish for you to stay away.*

An honorable man probably would, he privately agreed, but being honorable had provided cold comfort on those days and nights when he'd been alone. Being honorable had cost him a great deal more than he was willing to pay. Being honorable had turned him into a bitter, frustrated man and he wanted to regain his old self. The only way to do that was to coax Sabrina back into his life.

He knocked. At the answering reply of "It's open," he strode in and found Sabrina feeding Jeremy something yellow. From the frowns on the baby's face, he clearly didn't approve of what his mother was shoveling into his mouth as fast as he spit it out.

"What *is* that?" he asked as he approached to tug on Jeremy's socked foot.

The little boy smiled, kicked and waved his arms as if happy to see him, and Adrian's heart flip-flopped with love.

"Squash."

He grimaced. "I don't blame him. By the way, do you always leave the door unlocked?"

"No, I don't, but I knew you were coming. Besides, any self-respecting thief wouldn't waste his time barging in here. I don't own anything that's worth money on the street, unless they're looking for a baby stroller."

Her answer had pacified him, but her reasons had not. "You're assuming everyone who breaks in is a thief. Any pretty single woman living alone needs to be concerned about her personal security. Our Jane Doe should have convinced you of that."

"I'm fine, Adrian. As I said, the door is usually locked."

"Good," he said, recognizing the mulish set to her jaw

as a sign to drop the subject, and he did. "Do we need to make a list for the store?"

"We're only getting picnic food," she said, "not stocking the *Queen Mary*."

"No, but I noticed yesterday that your fridge was quite bare."

She shrugged. "One person doesn't eat that much."

He pressed on, determined to get answers. "I recall a time when your refrigerator was full."

"It was also a time when we were together. We aren't, so I only buy half as much as I did before."

He might have believed her if she hadn't avoided his gaze and if he'd found a few of her favorite foods, but he hadn't. Instead, he'd only seen the items familiar to students who struggled to make ends meet—macaroni and cheese, instant oriental noodles, and cans of tuna.

In his mind, other observations fell into place—her lack of furniture, the absence of her prized stereo system, the tiny apartment in a not-so-good part of town. She hadn't been in these dire straits when she'd lived in Denver and worked at Mercy Memorial. Between the move here and the expense of a baby, she was clearly struggling financially.

Immediately, he felt guilty on many levels. While she might not have much in terms of possessions, one thing she had in abundance was her pride. She probably wouldn't confide in him but he had to try.

"You have a cash-flow problem," he stated.

"What makes you say that?" Once again, she concentrated on Jeremy as if to avoid his gaze.

"The signs are here," he said bluntly. "It took me a while to put them together, but I'm right, aren't I?"

"We have everything we need, Adrian." This time she

met his gaze and glared at him. "Don't imagine or imply that we don't."

"But you're doing without a lot of things."

"We have everything we need," she repeated firmly. "As for doing without, so what if we are? What I do isn't any of your business."

"If it concerns Jeremy, it concerns me."

"It doesn't concern Jeremy," she insisted.

"Tell me what I want to know or I'll ask other people my questions," he warned. "And I don't think you'd want that."

"Oh, all right," she groused, clearly irritated by his persistence. "Yes, money is tight. I ended up with a few more expenses than I'd anticipated, but I'm making headway in my debts."

"How?"

"Whatever you do, Adrian, do *not* offer money because I won't take it. I don't want anything from you. I won't be a charity case again."

He paused, surprised by her vehemence. "Is it that distasteful to accept a helping hand?"

She scoffed. "Absolutely. You pay for your so-called helping hand one way or another. Nothing is ever free."

"I wouldn't ask you to pay."

"Sometimes you pay with something more precious than money. You pay with a part of yourself. When I was growing up I wore my cousins' hand-me-downs because my aunt refused to spend money on new clothes for me. I was told to be grateful.

"I took a paper route so I could have money to buy what the other girls took for granted. I'll never forget the time I stood in the checkout lane and discovered I was a quarter short and had to choose which item I wouldn't buy while people waited impatiently in line for me to finish. A generous soul took pity on me and made up the difference. I was grateful, but had never been so embarrassed."

Now he understand where her strong sense of pride had been born. "OK, if you won't accept a gift, how about a loan?"

"I have all the loans I need. Save your money for Clay…or your redheaded girlfriend. How is she handling your separation these days?"

"I don't know. But as you've mentioned her, I spent last night thinking of all the women I know who fit your description. The only one I can recall was Clay's physical therapist."

"That must have been convenient for you."

Inwardly, he smiled at her sarcasm because he wanted to believe it implied she still cared, even if it was only subconsciously. "Actually, she never came to the house. In fact, once I thought of her, I remembered the day you saw us together. She'd just come from Clay's room to tell me that he could feel his toes. It was quite an emotional moment for all of us."

The anger on her face turned to surprised dismay. "Oh."

"It certainly makes me wonder how differently our lives would have turned out if you two had had better timing," he mused aloud.

"We'll never know, will we?" She took Jeremy out of his carrier. "I'll change his diaper and then we can go."

Adrian knew if he wanted to provide any sort of financial assistance, he'd have to be creative. And he was.

By the time they'd reached the checkout counter at the grocery store, he'd filled the cart to the heaped stage.

"We can't possibly take all this to our picnic tomorrow," she complained. "Apples *and* oranges? Three kinds of cheese. Two pounds of ham and turkey. And all your fresh vegetables will spoil before they're eaten. Unless you plan to invite the entire ER staff to join us."

"Then we'll both be able to pack our lunches," he said, unconcerned.

She tried to separate the package of disposable diapers and the cans of formula away from his items, but he stopped her. "Leave them," he ordered.

"I can pay for Jeremy's things," she protested.

"I'm sure you can," he said smoothly, "but consider this a belated baby-shower present."

"That isn't necessary."

"No, it isn't, but unless you want to make a scene, I'd suggest you simply smile and say 'Thank you'."

For a moment he thought she'd argue. She'd squared her shoulders and looked ready to scold him, but then, as if she realized the futility, her stance relaxed and she offered a resigned half-smile. "Thanks."

The next day, as soon as Sabrina stepped out to take a well-deserved fifteen-minute break, Adrian cornered Hilary. "I saw Sabrina again last night," he commented.

"Again? I thought you two weren't going out at all until Friday?"

He flashed her a sheepish grin. "I jumped the gun. I couldn't wait."

She frowned at him. "As much as I'd like to see Sabrina with someone who'll appreciate her, with all due respect, you're one of those here-today-gone-tomorrow fellas. She doesn't need someone who'll cut out on her just when she's starting to depend on him."

"No, she doesn't," he agreed.

"Long-distance relationships usually don't work out, either."

"Ours will."

"You sound awfully certain."

He was, but of all the things he and Sabrina had discussed, announcing to the world that he was Jeremy's father hadn't been one of them. Once word leaked out—and it would, either by choice or by accident—the staff would treat him differently because their loyalties lay with Sabrina. After enjoying a more congenial work atmosphere and being treated like one of the guys, he selfishly didn't want to ruin a good thing until he proved himself to Sabrina and every one else.

He shrugged. "I have a gut feeling."

"Hmmm. Time will tell," she said ominously before she changed the subject. "What do you think of her little boy?"

"He's great," Adrian said, warming to the subject just as Sabrina always did. "He's so much fun to be around and he does the most interesting things for a baby his age. I've not seen a kid so inquisitive. Why, just last night, he jabbered for so long and was so serious about the noises he was making, it was like having a conversation. And he's so determined to start crawling." He grinned, remembering how Jeremy had maneuvered himself to his hands and knees before looking at Adrian as if to ask, What comes next?

He felt Hilary's careful study, her black-eyed gaze sharp, and hoped he hadn't blown his cover by sounding more like a proud papa than Bree's prospective suitor. "What can I say?" He shrugged. "I like kids."

"You know," she mused aloud, "a lot of men would consider that child as baggage or a necessary evil to get to his mama."

"They would," he agreed, "but I'm not one of them."

"Hmmm." The speculation in her eyes suddenly took on a knowing gleam. "You're his daddy, aren't you?" she asked in her southern drawl.

Startled by her insight as well as her daring, he struggled to frame an answer.

"By the way you're flapping your jaw, I'd say so," the charge nurse decided. She crossed her arms and a mulish expression appeared on her pudgy features. "If you ask me, that girl is far too forgiving, especially after everything she's handled by herself."

"We had a falling out," he said stiffly, "and I didn't know she was pregnant when she left. I'm not proud of the way she had to handle things on her own, but she won't go it alone from now on."

He felt Hilary's gaze as if she was trying to determine his sincerity, then she nodded.

"Good."

"The problem is, I know she's having financial difficulties, but she won't be specific—at least, not to me. Which is why I've come to you for answers."

Sabrina's reasons involved more than pride, he decided. A year's worth of mistrust tagged along, too. He hadn't helped matters either when he'd hinted at pursuing legal action by his fathers-have-rights-too comment. No doubt she was afraid that his more secure financial position would give him an edge with the courts.

So much for hoping she'd tell him about her troubles herself.

"If she won't talk, then I shouldn't, either. Every woman is entitled to her secrets."

"I'm not asking for her account numbers or her bank

balance," he said sharply. "Why don't I tell you what I think and you can tell me if I'm right or wrong?"

Hilary pinched her bottom lip in obvious indecision. "This is against my better judgement," she finally said, "but if you're that boy's daddy, you should know the facts. Just remember, though. You didn't hear this from me."

He pantomimed locking his mouth. "My lips are sealed."

Thinking of the photo he'd seen in her album, he began. "She probably had a rough pregnancy and missed a lot of work."

Hilary clutched the clipboard to her chest. "That isn't the half of it. At first she just had morning sickness, but it lasted all day. There were times I found her retching in the bathroom between patients. In fact, sometimes I thought she was sicker than most of the folks who came in by ambulance. The doctor wanted to admit her, but she refused. She finally agreed to cut her hours to part time and sold a lot of her furniture to make ends meet.

"After that stage finally passed, her blood pressure went haywire. This time she gave in when the doctor told her to stop working because, as she told me, she couldn't afford to lose her baby."

He was all I had. Hilary's words twisted the knife that Sabrina had thrust into his gut. "So Sabrina spent the final months of her pregnancy at home and probably took out a loan for her living expenses," he guessed.

Hilary's nod confirmed his theory.

"But that doesn't explain why she's still broke. Doesn't Pinehaven pay for the employees' single coverage health insurance policies?"

"They do," Hilary agreed, "except for maternity benefits within one year of enrollment in the plan."

That explained it. The situation was worse than he'd thought. A high-interest loan for living expenses, a huge hospital and doctor's bill, as well as expenses associated with a baby meant Sabrina had to stretch her dollar beyond the breaking point. Considering he was responsible for her circumstances, he was surprised Sabrina spoke to him at all.

"So," Hilary said after a soft sigh, "she picks up extra shifts whenever she can."

"How often?"

"Once, sometimes twice a week. In fact, she shouldn't be here today, but one of the nurses wanted to attend her niece's wedding, so Sabrina agreed to cover."

His head reeled from what he'd heard. No wonder she looked as if a strong wind would blow her into the next state. "I knew money was tight," he said hoarsely, "but I had no idea her finances were this bad."

"You aren't going to get all high and mighty, are you?" she asked, frowning. "Because if you do, you can forget having picnics or anything else with her. The girl doesn't have much, but she's got plenty of pride."

"More than enough," he agreed. But, pride or not, he knew his duty. It was time to take matters into his own hands and proceed with the rest of his plan.

"What are you going to do?" Hilary asked. "She has this aversion to accepting charity."

"There's more than one way to take a temperature, but it's best you don't know the details. That way, if she questions you, you can honestly tell her you don't know anything."

"Oh, good idea."

"Rest assured, her circumstances will improve."

Hilary's grin slowly grew to spread across her entire face. "This I can't wait to see."

"And you won't breathe a word about this to anyone?"

"Not one word," she agreed, "but I never would have guessed I'd run into Santa Claus in August."

Santa Claus he wasn't. Writing a check wouldn't come close to putting him in the same league as the jolly, benevolent fellow but it would serve as the first installment toward paying for his sins.

"It was a good idea to come here this evening." Sabrina sat on the blanket under the shade of the tree Adrian had chosen and stared at Jeremy, who was sitting contentedly between Adrian's spread legs, apparently fascinated by the hem of Adrian's khaki shorts.

"It was Jeremy's, not mine," he said.

If he wanted to give their son the credit, that was his prerogative. She was too relaxed to argue. "I don't care whose idea it was, it was a good one."

"I'm not so sure," he admitted, wiping the beads of perspiration off his forehead. "It's still over ninety degrees. We should either be lounging in a pool or sitting in air-conditioned comfort."

"We don't mind the heat, do we, sprout?" She leaned over and smoothed down Jeremy's wispy hair, eliciting a toothy grin. "This way, we have the park to ourselves. Right now, a pool would be too crowded for us to enjoy."

"Not true," he protested. "And the view would be great. You always did look fantastic in a swimsuit."

Her face warmed under his hungry gaze, as much a result of his compliment as her own heated thoughts. She hadn't forgotten their last trip to a pool even though it seemed like a lifetime ago. Adrian's knee-length trunks had covered a fair amount of skin, but the black Spandex had outlined well-defined quadriceps and a trim gluteus maximus to mouth-drooling, take-a-second-look perfection.

"That was before I had a baby," she said lightly, before she felt his perusal.

"Every pound you gained must have been Junior here, because it looks as if you've lost weight."

"A little," she admitted, "but keeping up with an infant and a hectic work schedule will do that."

"Hmmm," he said, sounding unconvinced. In the next instant his expression changed as he yelped.

Concern brought her to her feet as she watched him rub at a spot on his shin. "What's wrong? Was it a bee? Did you get stung? Is Jeremy—?"

"Jeremy's fine," Adrian said calmly. "He just discovered the hair on my leg."

"Oh. Is that all?" she teased, relieved there hadn't been any danger. "From the sound of your scream, I thought you were mortally wounded."

"I didn't scream. I yelped," he pointed out.

"There's a difference?" she teased.

"You bet there is. Women scream. Men yelp." Jeremy grabbed at his leg again, and Adrian grabbed his little hand and kissed it. "Our son needs a new toy. Pass his bag, will you?"

Sabrina handed the drawstring tote to him and tried not to like the sound of "our son" too much. That particular pronoun implied a connection—a bond—that went beyond the two of them physically creating a baby together.

Idly, she wondered if Jeremy himself wasn't providing the healing balm they needed to truly bury the past. Time would tell.

Adrian dug inside the bag and pulled out a set of plastic

rings, but Jeremy batted them away. "OK, try this." He held out a stuffed mouse and pinched its sides until it squeaked. Again, Jeremy refused his offering.

"One more time," he said as he thrust his hand back into the bag and drew out another item. "Well, well, what do you know? My toothbrush." He studied it with a furrowed brow as if trying to figure out how this particular item had become a toy, especially a toy with deep gouges in the plastic grip. "There are tooth marks on it."

They'd been caught, her secret was out! "When I was collecting your things while you were in hospital, Jeremy wanted to hold it. By the time I got it away from him, he'd left his mark. I couldn't let you see it without explaining everything, so it became his."

"And you bought me a new one."

"Yes."

Immediately, Jeremy reached for the brush and grunted. As soon as Adrian handed it over, Jeremy began gnawing on the bright blue handle.

"I think he likes the color," she said tentatively, hoping Adrian wouldn't comment on her duplicity.

Instead he smiled. "We'll have to teach him the other end belongs in his mouth."

"You're not upset?"

"About him playing with my toothbrush? No. For you not using it as an opportunity to tell me about him? I'm more disappointed than upset, but I'll get over it."

Jeremy alternated between beating the brush against his leg like a drumstick and chewing on it as if it were a teething ring. "I'm just grateful you didn't recycle it as a toilet brush," Adrian added.

"There is that possibility," she said lightly.

"So what *do* you do on your days off?"

"Clean the house, go to the laundromat, sew, take care of Jeremy."

"I didn't hear you mention golf."

"After the way I sliced the ball the other day, isn't it rather obvious I haven't played for a long time?" she asked wryly.

"Everyone slices the ball. I'll bet Tiger Woods does every now and then, too."

She laughed. "Somehow, I doubt it, but thanks for being so forgiving. If you must know, the benefit tournament was the first time I'd set foot on the Pinehaven course. Green fees are horrific and I don't golf enough to justify paying for membership. I'd also have to pay a babysitter, which I'm not able, er, willing to do." She hoped he hadn't noticed her slip of the tongue. It was bad enough that he knew she was having trouble making ends meet; he didn't need to know just how financially strapped she was. With information like that, it would be hard to say what a judge might decide if Adrian forced a custody issue.

"Honestly, though," she continued, "I'd rather spend my free hours with Jeremy. The hospital day care is great, but it makes his day rather long. On the other hand, working twelve-hour stretches means I usually work three days a week instead of four or five."

"Unless you fill in for someone else."

"It happens from time to time," she agreed.

His blue-eyed gaze seemed to see into her thoughts. "Hilary mentioned you tend to pick up at least one extra shift a week, sometimes two."

Surely the well-meaning nurse hadn't explained that her bills were her main reason for working those additional hours. "A lot of nurses covered for me when I was pregnant, so I reciprocate whenever I can." She raised her chin in defiance. "Jeremy doesn't suffer for it. Our hospital day care is excellent."

He raised an eyebrow. "I'm sure it is. Did I imply that he seemed deprived because he spent the day without his mother?"

"No," she said slowly, "but you'd always said…" Her voice died before she could complete her sentence.

"I always said what?"

"It doesn't matter."

"It does. I want you to finish. I'd always said what?"

"That you wanted your wife to stay at home for the kids. That you didn't want a sitter to raise them."

"What's wrong with that? If I had a wife, it would be the ideal situation, but we both know life doesn't allow for many ideal situations. Who knows?" He shrugged. "She may pursue a career instead of being a stay-at-home mom, and if that's the case, I wouldn't stand in her way. As for Jeremy, if he's at the best day care possible, I'm satisfied."

Suddenly the discussion took on an ominous tone. She didn't want to think about Adrian getting married. The notion of sending her baby for another woman to love— or possibly mistreat—sent a cold shiver down her spine. But she had to know how imminent or remote the possibility was.

"Now that I know about the woman I saw you with that time," she said lightly to hide her concern, "you've been footloose for the past year. I'm sure you've dated. Did you meet a potential candidate for a wife?"

"No," he admitted as he placed Jeremy on his tummy and shifted positions. "I've been too busy with work and Clay's therapy to see anyone. Plus, I haven't been the nicest of guys, so even if I'd wanted to go out, women have steered clear of me."

"Really? I find that hard to believe. As I recall, the nurses collectively drooled over you." At the time, she could hardly believe someone so handsome and debonair who could have had his pick of available—and the not-so-available—women had chosen *her*. Of course, he'd eventually dropped her like a hot potato, but that was beside the point.

He smiled. "Not any more. People tend to avoid bears with sore heads."

At that moment Jeremy began to fuss, and Sabrina was grateful for the interruption. She rose and stretched out the kinks in her back. "Sounds like he's had enough of the park experience for one evening."

"Probably so."

Back at her house, Sabrina prepared Jeremy's evening snack of cereal with a dollop of strained fruit while Adrian bounced the fussy baby as they paced her tiny living room like a pair of caged tigers. "How much longer?" Adrian asked.

"It's ready now." She set the bowl on the table. "And if I remember correctly, it's your turn to feed him."

"Oh, sure," Adrian commented good-naturedly. "When he's in a grumpy mood, I get the honor."

"Hey, I'm just giving what you asked for, and that was to share the routine. Would you rather unpack and sterilize his bottles?"

He grimaced. "Pass the spoon."

So, while Adrian fed Jeremy, Sabrina took care of her tasks at the sink. As she listened to Adrian's one-sided conversation with their son and Jeremy's smacking lips, she realized how family-like this scene seemed. Mom and Dad sharing in the care of a baby. This was what she would have had from the beginning and it would be what she'd have in the years ahead if only events had transpired differently...

No, she told herself. Don't go there. The "what if" and "if only" paths only led to unfulfilled dreams and disappointment. But for a long moment she wished that *she* could be the recipient of Adrian's attention, that he'd come for the sole purpose to visit *her* and not Jeremy.

She was being ridiculous. Why *would* he bother? She'd already warned him away after he'd kissed her so why would he break the rules and risk not being able to see his son?

As impossible as their circumstances were, she wanted him to break the rules.

Pathetic. She was positively pathetic. In a few short months they'd go their separate ways again and she'd be left with more recent memories to haunt her.

Much later, after Jeremy had eaten, splashed in the sink, and drunk his last bottle for the evening nestled in Sabrina's lap, and after she'd carefully laid him in his crib, Adrian hesitated at the front door.

"What do you have planned tomorrow?" he asked.

"Chores, laundry. Like I told you earlier, the usual stuff."

"Do you mind if I spend the day here?"

"Do you want to?" she asked, surprised by his request.

"Spending a few hours every day with you and Jeremy isn't an obligation," he insisted. "It's something I want to do. Provided you agree."

Part of her was thrilled by his request because in these few short days she'd gotten spoiled by having him nearby. They still had unresolved issues, but they were talking like the friends they had once been instead of sparring like enemies.

It wouldn't be wise for her to fall in love with him again

because it could easily happen if he continued acting like the man she'd loved nearly two years ago.

Unwilling to say yes and hating to say no, she chose her words carefully. "Are you sure you don't want a few days to yourself in an apartment that's bigger than a postage stamp? One with more comfortable furniture than a broken-down recliner?"

"We had some good times in that recliner. Not as many as on your sofa, but enough. If I stayed in my quiet apartment, what would I do all day besides read the newspaper or watch television? The only people I know in town are those I work with, you and Jeremy, and I'd rather hang around with you two."

"I assumed you'd go back to Denver on the weekends. Back to your other life." Actually, she hadn't thought that far ahead, but her idea made sense.

"I'd planned to," he confessed, "but that was before I knew about Jeremy. As for my so-called 'other' life, it's so similar to this one, it's ridiculous. I go to work and I come home, watch the news, and eat take-out. The only difference is that I don't have any home maintenance projects or yardwork here."

For a man who liked to stay busy, she understood how stressful it would be to live a life of relative leisure. However, no matter how bored he might be, regardless of how much she'd come to enjoy his company, *she* needed some distance. Being in his near-constant presence was reviving her fairy-tale imagination where the prince found his Cinderella and everyone lived happily ever after. Those fantasies simply weren't going to happen.

"In any case, I need to drive back on Sunday to pick up my mail and make new arrangements with my neighbor who's watching the house. I was hoping you and Jeremy would come along."

Logically, it wasn't a wise idea to go anywhere with Adrian. In her heart, though, she wanted it more than she should. "It isn't a good idea for us to spend so much time together," she said gently.

"Are you saying I can't see Jeremy?"

"No, I just don't think we should be together every single day."

"I'm only in town for a few months, remember? I'd like to create as many memories as I can in the short time I have."

Phrased like that, she couldn't argue with or deny his request. If the situation were reversed, she'd ask for the same consideration. However, at the same time she didn't have to ask what his future plans were. He'd stated plainly he would leave at the end of his contract period.

Surprisingly enough, the idea irritated her. How could he think it would be acceptable to breeze in, make himself indispensable for a few months, then disappear?

For that reason alone she wanted to pass the weekend like all the previous ones—just her and her son. Cooperating with him might be in her future best interests, but cooperation would also come at great emotional expense. After being around him for less than a week, she didn't know if she could guard against falling for his charm again. She was in a no-win situation.

Reluctantly and against her better judgement, she consented. "OK. We'll go with you."

His eyes lit up and a smile spread across his face. "Great. We don't have to leave too early and we'll be back in plenty of time so we won't disrupt Jeremy's bedtime schedule. Thanks, Bree."

He stepped forward and planted a firm but swift kiss on her mouth before he withdrew. "Sorry," he said, clearly unrepentant. "Don't be angry, but I couldn't help myself."

The kiss had ended before it had really begun, but it had lasted long enough to stir those unwanted and unrealistic romantic feelings. Irritated by her weakness for a man who'd once shattered her world, she simply pretended to be exasperated by his blatant disregard for their rules. "Yeah right."

"It's true," he insisted, his eyes twinkling. "Thanks for being so understanding and generous. We're going to have a wonderful weekend. Wait and see."

Understanding and generous, hah! He should have described her as a pushover—a sucker for a sad story—but it was too late to change her mind when she'd already agreed. She only hoped she wouldn't live to regret her hasty and completely irrational decision.

CHAPTER SIX

ADRIAN bounded up the walk on Sunday morning, eager for the impending trip. He'd already phoned Clay and invited him to his house that afternoon for a surprise, and he couldn't wait to see the look on his brother's face when he discovered he was an uncle!

He knocked impatiently on Sabrina's door and heard Jeremy's muted wail. Smiling at the volume, he began to worry when she didn't answer and Jeremy didn't stop crying. Taking a chance, because Sabrina knew when he'd arrive, he tried the knob and found it unlocked. Pushing his way inside, he went straight to Jeremy's playpen where he lay kicking and screaming.

"What's wrong, big fella?" he crooned as he hoisted Jeremy into his arms. "Are you hungry, wet, or just tired of being stuck in your playpen alone?"

Jeremy sniffled and bobbed his head against Adrian's shoulder.

"Sabrina?" Adrian called.

She came out of the bathroom, still wearing a short-sleeved sleep shirt that fell to mid-thigh and revealed plenty of long leg. "You're here," she said inanely as she finger-combed her hair.

"It's ten o'clock," he pointed out. "We'd planned to leave for our trip, remember?"

She visibly winced. "We can't go."

He bounced Jeremy and frowned. "Why not?"

"I'm not able to take a trip today. I'm sorry."

Disappointment sent his upbeat spirits into a downward spiral, but he suddenly noticed the dark circles under her eyes, her abnormally pale face and shaky hands. Immediately concerned, he asked, "What's wrong?"

She heaved a sigh, almost as if she hated to admit her problem. "Migraine."

He'd forgotten she suffered from those intense headaches. "When did it start?"

"Last night, after you left. I thought it would ease if I went to bed early, but it hasn't."

He'd seen her like this before. Nothing had cut the pain except medication and rest. "Did you take your pills?"

Slowly, she headed for the kitchen and he followed, watching her gingerly grab a bag of peas from the freezer and place it just as carefully on her forehead. "Well?" he demanded.

"No."

He cursed. "Why not?"

"I don't have a prescription."

"Why don't you?"

"Because it expired and I haven't asked my doctor to write another. Even if I did, I wouldn't fill it because those pills are too expensive." She repositioned the frozen peas to cover the right side of her head. "I'll be fine in a few hours."

"You and I both know an ice pack won't do the trick," he said bluntly.

"Yes, well, ice and over-the-counter pain relievers and

anti-inflammatories are all I have. They worked before and they'll work again."

"On an attack this severe? How often do you get them? Are you avoiding your triggers?"

She held up one hand. "Turn down the volume, please."

Instantly contrite, he lowered his voice. "Sorry. How often are you getting these headaches?"

"Not often. Every couple of months."

"What can I do?"

"Nothing. I'm really sorry we can't go with you, but have fun and call us when you get back into town."

Leave her like this? When she could hardly walk, much less take care of Jeremy? His trip didn't seem important right now. "You're not in any shape to look after yourself, much less a baby."

"I can handle it," she insisted. "I've done it before and I'll do it again. Don't give us another thought."

"Sorry, Bree, but there's no way I'm leaving you to manage on your own. You can hardly stand. How are you going to lift or carry him?"

"I'll call Kate if I run into a problem."

"You already had a problem," he said flatly. "How long would Jeremy have cried in his playpen if I hadn't walked in when I did?"

"Not long," she said defensively.

"Why call Kate when I'm already here?" He tried not to feel hurt by her obvious rejection. Apparently these past few days hadn't convinced her to rely on him. How ironic to realize he'd finally tasted a dose of his own medicine.

"My trip to Denver can wait for another day. You…" he grabbed her arm as much to steady her as to lead her "…are going straight to bed."

"I can't. Too many chores."

"We did everything yesterday from laundry to grocery shopping to vacuuming," he reminded her. "I can't imagine what we left undone, but whatever it is can wait another day or two."

"Jeremy's hungry," she said.

"Then I'll feed him."

"But—"

"If you don't trust me to take care of him, then tell me how to contact Kate," he said, hoping she wouldn't.

To his great relief, she didn't. "Fine." She gave in wearily. "Go for it. But if you have a question…"

"I'll ask you," he promised.

"Emergency numbers are posted by the phone. Poison control, his pediatrician, the hospital."

He wanted to remind her of his own medical degree, then decided it was simpler and faster to listen to her spiel about where to find the teething rings, extra diapers and a spare pacifier in case the primary binky got lost—in the freezer, under the bathroom sink, and in his dresser, respectively.

While she wrapped up her instructions, he placed Jeremy in the swing contraption, wound the handle and set the seat in motion before guiding her into the bedroom. "Come on. You'll feel better after you lie down."

He'd expected more of an argument, but she obviously felt terrible because she meekly let him help her onto the mattress. An instant later, he closed the blinds against the morning sun and left the room.

"It's you and me, bud," he told Jeremy. "Hang tight and I'll be right back."

A phone call, a diaper change and a bottle of warm formula later, Jeremy was fast asleep.

Debating on whether or not to cart him along on his errand of mercy, he wondered what would be worse. Sabrina waking up and discovering Jeremy was missing, or Jeremy crying and she couldn't respond? He chose to haul the baby with him.

Just in case she did stir before he got home again, he scribbled a note and placed it in Jeremy's crib, then quietly left the house. After some struggles due to inexperience, he strapped the baby carrier in backwards as he'd seen his friends do with their children's safety seats, and carefully drove to a nearby pharmacy.

By the time he returned, both mother and baby were still asleep. He opted to address Sabrina's needs first.

"Sabrina," he said softly, as he shook one large, white tablet out of the prescription bottle, "swallow this."

She opened bleary eyes. "What is it?"

"Your migraine pill."

"How…? Where…?"

"Don't ask questions, just sit up and swallow."

As soon as she'd downed the medicine, along with a liberal amount of water, she sank back onto her pillow. "Thanks," she mumbled, closing her eyes.

Suddenly hesitant to leave, he watched her and noticed the lines of strain around her eyes and mouth. In days past she would have welcomed one of his head and neck massages until the pill took the edge off her pain. Now she wouldn't appreciate his efforts.

As he settled Jeremy in his crib, he heard her whimper in her sleep. *Oh, what the hell*, he thought. She might not want his non-traditional therapy, but he had to do more than twiddle his thumbs and watch her suffer.

He perched on the edge of the bed, touched her temples

with a feather-light caress, then began his gentle massage. If she only took her over-the-counter meds every few months instead of two or three times a week, then she wasn't setting herself up for a complication known as "rebound" headaches—a condition when the treatment actually caused the headache instead of relieving it.

As he ran through his med-school lecture by a neurologist on this very subject, he remembered how migraines loved change. Any variations in one's life, whether it involved a disruption in the sleep cycle, missed meals or being exposed to sudden stress, could easily act as the trigger.

From what he'd seen during the past week, any one or all of those things could be the culprit. Babies weren't known to have regular sleeping habits; Sabrina obviously didn't eat properly or regularly; and his appearance in her life had clearly raised her stress level.

With painstaking care, he gradually smoothed away the tension with slow, soothing strokes. By the time the furrows between her brows became less pronounced, he began noticing as well as remembering other things—like how soft her skin felt. How her hair smelled like spring flowers. How it felt to have her long legs wrapped around him. How the curve of her breasts beckoned for his hands…

He wanted her badly, but he didn't feel worthy of this woman. He'd failed her in so many ways and he considered himself lucky that he'd wriggled his way this far into her good graces. Unfortunately, he still wasn't to the point where she willingly depended on him. The only reason he was sitting beside her now was because she'd been too wiped out from the pain to protest.

He wanted to be her first choice, not the consolation prize. Dammit, he *wanted* to be here with her and their son twenty-four seven, not just for a few hours every evening. He wanted to watch Jeremy take his first steps, to hear his first recognizable words, to teach him new things and see his wide-eyed wonderment. He wanted to give Jeremy a brother or a sister.

Family meant everything to him. It always had and always would. His father had passed his responsibility for his children to Adrian and he'd willingly accepted them. Now he wanted to accept one more. Regardless of the details surrounding Jeremy's conception, that small child was *his* to nurture and to take care of. He simply had to figure out a way to juggle both sets of commitments in two different locations.

He leaned over and brushed his mouth against hers. "We *will* work something out, Bree," he whispered. "Count on it."

To his surprise, she murmured, "I waited for you…but you took so long. So very long…"

It had only been twelve hours since he'd last seen her and she considered that to be a long time? She could have called him and he would have broken speed records to drive across town, until he realized he'd never given her his cellphone number and she'd never asked.

"I'm here now, Bree," he said instead.

Her hand moved to her abdomen. "Can you feel our baby kicking? Do you want a boy or a girl?"

In that instant, he realized she was caught up in a state where dreams and memories intermingled and she was talking in her sleep.

"I don't care," he said hoarsely, "as long as it's healthy."

"Me, too." She sighed. "I'm so tired."

"Then sleep."

"You'll stay? Beside me?"

He hesitated, knowing how tough it would be to lie next to her without driving himself utterly crazy, but there was no other place he'd rather be at this particular moment.

"I'll stay." Carefully, he got in to bed from the other side, then pulled her against him.

"Love you," she mumbled.

The words caught him by surprise before he decided she had to be dreaming. He may have made progress in paying for his sins, but she was still too wary to hand her heart over to him so easily.

She would, though. He'd failed at other things in his life, but he wouldn't at this one.

Sabrina slowly drifted awake with the most wonderful sense of well-being. It was unbelievable because normally, when the migraine pain faded, she woke up feeling exhausted. She grabbed her watch off the bedside table and read the display. Twelve-fifteen.

How could she feel this good after a two-hour nap? But it had to be, because the sun was shining. She couldn't have slept for twenty-four hours, but as she glanced at the date on her watch face, she realized it was true. A full day had passed.

Jeremy! Dear heavens, who'd taken care of him if she'd slept that long?

Fear speared her chest as she took in the empty bed and she bolted upright. The diaper bag was missing, too. Ready to call 911 and report a child abduction, she noticed a piece of paper taped to the crib's headboard.

The note was in Adrian's handwriting.

She snatched it free and scanned it. *Dear Bree*, it began. *Don't worry about Jeremy. I took him to the hospital day care. He'll be there, waiting for you to pick him up, but if*

*you don't find this before I get off duty, I'll bring him by
on my way home. Adrian.*

*P.s. You're officially on a sick day today. Hilary says to
take care of yourself.*

Relieved Jeremy was in a safe place, she was also
furious with Adrian's presumptuous decision to report her
as sick. He didn't have the right!

Common sense, however, said she was fighting a
foolish battle. Those extra hours of uninterrupted sleep
had been exactly what she'd needed; on previous occasions, she'd carried on as usual and had felt drained for
days. Instead of finding fault, she should thank him from
the bottom of her heart.

She sank onto the edge of the bed and tried to recall
the previous day, but only bits and pieces came to mind.
Adrian had come by for their trip, but she'd sent him
away. He couldn't have gone to Denver, because he'd
always seemed to be waking her to take a pill or to drink
something. Which reminded her…she'd have to reimburse him for her prescription.

At one point, she was certain he'd kissed her, because
she'd imagined the feel of his lips on hers, but that had
surely been a dream, hadn't it?

She'd also felt cozy and secure, almost as if he'd held
her, but either her subconscious had worked overtime or
she'd dredged up ancient memories. Yet, as she gazed at
the pillow beside hers and noticed a faint indentation as if
someone's head had rested there, she came to an undeni-
able conclusion.

Adrian had spent the night there. He hadn't just spent
the night, either. He'd *slept* with her, in her room, in her bed.

Oh, my. No wonder she'd felt so warm and cozy. She'd

always gravitated to his warmth because she was usually cold, so she had probably used him as her pillow and blanket. For a woman who'd tried to maintain emotional distance, how would she face him?

There was nothing *to* face, she scolded herself. She'd practically been unconscious, and if she'd made any inappropriate overtures, Adrian would chalk them up to her being out of her mind with pain. He wouldn't have taken advantage of her, because at heart he *was* an honorable man.

As she gazed at Jeremy's crib, she couldn't quite decide if she should feel grateful for Adrian's help or not. The truth of the matter was that she'd tried calling Kate as soon as she'd noticed the blind spots in her vision some thirty minutes before the pain had hit, but Kate hadn't answered. While she'd battled with her pride about contacting Adrian because she hated to give him any reason to doubt her ability to take care of Jeremy, her migraine struck full force. In the end, she'd had to rely on him.

That wasn't quite true. She hadn't *had* to do anything. She could have insisted that he track down Kate. Even though he wouldn't have wanted to, he would have because she'd asked.

She wasn't reluctant to trust him with Jeremy; even in the middle of her migraine attack, she'd known her son had been safe with him. What wasn't safe, though, was her heart because much as it pained her to admit it, she was falling in love with him all over again. And that fact made it far too easy to pretend they were a happy family.

The problem was, she *shouldn't* love him. She did once, and look where it had gotten her. Starting over in a new community with a new job, pregnant, all sorts of expenses. In her opinion, it was far too dangerous, not to mention horribly one-sided to love him again when Jeremy was the only glue holding them together. She simply had to rein in her wishful thinking. Maybe she could reluctantly accept that his motives had been altruistic and he'd only been trying to spare her, but what would happen the next time?

OK, so she knew he took his familial responsibilities seriously and probably wouldn't repeat his past mistake, but it was all about Jeremy. No matter what happened and to whom, he'd never push Jeremy away because he wanted him in his life in the worst way. To Adrian, she would simply be the means to his end because to get to Jeremy, he had to go through her first.

How pitiful for her to be jealous of her own son!

But thinking of her energetic baby with his ready smile and sweet temperament made her realize how badly she wanted him in her arms, at home. If she had gotten an extra day off, she intended to spend as much of it as possible with the little boy who was her entire life.

Adrian had never considered himself a clock-watcher, but he did today. He'd wanted to call Sabrina to see how she was doing, but if she was sleeping—and he hoped she was—he didn't want to wake her. He also hoped that his efforts yesterday would finally break through their relationship stalemate.

The sudden appearance of a tall fellow with a haggard expression on his face interrupted his thoughts. "I'm Dr Malloy. Thomas Malloy. I understand you treated a Jane Doe last week?"

"Yes, I did. How can I help you?"

"I'm her husband. May we talk privately?"

"Sure." Adrian led him to the small medical staff office

and closed the door. "I probably can't tell you much because of the privacy acts."

"I know. I've already spoken to the police and they told me everything. What I'd like to know is your impression of her mental state."

"Her amnesia," Adrian guessed.

"Yes."

"Her neurologist and psychiatrist could give you more information than I can," he began.

"Probably, if I could reach them," Thomas said impatiently. "According to their secretaries, both are tied up until late this afternoon. I'd like to know something *now*."

Adrian understood the man's frustration. "Have you seen your wife yet?"

Thomas shook his head. "I was out of town at a conference when I got the news my wife was missing. You see, before I left, Abigail told me she was seeing an attorney and wanted to file for a divorce. She asked me to cancel my trip so we could talk but as one of the conference organizers, I couldn't. So…" He sighed heavily. "She arranged to visit a friend in Breckenridge while I was gone. Supposedly to think.

"Unfortunately," Thomas continued, "she hadn't confirmed her plans with her old roommate, so when Abby didn't arrive, Rosie just thought she'd changed her mind and didn't question her absence until Abby's mother called because she hadn't been able to reach her. We started searching and found her here." He paused. "When I think of what that bastard did…what happened to her…." His voice broke. "Part of me is glad she forgot all that and part of me wants her to remember this guy so he can pay."

Adrian felt for the man's pain. "I understand, but if it's

any consolation, when she was in our ED, she seemed to be handling herself well. She was scared because she couldn't remember the details of her life that we take for granted, but she was calm and in relatively good health. I haven't seen her since we transferred her upstairs, so she may have regained some of her memory."

"According to the detective, she hasn't." He ran his hands through his hair. "The question is, if she wanted a divorce, do I let her go through with it, even though she can't remember?"

Adrian hesitated. He was the last person on earth to ask for marital advice. "I'm not the best person to advise you," he began. "I'm not—"

"I'm not asking for a medical opinion. I guess I'm just thinking out loud, one man to another."

Although Adrian didn't know this man, he couldn't turn his back on a fellow physician. If Malloy wanted a sounding board, Adrian would oblige. "What do *you* want to do?"

"I don't want her to leave," he said hoarsely. "The police told me we have a baby coming—our first—so I'll do whatever it takes to convince her to change her mind. I'll cut my hours, spend more time with her and the baby when it arrives, whatever. I want a second chance."

Although his own situation wasn't as dramatic as Thomas Malloy's, Adrian knew exactly how the man felt. "If that's what you want, then you should take it."

Thomas nodded. "I almost feel guilty, as if I'm tricking her, but her amnesia gives us a clean slate. We can write an entirely new future for our marriage on it."

"And if she ever does remember?" Adrian hated playing the devil's advocate, but the man needed to think of every angle.

"By then, I hope we'll have restored enough of our relationship to make her wonder why she wanted a divorce in the first place."

Adrian held out his hand. "Good luck, then. Let me know how everything turns out."

"Thanks," Thomas said, shaking Adrian's hand with a firm grip. "I will."

For the rest of the morning, Malloy's words echoed in Adrian's head. *You have a clean slate. A clean slate. A clean slate.* Several patients later, he decided to take Malloy's comment to heart.

After lunch, and after he'd explained to Maria Rios that her blood pressure was still too high and she needed to stay until they saw a response to her hypertension medication, he opened the exam-room door and heard a familiar baby laugh.

Immediately he smiled and strode toward the nurses' station, marveling at how quickly he'd learned to recognize his son's voice. "Someone's happy," he remarked as he came up to the staff gathered there.

"He loves the attention," Sabrina said, looking like a completely different woman from the one he'd seen yesterday. From the glow on her face, no one would ever know she'd suffered a debilitating migraine twenty-four hours ago.

"A typical male response when surrounded by adoring women," he said as he tugged on one of Jeremy's socked feet, eliciting another giggle and a fair amount of joyful kicking. "Lucky fellow."

"I'll say." Hilary smiled fondly at Jeremy. "Makes me eager for grandkids. Until then, I'll just have to spoil this one." She addressed Adrian. "Is Mrs Rios ready to go home?"

"Not until her blood pressure comes down. I want it taken every fifteen minutes. Call me as soon as there's a change."

"Will do." Hilary snapped her fingers at the staff still hovering around the desk. "Come on, people, back to work."

The group scattered, leaving Adrian and Sabrina behind. "I see you stopped at day care. I hope I sent enough stuff with him."

"You did. I just stopped by to let you know you didn't have to bring him home."

"I wouldn't have minded."

"Now you don't need to. Anyway, I just wanted to say thanks, for yesterday. For everything."

"You're welcome. It was my pleasure."

"You should have woke me this morning, though. I could have managed Jeremy myself."

Sensing she was trying to prove a point, he simply nodded. "Probably, but I'd say those few extra hours of sleep made a difference."

"I appreciate it, but I'm sorry you missed your trip on my account."

"I took care of nearly everything by phone. Clay's coming by tonight with my mail and to have dinner with us, so no harm done."

"Dinner? With us?"

"Yeah. I invited him to your place so I hope you don't mind, but it seemed easier for Jeremy's schedule if we spent the evening there rather than at my apartment. By the way, did you notice the steaks in your refrigerator?"

She shook her head. "No. But, Adrian," she protested, "I don't have a grill and—"

"Not to worry. Harvey's Hardware will deliver one this afternoon."

Her gaze narrowed. "What happens to the grill when you leave? I can't keep—"

"You'll use it and if you don't want the hassle when you're alone, I'll fire it up when I visit on the weekends. Remember?" He grabbed the handle on Jeremy's carrier and lifted him off the counter. "I hate to run, but if I don't get back to work, Hilary will scold me. I've learned it's not a good thing to land on the head nurse's bad side. So, I'll see you both tonight."

He strolled away, laughing inside at how he'd left Sabrina speechless. He'd enjoy his small victory while he could because when he arrived at her house tonight, the tables would be turned and he wouldn't get a word in edgewise.

CHAPTER SEVEN

"THANKS for the nice evening," Clay told Sabrina as he prepared to leave. "I had a great time meeting my nephew. I hope we can do this again."

"Absolutely," she said as she matched his uneven gait down the sidewalk while Adrian remained inside to give Jeremy his last bottle for the night. "You're welcome to drop by whenever you're in town."

"Thanks." He paused before he slid inside his blue Ford Mustang. "For what it's worth, I hope you two get back together."

She'd like that too, but only for the right reasons. "It's hard to say what will happen," she prevaricated. "Too many roadblocks are in the way." She didn't feel inclined to say that beyond the obvious issue of the physical distance between them, the biggest speed bump on her highway to happiness would be his motive.

"Road blocks are usually temporary and can be moved," he reminded her.

She laughed at his hopeful tone. "True, but it's dangerous to move them if the hazard is still on the other side."

He met her gaze calmly. "A preacher once told me that love covers a multitude of sins. Do you love him?"

Heaven help her, but she did. Every kind thing he'd done in the past week had built on the one before, but his selfless act on Sunday had turned the tide in his favor. The only problem was, he only did those kind things out of concern for Jeremy's welfare, not because he wanted to do them for *her*.

"My feelings aren't the issue," she countered as she met Clay's gaze. "Adrian's interest lies solely with Jeremy. As you know, he's fanatical about meeting his responsibilities. Right now, every choice he makes is with him in mind."

"If you say so," he said dubiously, "but I think you're wrong."

"We'll see," she said as she hugged him goodbye to purposely end the conversation. "Drive carefully and don't be a stranger. Jeremy wants to spend time with his favorite uncle."

She waited until Clay drove off before she went inside to find Adrian coming out of her bedroom. Funny, how it seemed so natural for him to have full rein of her whole house. What would it be like when he wasn't there? She didn't want to think of how empty the place would seem.

"He's asleep so soon?" she asked.

"He's had a busy day. I presume Clay's on his way home?"

"Yeah. I was glad to see him."

"Me, too. Did you think he looked OK?"

"I haven't seen him in over a year," she reminded him. "And he doesn't look anything like he did when I saw him in hospital. Why do you ask?"

"I thought he seemed a bit pale. He didn't have much of an appetite, either."

"He polished off a salad, a large steak and a baked potato. If that wasn't much of an appetite, then I'd hate to feed him when he has one."

"You're right. It's my imagination. By the way, I found out who our Jane Doe is. Her husband stopped by to see me today."

"Really? Who is she?"

"Abigail Malloy. Before her attack, she'd apparently told her husband she was going to file for a divorce. Now that she doesn't remember, Thomas intends to fight for his marriage."

"Oh?"

"Abby's amnesia gave him a clean slate and he wants to take advantage of it. Time will tell if he's successful."

"Or if his plan backfires when she remembers."

"That, too. With any luck, when that day comes, Thomas will have shown her he's not such a bad guy after all." He hesitated. "OK, let's have it."

"Have what?"

"The tongue-lashing you've been dying to give me all evening."

She sank onto the brand-new sofa that had arrived at four o'clock, right before the hardware store had delivered the gas grill. "Patience is a virtue. Besides, knowing you're waiting for the bomb to fall is half the fun."

"Gee, thanks," he said wryly as he sat on the other end of the sofa. "I think I'd rather hear you yelling."

"I do not yell," she said loftily.

"Point taken, but you have to admit you weren't very happy with me when I got home tonight."

And she'd thought she'd hidden her feelings so well. "I wasn't."

"I assume you didn't like Jeremy's gifts."

"I completely understand why you bought presents for him. What boy wouldn't want a play golf set, a baseball mitt or a tricycle? Those were thoughtful things and I certainly wouldn't deny him a single one, even if they are several years ahead of their time."

"It never hurts to be prepared. If you don't care about Jeremy's toys, what's the problem?"

She stared at him, incredulous. "The problem is the *other* stuff. The stuff you had delivered," she reminded him.

"You didn't like the grill? I bought it because it was a lot like your old one. The one you don't own any more."

She paused, surprised he'd noticed. "It's very nice and I love it, but…"

"But what?"

"You can't buy expensive things like that."

"Would it help if I told you I'd purchased it for Jeremy?"

She raised an eyebrow. "No."

"I did," he insisted. "He has to eat and you've always liked to cook outdoors, so it seemed logical to buy something you can use on his behalf."

"Aren't you stretching your justification a bit? It will be a while before he can sink his teeth into a steak."

"Maybe so, but the point is he'll benefit in the long run."

"How do you justify the television?"

"Cartoons," he said promptly. "You don't want our child to be the only one who hasn't seen or heard of *Sesame Street*, *Dora the Explorer*, or whatever the latest kid show is, do you?"

She folded her arms. "Then explain your rationale for this sofa. I suppose you thought Jeremy needed it, too."

His smile was boyishly handsome. "He does. On rainy days, we'd pull off the sofa cushions and build forts and rafts and all kinds of things. They're also perfect for protecting furniture from suction-cup darts, woofle balls and every other projectile a boy can shoot out of a toy gun."

"You obviously gave your purchases a great deal of thought."

"I did."

"Did you give any thought as to how *I'd* feel when these things arrived? Did you consider how your gesture looks from my point of view? Aren't my household furnishings meeting your exalted standards? Or maybe you think I'm not a good provider? Because that's exactly how your so-called gifts make me feel, Adrian."

He looked horrified. "I didn't intend to question your ability to provide. I bought those things strictly because they were things you could use, although I did have a few selfish motives."

"Oh, really? What were they?"

"For one, I like to watch the evening news and I can't."

"You can always go to your apartment."

"And miss being with Jeremy? Not a chance. As for the couch, I've spent a lot of time here and will spend more in the future. In case you haven't noticed, your chairs aren't the most comfortable in the world," he said wryly.

"OK, they're not, but you can't decide what I need, Adrian, then deliver it without giving me an option or the opportunity for discussion. That's what got us into this mess in the first place!"

He raised an eyebrow. "Would you have gone shopping with me if you'd known what I wanted to buy?"

"No."

He looked smug. "I rest my case."

"OK, so I would have refused," she admitted, stroking the soft fabric with one hand, "but don't you see, Adrian? I can't accept your gifts."

"Why not?"

"Because I don't feel comfortable accepting them," she said firmly. "I can't explain it, but it doesn't feel right." She ran her palm over a cushion and marveled at the fabric's softness. "Even if it did, though, as much as I love this sofa and can use the extra seating, it's far too big."

He glanced around the room. "It does cover a lot of floor space. Poor Jeremy won't be able to crawl far, will he?"

"Not without bumping into something," she agreed. "Next, you'll want to move us to a larger apartment."

She'd spoken facetiously, but to her dismay his guilty expression spoke volumes. "Please tell me you didn't sign a lease for a new apartment."

"I didn't," he replied defensively. "I've been considering it, though."

"Adrian, so help me…" she warned.

"Now, Bree, calm down. Give me an ounce of credit, would you? I intended for the three of us to hunt for a house or an apartment together."

"I don't want to move," she insisted. Actually, she did, but she couldn't afford to.

"I'm only thinking about the future," he countered. "Jeremy will eventually need his own bedroom for privacy and for little-boy sleepovers. But even before then, I'll be visiting on a regular basis. As much as I'm willing to do whatever it takes to spend time with Jeremy, I'm past the age when spending the night on the cold, hard floor is fun."

Obviously, the future he had in mind was for her to provide him with what basically amounted to a home away from home. If he actually paid for the apartment, it would only worsen the situation. She might as well stamp "mistress" on her forehead, she thought in disgust.

"The floor wouldn't be so terrible," she countered.

"You two could use sleeping bags. It would be your weekend adventure."

"Adventure is right. An adventure in pain."

"If the floor isn't an option, you can always have the sofa." She patted the cushion beside her. "Or stay in a real hotel."

He looked thoughtful. "You're right. Jeremy and I could camp out in luxury. Between the indoor pool, room service and the on-site restaurant, we wouldn't have to leave the building the entire time I'm in town."

The thought of being excluded didn't sit well in her chest. She'd like to think they were years away from that scenario, but she knew of one divorced couple who shuttled their two-year-old from his mother's house during the week to his father's on the weekend. Her stomach churned just thinking about it.

"On the other hand," he continued, "if you consider my original plan, which gave you a large enough place for all of us, when Jeremy and I did our guy things together, he'd still be at home and I wouldn't disrupt your routine. You'd hardly know I was there."

Oh, she'd know if he was there or not. In the short time he'd been visiting, he'd created such a presence in her house that it seemed remarkably empty whenever he was gone. For a woman who was used to being alone, she was amazed at how easily she'd grown to enjoy having him around.

As for her routine, Adrian may have slipped into their lives without causing a ripple, but he'd certainly disrupted her peace of mind.

Obviously, when the time came for Adrian's visits, she would have to choose between the lesser of two evils— constant exposure to Adrian or rattling around in an empty house and missing the only family member she had. From his too-innocent expression, he'd already guessed which option she would favor.

"I'll admit we'll need a larger house," she began, "but it won't happen until I pay off my bills and save some money."

"I could help," he began.

She shook her head. "If Jeremy needs something beyond my means, I'll let you know. Until then, forget it."

She saw the unhappiness in his eyes and the disapproving set to his mouth, so she bargained. "I'll agree to keep the grill and the TV if I can reimburse you for my medication."

"Throw in the sofa, and you have a deal."

She hated being beholden to him, but it was so very nice and functional, even if it was a trifle too large. "OK, but no more purchases until we discuss them first."

"Agreed," he said. "Now that we've settled that, is there any chocolate cake left?"

"You're still hungry?"

"I'm a growing boy." He grinned as he bounded to his feet. "Would you like a piece?"

"I'll pass. I'm still stuffed from dinner."

As he disappeared in the kitchen to serve himself, she heard Jeremy stirring in the other room. Immediately she rose to check on him. When she saw he was restless and wouldn't go back to sleep on his own even with his pacifier, she cuddled him against her shoulder.

"Did you have a nightmare, my little man?" she crooned.

Adrian appeared beside her. "What's wrong?"

"Bad dream, I guess," she whispered. "In another minute he'll be asleep."

He was. She laid him in his crib and tiptoed out of the room after Adrian. Expecting him to say goodnight, she was surprised when he snaked both arms around her waist and captured her in his embrace.

"You know something?" he asked. "I always knew we'd make beautiful babies, and we did."

She smiled. "One, anyway."

"He is such a miracle."

"All babies are."

"I didn't have a chance to thank you for the past couple of days. They were…special."

"I'm glad someone had a good time," she said dryly, thinking of her miserable Sunday.

"I know you didn't, but I was able to experience what you go through on a twenty-four seven basis. I appreciate that you allowed me to take care of him instead of someone else. Whether you realize it or not, you gave me a gift beyond compare."

His sincerity touched her heart. "I'm glad," she said simply, before she grinned. "Hold that thought, though, when you're in the middle of a tie-score football game with your team on the five-yard line, and your son decides he's hungry or wants your undivided attention."

He chuckled. "Then I'll have to negotiate another deal with his mom."

"Really? Negotiate with what?"

"With this." He bent his head and kissed her.

She'd told herself how dangerous it would be to kiss him again and he'd proved her correct. In spite of the minefield still lying between them, his need ignited her own and she felt as if she were bursting into flame. Everything faded into the background, leaving her senses free to fully appreciate Adrian.

His warmth surrounded her as he tugged her close and

pressed one hand against her spine so that she rested full length against him. He tasted of chocolate and smelled of sandalwood, and she felt a light rasp of five-o'clock shadow as he trailed kisses down her neck.

"I should go," he muttered against her skin.

"Probably," she agreed, although she didn't make any effort to break out of his hold. In fact, being in his arms was completely intoxicating. Sending him home seemed too horrible an act to contemplate.

"I don't want to." His hands roamed to the edge of her shirt. His fingers slipped under the fabric and skimmed the bare skin above the waistband of her Bermuda shorts.

"I don't want you to, either," she breathed, wondering if yesterday's migraine had caused her to lose her mind and all of her inhibitions. No, even if all her faculties were intact, she couldn't refuse him because she wanted their special brand of intimacy as much as he did.

Heaven help her.

His hands slowly inched upward until he reached the soft swells of her breasts. Instinctively, she arched her back to grant him fuller access, and a half-groan came from his throat.

"Do you know my real reasons for buying that sofa?" he asked.

"No."

"Because I imagined you sprawled on it. Wearing nothing but me."

"Hmmm."

"The colors reminded me of—"

"You're talking too much," she said breathlessly as his hands released the clasp of her bra.

"I am," he agreed.

"Make love to me, Adrian," she begged, noticing her

voice sounded husky, as if it belonged to someone more exotic and alluring than everyday, average Sabrina.

"I thought you'd never ask."

Within minutes, their clothes disappeared and he lowered her onto the sofa cushions, fitting her body beneath his. His hands masterfully and magically made her body quiver. Needing to ground herself, she flung her arms around his neck and tried to ride out the building storm.

Suddenly, he pulled away. "Wait."

"For what?" She grumbled at the interruption.

He rustled through the clothing on the floor, dug in his jeans pocket and as soon as he removed a foil packet, she understood.

Fumbling with the package, he mumbled an uncomplimentary "Damn" before she took pity on him and ripped it open herself. Although his clumsiness with protection didn't prove anything, his ten-thumbed dexterity seemed to corroborate his story that he hadn't seen anyone since she'd left. He was as out of practice as she was and the thought was comforting.

Yet, when he repositioned himself between her legs, ineptitude became skill, awkwardness became grace and every action became perfection, as if their instincts were so tuned to each other that months of celibacy didn't matter.

She squirmed beneath him, eager to receive him, begging him to hurry. When she thought she couldn't stand another second of this torment, he slipped inside her and she groaned with delight.

He moved slowly, then built to a steady rhythm that seemed choreographed specifically for them.

Suddenly she shattered as tsunami waves of pleasure

surged through her. Another thrust sent Adrian surfing with her.

He collapsed, pressing her into the cushions, but she hardly noticed. It could have been a minute later, or an hour, but still buried deeply inside her, he raised himself on his elbows.

"I didn't mean to crush you."

"You didn't."

"I didn't hurt you, did I?"

He sounded so concerned she smiled. "I'm fine. More than fine, actually. I'm great."

He kissed her temple. "Me, too. That was amazing."

What she thought more amazing was how easily the barriers and hurts of the past year had disappeared during this magical interlude, although she didn't delude herself by thinking these moments signaled a happily-ever-after ending. Then an unwelcome thought popped into her head.

"Did you plan this?"

"No." He was aghast. "What makes you think I did?"

"The condom in your pocket."

His boyish smile appeared. "Wishful thinking on my part. Apparently my fairy godfather chose to grant my wish."

"I didn't know fairies were of the male persuasion."

"How else does one get little fairies?" he teased.

"How else, indeed?" she said wryly.

A car door slammed in the distance. "I suppose that's my cue to get up." He brushed a stray lock of hair off her cheek before he planted a swift, hard kiss on her mouth. "I must say, though, I feel like a teenager who's hoping his parents won't come home unexpectedly."

"The joys of necking in the living room."

"All the more reason to move," he countered. "As much

as I enjoyed the sofa, I'd prefer a bed, especially in a room without impressionable ears."

"Aren't you assuming there will be a next time?" she asked as she dressed quickly, aware of Adrian doing the same.

"Yes, I am," he said boldly. "Which is why we need to talk." He plopped back on the couch and patted the cushion beside him in an invitation to join him.

Suddenly wary, she sat at the opposite end. "About what?"

"About what comes next. I want to acknowledge Jeremy as my son."

She'd expected this discussion, but she'd hoped to postpone it for a few more weeks. While unveiling him as Jeremy's father wouldn't be easy and she didn't know what sort of reception he'd receive afterwards from the staff who'd taken her under their wings, she was willing to tell the world. "If you want to announce you're his father, go ahead, but I'd like some advance notice."

"I don't want to just go public," he said. "I want my position to be recognized legally."

She'd always anticipated his request and, in fact, she was surprised he'd warned her of his intention, but she'd hoped to postpone any official action for a while. Sharing Jeremy on paper seemed to bring her one step closer to losing control over her son's life. Apparently she suffered from the same control issues that Adrian did.

"Is it really necessary?" she asked. "I'm willing to work with you and I thought I'd proved it this past week."

"A verbal agreement isn't good enough. What if you met another guy and changed your mind? Moved to the other side of the country?"

She smiled at his concerns. Although she'd never admit it, no other man would ever compare to Adrian. "I won't."

He raised an eyebrow, as if unconvinced. "You also have Jeremy to consider. What if the unthinkable happened to you? What if you landed in the hospital, were in a car accident or became a victim, like our Jane Doe? Who would look after Jeremy? The bigger question is, who would know to contact me?"

As tempted as she was to play the odds that nothing untoward would ever happen, if the worst-case scenario did unfold, Jeremy would suffer the trauma of being left in limbo. She'd already considered that herself when their Jane Doe had walked through the ED doors.

"Do you have a will naming Jeremy's guardian?" he asked.

"No."

"Who's listed as next of kin on your medical and employment records?"

She'd been so determined to wipe all traces of Adrian out of her life that she'd left those spaces blank. An omission she'd already recognized but hadn't taken time to correct. "No one."

He paused. "You didn't list me as the father on his birth certificate either, did you?"

She'd completed the application form by printing "Unknown" in that particular blank. At the time she'd been intent on forgetting Adrian existed, although without him, Jeremy would never have been born.

"I refuse to feel guilty about my decision," she said stiffly. "You didn't want to be a part of my life, remember? Why would I mention you under those circumstances?"

He hesitated, as if carefully choosing his words. "The real question is, what do you want to do now?"

She had to give him credit for asking even though the determined lines on his face indicated he would take matters into his own hands if she didn't voluntarily acknowledge his rightful access to Jeremy.

"I'll make the changes you'd mentioned."

"And the legal issue? Modifying his birth certificate?"

Telling herself everything would work out, that she didn't have anything to fear, she nodded. "I'll take care of it."

"When?"

"Soon."

He frowned, eyes narrowed. "When?" he repeated, clearly impatient.

"Soon," she emphasized, already wondering how she would squeeze attorney's fees out of her too-tight budget. "Although, as I recall, you said we had several months before we had to address the legalities."

"The legal system grinds slowly; nothing happens overnight. The sooner we start the process the sooner Jeremy will be protected in a worst-case scenario."

Although he was right, it grated to hear him point out the obvious. "Fine. I will."

Adrian shifted positions to face her. "You know," he said, offhandedly, "there is another option."

"Another option?"

"We could get married."

Married! Her breath immediately caught in her throat. They were the words she'd heard in her dreams when Adrian swooped in to admit he'd always loved her and would take her away from all this à la Cinderella, but fairy-tales only existed in books and reality wasn't filled with emotional warm fuzzies. Her flash of excitement died as his sentence hung in the air like smog.

Sabrina felt his gaze as he waited for her reaction. Unfortunately, she didn't know if she was happy, sad, or just plain surprised, but the longer she thought about it, the more bitter-sweet his offer became.

She stared at him, trying to read his body language for a clue as to if he was simply trying to create a joke to lighten the mood or if he meant what he'd said. His steady and unflinching gaze indicated the latter and the prospect unnerved her. Surely she'd misread him. "Are you serious?"

"Very."

Sabrina couldn't think of an appropriate answer. "I don't know what to say."

"Say yes."

As if she could. "Is this a spur-of-the-moment suggestion, or—?"

"I've thought about this all day," he admitted. "Marriage would solve a lot of issues."

She wondered if he realized that suggesting marriage as a solution wasn't the way to win a girl's heart. Then again, he didn't want her heart. He wanted his son.

"Marriage would also create others," she pointed out. "You can still be the father Jeremy needs without having that particular piece of paper."

"We're going to have one piece of paper or another," he said firmly. "You can choose between a marriage certificate or a custody decree. The certificate would be a lot easier to obtain and we wouldn't have the third-party court system looking over our shoulders to ensure we obey the letter of the law as far as visitation schedules and child-support payments went."

He was a private man, so she understood why he hated the idea of dragging his personal affairs before judges and lawyers. "That's what prompted your idea? You're looking for an easy fix?"

He started to speak, then stopped, as if he'd realized how close he was to stepping into something nasty. "I want what's best for Jeremy," he said. "If there's a simple way to accomplish that, why not take advantage of it?"

"Because 'easy' isn't the same as 'best'."

"Jeremy needs us."

"And we'll be there for him," she said. "We don't have to live together to accomplish that objective."

"Do you really want to put Jeremy in a position where he has to explain why his parents aren't married?"

"We're talking about *our* relationship, Adrian. You say this is what Jeremy needs, but…but I can't marry someone who thinks of me as an obligation or a means to an end."

"I don't," he insisted.

She wasn't convinced. "Are you sure?"

"Hell, yes! Have you already forgotten what we've been doing on this sofa? That didn't feel like an obligation to me and from your moans, I'd say it didn't feel like that to you either."

He would have to remind her of her uninhibited response. "We had great times in bed before, too, but those weren't enough to hold us together, were they? What we had was just sex."

"Just…?" He ran his hand through his hair until a few strands had spiked. "You're accusing me of having casual sex?"

"No, but—"

"Or could it be you think I'm the sort who'd sleep with a woman in order to get what I want?"

She spoke without thinking. "I think you're willing to do whatever is necessary to achieve your goal." As soon as she heard herself, she realized she'd crossed the line.

As expected, his response was immediate. His nostrils flared, his eyes burned with anger, and his tone grew quiet—all warning signs of his temper erupting with hurricane-force fury. "Trust me, Sabrina, if I only wanted *my son*, I would have hauled you into court faster than you can blink. I certainly wouldn't have bothered to break in the sofa."

For a long, painful moment, she didn't answer. Even with Jeremy shaking his rattle and jabbering to himself, the silence between them was deafening. "Tell me this," she said quietly, "if Jeremy hadn't been born and everything else was equal, would you be asking me to marry you?" She raised an eyebrow.

The anger faded from his eyes and puzzlement replaced it. He started to speak, then stopped as if to weigh his words. "Probably not, but…"

Her head had warned her to expect this particular response but her heart had encouraged her to think positively. Now he'd confirmed what she'd believed—if not for Jeremy, they'd simply be two people who shared a past— and the ember of hope residing in her chest winked out, leaving a smoky trail of disappointment behind.

This wasn't the first time she'd been rejected in life, she consoled herself. Neither was it the first time Adrian had rejected her. If she hadn't wanted the truth, she should have kept her thoughts and her questions to herself.

Her gaze didn't waver as she nodded. "That's what I thought."

"Let me finish. No, marriage wasn't on my mind when I came here because all I could think about was finding an opportunity to talk to you. I didn't allow myself to plan after that because everything hinged on how you reacted and if you forgave me. Between the golf-ball incident and finding out about Jeremy, I moved into fast forward."

"Now you can return to normal speed," she said crisply. "It's commendable of you to sacrifice your future with a woman you love for Jeremy, but it's unnecessary. I don't want to marry you."

"We could make it work," he insisted.

"It's nice of you to want to try," she said politely, aware that he'd missed the perfect opportunity to tell her that *she* was the woman he loved. Because he didn't, she knew she'd made the right decision. "We're both saving ourselves a lot of grief."

"We'd be good together," he insisted. "We proved that tonight, right here on this very sofa."

But do you love me? She wanted to ask outright, but she'd learned her lesson—don't ask questions if you don't want the truth.

"We generate a lot of sparks," she agreed, "but what happens when the sparks burn out? A commitment should be based on more than parenthood because we certainly don't need to live together or share wedding rings for you to assume a father's role. Besides, we've only been talking to each other for a week after a year's worth of hard feelings. We'd be foolish to rush into a situation we'd later regret."

He leaned forward. "I care about you, Sabrina. I really do. Maybe I did move faster than I should have, but I won't rescind my proposal. Just think about it. OK?"

Caring was nice, but she cared about Clay as well as a host of other people from colleagues and staff to patients. It didn't mean she should marry them.

"We'll see," she said, aware she hadn't technically

agreed to weigh his offer. She had to hear three magical words before she'd alter her decision. Only time would tell if he'd say them.

CHAPTER EIGHT

AFTER the conversation that hadn't gone as well as Adrian had hoped, he hated to leave. Once the door closed behind him, she wouldn't waste a minute of her time considering the possibilities. Knowing how devoted she was to Jeremy, he'd hoped the what's-best-for-Jeremy argument would carry more weight than if he'd professed how much he wanted her for himself. His strategy clearly hadn't netted the instant results he'd wanted.

Although he hadn't planned to make love with Sabrina before asking her to marry him, the timing had seemed perfect. Obviously she'd decided that he'd only been scratching an itch.

He didn't blame her for being wary. It *was* far-fetched to believe a man who'd disappeared from her life a year ago would have suddenly and miraculously had an epiphany after being reunited for a week. Perhaps when she calmed down and reflected on their conversation—that he didn't *have* to sleep with her to gain access to his son— she'd take his proposal more seriously.

He hadn't realized it before, but he'd plainly poked the bruises of her self-esteem issues and had to wait for the pain to fade. Meanwhile, he'd insert himself into every aspect of her life and slowly chip away at her defenses.

As luck would have it, Jeremy helped matters along when he woke up inconsolable a few minutes later. Adrian couldn't leave.

Sabrina touched his forehead. "He feels warm. I wonder if he's teething again." The baby tugged at his ear and bellowed.

"Or he has an earache," Adrian offered.

Jeremy immediately held out his chubby little arms to Adrian and leaned out of Sabrina's hold with large tears clinging to his eyelashes.

"You'd better take him," Sabrina said. "It's obvious he wants you."

As soon as she'd handed him the baby, Adrian sat in the recliner and waited for Sabrina to return with a cold gel-filled plastic ring designed to soothe sore little gums. Jeremy greedily gnawed on it like a dog with its favorite bone.

"I hope you have more where this one came from," he said lightly.

"In the freezer. Would you like me to take him now?"

"I don't mind holding him. He's starting to settle down so the less jostling the better, don't you think?"

"Yes, but it's getting late and you—"

"I'm fine right here," he said.

"But you have to go to work in the morning."

"So do you."

"I can handle him by myself."

For some reason, Sabrina seemed determined to prove herself and he was tired of her believing he was always looking to find fault with her parenting skills. Would they never get past that?

"I know you can, but why should you when we can share the load?" he asked calmly. "This way we both get some sleep."

She hesitated and he tried harder. "How about this? I'll stick around to take the first shift and you can take the second."

"OK," she finally said. "Wake me when it's my turn."

In the end, he didn't have to. By one a.m., Jeremy's pain had subsided enough for him to sleep, and although there was plenty of time for Adrian to drive to his apartment and catch a few winks in a comfortable bed, he didn't. With his clothes still in the car from his excursion to the dry cleaner's earlier in the day, his toothbrush and electric razor still in Sabrina's bathroom from the weekend, he had everything he possibly needed within reach.

Other than a bed, of course. Not wanting to risk upsetting Sabrina if she found him lying next to her, he grabbed an extra pillow and stretched out on the sofa.

Amazingly enough, Sabrina didn't seem surprised to find him there the next morning when she walked through on her way to the kitchen for Jeremy's bottle. She'd simply said, "The bathroom is free for the next fifteen minutes."

Even more amazing was how the next evening was a repeat of the one before.

"Why is it that his teeth only bother him at night?" Sabrina muttered at eleven o'clock as she paced the floor with Jeremy in her arms.

"It could be worse," Adrian said as he took a few minutes to flip through the twenty-four-hour television news channels to catch up on any world or national events he'd missed.

"How?"

"He could be fussy from the time we get home, but he waits until after we've had a nice, relaxing evening, a walk around the block or through the park, and a fun-filled swim in the sink."

Call him a masochist, but he was quite happy with Jeremy's schedule and if he didn't know better, he'd think the baby had planned it this way. Adrian was now spending the night without resistance, his clothes hung in Sabrina's closet rather than in his car, his underwear and socks were tucked in the bottom dresser drawer, and his shoes shared floor space with her tennis shoes, sandals, and high heels.

The only thing that would make him happier would be if the ring he'd purchased today was displayed on her finger rather than buried inside the outer pocket of his suitcase which he'd stored under her bed.

Actually, there was another thing that would make him happy, too—if he didn't sleep alone.

Even so, he wasn't complaining. With luck, Sabrina would realize just how handy he was to have around and his worries would be over.

He clicked off the TV with the remote control. "Do you want me to take him for a while?"

"Thanks, but it's my turn for the first shift," she said. "You can sack out on my bed because you won't get any sleep if you stay out here."

"Are you sure?"

"Yeah. I didn't change the sheets, though, so if you want fresh linen, you can strip the bed yourself."

She shouldn't have used the word "strip" because it evoked all sorts of pleasant images. Knowing he'd also be surrounded by her scent as he lay on her pillows, he doubted if he'd sleep at all. If he did, he'd have the most erotic dreams of his entire life. "It's fine the way it is," he said instead. "Goodnight."

"Goodnight. Oh, I forgot to ask. Did you ever get in touch with Clay?"

"I left a voice message. I'm sure he'll call me tomorrow."

They had an unwritten rule of touching base with each other every few days, especially after Clay had moved into his own apartment. Clay had balked at first, but after Adrian had appeared unexpectedly on his doorstep during a most inopportune time when Clay was "entertaining" a pretty young woman, he'd agreed.

"OK. Goodnight."

He sank onto her bed and, as he'd imagined, his keen sense of smell detected Sabrina's trademark gingery citrus scent in the room. This could have been his for the last year if he hadn't screwed things up—if he hadn't felt so guilty over Clay's accident and been so determined to pay for his sins alone. In the end, Sabrina had paid for them, too.

Confessing his innermost thoughts had never been easy for him and it had only gotten worse after his parents had died. Although his aunts, teachers and other well-meaning neighbors had encouraged him to open up, he couldn't. Describing his father's last moments, talking about the promise he'd made, and voicing his fears, only cultivated his sense of being powerless and out of control. So, as the proverbial man of the house, he'd continued to hide his emotions behind silence and stoicism, noticing how his training had come in handy for those times when he had to deliver bad news to patients or their family members.

Unfortunately, his reticence wasn't helping mend his relationship with Sabrina and he wanted to mend it badly.

With a son to consider, he wanted to rekindle the tender feelings they'd had for each other.

Unfortunately, it would take time for Sabrina to believe he had special care for her. Trust wasn't earned overnight, although he wished otherwise.

By Friday, Sabrina had to face facts. Adrian had moved in, lock, stock, and barrel. His change of residence was unofficial, of course, because he hadn't asked and she hadn't given permission. It had simply happened, taking place over the several days since her migraine attack. A single scrub suit in her closet suddenly became two weeks' worth of scrub suits and casual dress apparel. Both white and dark socks were tucked in the same drawer as Jeremy's undershirts and one-piece body suits. Adrian had even started to hang his toothbrush next to hers on the special holder instead of using his travel case.

He was there for the duration.

She should ask him to leave. It was too distracting to "play house" with him when she knew his reason for moving in. It was simple, really. He intended to prove they could make their marriage work by giving her a taste of the future as he saw it. No doubt he'd thought a woman who'd been raised by relatives who hadn't wanted her would jump at the chance to have her own family.

Sadly, he was right.

But she wasn't going to sacrifice her self-esteem to have that family. She wouldn't marry him, no matter how enticing the prospect was and no matter how hard he tried to convince her otherwise. Until he left, she simply had to protect herself emotionally and hope that when that day came, she'd handle it with grace and aplomb.

Meanwhile, she couldn't deny the gift of time that he provided. She could indulge in a leisurely bubble bath, read the newspaper or paint her toenails without waiting until Jeremy was asleep. She could sweep the floor without Jeremy perched on one hip. She could also retrieve her mail from the box at the curb without dashing down the sidewalk and keeping one ear open in case her son should notice her missing. She could actually run to the store by herself and not juggle a baby with her purchases.

Best of all, Adrian shared night-time duty so she was assured of a few hours of sleep each night.

Selfishly, she decided to let things ride while warning herself to remain objective and not grow attached to these temporary living arrangements.

But after watching the joy appear on Adrian's face as he put Jeremy to bed or helped bundle him off to day care, she didn't have the heart to take those simple pleasures away from him. That loss would come soon enough when he returned to Denver.

Fortunately, his departure was a problem for another day. The one facing her now was far more immediate.

"Someone made a mistake with my paycheck," Sabrina told the hospital's Accounts Receivable clerk. "The net amount doesn't reflect my payroll deduction for my hospital bill."

As soon as Sabrina had opened her direct deposit pay stub envelope, she'd been surprised to note the net amount was far greater than it had been since her last check two weeks ago. Knowing she wasn't due a raise for some time, she examined the deductions until she found a crucial one missing.

The girl clicked a few computer keys, then shook her head. "According to this, your account is paid in full."

"That's impossible," she said flatly. "I still have two years to go."

"My computer says otherwise."

"There has to be a mistake. Someone else's payment must have been posted because I didn't—"

"There's no mistake. A check was received and the money credited to your account."

Adrian, she thought irritably. How could he do this when she'd made it plain she didn't need his help? OK, maybe she could use a temporary boost in her finances, but she didn't *want* it coming from him. Somehow it made her feel beholden when she craved her independence.

"If you'll give me a second, I can give you more information." The clerk studied her screen. "Here it is. According to this, the balance was paid last week. Friday, to be exact."

She thought back to their conversation on Monday and how money had been discussed, but only in the most general terms. And even if she'd been specific, Adrian couldn't be responsible if her bill had been paid on the previous Friday. For all he'd known, her health insurance had covered all her expenses.

"Can you tell who paid it?"

"Sorry. All I have is a copy of a cashier's check made out to the hospital with your name in the memo line."

Sabrina could hardly take in her good fortune. Things like this didn't normally happen to her. "I wish I knew who it was. I'd love to thank them."

"Check with Alice. She's the one who handles the actual posting. Maybe she'll remember details."

"Thanks. I will."

Alice, however, wasn't helpful either. "An attorney

brought it by. Said one of his clients had wanted to give an anonymous donation to you, so I didn't question him."

"Isn't it against hospital policy for staff to receive gifts from patients?"

"Yes, but technically I can't prove the gift came from a patient, so if I were you, I'd take the money and run." She grinned. 'Honestly, the bean counters aren't concerned about *who* pays the bill, only that it gets paid. And yours is."

"Who was the attorney?"

Alice was apologetic. "Sorry. He didn't mention his name and as I don't run in legal circles, I didn't recognize him. If I were you, though, I'd say a prayer for the person responsible."

"Oh, I will," she assured Alice. "Don't worry."

As she walked from the accounting department, her mind raced with possibilities of what she could do with the extra money each month. She could finally have a mechanic diagnose the strange knock in her car's engine, replace her lumpy recliner, or just save her money for a larger apartment. Better yet, she could apply it to her other loan and pay it off sooner.

By the time she returned to the ED, she still hadn't come down from her financial windfall high.

"Good news?" Adrian asked as she approached the nurses' station.

"The best," she said with a smile. "Excellent, in fact. So excellent that we're going to celebrate. Any requests for the weekend?"

"Celebrate? Wow. What happened? You didn't win the lottery, did you?"

She giggled. "Almost, but not quite. Someone paid off my hospital bill and it wasn't a small amount either."

"No kidding. Who would do such a thing?"

"I don't know. It was an anonymous donation, but…" she smiled "…I'll take it and rejoice in my unknown benefactor's generosity. So, what do you say we find a sitter and go someplace nice for dinner?"

"I'm game. Where do you have in mind?"

"How does Mexican food sound? I'm hungry for a beef enchilada smothered in cheese," she confessed.

"Perfect." He glanced at the wall clock. "Things are quiet for the moment, so I'm headed to Radiology."

"Still waiting for the MRI results on the patient in room three?" At his nod, she continued, "Do you really think the scans will show something they didn't a week ago?" Alan Cavendish had been brought in by his wife for the second time in as many weeks because of severe headaches and dizzy spells. Sabrina had arranged for a second scan before she'd slipped away to straighten out her paycheck problems.

"Who knows? He came in at the end of my shift last week and the evening-shift doc handled his case. According to the records, he was treated for migraine and released. So, if he's still having a problem, something's going on. I intend to convince the radiologist to move my case to the top of his to-be-read pile and to go over it with a fine-toothed comb."

"I can do that for you," she offered.

"Thanks, but I'd like to see the fellow myself." He grinned. "The coffee over there is better than ours anyway and I'm hoping to bum a cup off them." He strolled away, whistling.

A few minutes later, just as she was about to check on Mr Cavendish, the exam-room door opened and his wife nearly knocked her over in her rush.

"Thank God you're here," she said, her eyes wide. "He's having a seizure."

Sabrina pushed past her and in a brief glance saw her husband's clenched jaw and twitching movements. "Pull the call cord," she instructed the woman as she began first aid until Adrian or one of the physicians' assistants arrived.

Cavendish was already in a bed with the rails raised, so she didn't have to worry about him falling, but vomiting could be a problem, so she rolled him onto his side to prevent the possibility of aspiration.

During her initial assessment, both he and his wife had denied this question, but she had to ask again. "He hasn't had any seizures before, has he?"

"No. None. Is he going to be OK?"

"We'll do everything we can." Sabrina held him in place as best she could, trying to keep his arms from banging on the aluminum side rails while she noted his respirations.

The door opened and Hilary came in, took one look, and said, "I'll get Doctor," before she scurried out and returned a minute later with Adrian.

"How long?" he asked tersely.

"Since you went to Radiology."

Grimly, he glanced at Hilary as he inclined his head in Mrs Cavendish's direction. "He'll need help, then." He rattled off a dosage while Hilary gently guided Alan's shocked wife from the room.

Sabrina hated to question his order but she wanted to be sure she hadn't misunderstood. "That's a high dose," she commented.

His gaze steadily met hers. "I know."

"OK." Sabrina pulled the medication from the drug cart, double-checked the vial's label before she drew off the required amount, then injected it into Cavendish's IV port.

At first nothing happened, then gradually Cavendish's

seizure eased under their watchful eyes. Sabrina gently rolled him onto his back and covered him with a blanket.

"Did you get your report?"

He nodded, his expression still grim.

Headaches, dizziness, and now a seizure added up to a serious problem. "What did the test show?"

"Brain tumor."

Her heart sank. "Oh, no. How bad is it?"

"All brain tumors are bad."

"I know, but is it operable?"

"Mr Cavendish will need a lot more tests before the neurosurgeon can decide." He heaved a sigh. "In the meantime, call whichever neurologist, neurosurgeon and oncologist is available and arrange for a transfer to a medical floor."

"Will do."

"Oh, and schedule him for the next available EEG while I break the news to his wife."

The electroencephalogram would record the electrical activity in the brain and convert those impulses into a tracing pattern which would then reflect the state of the brain. A tumor or other structural abnormality would shortcircuit those impulses, giving valuable information as to the location of the growth. She hoped Cavendish's tumor would be treatable.

Sabrina contacted the on-call neuro people and spent the rest of the afternoon in a flurry of doctors' orders and test procedures while monitoring her patient and giving moral support to Alan's wife. By the end of the afternoon, his doctors were trying to decide between surgery and radiation or a combination of the two.

Although this wasn't the first tragic case Sabrina had ever encountered, this one affected her more than most. Young people, young couples, always tugged at her heart.

She quietly went about her business and when she got home she gave Jeremy an extra-long cuddle until he eventually squealed a protest.

"My turn," Adrian said with a smile as he took Jeremy from her.

"Maybe we shouldn't go out tonight," she said.

"Why not? We're celebrating, remember?"

"I know, but I just feel as if we…shouldn't. It just seems so *wrong* to have a good time when people like the Cavendishes are in crisis mode."

"Moping won't change their situation," he told her.

"I suppose not." She let out a long breath. "OK, we'll go."

Yet as they sat in the fragrantly spicy atmosphere of Casa Ramon, enjoying a Mariachi band and eating their way through an appetizer of chips and three kinds of salsa as well as their dinner entrees, she realized Adrian's mood was more quiet and somber than usual and she wondered why.

Was he more upset over the Cavendish case than he'd admitted? In all the time she'd known him, he'd never acted as if the tragedies he'd encountered at the hospital had ever weighed him down, although she did remember a few times when he'd been quiet and withdrawn. Naturally, he'd given any number of excuses for his mood—he was tired, had nothing to say, etc. and she'd accepted them without question.

However, now she wondered if he'd felt the same sadness and disappointment as everyone else. Could it be that he'd simply been suffering in silence and hadn't wanted her, or anyone else for that matter, to know just how deeply he felt about his patients? That sort of behavior would certainly have ruined his tough, nothing-bothers-me macho image. The more she pondered, the more she could examine his character in a completely different light.

"Do you want to talk about it?" she asked softly.

He looked startled. "Talk about what?"

"Whatever's bothering you."

"Nothing's bothering me."

She'd heard that one before. "You're quiet."

"It's been a long day."

That, too, was a familiar refrain.

She spoke as if he'd answered her question. Instead of receiving encouragement, she chose to give it. "Alan Cavendish is in good hands. Dr Graham is an excellent oncologist and all the staff think highly of Dr James's neurosurgery skills."

"So I've heard."

"Did you know Alan and Nicole—that's his wife—have a two-year-old daughter? Apparently they'd been married for years and weren't able to have children, and then, bingo, along comes Lily."

"Did Jeremy do anything special today at day care?"

His abrupt change of subject suggested that she'd hit a sore spot. "He's seven months old, Adrian. He eats, sleeps and plays with his toys."

"He's due for a lot of 'firsts', Bree," he said, as if she needed a reminder.

"True, but—"

"He could crawl any day," he said, sounding determined to focus the conversation on someone other than himself. "You can tell from looking at him that he's eager to go, but he hasn't quite figured out how to start his engine yet."

Sweet baby Jane! How self-absorbed had she been to not have recognized his distraction techniques for what they were? How many other patients had caused him to internalize his struggles because he wouldn't talk about them? In fact, she now suspected why he'd been so close-lipped about Clay's accident, especially when he'd helped pay for the motorcycle in the first place. It had been too painful and the drastic events had only reinforced Adrian's lack of control over the situation.

She leaned across the table to place her hand on his forearm, noting his tense muscles. "It's OK to be upset about our patient. You don't have to hide it from me."

"I'm not upset." He fingered the condensation on his bottle. "We've seen thousands of cases like his. Life is short and doesn't come with any guarantees. Period."

"Life *is* short, especially for some," she agreed, "but that doesn't mean we shouldn't feel badly at the injustice."

He studied a point over her shoulder for several drawn-out seconds before he met her gaze. The pain in his eyes caused her heart to ache. But before she could think of something to say, he wiped all expression off his face.

"Can we go?" he asked abruptly.

"Sure. Just let me ask the waiter for the—"

"I got it." He rose, pulled out his wallet and tossed enough bills on the table to cover the meal and a generous tip.

"This was my treat, remember?" she said as he ushered her to his vehicle as quickly as if they were racing to attend a code blue.

"Considering all the meals I've eaten at your house, I owe you." He opened her car door.

"You don't owe me anything," she said, sliding inside. "We had a nice dinner by ourselves and in wonderful surroundings."

"When do we have to relieve Kate?"

Kate was babysitting and she'd pulled Sabrina aside

before they'd left the house to whisper her willingness to stay as late as Sabrina needed her…then she'd winked.

"Whenever," she said airily. "I have a television now so Kate won't be bored after Jeremy goes to sleep."

"There's a walking trail around my apartment complex," he said. "Do you mind if we go there for a while?"

He obviously needed physical activity to release his tension. She was glad he'd suggested walking rather than working out at the gym because she'd rather be outdoors. "Not at all."

Within twenty minutes they were moving along the paved walkway at a steady clip. Thank goodness her sandals were comfortable enough for walking, although if she'd suspected he'd planned a workout this evening, she would have worn her exercise clothes instead of a denim skirt and sleeveless blouse.

"It's a lovely evening," she said as they passed through a shady grove of oak trees. "Not many people out yet, I see."

She tried to keep up with his long-legged stride, but after she began huffing and puffing and earned a stitch in her side, she gave up and came to a dead stop. "That's it. If you want to play the tortoise and the hare, I'm game. When you're finished loping around the path, you can come back to me."

"Sorry."

As soon as she caught her breath, she started off and this time he matched her pace rather than set it.

Once again she waited for him to initiate conversation and when he didn't, she took matters into her own hands and played on a hunch.

"Tell me about your parents," she said.

"They're both dead. You know that."

She nodded. "I also know you raised your brother and sisters, but what were your folks like? Did they laugh a lot, get along with each other? Did your dad take you fishing, teach you how to change the oil in your car, or scold you if you stayed out too late?"

He thought for a minute. "I remember Mom being happy all the time. She gave lots of hugs and baked the best peanut-butter cookies. She let me flatten them right out of the oven with a fork. If I had to describe her, I'd say she was more of a free spirit, artsy type."

"She sounds wonderful."

"Dad, on the other hand, was serious, although Mom always could get him to smile. He wasn't a talkative guy, but his love for us showed in the things he did and taught us. He always made time when we needed him. He was a good man, a hard worker, our biggest fan at baseball and football games, and he drilled responsibility into us. After his accident, I stepped into his shoes."

"It sounds as if he had big shoes to fill."

"To an eighteen year-old, they were *huge*. They still are, in fact."

"Did Clay and your sisters balk at you being in charge?"

"Not really. The girls had the usual teenage histrionics and angst, but my aunts helped me handle those episodes. Everything worked out in the end. We all earned college degrees, have good jobs, and didn't land in jail." He grinned. "Not bad, if I say so myself."

"I'd have to agree." She threaded her arm through his as they strolled down the path. If their relaxed pace reflected his mood, then their near-Olympic sprint had been the perfect means to release some of his frustration.

The cicadas sang louder and for several minutes Sabrina

simply listened to the sounds of nature and enjoyed the sense of companionship she felt as she remained tucked against his side.

The pastoral setting convinced her to bring up the subject he wanted to avoid. "What do you think of Alan Cavendish's chances?"

Adrian tensed ever so slightly and if she hadn't been hanging onto his arm like a leech, she never would have known. "Not good."

"How do you feel about that?"

"You're a psychologist now?"

"Just someone who's concerned about you."

"Don't be. There's nothing either of us can say that will make a difference."

From Adrian's flat tone, Alan Cavendish's diagnosis had clearly hit Adrian hard, either for the same reasons as hers or because his earlier test results hadn't indicated such a serious problem. Whatever the cause, she wanted to comfort a man who needed comforting but didn't want it.

Sensing he wouldn't appreciate the usual platitudes, she simply held onto him and refused to let go. The cicadas' song faded into the background as she stroked Adrian's arm in an effort to soothe him when words seemed trite.

"No, but it might make a difference to *you*. You must have a thought or an impression of some sort."

He stopped. "My thoughts and impressions are my own."

Once again he was shutting her out and she was slowly seeing a pattern. "Venting is better than bottling up your frustration. I, for one, am very frustrated and angry about the situation."

He didn't answer, so she pressed on. "But, then, I have

to ask myself, if we'd diagnosed him a week sooner, would it have made a difference? Would it?" she demanded.

"Maybe. Maybe not," he admitted.

"No matter what, you did your best."

"Did I?" He turned a wounded gaze on her. "I turned him over to someone else so I could go home."

"The evening physician is every bit as capable as you. He's the one who interpreted the results."

"Last week's report stated 'No abnormalities found'," Adrian said. "This week the radiologist found the spot so he compared the two sets of scans. The lesion had been there all along."

"Oh, dear."

"No kidding."

"Hindsight is always twenty-twenty," she told him.

"The point is, whether a week would have made a difference or not, we shouldn't have made the mistake."

"Maybe the radiologist was tired when he read the first set of pictures. Maybe he had a stack of films waiting and was in a hurry. Maybe he was interrupted and thought he'd come back to it and for some reason never did. Maybe the transcriptionist confused her cases. Who knows? There could be any number of extenuating circumstances. You weren't to blame."

"I still feel somewhat responsible."

"You can't take on the entire world, Adrian, even if you think you should. Did—?"

"Can we talk about something else?" he asked impatiently. "A topic other than medicine?"

Oh…damn it! She'd finally made progress but he'd clammed up before her eyes. Still, Rome wasn't built in a day… "If that's what you want."

They'd come full circle and stopped in front of his building. As he hesitated, she asked, "Do you want another jaunt around the complex or should we go home?"

"Come inside with me."

He stood tall and stoic, waiting for her reply with a plea in his eyes. Immediately and without hearing specifics, she knew what he wanted. He could deny it with his last breath, but he was hurting and needed her to help him feel less subject to the whims of fate and more in control.

She rose on tiptoe to brush a soft kiss against his mouth. "Last one in is a rotten egg."

CHAPTER NINE

ADRIAN'S apartment hadn't changed since she'd been here last, although now his belongings were noticeably absent. It still resembled a hotel and had that same, unaired, vacant quality, but at the moment she didn't care because it had one major point in its favor.

Privacy.

The minute the door closed behind her, he took her in his arms and kissed her with a starving-man greediness that caught her by surprise and raised her spirits. He wanted *her*.

She tugged on his shirt as he did likewise, but before she could do more than unsnap his shorts, he'd hoisted her into the air. She gasped from the sudden weightlessness, only to realize he was carrying her into the bedroom.

"We're going to do this right," he mumbled against her mouth.

"The sofa would have…" she gasped as he nipped her neck "…been fine," she finished when she caught her breath.

"Not this time."

Somehow, without ever breaking contact, clothes disappeared and the comforter sailed onto the floor a few seconds before he followed her onto the slick, cool sheets and covered her body with his.

He made love with a desperation she recognized and understood, giving of herself freely until he found his release. When it was over, when he'd collapsed on the sheets beside her, she simply snuggled against him.

He flung one arm over his eyes. "I'm sorry."

"What for?" she asked, although she knew.

"I went too fast."

"Am I complaining?"

"No."

"Then don't worry about it." She craned her neck to see his expression. "There's always next time."

"True." He squeezed her arm.

Deciding she could get away with asking a few questions now that he was relaxed and his defenses were down, she did. "Your dad didn't encourage you to show your emotions, did he?"

"He wasn't a demonstrative sort, more of an introspective, quiet type. I've been told I take after him," he said wryly.

"Oh, I don't know." She traced a circle on his chest. "You can be demonstrative and noisy on occasion. Like now. Or when you're with Jeremy."

"That's different."

"Is it?"

"Of course it is. What patient wants to see their doctor blubbering all over him? People lose faith if I can't be objective."

"True, but that doesn't mean you can't share your worries and concerns with someone. It isn't healthy to bottle all your feelings up inside. People aren't supposed to suffer alone."

"Speaking of suffering…" he flipped her on top of him "…I have this ache."

She felt his body's response and smiled. "How bad is it?"

"Bad enough we'll have to take it slow and easy."

She threaded her arms behind his neck. "If you say so. I always follow doctor's orders."

"I'm worried about you," Kate told Sabrina on Sunday after she and Adrian had returned home from finishing their round of golf. Adrian had gone to the back yard so he could call Clay and enjoy an uninterrupted conversation.

"What do you mean?"

"Aren't you two getting rather chummy? He's only been in town for two weeks."

Sabrina smiled, touched by her friend's concern. "I know, but—"

"And, honestly, I wasn't snooping, but when I put Jeremy down for his nap, well…" she grimaced "…it's obvious he's moved in with you."

"He has."

"Oh, Sabrina." Kate's distress shone as brightly as a neon sign. "Aren't you rushing things? I mean, you're a single mom with a baby who hasn't celebrated his first birthday. Do you want to run the risk of having a second?"

While Sabrina would dearly love Jeremy to have a sibling, she wasn't foolish enough to provide him with one within weeks of Adrian resurfacing in her life. "You worry too much."

"Of course I do. That's what friends are for. Whatever you do," she begged, "don't forget the last guy you dated. He left you high and dry and—"

"He's outside."

Kate stopped short and blinked owlishly. "Who's outside?"

"The guy who left me high and dry."

She frowned. "Adrian's outside."

Sabrina smiled. "Exactly."

Understanding crept across Kate's features. "Oh. My. God. Are you telling me—?"

"Yes."

"The creep who ran out on you is the hospital's current heartthrob stud muffin?"

Sabrina nodded. "That's him."

Kate sank bonelessly onto the sofa. "Oh. My. God," she repeated. "You actually let him back into your life?"

"I didn't have a choice. He *is* Jeremy's father."

Kate stared at her, clearly stupefied. "I can't believe this."

"It is rather unbelievable."

"If we hadn't been through so much together, I wouldn't ask, but what happened?" Kate's eyes grew saucer-sized. "Please don't tell me you had a one-night stand."

Sabrina perched on the edge of the recliner. "We were dating, rather seriously I thought, but our relationship fell apart after his brother landed in hospital." She told the entire story, beginning with Adrian's fatefully misguided decision to her arrival in Pinehaven.

By the end, Kate was plainly stunned. "Oh, Sabrina. What are you going to do next?"

Jeremy threw his ring of plastic keys on the floor and while Sabrina retrieved them, she pondered her answer.

"I'm not sure." She hesitated. "He's asked me to marry him."

Kate's gaze grew intent. "Is that what you want?"

Sabrina shrugged as she balanced Jeremy on her lap and breathed in his baby scent.

"Do you love him?"

She didn't waver. "Yes. I almost wish I didn't, but I do."

"And that means…?" Kate raised an eyebrow.

"It means nothing," she said firmly. "My feelings are one-sided. Adrian doesn't love me."

Kate frowned. "Are you sure?"

Sabrina rolled her eyes. "Does the sun set in the west? Of course I'm positive."

"So what are you going to do? It isn't wise to let him stay here."

"From my perspective, it isn't," she agreed. "But he's good for Jeremy, so what else *can* I do? I'll just have to tolerate the situation for my son's sake."

Kate rose. "I don't know, dearie. If you ask me, you're setting yourself up for a major meltdown, but whatever happens, I'm here for you."

"Thanks, Kate. You're the best friend ever."

The back door squeaked, followed by the squish of Adrian's tennis shoes on the linoleum floor. "Let me know if you have any problems with the situation we just discussed," Kate said as Adrian appeared in the living room. "One of my former patients comes from a family with mob connections. She had a difficult delivery and the grateful parents will be more than happy to do a favor for me." She glanced pointedly at Adrian.

Sabrina smiled. "I'll keep it in mind."

Kate leaned over and kissed Jeremy's head. "See you later, short stuff. Any time you need a sitter, let me know. And, Adrian…" her smile was too sweet. "Do you have a bulletproof vest?"

His brow furrowed. "No, why?"

"Just wondering," she said airily. "Take care and I'll see you later."

"Mob connections and bulletproof vests?" Adrian asked with stunned curiosity as Kate walked toward her car. "What was that about?"

"I think she was delivering a warning."

"Why? What did I do?"

"You moved in," she said wryly.

"Ahh."

"I also told her you were Jeremy's father."

He nodded slowly. "Makes sense. She can finally put a name and a face to the 'dirty rotten scoundrel who left you high and dry when you were pregnant'," he said dryly.

"I hate to agree, but yes."

"I assume every move I make will be scrutinized from now on?"

"Probably. Does it bother you?"

He shrugged. "I have nothing to hide."

"Things might be a little chilly for you at work," she said. "You should prepare yourself."

"I can handle it."

She didn't doubt it at all. Adrian had charmed the staff since he'd arrived, so a few might study him with curiosity and wariness, but he'd win them over again.

"Did you get in touch with Clay?" she asked.

"Yeah. He finally answered his phone." He held out his arms to Jeremy and the little scamp giggled and dove forward for Adrian to catch him.

"How's he been?"

Adrian sat on the sofa and laid Jeremy on his lap in order to tickle his tummy. "He claims he's fine. Said his stomach has been acting up the past few days. He thinks he contracted some sort of food poisoning from a little taco stand he visited."

"Did he see a doctor?"

He shook his head. "According to him, he's doing better."

"Do you want to drive to Denver and check on him?" she asked. "It's early enough. We can."

He looked thoughtful for moment. "I'd like to, but I know he'll get upset if I do." He grinned. "Who wants to have his big brother running over to check on him just because he has a stomachache and diarrhea?"

She laughed as she sat beside her men. "Not the best time to have a visitor."

"Exactly. I'll call him tomorrow. Maybe we could plan to drive to Denver next weekend. We both have four days off."

She leaned over. "Hear that, Jeremy? You're going to have your first road trip."

"We could make it a honeymoon." He sounded hopeful.

"Why should we?" She didn't just want a *good* reason, she wanted the *right* reason.

"I'm introducing Jeremy to my family. It would be nice to introduce my wife at the same time."

Wrong answer. "Ah, the kill-two-birds-with-one-stone philosophy. Well, it would be nice if I won the lottery, too, but that isn't going to happen."

"You're being stubborn." He spoke without rancor, almost as if he hadn't expected her to agree, but had felt obliged to ask…just in case.

"I'm being prudent."

"For how long?"

"I try my best to always be prudent," she said primly, aware she hadn't answered his question.

"I can't believe you won't do what's best for Jeremy." He spoke calmly, without any trace of surprise or anger, which indicated he was fishing.

"Save your guilt trip," she advised. "Besides, I don't under-stand your rush. You're enjoying the perks of married life. You have a son, a pseudo-wife—and don't think I haven't noticed how you've given up sleeping on the sofa every night."

Ever since they'd warmed the sheets in his apartment on Friday, he'd taken it on himself to slide into bed beside her at the end of each day. She wasn't complaining, but that evening had effectively ended an on-again, off-again sleeping arrangement.

"Plus," she continued, "you're still able to leave any time you'd like."

"What if I don't intend to go?"

She hesitated, hating to raise her hopes. "Is that your plan? To give up everything you have in Denver, includ-ing your family, to move here, where I have a job I love and friends who support me?"

At his hesitation, she smiled weakly. "I didn't think so."

"I can draw up whatever custody arrangements you'd like, Ms. Hollister." Jonathan Gray steepled his fingers as he peered at her over his reading glasses. "The problem comes in asking the other party to sign them."

"This is a fair arrangement, isn't it? Jeremy's father can visit any time he wishes, but I keep sole custody."

"Have you discussed these terms with Dr McReynolds? Is he agreeable to them?"

She thought of the conversation that had led to her scheduling an appointment with a lawyer. "We haven't talked specifics," she admitted.

"I suggest you do, Ms. Hollister. While your offer seems generous, the family court in our county rarely awards sole custody until a parent is proven as unfit. Can you do that?"

Adrian, an unfit parent? Hardly. He could be the featured parent on fatherhood posters. "No. Definitely not."

"Then the court will most likely award joint custody. It can be joint legal custody in which you and Dr McReynolds share in any decisions regarding your son, or joint physical custody, in which case you share in the physical care and lodging with each of you having equal time."

"So Jeremy would have two homes."

"Basically. Although as young as he is, you might be granted primary physical custody. Keep in mind, though, if it's granted, Jeremy's father can ask the court to reconsider when Jeremy gets older. My advice is for the two of you to sit down and devise a parenting plan that specifies your agreed-on arrangement. Without it, the court will decide what they feel is in Jeremy's best interests. You may or may not like their ruling."

So much for this being a simple matter. "I see," she said.

"Tell me, has Dr McReynolds supported you in any way, either during your pregnancy or after?"

"No." She thought a moment, then backpedaled. "Though lately he's bought a few things for Jeremy and for our house."

"Hmmm. We could make the argument that he hasn't supported you and therefore you'd like primary physical custody, but the court takes a dim view of fathers who don't live up to their responsibilities."

Dad drilled responsibility into us.

Adrian's comment reverberated in her head. If not for his sense of responsibility, she wouldn't be sitting in an attorney's office now, looking at ways to change the status quo. That same sense of duty would interfere with the life she'd originally planned with Jeremy because she couldn't imagine Adrian being happy with an arrangement that afforded him anything less than fifty percent of his son's actual time, care, or lodging.

"May I make a suggestion?" Mr Gray asked.

"Of course."

"Is there any way you two can work out your differences? Seek counseling, perhaps?"

"I…I don't know."

"As I said, I would encourage you to try."

Sabrina left Jonathan Gray's office, completely uncertain as to what to do next. She didn't want to give up Jeremy for as much as a single day, but after seeing how much Adrian loved his son, could she expect him to willingly do what she couldn't?

What options did she have?

She mulled over Gray's advice for the next few days until Wednesday evening, when she finally found the courage to raise the subject with Adrian. After sliding a pan of his favorite brownies into the oven for dessert, she waited for her opportunity.

"I spoke to an attorney the other day," she said offhandedly.

"Oh?"

"He'll draw up a will that appoints you as Jeremy's guardian if anything should happen to me."

For several seconds he didn't answer, as if he was either choosing his words carefully or stopping himself from saying something he might later regret. "I suppose I should admit I did the same."

She was stunned. "You did?"

"Well, my will isn't quite like yours because of the guardianship issue, but if anything happens to me, everything I own will belong to you and Jeremy."

"You did that? For us?"

"Of course." He seemed surprised that she'd asked. "Why wouldn't I?"

"Well…" She hesitated. "What if you meet someone you want to marry?"

"If by some chance I do, wills can always be changed."

Once again, the thought of a stepmother appearing in her son's life didn't sit well in Sabrina's heart. The idea of another woman in *Adrian's* life was equally disconcerting.

"The point is," he continued while she stewed about the possibility, "we have Jeremy's future decided if one of us dies, but what do we do while we're both living?"

She toyed with her fork. "The attorney and I talked about that, too."

He studied her thoughtfully. "And?"

"He suggested we create a parenting plan."

For several seconds, he didn't answer. "Which means what?"

She drew a bracing breath. "We decide if I should have primary physical custody and if we'll share legal custody. That way, we're both involved in any major decisions like Jeremy's education or medical concerns."

"By primary physical custody, you mean he'll live with you three hundred and sixty-five days out of the year."

"More or less."

Once again, he fell silent. "I don't care for your solution."

"I didn't think you would," she said wryly.

"Out of curiosity, what happens if we don't agree on terms?"

"Then the court will decide for us. And…" her breath caught "…most likely, Jeremy will be shuttled back and forth between us." She met his gaze. "I've already made my feelings plain. I don't want Jeremy to be displaced every week."

He rose from the table and scraped his plate into the garbage disposal. "I'm not happy about it either, but what choice do we have?"

What choice, indeed? He already knew the answer by the calm way in which he spoke. He was simply waiting for her to accept and admit it, too.

But could she commit to a wedding because she didn't want to be separated from her son? After all, there was a slight chance the judge would rule in her favor. Adrian's cellphone interrupted her thoughts.

He glanced at the display and smiled. "My sister," he said before he answered.

"Hi, Marcy. I'm in the middle something monumentally earth-shattering and life-changing." His wink in her direction brought a warm glow to her face. "So this had better be good."

His teasing tone disappeared and his smile turned into a worried frown. "Room seven-fifteen. I'll be there. Call me if anything changes." He clicked off the connection.

"What's wrong?"

A cold, hard mask had settled on his face. "It's Clay. He's in hospital."

Her stomach clenched. "Oh, Adrian."

"Apparently he has peritonitis. His so-called food poisoning last week was apparently a leaky appendix. His temperature shot up and he went into a seizure." He jumped up. "I have to go."

"I'll help you pack your bag." After a quick swipe of Jeremy's messy face, she placed him in his playpen and went to the bedroom.

Adrian's suitcase lay open on the bed as he yanked clothes off hangers and tossed them haphazardly in its direction. "I'll do this," she ordered. "Fetch your shaving kit."

He left, presumably for the bathroom, and returned a minute later with his toiletry case in hand.

"Do you want all your clothes or just enough for a day or two?" she asked, poised in front of the closet.

"Enough for a few days. Just casual stuff. If I need anything else, I'll get it from my house."

She quickly folded the clothes meeting his criteria inside the soft-sided case and left the others to hang up later.

As soon as she'd packed his essentials, he zipped the piece of luggage closed and headed for the door.

"You'll drive carefully, won't you?" she asked, knowing his worry could make him inattentive and impatient behind the wheel.

"Yeah."

"And you'll call me. To tell me how he's doing?"

His "Yeah, sure," sounded so automatic, she wondered if he meant what he'd said. Although if he didn't call, she knew his number.

He paused at the playpen, bent down and kissed Jeremy's cheek, then hurried out of the house.

Sabrina tried not to feel rejected, but she did. Suddenly she was glad they hadn't had the conversation she'd hoped for because his action couldn't have spelled out his feelings any plainer.

She was only a convenience. A means to an end. A necessary evil to live with in order to have access to his son. Granted, he'd been in a hurry when he'd left, but he could have acknowledged her in some way, instead of ignoring her.

Fighting back tears, she began clearing the dishes when suddenly the front door slammed. She turned to see Adrian striding purposely toward her.

"I forgot something," he said.

She blinked the wetness out of her eyes and swallowed the lump in her throat. "I can't imagine what," she said, hating to hear the choked-up sound coming out of her throat.

He planted a hard kiss against her mouth. "I *will* call you," he said, and then he left.

He came back because he'd forgotten to *kiss her*?

Oh, my.

She wanted to laugh and cry at the same time. Tears streamed down her face as she sank onto the nearest chair. Adrian's one small action sent her spirits soaring before they crashed with chagrin and embarrassment at how quickly she'd thought the worst, and how badly she'd misjudged his actions.

If they were going to have any sort of future, she had to stop reading events through the veil of her insecurities and have more faith in him. If he was trying to put their past behind him, she couldn't do any less.

The kitchen clean and Jeremy happily entertaining himself, she began straightening the clothes Adrian had discarded in an untidy heap. It didn't take long, but as she retrieved a pair of trousers off the floor, a scrap of paper fell from a pocket. Thinking it might be a phone message or an appointment reminder, she unfolded the slip and saw it was a cashier's check receipt.

Certain he'd need it for business purposes, she laid it on the dresser. Just as she turned away, the amount caught her eye and she froze.

She hadn't misread those numbers. They matched her hospital bill down to the last cent.

Adrian had paid her bill. *Adrian* had been her anonymous benefactor. *Adrian* had wiped out her debt.

How could he do this to her? He *knew* she didn't want his financial support, but he gave it anyway. Accepting the television and the rest of his "surprises" had been difficult enough, but knowing he'd paid her bill was doubly hard to swallow.

What motive did he have?

Righteous anger built. Was he trying to prove she couldn't provide for Jeremy, whereas he could? Or was it strictly conscience money, a way to pay her off and feel good in the process?

Have faith, her conscience whispered.

Shamed by breaking her vow in less than five minutes, she sank weakly onto the bed and scolded herself for jumping to conclusions.

Yes, he was deeply committed to his family and didn't shirk his perceived responsibilities toward them. As Jeremy was now a part of that circle, Adrian probably felt obligated to carry his share of her financial load.

Obligated. Oh, how she hated that word. She didn't want to be anyone's obligation, especially not Adrian's. She wanted him to love her and she desperately wanted to hear those words.

His love for us showed in the things he did and taught us.... He always made time when we needed him.

Why Adrian's description of his father popped into her head at that moment, she didn't know, but now that it had, she judged Adrian's actions by a new standard. Apparently Adrian's father had quietly let his actions speak for himself, which was what Adrian had obviously spent his entire life doing. Carrying the responsibilities of a family was a labor of love, not obligation or duty.

No, Adrian hadn't said he loved her, but she knew he did. He'd come back to kiss her goodbye.

CHAPTER TEN

ADRIAN sat next to Clay's bed as he watched his brother sleep. IV tubes carried pain meds, fluids, and strong antibiotics while a urinary catheter and an abdominal drainage tube accomplished the opposite.

He paid close attention to the numbers flashing on the monitors. If a problem developed, he intended to catch it in the early stages. At the moment Clay's condition was stable, but he still felt powerless.

Clay would be fine. In his head, he recited those words like a mantra, but he couldn't stop thinking that he shouldn't have accepted his brother's self-diagnosis of food poisoning without asking more questions. He was the doctor in the family, dammit! His family relied on *him* for medical advice.

Some advice he gave. He'd simply told his brother to drink plenty of fluids and lay off the steaks for awhile. He may as well have recommended the famed take-two-aspirin-and-call-me-in-the-morning cure.

Marcy walked in, wearing her favorite hunter-green drawstring trousers and a colorful T-shirt that read, "Teachers have class". A huge bag hung off one shoulder and she balanced a steaming cup of coffee in each hand. "How's he doing?" she whispered.

"Resting comfortably. I see you're still carrying every-thing but the kitchen sink." He motioned to her purse.

"That's right," she whispered cheerfully as she handed over Adrian's latest dose of caffeine. "Teachers are like Boy Scouts. Our motto is 'Be prepared'. You never know what you'll need or when you'll need it." She nodded in Clay's direction. "What did the doctor say, or is telling me a breach of privacy regulations?"

"Jalil said Clay should be up and around in a few days." Jalil Kedar was Clay's general surgeon as well as Adrian's friend. "He'll be a sick puppy for a while, but they've loaded him with antibiotics so we should see improve-ment soon."

"Then he won't have any more seizures?"

"His was probably a reaction to his high temperature because he hasn't had any since his temp has come down to near normal. Jalil wants to take a wait-and-see attitude. If it happens again, we'll call in a neurologist."

"Clay's survived his share of medical problems, hasn't he?" she murmured.

"He's definitely met his quota," Adrian said wryly.

Marcy plopped down on a second chair. "It sounds as if he's on the mend, though."

"I think so."

"Then while we're waiting for Clay to finish his nap, I want to hear all about this earth-shattering, life-changing situation you were telling me about." Her eyes sparkled. "Does it have anything to do with a certain woman who's my nephew's mother?"

"You know about Sabrina? And Jeremy?"

She waved a hand. "Of course. Clay couldn't wait to call me with the news after your little dinner the other night. Frankly, bro, I'm disappointed you didn't invite Susan and me."

"It was a last-minute thing."

"So are you and Sabrina back together?" She sounded curious rather than upset or disappointed but, then, she'd told him he'd been a fool a year ago, immediately after he'd broken off their relationship.

"We're still working things out," he replied. "It's complicated."

She sighed. "It always is."

Sabrina waited all evening for Adrian's promised update and when the phone didn't ring, she lifted the receiver several times to verify she had a dial tone. Hating to contact him in case the situation was critical and he couldn't talk, she told herself not to worry.

He finally called her late Thursday morning. "Clay is doing OK. The antibiotics seem to be working, although he isn't too perky yet."

She heard the note of exhaustion in his voice and guessed at the cause. He probably hadn't left Clay's side, which meant he looked as rough as he sounded.

"I'm guessing you aren't too perky yourself," she said. "You stayed all night at the hospital, didn't you?"

"I slept a few hours here in the room."

Having worked at Mercy, she knew the sleeping arrangements available for family members. "In one of those awful recliners, I'll bet."

"Yeah, but I'll be fine."

"Are your sisters with you?"

"They were yesterday, but not today. Marcy has teacher inservices because school starts next week and Susan had an out-of-town audit she couldn't reschedule."

"I could drive down."

"No. It isn't necessary. Everything's under control."

Of course it was. Adrian would demand nothing but perfection and order. Meanwhile, he was probably driving the nurses crazy.

"Honestly, I don't mi—"

"Gotta go. I'll talk to you later." He disconnected before she could finish. Although she hadn't planned anything exciting for their four-day weekend, she hadn't dreamed they'd spend it in separate cities either.

He'd sounded so tired; he was obviously too intent on watching over Clay to take care of himself. Someone had to convince him to see reason and without any other candidates available, the task fell to her.

After several phone calls and two haphazardly packed bags later—one for Jeremy and one for herself—she exchanged her scruffy pair of denim shorts and formula-stained tank top for her favorite multicolored floral sundress. If she was going to barge into Clay's room without an invitation and brave Adrian's wrath for disobeying his wishes, she wanted the bolstering support of knowing she looked her best. A quick brush of her hair, a touch of eye-shadow, and she deemed herself ready.

As an afterthought, she added the matching lime-green sweater because hospital rooms were often chilly, then loaded Jeremy and their bags into her car. Within fifteen minutes the day-care staff at Pinehaven welcomed Jeremy into their fold and she headed southwest to Mercy Memorial.

An hour and a half later she stepped off the seventh floor elevator and onto her former nursing unit. Room seven-fifteen's door was slightly ajar, so she knocked, then waited a few seconds before strolling across the threshold.

Adrian's face registered surprise as his mouth curved into a welcoming smile. Before it stretched too far, though, he turned it into a frown. "Sabrina. What are you doing here?"

"Isn't it obvious? I came to visit," she said softly, aware of Clay sleeping a few feet away. "How's he doing?"

"The same as a few hours ago. You didn't have to come. I told you everything was fine."

"I know you did, but I wanted to see for myself." She eyed his wrinkled shirt, the dark shadow on his face. "I was right. You look as ragged around the edges as Clay does."

He shrugged, seemingly uncaring about his appearance. "Nothing that a little soap and water won't cure."

"Have you gone home?"

"I came straight here as soon as I arrived in town and I haven't left," he confessed. "My bag is still in the car."

"Maybe you should get it. I'm sure the shower in the doctors' lounge is free. You'll feel a lot better if—"

"I appreciate what you're trying to do, Bree, but I'm a big boy and don't need a mother hen telling me what to do."

She didn't allow his mood to bother her. "Testy today, aren't we?"

"Look," he said, more calmly than before. "I don't need company and, as you can see, neither does Clay."

So much for her mission of mercy. "Trying to give you moral support is like trying to force sour-tasting medicine down Jeremy's throat," she said lightly.

His eyes widened. "Speaking of Jeremy, where is he?"

"At day care. Kate will babysit after her shift ends and—"

"You left him over an hour away?" He sounded horrified.

"I couldn't bring him to the hospital for obvious reasons

and I certainly couldn't leave him at your house alone either. I don't have a child-care system here."

"Then you shouldn't have come."

"Jeremy is in good hands. I didn't leave him by the side of the road or alone in an empty house, and I never would. You know that."

He fell silent and she watched him clench and unclench his jaw. It was easy to see how Clay's condition weighed heavily on his mind.

"Talk to me, Adrian. What's really bothering you? Is there a complication you aren't telling me?" She whispered her last comment so Clay couldn't overhear.

He raked a hand through his hair. "No complications. He's doing fine."

"Then why are you acting this way? I love you, so we're supposed to handle problems together." She hadn't meant to blurt out her feelings when she'd wanted to share them under the proper ambience, but the best-laid plans....

"There isn't a problem," he insisted.

"Something is eating you up inside. Why won't you tell me?"

"Go home, Sabrina, where..." His tired voice broke. "Just go home."

"Where? Where I belong?" she asked, certain he would have finished with those words if he hadn't stopped himself.

He didn't answer.

As much as she wanted to argue, to remind him that she wanted to help him fight his demons, she'd plainly lost the battle before it had begun. Struggling with her own disappointment, she said, "OK, I'll leave you, then. Before I do, though, why don't you give yourself a break to shower and shave? I know you don't want to leave Clay by himself, so I'll sit with him in the meantime."

He hesitated, and she guessed why.

"Nothing will happen while you're gone," she told him. "I'll watch out for him."

For an instant his hesitation was obvious, but then he shook his head. "I'm staying."

For a long moment, she watched and waited, trying to sound calm when her emotions whirled like a tornado. "Why are you shutting me out, Adrian?"

"I'm not," he denied.

"You are," she insisted.

"Clay's my responsibility, not yours."

"I'm trying to help *you* help Clay. I'm not trying to take your place."

He fell silent.

Wondering how she would break through his hard-headedness, she gave a final argument.

"According to you, your father showed his love by the things he did for his family. You've obviously learned from his example because I've seen you do kind, thoughtful things for the people who mean a lot to you. So I don't understand why you won't allow anyone to support you in the same way."

To her disappointment, he didn't answer. "You're right. There isn't any reason for me to stay. I don't belong here."

He swiped his face tiredly. "You should be with Jeremy."

"Yes, I should be," she snapped. "He appreciates having me around all the time, not just when it's convenient. I'm curious, though. If I'd accepted your proposal, where would my place be today? Here with you, or at home, out of the way?"

She turned on one sandal and made a beeline for the door, but before she could pull it open, his hand held it shut.

"Clay's my brother," he said simply. "I have to be here. You don't."

"You're wrong, Adrian. It isn't about 'have to's.' It's about 'want to's.' Our place is *together*, but if you can't see that, then you deserve to hold your lonely vigil. Just don't expect me to welcome you back with open arms. In fact, don't expect me to welcome you *at all*, and I don't care how many times you're hit by a golf ball!"

Yanking at the handle, she broke his hold, then slipped into the hallway. Luckily, she didn't run into anyone she knew on her way to the elevator. Adrian McReynolds had driven her to tears in front of her colleagues before. He wouldn't do it again.

She punched the "down" button, overwhelmed by the sense of déjà vu. Once again, he'd rejected her, but she'd finally learned her lesson. As much as she'd admired him for his devotion to his family, it was obvious she'd always play second fiddle.

OK, so maybe she was being somewhat selfish, but she liked to think they'd handle family problems—or any problem for that matter—as a team, not as "his" or "hers". He obviously didn't hold the same philosophy but she wouldn't have it any other way.

The elevator arrived, then descended floor by agonizing floor. Chafing at the delay when she'd hoped for a quick exit, she blinked away the tears burning in her eyes. Now wasn't the time to feel the hurt—that would come later and in private. Right now anger propelled her forward and stopped her from falling on the floor and wailing like a two-year-old.

If Adrian wanted to shoulder his burdens by himself from now until eternity, he could do so with her blessing.

Ever since Marcy's phone call, Adrian had been racked by guilt for not recognizing Clay's symptoms. However, that black cloud was nothing compared to what he was feeling now.

"Idiot." Clay's weak voice broke through Adrian's misery. "You're an absolute, certifiable idiot."

Adrian privately agreed.

"You had a good thing and let it slip through your hands again." Clay rubbed his eyes. "For a man who always told us to learn from our mistakes, you don't follow your own advice."

He struggled to raise himself, but Adrian intervened. "What are you doing?"

"Trying to get up so I can punch your lights out," Clay retorted, although his shakiness contradicted his threat.

"Settle down. I got the message." Adrian gently pushed his brother onto his pillows and checked the IV lines to confirm Clay hadn't unseated them. "I assume you heard?"

"Enough to know my supposedly intelligent brother cornered the market on stupidity and insensitivity."

"OK, OK," Adrian said impatiently. "I got your point."

"Why *do* you keep pushing Sabrina away?" Clay's gaze narrowed. "What would have been wrong with letting her sit here while you cleaned up? Frankly, brother, you look worse than I feel."

"Gee, thanks."

"Honestly, I don't know why you think I need you to hold my hand."

"It's what Mom and Dad would have done."

"So you still intend to take their place until we're both gumming our food?" Clay muttered a harsh expletive. "Dammit, Adrian, I didn't ask you to sit beside me when I wrecked my cycle. I didn't ask you to come running now. I appreciate your time and concern, but you don't *have* to be here."

Adrian winced. "You heard that?"

"And a whole lot more. What I'm trying to say is I'll always need my big brother, but not in the way I did when I was eight years old. Your responsibilities have changed. Marcy and Susan and I shouldn't take first place. Sabrina and your son belong there."

For the last twenty-four hours Adrian had been struggling with how to juggle his responsibilities toward his old family with those of his new one, but now, losing Sabrina was more than he could bear.

"You know," Clay said kindly, as if their brotherly hierarchy were reversed, "Dad may have asked you to look after us, but he wouldn't have wanted you to stop living your own life."

Clearly he *had* gotten stuck in his surrogate father role. One thing was certain—if he'd been torn up by their separation before, he wouldn't survive it now.

Only a few minutes had passed; Sabrina couldn't have gotten far. He jumped to his feet and headed toward the hallway. "I have to catch her before she leaves."

"Don't come back unless she's with you," Clay called after him.

Adrian bolted for the elevator, but the display showed it had stopped on the second floor. He couldn't wait for it to meander back to the seventh. He sprinted for the stairs and flew down the twisting and turning steps as if he was running for his life.

Maybe he was.

He had to get to Sabrina before she drove away.

He burst onto the main floor, struggling for breath as he scanned the lobby for her brightly colored dress.

There she was, several feet from the front entrance! He sprinted forward, calling her name.

She paused to listen, but as he yelled her name again, she ignored him and went on.

He skirted several people in his race to intercept her before she reached the door. A heartbeat later, he grabbed her arm. "Sabrina, wait."

She stopped and stared coldly at him. "Let go of my arm or I can guarantee we'll both be on the evening news. You, *Dr McReynolds*, will be a public relations nightmare for Mercy Memorial."

He held on. "Please, wait. I have to talk to you. Explain."

"What's to explain? You don't want me sharing this part of your life, so I won't. I'm going home to *my* son, where *I* belong. By the way, don't worry about your things. They'll be waiting on the front lawn for you when you get back, so you'd better pray it won't rain in the meantime.

"Oh, and my attorney will be in touch with a visitation schedule. I'll warn you it won't be generous."

Adrian moved quickly to stand in front of her. "Don't go. Please."

She gave a most unladylike snort. "Why shouldn't I?"

"Because I love you."

Her eyes suddenly glistened, but she rapidly blinked away the moisture. "No, you don't. If you loved someone, you wouldn't hold a part of yourself back and you wouldn't push the other person away."

"I'm sorry."

"I'm sure you are. Now, either turn me loose or I'll scream."

He held on, his steely-eyed gaze unwavering as he met hers, hoping she'd see what lay in his heart.

Ready to follow through on her threat, Sabrina opened her mouth to draw in a breath, but before her lungs filled to capacity, his mouth covered hers in a hard, bruising kiss.

She resisted at first, then, too emotionally drained to protest, gave up. Attune to her surrender, he gentled himself, kissing her until she began kissing him back. Oh, how she hated her weakness where Adrian McReynolds was concerned.

"Oh, get a room," a blue-haired lady snapped as she walked by. "This is a hospital, not a seedy hotel."

A *seedy hotel?* The words snapped Sabrina out of her haze and she began to giggle, more as result of her conflicting emotions than from any humor.

"Come on." Adrian pulled her over to a cozy visitors' nook and guided her into an overstuffed chair. After she was settled, he perched on the edge of a solid walnut coffee table.

She wondered if he realized how he'd placed himself at her feet, then decided it didn't matter. "You're wasting your time, Adrian. I don't have the fortitude to go through this time after time. I'm saying enough."

"I want to tell you a story."

Crossing her arms petulantly, she snapped, "I don't want to hear it."

"I want to begin on a day about seventeen years ago,"

he continued as if she hadn't spoken. "A week before my eighteenth birthday."

She tapped her foot. "This has nothing to do with—"

"Bear with me, Bree. My parents and I had gone to a used-car lot to shop for a car for me. On the way home, I was driving. The driver of a cattle truck ran a red light and hit us. I'd swerved, but I wasn't fast enough. The passenger side of the vehicle was crushed. Mom was killed instantly."

He'd drawn her into his story and she could only gasp and keep listening. "I'm so sorry. You never told me the details."

"It was too painful, so I didn't. And I didn't get more than a few scratches and bruises. Someone called an ambulance and the fire department used the Jaws of Life to cut my dad out of the wreckage. I talked to him the whole time, holding his hand and begging him to hang on.

"He knew he wasn't in good shape. He made me promise to look after my sisters and Clay, no matter what. I did. I would have promised him whatever he'd asked for because I felt responsible. If I hadn't been so eager to buy that car, we wouldn't have been at that intersection. Maybe if my dad had been driving, he could have avoided the crash. Because of all that, I robbed my little brother and younger sisters of their parents."

"You never told me. You should have," she gently accused.

"Probably, but I don't talk about it. It brings up bad memories and old feelings I'd like to forget."

She leaned forward. "But the accident wasn't your fault. You didn't run that stoplight. And who knows if your father could have swerved in time? Maybe if he had, *you* would have been killed. You just don't know and you can't blame yourself for events outside your control."

"Maybe not, but since then I've taken my responsibilities toward my family seriously. When Clay got the idea to buy a motorcycle, he asked me for the money. He'd been scrimping for a long time, but he'd only saved half the amount. Then he found a used cycle advertised in the paper. It was such a good deal, he hated to pass it up. And I hated to see him spend more money for the identical thing, so I gave in and loaned him the balance.

"A few weeks later, he had the accident. Naturally, I felt guilty and was angry at myself for going against my better judgement. I'd failed him once, you see, and I was determined to work with him twenty-four seven if that's what it took to help him walk again. So I broke off things with you."

"And you did it again today," she reminded him. "Don't tell me you're holding yourself responsible for his peritonitis."

"I *am* the doctor in the family. I should have sensed something was seriously wrong with my brother."

"Adrian." She took his hand. "When you were a kid, did you have accidents or illnesses?"

He stared at her. "You have to ask? Of course I did. Who doesn't? I fell out of a tree and gashed my chin. It took ten stitches to close it. I broke my arm one summer playing football and broke off several teeth when I took a header into home plate during baseball season. I also had my tonsils removed because I had frequent sore throats."

"Did your parents feel guilty because you got hurt or because you needed surgery?"

"They didn't act like it." Understanding suddenly dawned in his eyes.

"I think you're trying to fill your parents' shoes and you've lost sight of several facts. One, life happens. We get sick, we need surgery, whatever it might be. Two, Clay and your sisters make their own decisions. They aren't children needing your protection."

He looked sheepish. "That what Clay said, too."

"They're adults and all they need is your love and support, which is all Jeremy and I want, too."

"You'll have it," he promised. "I love you, Bree."

Hearing the words thrilled her and yet they still had a few more issues to iron out. "Are you sure?"

"Absolutely. I lived without you for a year and I can't lose you again."

"Then you can't keep pushing me away, Adrian. Our relationship isn't like golf, where we each play individually. We should function like a football team where we work together. What concerns you concerns me."

He nodded. "I know I've screwed up twice, but can we try this again?"

As she gazed into his face, she knew she owed it to herself and to Jeremy to give him another chance. Yes, they could fail, but somehow she sensed they wouldn't.

"You know what they say." Her voice was filled with emotion. "'Third time's the charm'."

His smile slowly grew. In a flash he rose, pulled her into his arms and kissed her until her toes curled.

Finally, he raised his head. "It will be, Bree. It will be."

EPILOGUE

Two years later

"I REALLY think you should rest in the clubhouse," Adrian said as he eased off the brake and headed the golf cart toward the twelfth hole of the Pinehaven Public Golf Course. "You're nine months pregnant and have absolutely no business riding around the links."

Sabrina rested her hands on her massive tummy and rubbed away another twinge. She'd been having those pains off and on for the last two days but if she'd mentioned them, Adrian would have whisked her to the hospital faster than she could yell "Fore". She wasn't going to be stuck indoors because of Braxton-Hicks' contractions.

"I need the fresh air," she said instead. "Besides, bumping around in a cart might shake Junior loose. He's obviously forgotten he was supposed to arrive last week."

"Junior? It's probably a girl and she's late because she's still primping and preening."

She laughed. "For the record, I do not primp or preen."

"And Jeremy and I don't forget. We may get sidetracked or postpone things, but we don't forget."

"I stand corrected."

"But speaking of getting sidetracked, you're the reason why I'm playing badly today. I'd shoot a better score if I wasn't worrying about you."

"Excuses, excuses," she teased.

He swerved to avoid a pothole in the cart path and she grabbed the armrest to hold on. "Sorry," he said.

Her twinge felt stronger. "You should be," she said. "I think you sent Junior into a somersault."

"I still think you should be lounging in the clubhouse."

"And miss all the action?" She shook her head. "Not a chance. I can sit in the cart just as easily as I can sit in a chair."

"We've seen enough action the last two years," he informed her. "It's always our family who lands in the spotlight. I'm hoping this year's benefit tournament will be different."

Another twinge. "Keep hoping," she muttered under her breath. "Granted, the first year was unplanned excitement when I sliced the ball and beaned you. But it turned out well, I'd say." She smiled at him. "We got back together and Pinehaven Health Center recruited its very own full-time emergency services specialist.

"And you can't complain about last year's events because we planned our wedding in advance," she continued. "No unexpected surprises there." After the final team had completed their eighteen-hole round, Sabrina and Adrian had celebrated their wedding. The ceremony had been a well-kept secret and only a handful of people knew the couple had organized the service to take place after the tournament in the clubhouse where everyone had been invited.

"I don't want to deliver my own baby on a green," he said as he slowed down and parked near the tee box. "I personally think Kate's lottery is going to jinx us and we won't get to the hospital in time."

In light of the prominent role Sabrina and Adrian had played in previous tournaments and to generate interest in this year's event, Kate had started taking bets as to the precise hole where Sabrina would go into labor. Tickets were ten dollars each and all proceeds went into the patient benefit fund. Winners would have their pictures taken with the community's newest arrival.

"I don't believe in jinxes and, besides, the contest is for a good cause." Another cramp hit and she surreptitiously glanced at her watch. They were closer together than she'd thought.

Adrian drew his driver out of his bag, then joined the rest of his team on the tee box. Sabrina impatiently drummed her fingers on her knee.

By the time he returned to the cart with a smile on his face for his long drive, she held the armrest in a white-knuckled grip. As soon as the contraction eased, she said, "The twelfth hole is someone's lucky number."

He stared at her. "What?"

"We need to head to the hospital."

"I knew it. I knew it." He hit the accelerator pedal and the cart shot forward, careening along the path until he veered onto the course itself in an obvious attempt to take a shortcut.

"You can't cut across," she gasped. "You'll tear up the grass."

"Ask me if I care," he said grimly, gripping the steering-wheel as if he were participating in the Indy 500.

He rolled past a group of golfers who began to cheer as if they guessed why he was driving like a maniac. "Adrian, you can slow down. We have plenty of time."

He screeched to a halt in front of the clubhouse and a crowd of well-wishers, including Kate, hurried her to his car.

Fifteen minutes after Sabrina arrived at the hospital, Susannah Marie McReynolds made her appearance.

Sabrina watched as Adrian held the swaddled little body in his arms. "She's beautiful," he said.

"She is," Sabrina agreed. He perched on the edge of the bed and held the baby so she could see Susannah's face. "Oh, dear, she has my nose."

"And a gorgeous nose it is," he said, before he leaned over and kissed her. "Thank you for our daughter, my love."

Sabrina smiled tiredly at him. "You're welcome."

"There are a few people waiting outside the nursery to meet their new niece and sister. Do you mind if I show her off?"

Did she mind? Not at all. In fact, hardly anything upset her these days and the same applied to Adrian. Family and friends filled their life and love tied them all together.

MEDICAL™ 2-in-1

Coming next month

ITALIAN DOCTOR, DREAM PROPOSAL
by Margaret McDonagh

Gorgeous but shy Dr Ruth Baxter doesn't do relationships –
until a seductive encounter with her handsome new boss,
Dr Rico Linardi! An encounter that convinces Rico that
he wants Ruth not only as his lover...but his wife!

WANTED: A FATHER FOR HER TWINS
by Emily Forbes

Dr Rosie Jefferson's priority is caring for her orphaned twin
niece and nephew, not her appearance! But deliciously
attractive Dr Nick Masters makes her feel beautiful again and
this single mum finds herself wishing for the impossible...

BRIDE ON THE CHILDREN'S WARD
by Lucy Clark

Years ago, Dr David Montgomery and Eden Caplan shared
a soul-searing kiss. Now, gorgeous doctor David realises
that one kiss wasn't enough – he wants a lifetime,
with Eden as his bride!

MARRIAGE REUNITED: BABY ON THE WAY
by Sharon Archer

The Campbells' marriage fell apart when doctor Liz's gorgeou
firefighter husband Jack thought he couldn't give her the fami
she wanted. Now one miraculous night leaves Liz pregnant,
and Jack's determined to be the perfect husband and father

On sale 2nd October 2009

MEDICAL™

Single titles coming next month

THE REBEL OF PENHALLY BAY
by Caroline Anderson

Everyone remembers heartbreaking bad-boy Sam Cavendish
– especially shy practice nurse Gemma Johnson. She's
spent ten long years trying desperately to forget their
secret whirlwind wedding, but Sam's returned to Penhally
and is determined to win back the heart of the only
woman he's ever loved…

MARRYING THE PLAYBOY DOCTOR
by Laura Iding

Seth Taylor appreciates beautiful women, so he can't
wait to get to know his new colleague, paramedic
and single mum Kylie Germaine, better! Only for
the first time ever, Seth's smitten – this eligible bachelor
finds himself wanting to put a ring on Kylie's finger
and become a father to her little boy.

On sale 2nd October 2009

Available at WHSmith, Tesco, ASDA, Eason and all good bookshops.
For full Mills & Boon range including eBooks visit
www.millsandboon.co.uk

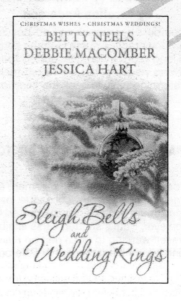

From No. 1 *New York Times* bestselling author Nora Roberts

Nightshade available 2nd January 2010

When a teenager gets caught up in making sadistic violent films, Colt Nightshade and Lieutenant Althea Grayson must find her before she winds up dead…

Night Smoke available 5th February 2010

When Natalie Fletcher's office is set ablaze, she must find out who wants her ruined – before someone is killed…

Night Shield available 5th March 2010

When a revengeful robber leaves blood-stained words on Detective Allison Fletcher's walls, she knows her cop's shield won't be enough to protect her…

Passion. Power. Suspense.
It's time to fall under the spell of Nora Roberts.

millsandboon.co.uk Community

Join Us!

The Community is the perfect place to meet and chat to kindred spirits who love books and reading as much as you do, but it's also the place to:

- Get the inside scoop from authors about their latest books
- Learn how to write a romance book with advice from our editors
- Help us to continue publishing the best in women's fiction
- Share your thoughts on the books we publish
- Befriend other users

Forums: Interact with each other as well as authors, editors and a whole host of other users worldwide.

Blogs: Every registered community member has their own blog to tell the world what they're up to and what's on their mind.

Book Challenge: We're aiming to read 5,000 books and have joined forces with The Reading Agency in our inaugural Book Challenge.

Profile Page: Showcase yourself and keep a record of your recent community activity.

Social Networking: We've added buttons at the end of every post to share via digg, Facebook, Google, Yahoo, technorati and de.licio.us.

www.millsandboon.co.uk

2 FREE BOOKS
AND A SURPRISE GIFT

We would like to take this opportunity to thank you for reading th
Mills & Boon® book by offering you the chance to take TWO mor
specially selected books from the Medical™ series absolutely FREI
We're also making this offer to introduce you to the benefits of th
Mills & Boon® Book Club™—

- **FREE home delivery**
- **FREE gifts and competitions**
- **FREE monthly Newsletter**
- **Exclusive Mills & Boon Book Club offers**
- **Books available before they're in the shops**

Accepting these FREE books and gift places you under no obliga
tion to buy, you may cancel at any time, even after receiving your fr
books. Simply complete your details below and return the entire pag
to the address below. You don't even need a stamp!

YES Please send me 2 free Medical books and a surprise gift. I
understand that unless you hear from me, I will receive 5 superb nev
stories every month including two 2-in-1 books priced at £4.9
each and a single book priced at £3.19, postage and packing free. I
am under no obligation to purchase any books and may cancel m
subscription at any time. The free books and gift will be mine to kee
in any case.

Ms/Mrs/Miss/Mr _____ Initials _____

_____

Surname _____

Address _____

_____

_____ Postcode _____

Send this whole page to: Mills & Boon Book Club, Free Book Offe
FREEPOST NAT 10298, Richmond, TW9 1BR

Offer valid in UK only and is not available to current Mills & Boon Book Club subscribers to this series.
Overseas and Eire please write for details.. We reserve the right to refuse an application and
applicants must be aged 18 years or over. Only one application per household. Terms and prices subject to
change without notice. Offer expires 30th November 2009. As a result of this application, you may receiv
offers from Harlequin Mills & Boon and other carefully selected companies. If you would prefer not to
share in this opportunity please write to The Data Manager, PO Box 676, Richmond, TW9 1WU.

Mills & Boon® is a registered trademark owned by Harlequin Mills & Boon Limited.
Medical™ is being used as a trademark. The Mills & Boon® Book Club™ is being used as a trademark.